James Harvey Mathes

The Old Guard in Gray

James Harvey Mathes

The Old Guard in Gray

ISBN/EAN: 9783337371845

Printed in Europe, USA, Canada, Australia, Japan

Cover: Foto ©Andreas Hilbeck / pixelio.de

More available books at **www.hansebooks.com**

THE
OLD GUARD IN GRAY

Researches in the Annals

OF THE

Confederate Historical Association.

SKETCHES OF MEMPHIS VETERANS WHO UPHELD HER
STANDARD IN THE WAR, AND OF OTHER
CONFEDERATE WORTHIES.

ILLUSTRATED.

BY

J. HARVEY MATHES.

HON. JEFFERSON DAVIS.

LIEUTENANT-GENERAL NATHAN BEDFORD FORREST.

TO MY COMRADES,

THE LIVING AND THE DEAD,

WHOSE NAMES ARE LINKED TOGETHER AS HEROES IN THE
GREATEST STRUGGLE OF ALL THE AGES FOR HOME
RULE AND CONSTITUTIONAL RIGHTS, AND
TO THEIR CHILDREN AND
DESCENDANTS,

THIS VOLUME IS RESPECTFULLY AND

AFFECTIONATELY INSCRIBED.

ACKNOWLEDGMENTS.

Acknowledgments are due for frequent reference in the compilation and writing of this book to Dr. J. Berrien Lindsley's "Military Annals of Tennessee;" J. P. Young's "Seventh Tennessee Cavalry;" "Campaigns and Battles of the Sixteenth Tennessee Infantry," by Colonel T. A. Head; "Hancock's Diary;" "Keating's History of Memphis;" various volumes of Government "Records of the Rebellion," S. A. Cunningham's "Confederate Veteran" magazine of Nashville; and especially to the officers and members of the Confederate Historical Association of Memphis, and other comrades and friends who have furnished data and offered kindly words of encouragement from time to time as the work progressed. To the papers of Memphis and other cities the author is indebted for flattering notices in advance, and he hopes to not altogether disappoint their many readers.

REPORT OF COMMITTEE.

Hon. C. W. Frazer, President Confederate Historical Association of Memphis:

The undersigned committee, appointed at a meeting of the Confederate Historical Association to inspect the manuscript work of Captain J. Harvey Mathes and examine the sketches and brief memorials which he has drafted of the various members of the Association, living and dead, respectfully report that they find Captain Mathes has with extreme care and painstaking labor compiled brief sketches of many members, past and present, showing their military records and frequently embellished with incidents illustrative of the devotion and daring energy of the Confederate soldier. The little book is replete with historical facts, and will not only entertain the general reader, but will prove of infinite value to the descendants of those whose deeds are therein narrated, in enabling them to trace the military career of their ancestors through the battles and campaigns of the great war. We therefore heartily commend the book to all Confederates who feel a pride in the deeds of their comrades in arms in the mighty struggle.

J. P. YOUNG,
Chairman of Committee.

MEMPHIS, TENN., January, 1897.

ILLUSTRATIONS.

INDEX TO SKETCHES.

Confederates Incidentally Mentioned.

CONDITIONS FOR MEMBERSHIP IN C. H. A.

The reorganization in May, 1884, referred to elsewhere, provided by by-law, that the petition for membership must give the company, regiment and brigade of the applicant; when enlisted or commissioned; when and where paroled or discharged: and that he should be recommended by a veteran; and that the petition should be presented only at a regular meeting; should be referred to the committee on credentials and lie over for one month; the qualification for membership being that applicant shall have actively served in the Confederate army, and that his record was blameless.

INTRODUCTORY.

THE original idea of this work was to get up a complete and reliable list of all the members of the Confederate Historical Association of Memphis under present and former charters, and give a brief history of the society. But research into old books and papers, interviews and correspondence with comrades and press notices, brought out an unexpected amount and variety of valuable historic material, enough indeed, with the reminiscences of men whose lives were a part of the late war, to fill many volumes. The oral testimony of such men cannot much longer be available ; some of it, in connection with their records and gleanings from various other sources, has been put together in the pages to follow. Thus condensed to encyclopædic form and arrangement, it may suggest to others more and better work in the same lines.

It will at least group the names and deeds of many representative ex-Confederates, regardless of rank, who exemplified the highest and best qualities of soldiers and citizens, and were willing to die for their principles, their honest beliefs, and the sanctity of ancestral homes. Such men in defeat or victory, living or dead, need no defense or glowing eulogy. It is sufficient that we preserve the actual facts of their lives, and as to the cause in which they fought to transmit as a heritage to posterity ; and it is a proud satisfaction to know that so many men and women, and even children, were faithful even unto death, in times of greatest trials and perils that can come to human hearts, and thus were an honor to their race and generation.

Many of the survivors of the civil war are still in the prime of life, and look back with wonder and thankfulness at the mercy of Providence, which preserved them in the midst of so many and great dangers ; and having done their part well

in war and in peace from a strict sense of duty, they are con-
tent with the results, and have no fear or doubt as to the
ultimate verdict of the world.

The Southern people have been too busy since the surrender
of the Confederate armies to devote much time to the writing,
reading or preservation of their own history. They have been
occupied in hard struggles to retrieve untoward fate; in building up homes, schools, churches, factories, reclaiming farms,
and planting vineyards, and have made a showing which
again excites the surprise if not envy of other sections and
the admiration of thinking people everywhere. A few persons
at least among us have held that we should write and preserve our own history, and not leave it to tradition as so
many of our forefathers did after the Revolutionary war, or
to outsiders who have a motive for perverting the facts. We
were an agricultural people before the war, with but few
great colleges or publishing houses, and permitted others to
supply most of our school books, histories and literature.
After the war school books again came into the hands of our
children that were written in a sectional, partisan, misleading
spirit. That some improvement has been made is admitted;
more is expected and demanded in the interest of truth and justice; simply that and nothing else. The humiliation of defeat
passed away with the Southern people long ago, and they are
as cheerful, industrious, loyal citizens as can be found in any
part of the country, but they none the less respect the deeds
and sacrifices of the men who wore the gray, whose names
will be honored as long as American valor and true manhood
endure. In their minds and hearts the bird's nest has been
built in the cannon's mouth, and the bloody chasm of history
is now a smiling landscape of teeming industries, waving
grain, fairest fruits and fragrant flowers. They vie with their
Northern brethren in loyalty to all that is meant, or that can
properly cluster in memory, around the stars and stripes; at
the same time they owe it to themselves and the generations
to come to honor the names of their fallen heroes and to
preserve a record of the deeds of those who fought under
the stars and bars. For these men were as true to their sense

of right as were Washington and Warren and Mad Anthony Wayne, as Marion and Sevier, as the Campbells, the Lees and Greens, the Shelbys and Robertsons and their compatriots, who also were classed as rebels against their government. The Southern States withdrew from the Union one by one, in the hope of escaping from aggressions and policies which violated the spirit of the Federal compact and trampled the constitution and all its traditions under foot. They fought for home rule and constitutional liberty and went down in the unequal struggle. But "time makes all things even" at last. They have been restored to their position in the Union with all disturbing causes removed, have rebuilt their waste places, and have set marvellous examples of thrift, patience and recuperative capacity. The bitter chalice has passed with its dregs, and been replaced by the wassail bowl of good fellowship, around which the veterans of both sides may meet to tell many a long-drawn-out story of weary march, of camp life, of surprise, ambush and shock of battle.

It is not possible in the limits of this book to give more than an outline of the military life of any one man. Where mention is made of the civil life of anyone before or after the war, it is merely put in as a record for posterity and to show what kind of men went out to fight the battles of the South as against the North.

In a few instances no data was found in the books of the Association, as some of these have been lost or mislaid. The sketches are meager enough, but are semi-official and deemed entirely reliable. Great pains have been taken to obtain actual facts. If any preference is shown, it is in favor of the privates and non-commissioned officers, as nearly all the generals and colonels have long since been given conspicuous places in current and permanent histories.

Just when the Confederate Historical Association of Memphis originated is a matter of doubt, owing to the loss of early minutes; some meetings of returned Confederates for social and relief purposes were held as early as 1866, a later book showing that B. J. Semmes joined in that year. The records in existence begin in 1869 and come on down to the present,

being kept in a strict business manner. The first charter
was obtained from the Legislature under an act passed February 17, 1870, found on page 393, Acts of 1869-70. The
incorporators named were W. D. Pickett, W. B. Wiggs, R.
W. Mitchell and John H. Erskine, and their associates and
successors, with succession for thirty-three years. The name
then was the Confederate Relief and Historical Association
of Memphis. The old association back of that had been reorganized July 15, 1869, as the minutes show, with Isham G.
Harris as President and a membership of 225; the membership now is 245. Gov. Harris served two years, and J. Harvey
Mathes was Secretary for one or more years, and Felix W.
Robertson was Treasurer. Mathes was succeeded in 1871 by
Major Minor Meriwether, who also became Treasurer. At
the end of the second term of President Harris in 1871, he
was succeeded by General John C. Fizer. It was about this
time that Jefferson Davis became a citizen of Memphis and
a member of the Association. He attended meetings regularly and was frequently called to the chair, in which he pre-
sided with that ease, grace and dignity so characteristic of
the man in higher places and under all circumstances. He
was in the home of his friends and took a lively interest in
their proceedings. Memphis was then a rendezvous for ex-
Confederates second only to New Orleans. The following
distinguished leaders, all or nearly all, belonged to the Association and attended the meetings:

    President Jefferson Davis,
    Admiral Raphael Semmes,
    Lieutenant-General Richard S. Ewell,
    Lieutenant-General N. B. Forrest,
    Major-General Gideon J. Pillow,
    Major-General W. Y. C. Humes,
    Major-General Patton Anderson,
    Brigadier-General Francis A. Shoup,
    Brigadier-General A. J. Vaughan,
    Brigadier-General Colton Greene,
    Brigadier-General E. W. Rucker,
    Brigadier-General J. W. Frazer,

Brigadier-General George W. Gordon,
Brigadier-General W. M. Brown,
Brigadier-General James R. Chalmers,
Brigadier-General Marcus J. Wright,
Brigadier-General J. C. Fizer, commanding brigade,
Colonel C. R. Barteau, commanding brigade,
General Thomas Jordan,
Hon. Jacob Thompson,
Isham G. Harris, the war Governor.

This is believed to be the oldest association of the kind in the South. For some years it maintained a relief fund, but this was finally discontinued. A general meeting was held at the Cotton Exchange, May 23, 1884, when it was determined to effect a reorganization. C. W. Frazer was chosen President and J. Harvey Mathes, Vice-President. Major Frazer has continued as President ever since. Mathes was succeeded the next year by R. B. Spillman, who has since filled the position. An application was made for a new charter, omitting the word "relief" from the title. It was signed by the following members, duly granted and recorded:

C. W. Frazer,	A. J. McLendon,	W. F. Taylor,
John F. McCallum,	R. J. Black,	J. C. McDavitt,
J. P. Young,	R. B. Spillman,	W. A. Collier,
M. J. Miller,	J. Harvey Mathes,	Charles G. Locke,
James E. Beasley,	W. F. Shippey,	G. V. Rambaut,
Daniel S. Levy,	John T. Willins,	A. J. Murray,
	Jno. W. Waynesburg.	

A few years ago this Association, without losing its identity, became Camp No. 28, Bivouac No. 18, United Confederate Veterans of Tennessee, and it is therefore part of the general organization of which General John B. Gordon is Commander-in-Chief. An excellent hall for an armory and the collection of war relics was secured in 1893, and is used jointly by the Association and its auxiliary, the Ladies' Confederate Memorial Association, and is an attractive gathering place for Confederates and their friends.

Whilst only scant measure is given the services of many gallant Confederates named, they represent a class and must stand as types of the greater number not mentioned. It will be noticed that some who made the very best soldiers were born north of the Ohio river, and some were from other lands, thus showing that human sympathies and courageous qualities are not exclusive privileges for any particular people. It may be mentioned without partiality or invidious intent that the Hebrews, who claim no country as their own, though usually good citizens wherever found, had many valiant soldiers in the Southern armies, as well as a representative in the cabinet of the Confederacy. Several of them are active and honored members of this Association. One of the oldest members is Comrade David Flannery, the veteran telegrapher, born in Limerick, Ireland, February 16, 1828, who rendered such valuable services during the war in his peculiar line. Another of the oldest is Comrade Daniel S. Levy, the artillerist, born in Prussia in the year 1826, a live, working member of Company A, Confederate Veterans, and was able to carry a gun and march in line many miles at Chattanooga last year and at Richmond this year (1896), when younger men fell by the wayside. There are several others, however, who are full seventy years old. The present organization really dates back only to 1884, but it is practically a continuation of the parent society, and it may be accepted as a fact that few or none ever become members without proper indorsement. The strictest scrutiny has always been exercised with regard to applicants, as a matter of proper precaution. This, however, would hardly seem necessary, as no one unworthy of fellowship would be likely to seek it. It will not be many years before the old soldiers will pass away to their eternal rest; others may come after to take up the threads of reminiscence and history as well as romance and poetry, and weave them into volumes of wider scope, to occupy space in the libraries of the future, and the descendants of Southern men and women will doubtless read in no narrow spirit the annals of their whole country's struggles with patriotic pride and satisfaction.

In a few years the ex-Confederates, still so active and potential in all the affairs of life, will sleep peacefully beneath the sod, and no more be seen than their banner which was furled forever. Many names are yet on the rolls of the living, but the final Appomattox must come to each man, and not far over in the next century. A younger generation is succeeding us if it has not done so already. We hope to transmit a respect for law and order and love of country to stronger arms and buoyant, noble hearts. May the sunset of every comrade leave a halo of soft, mellow light and memories of well-spent lives, worthy to be cherished and emulated in other days, is the sincere wish of

THE AUTHOR.

29 Cynthia Place,
Memphis, Tenn., December 12, 1896.

SKETCHES OF SOLDIERS

CONFEDERATE HISTORICAL
ASSOCIATION.

ALBRIGHT, CALVIN H., was born October 9, 1846, in Old Orange county, N. C. His ancestors were of Scotch-Irish Revolutionary stock on one side, coming from the Mebanes, Andersons and Bryans of North Carolina, while on the other he came from sturdy Dutch Protestants who settled in Pennsylvania over two centuries ago. He quit school November 4, 1861, and enlisted in Company H, Fifth North Carolina Volunteers, afterward Fifteenth North Carolina Regulars; served under Captain J. R. Stockard, Colonel McKinney, Brigadier-General Howell Cobb of Georgia, and Major-General Magruder; was in the battle of Lee Mills, near Yorktown Peninsula, of Virginia, April 16, 1862, where the regiment lost heavily and Colonel McKinney was killed. In this fight young Albright picked out and fired at a man, who was found dead at the spot where he had stood. Saw much hard service; was in the retreat from Yorktown to Richmond, and remembers vividly the encouragement given tired soldiers by General J. E. Johnston in the Chickahominy bottoms; at end of three days, marching and starving, he was broken down, and went to a hospital until after Malvern Hill. August 12, 1862, was discharged from the army on account of his age; attended school at Davidson College, North Carolina; re-entered the service in February, 1864, as clerk under Captain C. R. King at Graham, N. C.; remained until October 1, 1864; then enlisted in Company H, First North Carolina Cavalry, Captain George Dewy, Colonel W. H. Check, Brigadier-General Rufus Barrington, Major-General W. H. F. Lee, Hampton's Corps Army of North Virginia; was in several severe

fights while in this command; was at Wilson's Farm on Boydton plankroad, October 27, which was a hot fight, lasting
several hours, General Hampton losing a son, Preston Hampton, killed in this fight; that night he was one of three men
sent out on perilous service: next day he was highly complimented by Captain Dewy, who said, "Albright is too good a
soldier to hold horses when there is fighting to be done." He
was in several more engagements; his last fight was at Five
Forks, near Dinwiddie Courthouse, March 31, 1865; his regiment went into the fight that morning one hundred and
forty-seven strong, and lost, killed, wounded and captured,
eighty-seven men and officers, the Confederates driving Sheridan's command back for nearly two miles. This was young
Albright's last and hardest battle; after this fight he was
ordered to take charge of horses belonging to men killed,
wounded and captured, and he was not in any of the last
fights of the few days left to General Lee before Appomattox;
he did not surrender with General Lee's army, but escaped
across the river with other soldiers, and was paroled at Greensboro, N. C. He brought his cavalry sword home with him,
has it yet, and will leave it to his children to remind them of
their father's soldier days.

Mr. Albright left North Carolina January, 1866, with letters to Judge Archibald Wright and other prominent people.
After various business experiments more or less successful, he
engaged in the express business in 1871, first running as messenger between New Orleans and Humboldt, and in 1885 was
made agent at Memphis, where he has lived since. He has
shared in some degree the prosperity of the company he serves.
He is interested in various affairs; is president of a mining
company, is a director in a building and loan association, commissioner to the Tennessee Centennial, and a member of the
Shelby County Commission; is also a worker in the church,
being an elder in the Alabama Street Presbyterian Church,
and is superintendent of a Sunday-school. He has been married twice: his first wife was Miss Ella Hastings Moore of
Vicksburg, Miss., the daughter of Mr. Henry Moore, superintendent of public education for so many years. His second

wife was Miss Ellen Owen Stedman, the oldest daughter of Rev. James O. Stedman, D.D., of Memphis, Tenn. He had no children by his first wife; he has by his second wife three boys and one girl. He became a member of the Association in the spring of 1896.

ALLEN, AARON, enlisted early in the war and served in the Trans-Mississippi. Came to Memphis, became a member of this Association soon after it was organized, and lived in Memphis many years; was connected with railroads and other business, and is now a resident of Little Rock, Ark.

ALLIN, PHIL. T., Major in Forrest's old regiment; entered service early in 1861, and remained until the end. Proposed for membership by James E. Beasley, and elected February 8, 1870; died many years ago; is mentioned frequently on other pages of this work.

ANDERSON, JAMES H., enlisted May, 1861; was Major of the Nineteenth Mississippi Regiment Army North Virginia; served as Quartermaster Fifth Brigade, General Forney commanding, also on the staff of General Wheeler as Acting Quartermaster; was captured while on leave of absence and imprisoned at Helena, Ark; paroled without the right of exchange, but through the influence of friends in Memphis this was secured; finally paroled June, 1865. Joined this Association June 13, 1894.

ANDERSON, KELLAR, Captain Company I, Fifth Kentucky Infantry, Hanson's Brigade; enlisted April, 1861, and served in the Army of Virginia; was discharged with First Kentucky Infantry at the expiration of enlistment at Camp Winder, near Richmond; re-enlisted June, 1862, and was transferred from the Ninth Kentucky to the Fifth Kentucky Infantry, Hanson's Brigade; was wounded at Chickamauga; captured at Jonesboro, Ga., September 1, 1864; exchanged September 22, 1864; was sent to Kentucky April, 1865, to recruit for the Kentucky Brigade; surrendered and was paroled at New Castle, Ky., May 21, 1865. Afterward married in Helena, Ark., and has since lived in Memphis, and been prominent in connection with local military and State affairs, and commanded the State forces during the Coal Creek riots and troubles with a coolness and efficiency that gave him great distinction. He now holds (1896) a revenue appointment under President Cleveland, with headquarters in Memphis, but his duties extend over a wide field.

ANDERSON, PATTON, rank Major-General, entered the Confederate Army, from Florida, May 8, 1865; commanded Anderson Division Army of Tennessee; entered the service March 26, 1861, and was paroled May 8, 1865; was in the life insurance business in Memphis several years after the war, and died here. Was admitted to this Association upon his own application on the 1st of July, 1869.

ANDERSON, W. L., was First Sergeant of Company A, First Virginia Cavalry, Stuart's Regiment during the first year of the war; transferred to Company D, Southern Virginia Infantry, Hilton's Brigade, Pickett's Division, in June, 1863; commissioned in Confederate States Navy in autumn of 1863, and served in James River Squadron until the evacuation of Richmond; fell back with naval brigade and surrendered with it at Greensboro, N. C., April 26, 1865. Admitted to this Association November 4, 1869.

AUSTIN, J. A., Adjutant Thirty-First Tennessee Regiment, enlisted April, 1861; was appointed Adjutant by General Strahl; was wounded at Jonesboro, Ga.; served two years as Sergeant-Major; was ordered on detached service by General Hood after the battle of Franklin; paroled May, 1865; has since been an active and successful merchant of Memphis. Joined this Association October 9, 1894.

AVENT, B. W., Surgeon in General Rucker's command; entered the service May 7, 1861, and retired May 7, 1865; practiced his profession in Memphis after the war. Proposed for membership in this association by Dr. R. W. Mitchell and elected July 1, 1869. Has been dead for several years.

CAPT. T. H. ARNOLD.

ARNOLD, CAPTAIN T. H., was born in Brunswick county, Va., and reared in Mecklenburg, the adjoining county. In his early youth he took up his residence in Somerville, Tenn., a few years before the war. He joined Captain Wm. Burton's company, the Fayette Greys; was elected Second Lieutenant of this company; went into camp at Jackson, Tenn., where they were assigned to the Thirteenth Tennessee Regiment. Lieutenant Arnold, then in command of this company, drew the position of Company A in the regiment. From Jackson, Tenn., this company was ordered to Randolph, Tenn., then to New Madrid, Mo., and thence to Columbus, Ky. His company was engaged in the battle of Belmont, and by his side fell the gallant Matthew Ray; a braver soldier never drew a sword or gave a command. The company lost several killed and a number were wounded. Lieutenant Arnold himself was wounded, but he remained on the field until 2 o'clock in the night, removing the dead and wounded of his company to his camp on the east side of the Mississippi river.

Captain Wm. Burton resigned soon after the battle of Belmont, and Lieutenant Arnold was unanimously elected Captain. His company was engaged in the battle of Shiloh. Several of his company were killed and a number wounded. It was in this battle he lost his first lieutenant, the gallant Hamilton Whitmore, a scholar and a soldier. The army fell back to Corinth, Miss. About this time the Congress of the Confederate States of America passed the conscript law, wherein it was provided that all officers of the army were permitted to join any branch of the service they chose. Captain Arnold was granted leave of absence, on a sick furlough, and returned to Somerville, Tenn. After his furlough expired he was again offered his former command, but declined, preferring the cavalry branch of the service, and in company with Colonel Columbus Wilbourn of LaFayette, Miss., organized two companies of cavalry. By order of Colonel Hughes of Port Gibson, Miss., A. C. McKissick of Oxford, Miss., was elected Captain of one of these companies and T. H. Arnold First Lieutenant. This battalion of cavalry, under command now of Colonel Wilbourn, was ordered by General Pendleton to report at Port Hudson, La., to Colonel Logan, then in command of the cavalry of that department.

When General Banks besieged Port Hudson the cavalry operated in the rear of General Banks' army. Colonel Powers, in command of one of the regiments under Colonel Logan, conceived the idea to burn and destroy the camp and stores of General Banks on the Mississippi river. With one hundred picked men, traveling all night, they reached the banks of the Mississippi before day. Colonel Powers, Lieutenant Arnold and Lieutenant Buck of Port Gibson dismounting, approached on foot within sight of the enemy's pickets with twenty detailed men. Lieutenant Arnold was charged to capture their pickets without firing a gun, which command was carried out accordingly, and the pickets were captured.

The command then closed up, and Lieutenant Arnold was ordered by Colonel Powers to make a charge on the encampment and burn and destroy their stores and equipment. This order was promptly executed. It was a desperate but a successful effort, with the loss of but one officer, a lieutenant.

None but those who have traveled in the lowlands of Louisiana at about twilight, when the surrounding scenery was hiding from view the sun's departing rays, to faintly spot the hills and die away behind the king of the forest, can fully appreciate the somber, weird feeling that steals unconsciously over one as the sighing zephyrs creep through the long, waving moss that hangs from every tree, and seems to moan a requiem of departed joys of other days spent with home and friends, and the hoot of the owl tells of the approaching night.

It was in this land that Captain Arnold, on a night like this, was on the outpost picket duty. At the solemn hour of midnight the Sergeant woke the Captain up, for the last grand round to the vidette picket. The horses being saddled they were off to duty. Passing the first and second picket it was but a short while when the word Halt, who comes there? rang out on the stillness of the night. It was the vidette picket guard. Dismount; advance and give the countersign. This being done with bated breath they discussed the situation of the outer post, it being pretty close to General Banks' picket, as it was proved the next morning the picket was shot while on duty. He now sleeps in the land of the palms, and beneath the long, waving moss.

It was on this memorable night that Captain Arnold says he witnessed one of the grandest sights his eyes ever beheld. It was the bombardment of Port Hudson by General Farragut's fleet—hundreds of guns on each side—all sounds gave place to booming cannon; the shells like flaming serpents chased each other in such rapid succession that the elements became one blaze of fire. The shells seemed to meet sometimes in midair with their long fiery tails, and with the deadly hiss of reptiles to grapple as it were for the mastery. Finally a shell from our guns struck the magazine boat of the enemy, and such a terrific explosion he has never heard before or since. The heavens were lighted up for miles around, and after a little all was quiet. They folded their tents like the Arab and silently stole away.

Subsequently his command was in several engagements with Grierson's cavalry, and demoralized them to such an extent that they were obliged to keep close to their infantry. His company was engaged at Oxford, Miss., and falling back in front of Grant's army encamped at Grenada.

Lieutenant Arnold was with General Van Dorn in his famous raid on Holly Springs, Miss. His company was among the first to enter the place. It was here that Lieutenant Arnold captured a Federal cavalryman, depriving him of his saber, which trophy he still has. He was also with General Forrest on his raid to Johnsonville, Tenn., subsequently was ordered to report to General Wirt Adams, and was assigned to duty as Provost Marshal of his brigade. Afterward General Adams was appointed to the command of a division of the army, and General Mabry succeeded him. Lieutenant Arnold acted in the capacity of a Provost Marshal until the close of the war. Was in several engagements under General Forrest, and surrendered at Gainesville. Ala., on May 10, 1865. Since the war he has lived in Memphis, and been almost continuously connected with one leading house, in which he still holds a desirable and pleasant position. He became a member of this Association September 9, 1869, under the presidency of ex-Governor Isham G. Harris.

ASHFORD, JAMES A., Captain Company B, Second Confederate Tennessee Regiment; discharged before the close of the war on account of ill-health upon certificate by Surgeon Holcomb.

AVERY, W. T., originally Lieutenant-Colonel First Regiment Alabama, Tennessee and Mississippi Infantry; afterward Superintendent of Postoffice Department in Trans-Mississippi Department. Proposed for membership by Isham G. Harris and R. Dudley Frayser, and elected March 20, 1870; was afterward Clerk of the Criminal Court, but has been dead many years.

COL. C. R. BARTEAU,
In 1864.

BARTEAU, CLARK RUSSELL, was born April 7, 1835, in Cuyahoga county, near Cleveland, Ohio. His mother died in 1846, and his father, Russell W., in 1858, leaving four children—two sons and two daughters. C. R. Barteau remained on his father's farm until he was about sixteen years old, then entered the Wesleyan University at Delaware, Ohio, where he remained four years, then came South with some fellow students from Kentucky to learn something of Southern society and of slavery as it really existed. He became principal of the Male Academy at Hartsville, Tenn., in 1856, and continued as such for two years. In 1858 he began to edit and publish the *Hartsville Plaindealer*, ultra-Democratic and States-rights paper. He threw himself heart and soul on the side of the South, and denounced the anti-slavery crusade as the out-

3

growth of jealousy, falsehood and fanaticism. On the 20th of January, 1859, he was married to Miss Mary Cosby of Smith county, established a home, and continued both to teach and edit his paper until the outbreak of the war. In the meantime he had been studying law under Jno. W. Head, Esq., an eminent member of the bar. Having cast his lot with the people of the South, at a fearful cost of early friend- ship and family ties, he promptly espoused the cause of the young Confederacy, and risked his life and his all in its behalf. He arranged his affairs at home as best he could, and enlisted as a private in Company D, Seventh Battalion Tennessee Cav- alry, on the 17th day of October, 1861, and became a favorite at once with all the men. In a few weeks he was transferred to Company F, same battalion; this and the First Battalion were consolidated near Fulton, Miss., June 12, 1862, and pri- vate Barteau was elected Lieutenant - Colonel, and placed in command of the Second Tennessee Cavalry.

A pathetic incident is related in Hancock's Diary of Colo- nel Barteau's last interview with his wife. It was after the fall of Fort Donelson; he rode home, and on the 17th of February, 1862, spent one hour with his dear wife and infant child. The army was falling back; he could remain no longer. It was their last kiss and farewell. Mrs. Barteau lived to hear of her husband's promotion, but never to see him again.

Colonel Barteau was promoted to the full rank of colonel in 1863, and frequently commanded a brigade, so often indeed that he was known in the army as General Barteau, though never commissioned as such. He was known as a fighter from the start, and had the confidence of every man under him and officers above him in rank. If he cared for promotion or rank, he never made any sign; he was as modest as he was brave, and seemed to have no aspiration save to do his whole duty. He was mentioned frequently in official reports and in the various histories and accounts of the operations of Forrest's Cavalry. He was a very cool man, but impetuous in action, and always in the thick of the fight, and wounded in many battles, including Shiloh, Murfreesboro, Franklin, Harrisburg and Okolona. At the last-named place he was knocked from his horse while leading a charge through the town. In Hood's campaign he was so seriously wounded, December 6, 1864, that he was disabled for the rest of the war. After that he went to Aberdeen, Miss.: was paroled July 26, 1865; was admitted to the bar in 1866; removed to Bartlett, Shelby county, Tenn., in 1870, where he still has a home, and practices law in Memphis.

Colonel Barteau, or General, as he is known, has attended several reunions of the survivors of the "Old Second" at Gallatin and other places, and been received with open arms, not only by his comrades and followers, but by the people at large. He is an eloquent speaker, of fine physique, and well preserved, looking very young for his age, and his appearance at such reunions always creates the greatest enthusiasm. He was married the second time, near the close of the war, to Miss Zura Eckford of Macon, Miss., a young lady who had given up five brothers to the Southern cause and faced many hardships and dangers, and once at least was in the smoke of battle, as well as many times afterward in the hospitals, on missions of mercy and good deeds. He has three daughters grown and happily married, and the colonel has more than his share of welcomes and homes, and as the evening of life comes on he can look back over an eventful and honorable career of which any man or family might be justly proud.

It happened that his only brother fought in some of the same battles that he did, on the other side. After the war they corresponded, and the most cordial brotherly relations were restored.

The picture of Colonel Barteau above is from an old ambrotype taken in 1864, when he was recovering from a wound in the wrist and a severe illness. The mark of the bullet can be seen in his sleeve. **1746030**

BALLENTINE, JOHN G., Colonel of Ballentine's Regiment and Mississippi Cavalry; entered the service in May, 1861, and remained four years. Proposed by J. E. Beasley for membership in the Confederate Historical Association and elected April 28, 1870.

BAILEY, L., private Company I, Tenth Mississippi; enlisted June 15, 1861. The regiment was disbanded at Corinth, Miss., March 26, 1862. Returning home, Mr. Bailey re-enlisted with Battery A Army North Virginia, and served continuously with the Army of Virginia until the fall of Petersburg, where the battery was captured and he was wounded; was in the hospital when captured and paroled.

BAILEY, THOMAS F. private Company B, One Hundred and Fifty-fourth Tennessee Regiment; enlisted June, 1861; served through the war, and paroled May 11, 1865. Admitted to this Association October 9, 1894.

BAIN, JOHN, enlisted May, 1861, in Fifteenth Tennessee; was appointed Adjutant of the regiment and afterward elected Captain of Company H; was on detached service at the close of the war, and captured at Macon, Ga.

BARKER, J. O., enlisted in the Ninth Mississippi early in the war, and was discharged on account of ill-health; afterward re-enlisted in Company G, Adams' Regiment, and served until the end of the war. Paroled May 12, 1865.

BEASLEY, JAMES EDWARD, was born in the town of Plymouth, N. C., August 31, 1839; graduated at the University of North Carolina (Chapel Hill) June 2, 1859, and came to Memphis immediately afterward. Became a member of the Shelby Grays, a company organized in this city in February, 1861. This company became Company A of the Fourth Tennessee Infantry, was mustered into service by General W. H. Carroll of Germantown, on the 15th day of May, 1861. Served the last two years of the war in different positions at the Brigade Headquarters of Brigadier-General O. F. Strahl; was with General Strahl when he was killed, November 30, 1864, in the trenches at Franklin, Tenn.; was surrendered with General Johnston's army and paroled at Greensboro, N. C., April 26, 1865, and returned to Memphis to live, reaching here June 21, 1865. He was one of the original and most active members of the Association.

COL. JOSEPH BARBIERE.

BARBIERE, JOSEPH, Colonel of Third Alabama Reserves; was taken prisoner, and had some hard experience, which he afterward wrote up in a book entitled "Scraps From the Prison Table"; was a lawyer and a journalist, and genial, brilliant man; was at one time President of the Tennessee Press Association; lived a good many years in Pennsylvania, near Philadelphia, and died there in 1895. Joined this Association February 3, 1870.

BARBOUR, JAMES G., Captain in McDonald's Battalion; entered the service in April, 1861, and remained four years; was a merchant after the war. Admitted to this Association upon his own application July 15, 1870. Removed to Mississippi, and died at Yazoo City a few years ago.

BEASLEY, T. J., Lieutenant of Company E, Third Regiment of Arkansas Cavalry, Humes' Division, Wheeler's Command. Proposed for membership by J. E. Beasley and R. W. Mitchell, and elected May 12, 1870.

BENNETT, J. C., private in Company B., Jeff. Forrest's Regiment of Cavalry, and served through the war. Proposed for membership by J. G. Barbour and Henry Moode, and elected May 20, 1870.

BICKNELL, B. J., private Company A, First Mississippi Cavalry; enlisted May, 1861; was detailed as clerk of acting Quartermaster Department January, 1863; under Major J. A. Grant, March, 1863; later came under Brigadier-General F. C. Armstrong, and did staff duty in connection with other duties.

BLACK, A. J., private in the Twenty-eighth Mississippi Regiment. Elected a member of this Association July 1, 1869.

BLACK, R. J., Second Lieutenant Company B, Seventh Tennessee Cavalry; enlisted May 31, 1861; served actively throughout the war, and was paroled at Gainesville, Ala., May 12, 1865. The Seventh Tennessee was engaged in West Tennessee, West Kentucky, Middle Tennessee and North Alabama. He was in Rucker's Brigade, afterward Campbell's, W. H. Jackson's Division and Forrest's Corps; was with Forrest throughout the war, except about twelve months, when Company B, Captain J. P. Russell, was detailed as escort to General Loring and moved about Canton, Jackson, Yazoo City, Vicksburg and Meridian, after which the company rejoined the main command. Lieutenant Black was wounded three times—first at Lockridge's Mill, Ky.; second at Hernando, Miss., and third at Union City, Tenn. After the war he located in Memphis, married, served as Clerk and Master of the Chancery Court for several years, was successful in real estate, building and loan and other business; was Secretary of the Confederate Historical Association for many years, and finally removed to St. Louis in 1896, but will probably return to Memphis.

MAJ. HUGH L. BEDFORD.
At Richmond in 1863.

BEDFORD, HUGH L., is the son of Benjamin W. Bedford, and the grandson of Capt. Thomas Bedford, a soldier of the American Revolution, for whom Bedford county, Tenn., was named, and of Robert Whyte, for many years a judge of the Supreme Court of Tennessee. He was born June 11, 1836, in Fayette county, Tenn., and reared in Panola county, Miss. After finishing the classical course at the University of Mississippi, he went to Kentucky to study civil engineering under Col. E. W. Morgan, and graduated in 1855 at the Kentucky Military Institute. After reading law under Judge J. P. Caruthers, he took the full course at the Lebanon Law School. Before he reached the anniversary of his 22d birthday he had attained the collegiate degree of A.M., C.E. and L.B. In the spring of 1858 he opened a law office in Memphis,

Tenn., in partnership with his elder brother, Harry Hill, who had taken the same curriculum; but his brother, an exceptionally bright and promising young man, soon died.

When the "Shelby Grays," a company composed largely of his friends and associates, was ordered to rendezvous at Germantown, Tenn., he was suffering with an acute attack of measles, and was unable to go into service. He received in midsummer an invitation to organize a battalion of Missouri Light Artillery, with the promise of command, but after he had equipped one section of a battery he found that he was physically unable for active service, and resigned and returned home. In the autumn of that year he was summoned, through Colonel E. W. Munford, aid to General A. S. Johnson, to report to that commander at Bowling Green, Ky., by whom he was ordered to Fort Donelson as Instructor of Artillery, with the rank of Lieutenant. Finding none of the heavy guns in permanent batteries he was put on duty to mount them. Owing to the often-enforced absence of the engineer in charge, Captain Dixon, engineering skill was in much demand, and Lieutenant Bedford was kept constantly on duty in forwarding the defenses of the fort until after the investment of the enemy.

In the assignment of the guns of the water batteries to resist the attack of the gunboats, the 10-inch Columbiad, manned by detachment of twenty men of Captain Ross' light battery, under Lieutenant Sparkman, was assigned to the command of Lieutenant Bedford. For the performance of that piece, in the battle with the gunboats, reference is made to the reports of various officers, as contained in the seventh volume of "Records of the War of the Rebellion," but more especially to that of Captain Culberson, commander of the water batteries, wherein the defeat of the enemy's fleet is mainly attributed to the skillful direction of the Columbiad by Lieutenant Bedford, but by one of those mishaps, peculiarly annoying to the victim, the copyist or the compositor, by the substitution of an S for an L, gives the credit to Lieutenant H. S. Bedford, an officer "non in esse" at the batteries.

After seven months as a prisoner of war, first at Camp Chase, with ten days of parole in Columbus, O., and then at Johnson's Island, he was exchanged at Vicksburg, Miss., placed in command of a battalion of infantry that had become detached from the Fifty-first (Bowdre's) Regiment, which temporarily conferred the field rank of Major. When this detachment rejoined its regiment Lieutenant Bedford reported to the Ordnance Department, in which service he continued until the close of the war, with the single break when the exigency of the service placed him for that occasion in command of a light battery. At the time of the surrender he was Ordnance Officer of the Department of Mississippi.

After the war he resumed his profession, but experiencing the necessity of active, outdoor life, he abandoned his law office in Memphis and commenced farming, which vocation he is now following at Bailey, Shelby county, Tenn.

Major Bedford was one of the early members of the Confederate Historical Association. Was married to Miss Marie Louisa McLean at Grenada, Miss., May 23, 1867, and his wife is now serving her second term as President of the Ladies' Confederate Memorial Association of Memphis, which was organized as an auxiliary society to the Confederate Historical Association in 1889. They have two sons — Benjamin Watkins Lee and Hugh Lawson Bedford.

BLOCK, W. F., was a private in Company B, Seventh Tennessee Cavalry, Rucker's Brigade; enlisted while General W. H. Jackson's command was encamped at Coldwater, Miss., in 1862; was paroled at the end of the war. Joined the Confederate Historical Association October 25, 1889.

BOGGS, Rev. WM. E., D. D., was Chaplain of the Sixth South Carolina Volunteers, Bratton's Brigade, Army of Northern Virginia, and often took his musket and went into the trenches or into battle in the open field with his command. He served throughout the war; was afterward pastor of the Second Presbyterian Church of Memphis, and is now at the head of a leading theological college in Georgia. Was an early member of the Association.

BRENAN, FRED R., private Confederate States Army; in 1861 came to Memphis from Hamilton, Ohio, and joined the Bluff City Grays, Company B, One Hundred and Fifty-fourth Senior Tennessee Regiment, at outbreak of the war; was with the company at Randolph, New Madrid, Hickman and Columbus, Ky.; was transferred to the Hudson Battery of Panola county, Miss., and served with it at Camp Beauregard, Ky., under General Bowen, and was with the battery at Bowling Green, Corinth, in battle of Shiloh, siege of Vicksburg, battle of Baton Rouge, and in many engagements in Mississippi and Tennessee under General Forrest. After siege of Vicksburg, was transferred back to Bluff City Grays, who in the meantime had been mounted and transferred from the infantry to Forrest's Cavalry, and formed Company B of the Old Forrest Regiment; was with Forrest in many of his fights and raids in Mississippi and Tennessee—the storming of Fort Pillow, the advance to the Tennessee river, capture of gunboats and transports below Johnsonville; went with a detachment of Bluff City Grays, under Lieutenant James Sutherland, across the Tennessee river to keep telegraph wires cut between Nashville and Johnsonville while Forrest's Artillery attacked and destroyed gunboats and stores at Johnsonville; recrossed the Tennessee river at night in "dugouts," swimming the horses, rejoined the command, and marched to Florence, Ala., and from there went with the cavalry in the Nashville campaign under General Hood; was in the skirmishes and engagements along the pikes up to Spring Hill and Franklin; engaged in the battle of Franklin, the fighting around Nashville, and the subsequent retreat across the Tennessee river; served with the command in Mississippi, and went to the relief of Selma and to intercept the Wilson raid; the command then retired to Gainesville, Ala., and surrendered at the close of the war. Returned with parole to Memphis, and became a deputy chancery clerk under Clerk and Master Doctor Alston; practiced law a couple of years, then became a reporter on the old *Avalanche*, and subsequently was a reporter on the *Public Ledger*, the new *Avalanche*, the *Memphis Appeal*, the *Appeal-Avalanche*, and the *Commercial Appeal*. Is married and has an interesting family.

EDWARD BOURNE.
Taken in Montgomery, Ala., in 1863.

BOURNE, EDWARD, was born June 23, 1846, in Memphis, reared and educated here, and passed his examination for college in June and witnessed the taking of Memphis June 6, 1862. Instead of going off to college was kept at home and drilled with the Young Guards under Captain John F. Cameron. Owing to his youth and delicate physique he was not accepted as a soldier for some time; was finally sworn into the same company when his brother Wm. F. Bourne became its captain in the latter part of 1863, when the army was in winter quarters at Dalton. This company (B) was then a part of the Third Confederate Regiment, and afterward, near the end, was consolidated with the First Arkansas Regiment. Private Bourne was in most of the fighting from Dalton to Atlanta, where his brother, Captain Bourne, was

killed on the 22d of July, 1864, and Comrade Bourne buried
him with the assistance of Sergeant Pixley on the battlefield.
He continued with the regiment to the surrender; was with
Hood on his raid into Tennessee, and endured all the hardships of that and subsequent campaigns.

On the Georgia campaign the regiment was left on an outpost near Calhoun station with one piece of artillery, with the
expectation that it would cover the retreat and be captured.
Instead of that the men escaped at the last moment, bringing
with them one prisoner as a living trophy of their alertness
in a critical place. Near Limestone, Ga., Comrade Bourne
was wounded at short range by a ball that had passed through
a fence rail, but he was not disabled   He was captured with
his regiment at Jonesboro, after a sanguinary and hand to
hand fight, September 1, 1864. A month later the captured
Confederates were swapped by special arrangement between
Generals Hood and Sherman for an equal number of Federals.
Under a regular exchange the Confederates would have been
entitled to a furlough, but instead of that were furnished En-
field rifles and forty rounds of ammunition before rations were
issued to them. They followed the army and overtook it
near Decatur. Coming out of Tennessee Comrade Bourne
was literally barefooted and his feet were very much swollen.
At Pulaski he and others waded through Sweetwater Creek
with ice in it up to their necks, and that night slept on snow
several inches deep. They were thinly clad, and the wonder
is that they lived through such terrible sufferings. A few
days later several men froze to death in a train, while Comrade Bourne was riding and sleeping on top of a car. But
he got through it all; was in the battle of Bentonville, and
was paroled with General Johnston's army at Greensboro,
N. C., where the men were given $1.35 each out of what was
left of the Confederate treasury as a medal or souvenir, rather
than as pay, for their heroic services.

Comrade Bourne came home in the fall of '65, went into
business at once, and has been a very busy man ever since.
He served two years as President of Memphis Board of Underwriters, and was also President of the Memphis Salvage

Corps. In church matters he took an active part; was sometime President of the Shelby County Baptist Sunday-school Convention, and for three years President of the West Tennessee Baptist Sunday-school Convention, and was for a long time a member of the State Sunday-school and Colportage Board.

He was married March 11, 1869, to Miss Jennie Garth McGarvey of Hopkinsville, Ky., whose father, J. W. A. McGarvey, was also a Confederate soldier under John H. Morgan, and they have three children living out of five born to them. Comrade Bourne became a member of this Association several years ago, has been a member of Company A, Confederate Volunteers, from the first, has been First Lieutenant ever since the company went into the State National Guard of Tennessee, and has been with the company on its trips to Chattanooga, Richmond, Little Rock and other places. In his time he has belonged to several local military companies and held offices. In the Inter-State drill given in Memphis in May, 1895, he was a member of the Military Committee. He has always had strong inherited military tastes, and had the advantage of two years at a military school. His family on both sides came of noted Revolutionary stock. His father, James Treadwell Bourne, was born in Kennebunk, Me. His mother, Miss Martha Tucker Freeland, was born in Salem, Mass. They were married at Portsmouth, N. H. The father for a short time was engaged in the shoe business in Boston, but in 1837 came South, moving his family to Memphis, where he lived until his death in 1883. His grandfather, Bourne, married three times. His first wife was Miss Mary Treadwell, the second Clarissa Warren, a niece of General Warren, who fell at Bunker Hill, and his third wife was Narcissa Sewall of Bangor, Me. His mother was the daughter of John Freeland, and through her mother was a descendant of President John Adams' father.

BOND, LEE, private Company B, Twelfth Tennessee Cavalry; enlisted June, 1862; went through the war under Forrest; was at home on furlough at the time of the surrender; came to Memphis and was paroled in May, 1865.

BOBBITT, P. A., Orderly Sergeant Company F, Twelfth North Carolina Confederate Regiment, Army North Virginia; enlisted April, 1862; was wounded at Gettysburg and Fisher's Hill; captured at Gettysburg July 4, 1863, and released August 29, 1863; paroled April 14, 1865. Admitted to the Confederate Historical Association January 8, 1895.

BRENNEN, JOHN, enlisted as a private in Company C, Fourth Louisiana, May 25, 1861. No other entry except " dead."

BRIGHTWELL, THOS. H., enlisted in Company D, First Virginia Infantry, April 9, 1861, and became Adjutant of the Regiment; served through the war, and paroled June 25, 1865. Admitted to the Confederate Historical Association April 9, 1895.

BROWN, C. W., private Company L, One Hundred and Fifty-fourth Tennessee Regiment; enlisted in 1861; was wounded at the battle of Shiloh; captured, and escaped at Selma, Ala., April 2, 1862; paroled May 11, 1865. Admitted to Confederate Historical Association August 13, 1895.

BOWLES, ROBERT S., private Company B, One Hundred and Fifty-fourth Tennessee Regiment, enlisted April 26, 1861; was wounded twice at the battle of Shiloh, but served afterward, and was paroled April 26, 1865, just four years from date of enlistment. Admitted to this Association October 9, 1894.

BURFORD S., served in the Adjutant-General's department on General Wheeler's staff, with the rank of Major. After the war he became an Episcopal minister, and for several years was rector of Calvary Church, Memphis; was transferred back to a church in New York city and died there in 1895. Became a member of this Association some years ago.

BURROW, F. J., Second Sergeant Company D, Fourth Tennessee; enlisted May 15, 1861; was in Stewart's Brigade, Cheatham's Division; wounded at Murfreesboro December 31, 1862; taken prisoner and carried to Rock Island; paroled March 16, 1865. Admitted to the Confederate Historical Association May 4, 1895.

JUDGE T. W. BROWN,
In 1896.

BROWN, THOS. W., was born, reared and educated in Kentucky, and is a most loyal Kentuckian to this day, believing that it has in the past produced more great men than any State in the Union. The only State he is willing to admit to a parallelism in this regard is old Virginia. Just after he graduated at Center College he went to the Mexican war before there was a sprig of beard on his face. Is now a Mexican veteran, and as such receives a pension from the Government.

He came to Memphis to practice law just fourteen days before the fall of Fort Sumpter. He was in politics a Henry Clay Whig, and did not believe in the doctrine or policy of secession; and when Tennessee reversed her sentiment of February, 1861, he steadily refused to have anything to do with

the war. For this he was denounced by secession extremists.
To them he calmly replied: "If you think you can easily
whip the North you will find yourselves mistaken. But I
give each and every one of you this assurance, that when the
time comes that requires every man to save the South from
the humiliation of defeat, I will go and fight for her to the
last. Many of you now so clamorous for war and so full of
fight will then skulk." When Grant occupied Memphis T.
W. Brown thought it was time for every man in the South
to go into the fight. He went out of the lines for this purpose, while others who had denounced him remained, as he
had predicted. At the time he went out of Grant's lines
Bragg was moving into Kentucky. At Chattanooga he received authority from Richmond to follow the march of Bragg,
and raise either a regiment of infantry or a battery. General
Bragg did not occupy Kentucky long enough for this to be
done. Returning into East Tennessee Bragg moved his lines
to Murfreesboro, confronting Rosecrans. The Confederate
Congress created for the administration of military law in
the Confederate armies, corps courts, to be in the field, and
with the respective corps. T. W. Brown was appointed Judge
Advocate to the military court assigned to the corps, then
commanded by Lieutenant-General Polk, subsequently by
Lieutenant-General Hardee. The judge advocates of these
corps courts were commissioned captains in cavalry. The
court assigned to above named corps especially distinguished
itself in the discharge of its duties. It was ever with its
corps on the march and in battle. So marked was its excel-
lence that it attracted the attention of the commanding general of the army, who obtained the passage by the Confederate Congress of an act allowing him to use either of these
corps courts he might select for the general business of the
army, or for the work of any corps as he might assign. The
discipline of the corps now commonly known and called Hardee's Corps had become under the administration of its corps
court so perfect that the business of this court, which at first
was very arduous, had greatly eased off, to the great relief of
its Judge Advocate, upon whom the burden of the work fell.

But the procurement of the act mentioned, by General Joseph E. Johnston, again threw upon Judge Advocate Brown a flood of work. He, however, met his greatly increased labors with uncomplaining energy, and received from General Johnston complimentary recognition.

Two incidents somewhat humorous may with propriety be mentioned here. When the Army of Tennessee reached Atlanta, closing the bloody campaign from Dalton to the Chattahoochee, the military court of the corps was ordered to Liberty, a little hamlet in the rear of the army, around which were quartermaster and commissary encampments and some convalescing soldiers. In a few days McCook's Federal cavalry raided on the left wing of the Army of Tennessee and swooped down on quartermasters and commissaries. Judge Advocate Brown and Colonel Worthington, the only members of the court present (the others having been granted leave of absence for a few days), were captured after a gallant effort by Judge Advocate Brown to escape, in which he very nearly succeeded. By this time General Wheeler's command was in pursuit of the raiding column in a "stern chase." At Newnan Wheeler's advance caught up with McCook's forces and a severe battle ensued. During the battle the prisoners and their guards found themselves between the fires of the contending lines. The Federal officer made no effort to relieve this situation ; this however was not intentional—he had simply lost his head. Captain Brown suggested to him that he should change his position, to which he replied that he could not. The captain then told him he would order his fellow prisoners to dismount and lie on the ground, to which the officer assented. The order was given, the prisoners dismounted and hugged the ground; not one was struck, but a few horses were killed. Directly McCook's lines broke and started in full retreat. The prisoners dispersed toward the Confederate lines, leaving Colonel Worthington, the Judge Advocate and four convalescent soldiers by themselves. There were many loose horses roving about. If there was anything at that time a Confederate soldier wanted, it was a horse. The Judge Advocate and the four soldiers proceeded to cap-

4

ture a horse apiece, but found there were a good many loose
Federal soldiers around, as well as loose horses. The soldiers
were taken in as well as the horses. To the surprise of the
Judge Advocate, while he was careering over the late battle
field on a fairly good mount with which he had provided himself, his familiar schoolboy name Tom was shouted about one
hundred yards distant by a Federal officer. He rode at once
to the officer and found Dr. Burdett, an old college friend, a
Federal surgeon in charge of McCook's field hospital, with
his wounded. The Judge Advocate received the surrender
of the hospital, not refusing a nip of good French brandy
offered by his old college friend.

About this time one of the four soldiers called the Judge
Advocate's attention to a white flag in a bottom cornfield,
quite dense in growing corn. With the four veterans the
Judge Advocate marched to the white flag and found a regiment of Federals. The officer apparently in command an-
nounced the regiment to be the Eighth Iowa Cavalry, that
he was Major Istis, that their lieutenant - colonel was lying
mortally wounded in the adjacent woods, and that their colonel had left them. Confident that Wheeler's lines were close
up, the surrender of the regiment was taken in due form and
the wounded lieutenant colonel taken care of as well as could
be done at the time; but it turned out that Wheeler's lines
were not as close up as was thought at the time the surrender was taken. The surrender was taken at about 1 o'clock
P.M. The delay in appearance of the Confederate lines was
so long that the Yankees began to murmur. This of course
was dangerous to the Judge Advocate and his four veteran
associates. One of the four was sent to find some command
of Wheeler's and report the situation. In the meantime the
Judge Advocate held on to the surrendered regiment with a
stiff upper lip, but much trepidation, as he confesses. At a
little after 6 o'clock P.M., Colonel Ross' Texas Brigade came
up and settled the difficulty.

Judge Advocate Brown has always claimed that he got
more than even with General McCook for capturing him at
Liberty, Ga.

A joke is told of Hardee in connection with Judge Advocate Brown. When Hardee took command of the corps he found in it some brigades not satisfactory to him on the day of battle. Hardee wanted only fighting brigades and regiments in his corps. He had been quite importunate and successful with the commanding general in getting rid of the inferior commands and necessarily putting them on the other corps commanders. But there was one brigade he had not rid himself of. He went again to the general in command of the Army of Tennessee and urged the general to exchange this brigade for one in another corps. The general replied with some heat, it is said, to the application, calling his attention to the success he had achieved in getting out of his corps inferior commands, and telling him that he was as much bound to put up with poor soldiers as the other corps commanders. Hardee, stumped by this very just reply to his application, is said to have answered as follows: "General, I am influenced somewhat in this proposal by humanity." "How is that?" said the general. Hardee replied, "I am afraid, general, if that brigade is not taken from me my judge advocate will shoot all of them." Hardee did get rid of the obnoxious command.

Judge Advocate Brown was a great favorite with both Polk and Hardee. The former applied, when he left the Army of Tennessee for the Department of Mississippi, to Mr. Davis for permission to take him with him. This was refused, it being decided that he belonged to the corps, and not to the corps commander. The latter called him into his confidence when he was about to have a duel with Hood. He was one of the paroling officers at Trinity Church, Greensboro, N. C.

After the war Judge Advocate Brown was conspicuous in recovering the liberties of ex-Confederates from the reconstruction measures. He had the singular fortune to first present in 1868 at New York the impolicy and oppression of reconstruction administration in the South to the Northern constituencies; and also from the balcony of Peabody Hotel, at the request of the business men of Memphis, made the last speech in the drama of reconstruction. This was on the occasion of the celebrated McEnery controversy in Louisiana. Captain Brown prepared the resolutions for the Memphis merchants. The resolutions and speech were sent to President Grant. Then followed quickly the withdrawal of Federal military authority from Louisiana.

Judge Brown joined this Association April 12, 1884.

BOLINER. PATRICK McHENRY, son of James and Ann Boliner, was born in Staunton, Va., September 14, 1831. His ancestors were of Revolutionary stock, and his grandfather Boliner was in the war of 1812. He is a nephew of the late John McCullough, the tragedian, who was his mother's brother, they being the only two of the family who came over from Ireland, as far as he knows. The Mc in his name is for McCullough. In 1852 young Boliner, whose father had died in 1849, went to Fort Worth, Texas, and after working a few years started to college at McKenzie, where he was a student thirty years of age when the war began. When the news came of the firing on Fort Sumpter 300 young men dropped their books and rushed off for the war, Boliner among the rest. He says now that his class had a lesson ready in differential calculus that has never yet been recited. He enlisted in May, 1861, at Clarksville, Texas, in Company E, Ninth Texas Cavalry, and was in a brigade commanded by General McIntosh at the battle of Elk Horn, Ark., March 4, 1862, where both McIntosh and Ben McCulloch (no relative of Boliner) were killed; was in several engagements out West with the Indians. He came over with the regiment, without horses, with Price's army, and was in the battle of Corinth, on foot, October 4, 1862, and was severely wounded there. Later in the war his regiment became part of Ross' famous brigade, and he served in it under Jackson and Forrest until the surrender; was wounded at Dallas, Ga., and at Franklin, Tenn., by a sabre cut; was captured at Spring Hill, but knocked the guard in the head and escaped the same night; never missed a fight, except when absent on account of wound, which was only a short time; was paroled May 13, 1865, at Jackson, Miss.; has taught school and been variously engaged since; has made Memphis his home for thirty years; never married. Joined this Association October 9, 1894; became an active member of Company A, Confederate Veterans, at once, and was with it at the reunion in Richmond June and July, 1896.

J. J. BROWN.

BROWN, J. J., born in Hardeman county, Tenn., January 24, 1840; removed to Fayette county when a boy; joined a company of infantry in 1861, whose services were offered to the State but not accepted, as the quota desired was full. In November, 1861, he enlisted in Eldridge's Battery, made up from Fayette, Hardin and Wayne counties. At Nashville J. W. Eldridge was elected captain; E. E. Wright and T. W. Jones first lieutenants; J. W. Mebane and Joe Williamson second lieutenants, and J. W. Phillips orderly sergeant, with a company roll of 128 men; was ordered to report at Bowling Green, Ky., and assigned to Baker's Hill, an advanced position, which was occupied until the army fell back on Nashville. Then the battery and several siege guns blockaded the river several miles below Nashville and held the enemy's gunboats in check until the city was evacuated. At Murfreesboro the battery was assigned to Breckinridge's Division. Arriving at Corinth the subject of this sketch was ordered to report to the colonel commanding cavalry at Decatur, Ala., with two guns of the battery; remained on outpost duty with the cavalry until after the evacuation of Corinth, and then joined the other section of the battery at Saltillo, Miss., which had taken an active part in the campaign around Corinth. The battery also took an active part in the Kentucky campaign, but was not engaged in the battle of Perryville. After the army fell back to Knoxville the battery was ordered to Murfreesboro, where early in November, 1862, it reorganized by electing E. E. Wright captain, J. W. Mebane first lieutenant, J. W. Phillips second lieutenant, and J. C. Grant third lieutenant; took an active part in the campaign around Murfreesboro; was not engaged in the first day's battle, but held in reserve under a hot fire; was with Breckinridge in his desperate charge on the enemy's left on the 2d of January, 1863, where they lost Captain Wright and one-third of the company. The division went in 4000 strong and left 1800 on the field. The engagement lasted forty minutes.

About the first day of June, 1863, the division was ordered to Jackson, Miss., to reinforce General J. E. Johnston; took part in the Vicksburg campaign; had a light engagement with a division of the enemy at Jackson, Miss., in July, 1863. About the 1st of September, 1863, was ordered to reinforce Bragg, near Chattanooga; was engaged in the battles of Chickamauga, Missionary Ridge, and Rockyface Ridge (or Dalton), Resaca, Lafayette, and Kenesaw Ridge, where Captain Mebane was killed, having the top of his head blown off by an eight-inch Parrott shell while engaged in an artillery duel with the enemy. After Captain Mebane was killed Lieutenant Phillips was promoted to captain.

About the 16th of June, 1864, was engaged in the light-
ning bug fight at the dead angle. On the night of July 1,
1864, was engaged at Pine Mountain; July 4 at Peachtree
Creek; July 20–22 at Atlanta; also at Jonesboro, Lovejoy's
station, Franklin and Nashville, Tenn., and last but not least,
at Spanish Fort, one of the approaches to the city of Mobile,
in April, 1865. After the evacuation of Mobile the battery
went up to Demopolis, where the men were given muskets,
having left their guns in the fort; were ordered over to Meridian, Miss., where the company surrendered. Ten of them
not feeling disposed to do so, on that morning broke their
muskets over a tree and left for Tennessee. Reaching La-
Grange, Mr. Brown and some of his comrades surrendered
and received their paroles in June, 1865. He has lived in
Shelby county for the last thirteen years. He was in all the
campaigns of his battery and in some awful close places,
especially at Spanish Fort, where the Confederates were con-
fronted by a force of perhaps ten to one, but he was never
wounded. He became a member of this Association several
years ago; is a member of Company A, Confederate Veterans, and was on the trip to Richmond last summer. He was
married to Miss Belle Abernathy of Fayette county in 1871,
and they have two daughters, Miss Irene Fowler, a graduate
of Vassar College, and Miss Anna Belle A. Brown. The latter is a "daughter" of Company A. Their home is at
Buntyn, near this city.

BEECHER, EDWARD A., born in the State of New York
in 1834. A few years after his father moved out to Loraine
county, Ohio, and in co-operation with other Eastern men of
congenial ideas formed the community of Oberlin. In the
college of Oberlin Edward Beecher graduated before reaching his majority. After reading law under Salmon P. Chase
in Cincinnati, casting aside forever the associations and teach-
ings of childhood and youth, he turned his face southward,
making for himself a place among a people of whom he had
never perhaps heard a kind word. About the year 1856 he
landed in Memphis. Under the late E. M. Yerger and other
lawyers of ability he passed an examination said to have

been of an exceptional character. The late James Wickersham complimented the youthful member of the bar by making him a partner. Owing to a passionate love of the law, combined with what General Hood in later years called his matchless energy, an enviable degree of success crowned his efforts. Suddenly his onward and happy progress was checked; upon the secession of Tennessee duty pointed another way: he said that "A faithful discharge of duty is a strong foundation on which to build one's happiness."

He enlisted with Captain McDonald's Dragoons in 1861. In 1862 General Polk asked him to join his staff in the capacity of quartermaster, which he did, holding the position as a temporary one, as he thought; for this, he wrote, was not his idea of military service. His peculiar power of overcoming obstacles, his "matchless energy and activity," rendered his services in this line so needful that his work seemed cut out for him. It was said of him that in moving the army, while acting as military superintendent of railroads, his powers of providing ways and means were almost limitless. He was, with the exception of a few months after his marriage, always in the field. The few months were spent in Macon busily occupied in the office of the Master of Transportation.

Letters of appreciation from his superiors were not lacking. One from Richmond offered a broader field, with the rank of colonel, which was declined. To be called an "honest quartermaster" was his distinction. In common with all soldiers of Tennessee, he shared an unbounded devotion to Generals Vaughan and Cheatham; he wept over Preston Smith and was ever loyal to Joe Johnston. With his comrades he believed that the Army of Tennessee led the military field in courage and endurance. Few Southern born men felt the fatal termination of the war as did this adopted son. He took up the pursuit of his profession at the end, but under such changed circumstances, owing to the terrible period of so-called reconstruction, that, although financially successful, the practice of it was never the same pleasure again. Major Beecher died in 1873 of pneumonia. He became a member of this Association September 9, 1869.

DR. R. E. BULLINGTON.

BULLINGTON, R. E., was born in DeSoto county, Miss., the 2d day of April, 1847. His father was Dr. Edward Bullington, who came from Richmond, Va., many years ago; was a well known and highly popular citizen, and died of yellow fever at Hernando in 1878.   When the war broke out R. E. Bullington was a mere boy, but he enlisted in September, 1864, in Company K, Captain W. A. Rains, Eighteenth Mississippi Regiment, Colonel Alex. Chalmers, Rucker's Brigade, and saw eight or ten months' very arduous service.   He first took part in the recapture of a wagon train near Florence, Ala., which had been taken from the Confederates; was in an engagement at Cedar Grove, and next day was at the battle of Franklin. He was in various skirmishes on the raid to Nashville, and shared the hardships of the retreat of Hood's army from Tennessee, and came out with very little clothing. At one time his company and Chalmers' escort was cut off and in the rear of the Federal army, but by hard riding for three days and nights and swimming Duck river they escaped. He was with the command on down to Selma, and participated in a sharp engagement there. After the surrender he came through to Memphis and was paroled here. He lived for a time at Hernando and was in business; married Miss Sallie Peete, daughter of Dr. J. S. Peete, near Mason, Tenn., December 30, 1869, and they have reared an interesting family of seven children. A year after marriage the young doctor, as he was to be, went off to college, and was graduated in 1872 with first honors, and returning began the practice of his profession. He lived one year at Humboldt, Tenn., and twelve years at Hernando, Miss.; removed to Memphis in October, 1885, and has lived here ever since and been eminently successful. He became a member of this Association on the 13th of June, 1894.

BUCHANAN, J. W., first enlisted as a private in the Chickasaw Guards, a company organized by General W. F. Tucker, in Chickasaw county, Miss., in the fall of 1860. In January, 1861, this company, with other State troops, was ordered to Pensacola, Fla.; served one month and returned home. This company was one of the first to offer its services to the State, and was ordered to Corinth about the 1st of April, 1861, when it, with other companies, formed the famous Eleventh Mississippi and went from Corinth to Lynchburg, Va., and was there mustered into the Confederate service; from there went to Harper's Ferry. The Eleventh Mississippi, Second Mississippi, Fourth Alabama, First Tennessee (Colonel Turney) and Sixth North Carolina constituted General Bee's Brigade at the first battle of Manassas. Only a part of the Eleventh Mississippi was engaged in this battle. His company did not get to the battlefield until the fight was over, being delayed on a train. He was discharged, on account of a long spell of fever, in August, 1861, and returned home. Shortly after this he was elected captain of a new company, about the 1st of September, 1861. His company was ordered to Marion station, near Meridian, Miss., where

the Twenty-fourth Mississippi Regiment was organized, with
W. F. Dowd of Aberdeen as colonel. The regiment was
ordered to Fernandina, Fla., where it remained until ordered
to Chattanooga about the 1st of March, 1862. The regiment
became a part of General S. B. Maxey's Brigade, and was
ordered from there to Corinth, and reached there the day
after the battle of Shiloh. The Twenty-fourth Mississippi
Regiment became a part of the Army of Tennessee after
this. In the Kentucky campaign it formed a part of Marsh
Walker's Brigade, General Patton Anderson's Division, Hardee's Corps, and was engaged in the battle of Perryville, this
being its first regular battle. Just before the battle of Murfreesboro the Twenty-fourth, Twenty-seventh, Twenty-ninth,
Thirtieth and Thirty-fourth Mississippi Regiments became
Walthall's Brigade, but was under command of General Patton Anderson in the battle of Murfreesboro, General Walthall being absent on leave. On the promotion of General
Walthall to Major-General, Colonel Sam. Benton, colonel of
the Thirty-fourth Mississippi, was made brigadier-general,
and was fatally wounded at Atlanta on the 22d of July, 1864,
and lived only a few days. Colonel W. F. Brantly of the
Twenty-ninth Mississippi was promoted to brigadier-general.
Captain Buchanan was wounded at the battle of Jonesboro,
Ga., the 31st of August, 1864, and was never able to return
to his company. He was confined to his bed from this wound
until July, 1868.

He had graduated at the University of Mississippi in 1860,
and commenced the study of law before the war and during
his confinement in bed from his wounds, and began the practice in December, 1868. He was elected to the Mississippi
Legislature in 1879 and again in 1881, and in March, 1882,
was appointed circuit judge for the First District of Mississippi by Gov. Lowrey. In March, 1887, he resigned the office
of circuit judge to take the position now held with the Kansas City, Memphis & Birmingham Railroad Company, and in
January, 1888, he removed to Memphis.

BUFORD, SMITH, enlisted as a private in Company F,
Thirteenth Mississippi, early in 1861. Served until the end

of the war. He is a practicing physician at Raleigh, and is an active member of Company A, Confederate Veterans.

BUNCH, GEORGE H., Sergeant-Major Fifth Virginia, Army North Virginia; enlisted April 9, 1861; paroled June 7, 1865. Admitted to the C. H. A. January 8, 1895.

BUTLER, A. R., private Company H, Fifteenth Arkansas Regiment; entered service April 27, 1861, and paroled May, 1865. Proposed for membership by L. O. Rivers and C. G. Locke, and elected May 20, 1870.

CAMPBELL, D. A., enlisted August 19, 1862, in Company F, Second Kentucky Cavalry, John H. Morgan's command. Discharged January 8, 1865.

CAMERON, WILLIAM L., was a member of Company A, Young Guards, and afterward assistant paymaster in the Confederate States Navy. Served on the gunboat Savannah at Savannah; on the gunboats Huntsville, Baltic and Nashville at Mobile, and was captured at Naura Hubber Bluffs and paroled there May 10, 1865. Admitted to this Association August 13, 1895.

CANNON, H. E., private Company A, Seventh Tennessee Cavalry; enlisted May 16, 1861; was wounded while scouting around Lost Mountain and Powder Springs, Ga.; paroled May 11, 1865. Admitted to C. H. A. June 1, 1895.

CARMICHAEL, J., chaplain Thirtieth Regiment Virginia Infantry; entered service April 11, 1861; paroled July 5, 1865; was rector of Grace Church, Memphis, for several years, and took an active, heroic part in the relief of yellow fever sufferers in 1873; afterward returned to Virginia. Proposed for membership in this Association by R. J. Black and J. Harvey Mathes, and elected March 17, 1870.

CARPENTER, A. S., Orderly Sergeant Company B, Thirty-second North Carolina Regiment; enlisted May 20, 1861; was in D. H. Hill's and Rhodes' Divisions, Jackson's, Ewell's and Gordon's Corps; never missed a battle except when in prison; paroled May, 1865.

CAPT. W. W. CARNES.
In 1862.

CARNES, WILLIAM W., was born September 18, 1841, at Somerville, in Fayette county, Tenn. Some years later his family moved to Memphis, and he passed his boyhood days in this city. He was the eldest son of General James A. Carnes, a prominent citizen of Memphis before the war, whose military title was due to his being brigade commander of the State militia, the rank held in recent years by his younger son, S. T. Carnes. "Will Carnes," as he was and is known, was appointed to the U. S. Naval Academy at Annapolis when fifteen years old, and was in the graduating class there when the secession of the Southern States caused him to send in his resignation, that he might be free to aid his native Southland in the conflict he believed to be inevitable. After a short period of service in the first organization and drilling of companies, while on staff duty at the headquarters of General Gideon J. Pillow in this city, he was appointed by Governor Harris as Drill Master of Tennessee State troops, with the rank of First Lieutenant of infantry, assigned to Cheatham's Brigade at Union City, and attached to the Fifth Tennessee Regiment, commanded by Colonel Travis; was next appointed First Lieutenant of Artillery and assigned to Captain (afterward General) W. H. Jackson's battery of light artillery, at New Madrid, Mo. Captain Jackson was wounded at Belmont and Lieutenant Carnes placed in command of the battery. Upon Captain Jackson's return to duty he was made Colonel of Cavalry and Lieutenant Carnes succeeded him as Captain of Artillery early in 1862, when he was but twenty years of age. It was stated in *The Confederate Veteran* of June, 1895, published at Nashville, that "the youngest captains of artillery in the Confederate army were W. W. Carnes of Memphis, John W. Morton of Nashville, Tenn., and Willie Pegram of Virginia." "I think," says the writer, "John Morton was the youngest of these three; but Captain Carnes had been commanding a battery some time before Morton was promoted from Lieutenant to the rank of Captain. Both were captains in active command of field batteries at twenty years of age."

Carnes' Battery was first attached to a brigade commanded by General Clarke, of Mississippi, till after the battle of Shiloh. Soon after, General Daniel S. Donelson was assigned to the command of a brigade of Tennessee troops in Cheatham's Division, and the battery thereafter served with that brigade under Gen. Donelson, and afterward under Marcus J. Wright, who succeeded Donelson.

The first important field service this battery saw was at Perryville, October 8, 1862. Carnes' Battery brought on the fight on the left and was very hotly engaged in an artillery duel for more than an hour. After being ordered back to refit and prepare for a hotter contest still, the battery (of four guns) was transferred rapidly to the extreme right with Polk's Corps. There, supported by the Eighth and Fifty-first Tennessee regiments, and Wharton's regiment of Texas Cavalry, they attacked the extreme left of the Federal line, throwing them into great confusion. Wharton's Texas Rangers and Maney's and Donelson's Brigades followed up the advantage gained and the fight was won on that part of the field with comparatively light loss on the Confederate side. The Confederates had 13,000 men engaged, all told, against a force of 55,000 on the Federal side, available if not engaged. Captain Carnes was famous from that day, and his reputation was earned by hard, skillful fighting. In this battle he received his first and only wound during the war, being shot in the foot. He remained with his command and rode in an ambulance the greater part of the time on the retreat. He had been sick most of the campaign, and reaching Knoxville was given sick leave of absence to go to Macon, Ga., where his sisters were at school. There he met the lady to whom he was married soon after the war, and the Captain says he has never had any spite against the Yankee rifleman who helped to send him there.

Rumors of an approaching battle caused him to return to his command before his leave of absence expired, and he commanded his battery in his usual effective way in the battle of Murfreesboro. (See " Campaigns and Battles of the Sixteenth Tennessee Volunteers," by Thomas A. Head, also Lindsley's " Military Annals of Tennessee.") After the retreat from Murfreesboro the battery was camped at Shelbyville and Tullahoma. Colonel Head, in his book, states that on the retreat to Chattanooga, July, 1863, when the army reached the Tennessee river, near the mouth of Battle creek, after hard rains, they found it much swollen and the pontoon bridge broken in the middle—half being on each side of the river. The engineer officers in charge were at a loss what to do. At the suggestion of General Cheatham, Captain Carnes was placed in charge, and by his knowledge of ropes, boats and water, acquired in the navy, he quickly replaced the broken bridge and the army passed over in safety. For this he was highly complimented by Generals Cheatham, Hardee, Walthall and others, who were anxious spectators of his work. The part that Carnes' Battery took at Chickamauga is a matter of history. In the fight of Saturday afternoon, September 19, it suffered terribly in men and horses killed and wounded, and when the supporting infantry fell back the guns fell into the hands of the Federals. They were retaken, however, soon after, by Brown's and Bates' Brigades of Stewart's Division. Of seventy-eight men, thirty-eight were killed and wounded, and the battery also lost forty-nine horses in the short engagement of Saturday. The recaptured guns, with carriages badly used up, were carried to the rear, across Chickamauga creek, and, the battery being unfit for service, the remaining men were temporarily assigned to other commands, Captain Carnes being ordered to report for staff duty with General Leonidas Polk, who was very fond of him. General Bragg rode over the ground Sunday morning, and complimented Captain Carnes very highly for his work. After the battle he was given thirty days' leave of absence to fit out a new battery, having been allowed the privilege of making his selection from the fifty-nine guns taken from the field of Chickamauga, and on his return to the army he was placed in command of a battalion of four batteries. He continued in command of the battalion attached to the division commanded by General C. L. Stevenson until early in 1864, when, at Dalton, he was ordered to report for duty in the navy. He had been appointed to the regular Confederate States Navy, along with other officers who resigned from the United States Navy at the beginning of the war, and while commanding his battery he was borne on the Confederate States Navy register as Lieutenant, but noted there as "furloughed without pay, serving with the army." Being ordered to Savannah, Ga., he became executive officer of the iron-clad "Savannah," and afterward commanded the steamer "Samson." In command of this latter vessel he was guarding the river above Savannah when that city fell into the enemy's hands, and he carried his boat up to Augusta on a very full river caused by heavy rains at that time; thence was ordered to Columbus, Ga., to assist in equipping an iron-clad there, and when that place fell he escaped and started to join Forrest; met Grierson's raid at Eufaula, Ala., went back to Smithville, Ga., learned there that the army had surrendered, and then reported to

Macon, Ga., to be paroled on May 10, 1865. It was a pleasant place to him. Captain Carnes returned to Memphis in June, 1865, and engaged in business here. In 1866 he married in Macon, Ga., and in the winter of 1867 he left Memphis to make his home in Macon. There he became actively connected with the local military, and was for many years captain of the famous " Macon Volunteers," a crack company, whose organization dates back to 1825. In 1888 Captain Carnes returned to Memphis, bringing with him quite a large family reared in Georgia, and engaged in business here. In the course of time he became captain of " Company A, Confederate Veterans," which he now commands. At the August election, 1896, as the Democratic nominee, he was elected Sheriff of Shelby county under the most complimentary circumstances and conditions, and is now filling that office to the great satisfaction of all law-abiding and respectable elements of the community, who feel that they have in him a fearless, faithful and efficient public servant. He is a quiet, modest man, a good disciplinarian, without being a martinet, and enjoying the fullest confidence and respect of all the people.

One of the memories of the war which Captain Carnes cherishes with commendable pride is the fact that General Forrest made special application for Carnes' assignment to his command. In a communication addressed to Adjutant-General Cooper, at Richmond, General Forrest asked permission to leave the Army of Tennessee to come west and raise a command for special purposes set forth. He desired only a force of four hundred men from his own command and a first-class battery of Dahlgren or Parrott guns, and he designated Captain Carnes, then commanding a battery in Polk's Corps, as the artillery officer preferred by him. His suggestions were not then approved, but this did not lessen the compliment to Captain Carnes. This correspondence begins on page 507, Series 1, volume 30, of the " Official War Records," as published by the United States Government.

Another pleasing memento, now old and faded, is a letter from his former brigade commander, General Marcus J.

5

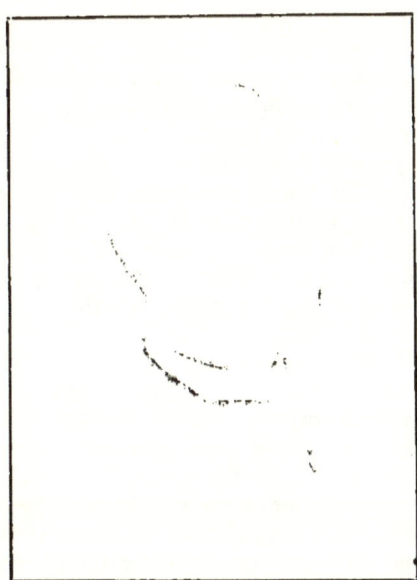

CAPT. W. W. CARNES,
In 1862.

Wright, written December 20, 1863, to Captain Carnes when he was about to leave the army in obedience to his orders for duty in the navy. Other highly prized letters from Generals Polk, Hardee and Cheatham were sent on to the Navy Department at Richmond, and were lost there.

One of his great friends and admirers was old Colonel Oladowski, General Bragg's Chief of Ordnance. From the battle of Perryville on through its career, Carnes' Battery used large quantities of canister shot at close quarters. This accorded so well with Colonel Oladowski's notions that he called Carnes his " canister shot captain " and was ready to sound his praises on all occasions.

In connection with this sketch we give two pictures of Captain Carnes. The first shows him as a young captain of artillery at the age of 21, the other as a citizen of Memphis thirty years later.

CARTER, A. B., Captain Company F, Sixth Virginia Cavalry, Army North Virginia; enlisted August, 1861, in the Black Horse Cavalry; was afterward elected first lieutenant Company F; was wounded five times—at Spottsylvania Court House, Winchester and in skirmishes in the Valley of Virginia; was promoted to captaincy of Company F in 1863; lost an arm at Winchester October 9, 1864, and was unfitted by this and other wounds until the close of the war; paroled from hospital May, 1865; is a native of Virginia, but lived in Mississippi at the outbreak of the war, and has lived in Memphis nearly twenty years. Joined the C. H. A. in 1895.

CHEATHAM, Major JOHN A., born June 6, 1826, in a home overlooking a part of the old graveyard now included in South Nashville. He was the fifth of eleven children. There were three sons, General Frank, Felix and John—the youngest. He was a son of Leonard P. Cheatham, who was postmaster at Nashville during President Polk's administration. His grandfather, Anderson Cheatham, with seven brothers were among the very early settlers in Robertson county, coming from Virginia. His mother, Elizabeth R., was granddaughter of the leader of the pioneer settlement on the " Bluffs," or " French Lick," now Nashville, General James Robertson.

Most of his boyhood was spent on a farm. He was not fond of books—did not graduate. At the age of 20 he became a planter in Arkansas; returned to take a clerkship in the Nashville postoffice under his father, during the Polk administration; was chief clerk for two years; returned to Arkansas and became a merchant. Being slightly lame from an accident in childhood, he did not enter the Confederate service until 1862; then joined a company of the Eighteenth Arkansas Regiment at Little Rock. He says now (1896) that he did nothing very brilliant, but that his promotions were numerous and in quick succession.

Reaching Fort Pillow he was made fourth sergeant; next assigned to duty as adjutant. After the retreat from Corinth reported to General Cheatham and was made division ord-

nance officer with the rank of major; was in the Kentucky
campaign and at Chickamauga; served as aide-de-camp on
General Cheatham's staff on down to the surrender in North
Carolina. After the war lived in Middle Tennessee and Mississippi; married for the first time in 1876; came to Memphis
in 1882. Settled under his own vine and fig tree in a sub-
urban village, joined the Confederate Historical Association,
became a member of Company A, to which he still belongs,
and is a fine type of the philosophic, entertaining Confederate veteran and old-time Southern gentleman.

CRUMP, JAMES M., Captain Company B, Seventeenth
Mississippi Regiment; was wounded four times—in the two
days' fight in front of Richmond, Va., at Gettysburg, Pa.. and
twice at Chickamauga. In application he says: "I served
with one command from beginning to end, and the only regret
I have now is that we did not succeed in our undertaking."
Admitted to C. H. A. October 9, 1894.

CULBERSON, J. H., private Company C, Third South
Carolina Cavalry; enlisted March, 1864; was always in the
same regiment. After the explosion of the mine at the crater
in front of Petersburg, Va., the regiment was sent to South
Carolina to meet Sherman's raid, and was surrendered at
Salisbury, N. C., April 17, 1865.

CUMMINS, HOLMES, was born 7th day of August, 1844,
in Tipton county, Tenn.; enlisted as a private in Company C,
Ninth Tennessee Infantry, May 24, 1861; served in Cheatham's Division under Bragg, Johnston and Hood; he was
wounded in the battles of Shiloh, Chickamauga, Resaca and
Jonesboro; at close of the war was Adjutant of the Ninth
Tennessee; paroled May, 1865; afterward read law; served
two terms in the Legislature; located in Memphis and became
a very prominent lawyer, and died here October 24, 1896.
His remains, in accordance with his instructions, were cre-
mated in St. Louis and his ashes interred in the cemetery of
his old home, Covington, Tennessee. He was one of the
early members of this Association.

GEN. JAMES R. CHALMERS.

CHALMERS, JAMES R., was born in Halifax county, Va., January 11, 1831; the oldest son of Hon. Jos. W. Chalmers, who succeeded Robert J. Walker as United States Senator from Mississippi. General Chalmers graduated with the second honors in the class of 1850 of the South Carolina College. Commenced the practice of law in Holly Springs, Miss., where he resided from childhood, in January, 1853. In 1857 he was elected district attorney of the Seventh Judicial District of Mississippi. In 1860 was elected to the State Convention which declared the secession of Mississippi, and was chairman of the committee on military affairs in that body. When John Brown made his raid into Virginia General Chalmers made a speech to the people at Hernando, declaring that it was time to prepare for war, and a company was then and there organized, of which he was elected captain, and this company he carried out on the first call for Confederate troops from Mississippi. In March, 1861, at Pensacola, Fla., he was elected colonel of the Ninth Mississippi Regiment. On the 12th of February, 1862, he was made a brigadier-general, and commanded the right brigade of Sidney Johnson's army at the battle of Shiloh, which got nearer to Pittsburg Landing than any other Confederate command in that engagement. He was wounded at the battle of Murfreesboro on Stone river, and after his recovery ordered to command of North Mississippi in 1863, where he commanded the cavalry until the arrival of General Forrest, when he took command of the First Division of Forrest's Cavalry, which position he held until the surrender.

He was elected to Congress in 1876, 1878, 1880 and 1882. He is a resident of Mississippi, but has his law office in Memphis, Tenn., in partnership with W. H. Carroll, who commanded his escort company when he took command of North Mississippi.

CLEARY, JAMES, was born in Ireland January 22, 1844: came to this country with his parents when an infant; was left an orphan in Memphis, without brothers or sisters, at the age of 8 years. At the beginning of the war he ran off to follow the Memphis boys at Columbus, Ky.; was rejected on account of youth, but on the 6th of April, 1861, he was sworn into Captain Marsh Patrick's Company H, One Hundred and Fifty-fourth Tennessee Regiment. He was with the command and in all engagements until after the battle of Missionary Ridge, when he was furloughed indefinitely and sent to the hospital at Montgomery, Ala., on account of a serious scalp trouble which threatened his eyesight. From thence he passed through the lines and went to Hot Springs, where he remained some time and apparently recovered; returned to the army, relapsed, went back to Hot Springs for a time, and was on his second return to the front when he heard of the surrender, and returned to what he called home.

Comrade Cleary had no blood kin in Memphis when he went into the army and none when he returned. A gallant fireman offered to secure him a job, and soon afterward he became a member of the fire department and distinguished himself for coolness and bravery. In time he became chief, and filled the place with distinction for many years. In 1884 he was taken from this position by the Board of Underwriters and given the important position of inspector, and has filled it ever since. In all his life he has never had but four different employments, including his army service. This indicates his staying qualities, if he did run away once. He is quiet and modest, as he is courageous, and enjoys the implicit confidence of all who know him.

During the war an uncle of whom he had never heard came to Memphis in a Federal regiment and inquired for him; he left his own address, away up in Massachusetts. After the war a pleasant correspondence ensued. The old uncle is alive yet, is some 80 odd years of age and draws a pension.

Captain Cleary, as he became before he was "chief," is not without some of his own blood and kin here now. He married after the war, and has an interesting family of nine children. He joined this Association soon after it came into existence and has been a regular attendant almost ever since, and has rendered much valuable service, especially on memorial or decoration occasions.

COLE, EDMUND ANDERSON, was born in Giles county, Tenn., on the 5th day of December, 1824. His mother was Mary Anderson, the daughter of Colonel Robert Anderson and Mary Read. His father was David R. Cole, and his grandmother on his father's side was a Miss Wills. They were all Virginians, but his grandfather Anderson and his father moved to Kentucky at an early period. His mother was of Scotch and his father of English descent. Both of his grandfathers fought in the Revolution.

He was licensed to practice law by Alexander M. Clayton of the High Court of Errors and Appeals the day he was 21 years old, but practiced only a short time, when he went to Mexico, being one of four brothers who enlisted in that war, one of whom fell a victim to disease and hardship incident to a soldier's life, and one other, now Dr. Robert A. Cole of Texas, was wounded. In 1849 he crossed the plains to California and engaged in mining. On his return home by way of Panama he was shipwrecked and returned with five companions through Mexico and Texas to Holly Springs, Miss., where he became in a business way connected with the Northern Bank of Mississippi. Afterward he became engaged in planting on the Mississippi river and moved to Memphis in 1857. In March, 1862, was elected and served as Captain of Maynard Rifles (Company L) in the One Hundred and Fifty-fourth Sr. Regiment, Tennessee Volunteers, and took part in the battles of Shiloh, Richmond, Ky., and Perryville. A complimentary notice of him and his company can be found in the tenth volume of the Government War Records. After the battle of Murfreesboro and the army had fallen back to Chattanooga, he was a member of one of General Bragg's court-martials, with the gallant General Carter as president, until his health became so impaired that he was unable to act. He, according to the opinion of army surgeons, was in so dangerous a condition as to be liable to drop dead at any moment, having rheumatism of the heart, and was advised to resign, but refused for several months to do so. Finally, despairing of ever getting well, he tendered his resignation, which was accepted. He remained in Mississippi, however, until the surrender and then returned to his home in Memphis, where he found that he had been complimented with an indictment for treason. He is at present secretary of the Memphis Bar and Law Library Association, and is of himself a walking encyclopedia of war reminiscences and varied thrilling experiences in the far West and South. He was one of the earliest members of the old Confederate Relief and Historical Association, but delicate health has prevented him from taking an active part.

CROFFORD, J. A., was a private in Company D, McDonald's Battalion, Forrest's old regiment; enlisted July, 1863, in Mississippi, but did not reach his regiment until September following; was wounded once in a battle south of and near Columbia, Tenn. His parole and other papers were burned in his home.

THOS. H. CHILTON.
In 1861.

CHILTON, THOS. H., was born in Benton, now Calhoun county, Ala., and removed to Mississippi when a child with his father and grew up at Byhalia and Oxford. Enlisted in the Lamar Rifles under Captain Green early in 1861. The company was afterward Company G, Eleventh Mississippi Regiment. It went into Virginia in the spring, but as young Chilton had been elected speaker for his (sophomore) class in the University of Mississippi he was induced to remain over for the commencement exercises, which never came off. The war spirit was so high that the university was suspended and he soon joined his company at Bristow's Station, near Manassas Plains, and was there sworn into the Confederate service July 7, 1861, at the age of 18 years. His first enlistment was for twelve months. At the end of that time he re-enlisted for the war and on that account was given a thirty days' furlough.

He served in Generals Bee's, Whiting's, Law's and Davis' Brigades, and in Joseph E. Johnston's, Stonewall Jackson's, Longstreet's, Hood's and A. P. Hill's Corps; was wounded at the battle of Seven Pines; wound not serious enough to cause him to leave his company. The division in which he served was transferred to Stonewall Jackson's command in the Valley of Virginia and made the famous march in the valley and over Blue Ridge to the rear of McClellan's army, and was again wounded in the battle of Gains' Mill on Frazer's farm; still kept on with the command and participated in the battle of Malvern Hill. The next battle he was in was the second battle of Manassas, in which he took part two days. He was under General Lee in his first and second invasions of Maryland and Pennsylvania.

On the first advance across the Potomac, when the army reached Hagerstown, Md., the quartermasters bought up all the shoes in the place. Only two pairs could be issued to his company. An inspection was made and he was selected as one of the two men suffering most for shoes and was given a light pair of gaiters, too large for his bleeding feet; went on and was in the battle of Boonsboro and South Mountain. He was wounded a few days afterward at Sharpsburg, where twelve bullets passed through his clothes; there he was given a sixty days' wounded furlough.

An incident at Sharpsburg illustrates the dire extremities to which the young men of the South were often reduced in the field. After the first day's fight he was detailed with others to go out at night in search of food for the company. They found only green corn and raw Irish potatoes in a field between the lines, and the men gladly ate these rations without cooking them. Next day in the fight in the same field young Chilton fell wounded and had only two raw potatoes in his haversack. Such were some of the privations and sufferings of Southern soldiers who had been accustomed at home to all the comforts and luxuries that easy circumstances or wealth command. On the second advance into Pennsylvania he was at the battle of Gettysburg and was in nearly all the general and minor engagements in which the army of Northern Virginia participated for four years.

THOS. H. CHILTON,
In 1896.

Finally he was captured in the last fight at Petersburg
down on the extreme right at daylight April 2, 1865. Before
that he had been detailed as commissary of the regiment and
properly could have kept out of the battle, but hearing that
one was coming on got a gun and fifty rounds of ammunition
and went into it. After this he endured eleven weeks' harsh
imprisonment at Fort Delaware and was released June 11,
1865. Box car transportation was furnished him to Cairo;
he came down the river in a boat to Memphis and slept the
first night, June 27th, on the ground at the Memphis &
Charleston depot. Next morning, hungry and half fainting,
he met an old negro named Newt Chilton, a former slave of
his father, who was overjoyed to meet his "young master,"
as he still addressed him, and took him to a restaurant where
he was employed and ordered the best in the house and gave

the famished young soldier the first full meal he had touched in many months.

He walked to Oxford through the country; returned to Memphis the same summer; became employed in a leading drug house on Main street; was admitted as a member of the firm six years later and has been so connected and actively engaged ever since. He has other interests, and for several years past has been president of one of the largest financial institutions of the city. Has been a member of the Confederate Relief and Historical Association and its successor since the first organization. and is a member of the Central Methodist Church; was married to Miss Blanche M. Blair of this city December 13, 1871, and they have two living children, a son and daughter.

COLLIER, DABNEY W., born in Haywood county, Tenn., February 20, 1841, and came from Revolutionary ancestry on all sides. He left the sophomore class at school to join the Bluff City Grays under Captain James H. Edmondson. The company was splendidly armed and equipped. The officers were: James H. Edmondson, Captain; Chris Sherwin, First Lieutenant; John R. J. Creighton, Second Lieutenant; Phil. T. Allin, Brevet Second Lieutenant; Thomas F. Patterson, First Sergeant; John H. Mitchell, Second Sergeant; L. A. Spicer, Third Sergeant; M. R. Marshall, Fourth Sergeant; W. J. P. Doyle, First Corporal; R. H. Flournoy, Second Corporal; James McClain, Third Corporal; R. J. Eyrich, Fourth Corporal. In April, 1861, the company fully equipped filed into Court Square to receive a beautiful flag presented with a patriotic and eloquent address by Mrs. Judge Dixon, after which the boys marched away under a shower of bouquets and adieus.

Chris Sherwin the First Lieutenant, was a finely drilled soldier, an ex-member of Ellsworth's famous Zouaves, and possessed that peculiar faculty and magnetism to impart his instruction to others.

D. W. Collier entered active service with his company, which was placed with the One Hundred and Fifty-fourth, as Company B, May 5, 1861, at Randolph, and took part in the battle of Belmont : was on outpost duty with Preston Smith's Brigade at Purdy, Tennessee, and participated in the battle of Shiloh. At the end of twelve months the company reorganized as sharpshooters for General Preston Smith's Brigade and moved with the brigade to Chattanooga. The brigade was here detached and with Cleburne's Brigade formed a division, commanded by Brigadier-General Cleburne, and was engaged in the battle of Richmond, Ky., August 31, 1862, and was with the command which threatened Covington, Ky.; rejoined the Army of Tennessee at Harrodsburg, Ky., returning to former division (Cheatham's) in time to take part in the battle of Perryville ; was in the battle of Murfreesboro December 31, 1862, and January 1 and 4, 1863, in which Lieutenants John Creighton and Albert Bunch were killed, after which W. J. P. Doyle and Dabney W. Collier were elected to fill the two vacancies, at Shelbyville. The company was mounted and transferred to the cavalry service January 15, 1863, and placed in the Eleventh Tennessee, commanded by Colonel James H. Edmondson.

Lieutenant Collier took part in the following engagements, after being mounted : Thompson's Station, Tenn., March 4, 1863 ; Brentwood, Tenn., Davis's Mill, April 5, 1863 ; Franklin, Tenn., Leighton, Ala., Day's Gap, Ala., April 30 ; Town Creek, Ala., Triune, Tenn., in May : Harpeth river, in May ; Triune, Tenn., Franklin and near Franklin June 26 ; Tullahoma, Tenn., July 1, 1863 ; Gordon's Mill, Ga., September 18. 1863 ; Chickamauga, Tenn., September 19 and 20 ; Mission Ridge, Tenn., September 21 ; Charleston and Athens, Tenn., September 26. After the engagement of the 21st at Mission Ridge General Forrest was ordered with his command into East Tennessee, and had much hard fighting. Near Athens a shell struck Lieutenant Collier's left ankle and passed through his horse, exploding at the same time. The horse fell on Collier's right leg. Phil. Mallon, a member of the company, pulled the animal off and it immediately expired. The wounded man was taken to a farm house, where, after the fight was over, General Forrest and staff made headquarters that night. September 26, 1863, Lieutenant Collier's leg was amputated just below the knee, General Forrest assisting to hold him. The general manifested great sympathy and sent the young man back to Cleveland in his private ambulance; thence he was sent to the hospital at Marietta, Ga., and rapidly recuperated. As a matter of history it may be mentioned here that two weeks after this event Major McDonald was killed at the battle of Farmington. Captain Phil. Allin succeeded him. T. F. Patterson became captain and W. J. P. Doyle was made adjutant.

Lieutenant Collier has lived in and near Memphis since the war and became a member of this Association many years ago.

COLLIER, C. M., is a native of Hampton, Va. His first service was with Commodore Pendergrast, on the frigate Columbia, having joined the navy at the age of 16. Later he served under Commodore Barron on the frigate Wabash on the Mediterranean station. Upon his return home he was transferred to the coast survey service commanded by Captain John N. Maffitt, who during the civil war commanded the Confederate steamship Florida.

When the war opened Captain Collier was in command of the coast survey schooner Varina, in New York harbor. He repaired to Richmond and was commissioned lieutenant in the Confederate States Marine Corps, but was soon after transferred to the regular army as lieutenant of artillery and placed in command of Fort Powhatan on James river. He participated in the first battle of Bull Run as aid to General Joseph E. Johnston and remained with the army of Northern Virginia until made Superintendent of the Powder Works at Augusta, Ga.; was next with General Stephen D. Lee in the ordnance department, and when paroled in Georgia he had attained the rank of lieutenant-colonel. He married a Georgia lady and since the war has lived in Memphis. He became a member of this Association at an early day in its history.

CLUSKEY, M. W., Captain and A. A. I. G., and afterward A. A. G. of Preston Smith's Brigade; was severely wounded in the Georgia campaign, and never entirely recovered; was elected by soldiers in the Army of Tennessee to the Confederate Congress at Richmond in August, 1864, and served there until the end of the war. Afterward was one of the editors of the *Avalanche* for a year or two; also edited a paper in Louisville, Ky.; married there, and died some years afterward in the 79s. Was proposed for membership by Colonel John W. Dawson of this Association and elected February 3, 1870.

COX, J. J., born March 1, 1848, in Washington county, Miss., sent to the University of Mississippi, at Oxford, and was there when the war broke out. He tried to enlist, but was rejected on account of his youth. June 22, 1862, he enlisted in Company D, Twenty-eighth Mississippi Cavalry, and was in all the campaigns of his command until the 30th of November, 1863, when discharged. While a member of Company D he was frequently complimented by his officers and mentioned in general orders. Both General S. W. Ferguson and Major-General W. T. Martin requested that he be commissioned and assigned to duty on their staffs, but was rejected on account of his youth. He re-entered the army and was assigned to the secret service. He made a trip into Vicksburg, staying a week at the headquarters of General George B. McPherson; going up to Memphis he was arrested and ordered to prison in the "Irving Block," but escaped on the street, ran into the old Worsham Hotel and was secreted by a young lady. Making his way to the trans-Mississippi he served one year on the staff of Brevet-Brigadier General O. P. Lyles, by whom he was promoted to first lieutenant for leading a forlorn hope, and was assigned to duty as Acting Adjutant of the Twenty-third Arkansas Light Infantry. In January, 1865, he resigned and was appointed master's mate in the navy by Commodore Robinson, in command at Mobile, Ala., and assigned to the Alabama, but finding the blockade of Mobile impassable he rejoined his old company in the Twenty-eighth Mississippi Cavalry. As General Forrest was about to surrender he ran away to avoid being paroled, and returned home. Soon after the close of the war he went to Frankfort, Ky., and entered the Kentucky

Military Institute, where he finished his education. He then went to planting cotton on his father's old plantation in Washington county, Miss.; remained until 1873, when he went to Dallas, Texas. In 1874 he joined the Texas State service as a private in the First Infantry; was soon promoted to first lieutenant and captain, in which rank he served until 1878, when he was promoted by Governor R. B. Hubbard, and the appointment was confirmed by an election by the officers, to be colonel of the Third Infantry, Texas State Troops. In 1878 he obtained leave of absence and joined the Mexican revolution against Diaz, holding the rank of colonel of cavalry. While serving in Mexico he lost his wife, who died at Greenville, Miss., with yellow fever. He then resigned his commission in the Texas service and returned to cotton planting on his grandfather's old plantation in Washington county, Miss. In 1885 he went to Marion, Crittenden county, Ark., and became the editor of the *Marion Reform* newspaper. In 1895 sold out and settled in Memphis. In 1885 he joined the National Guards, State of Arkansas, as first lieutenant, was promoted to captain in 1891, and at present holds that rank, being Captain of Company E, Second Regiment, Infantry. Captain Cox is in business in Memphis.

He joined this Association in June, 1896, and accompanied Company A, Confederate Veterans, to the reunion at Richmond. He was in the cast of the drama of " Johnson's Island," a war play written by Colonel C. W. Frazer and produced successfully both in Memphis and Richmond, he taking the part of General Trimble.

DAWSON, JOHN W., Lieutenant-Colonel One Hundred and Fifty-fourth Tennessee; entered the service in April, 1861, and served for four years when not incapacitated by wounds. Admitted to membership in this Association July 15, 1870; was a wholesale merchant; served as Vice-President and as Secretary of this Association, but lived only a few years afterward, as he never fully recovered from his wounds; was married, but left no children. The universal testimony of his men and comrades was that a more gallant man never lived.

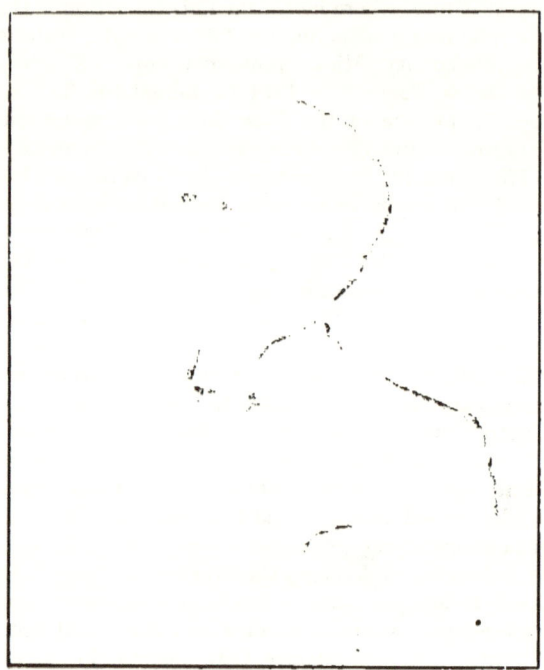

CAPT. JAMES DINKINS.

DINKINS, JAMES, was born near Canton, in Madison county, Miss., April 18, 1845. In 1860 was sent by his parents to the North Carolina Military Institute at Charlotte, from which place he enlisted with about 100 other cadets for six months in the First North Carolina Regiment, which was organized at Raleigh April 11, 1861, with D. H. Hill as colonel. Served in that regiment until term of enlistment expired, having participated in the first battle of the war, " Big Bethel ;" joined Company C, Eighteenth Mississippi Regiment, Griffith's Brigade (subsequently Barksdale's and Humphries') ; served as private in Company C until April 22, 1863. Took part in all the battles in which the regiment was engaged, including Leesburg, Gain's Mill, Malvern Hill,

6

Harper's Ferry, Sharpsburg and Fredericksburg. He was appointed first lieutenant of cavalry in the Confederate States army April 22, 1863. The appointment was made at the request of General Sims of Georgia. The latter was wounded at Sharpsburg some distance in advance of the line. Young Dinkins ran to his assistance and succeeded in getting him under cover, which circumstance attracted General Sim's attention.

During his term of service in the Eighteenth Mississippi he was known by the title of "Little Horse," because he never broke down on the march, nor was he ever sick during the war; was always cheerful and ready to play a joke on the others. After appointment in the regular army was ordered by the President to report to General J. R. Chalmers, commanding the troops in North Mississippi. After reporting to General Chalmers he was appointed to staff duty, in which capacity he served until the battle of Nashville, when he was assigned to Company C, Eighteenth Mississippi Cavalry, and commanded that company at the close of the war. Was with General Chalmers in all the exciting and daring movements under General Forrest, from Fort Pillow, Okolona, Harrisburg, Brices Cross Roads, Paris Landing, Johnsonville, Columbia, Spring Hill, Franklin on to Nashville.

Married in November, 1866, to Miss Sue Hart of Canton, Miss., and has two children, boy and girl. On his maternal side is related to the Davidsons, Baxters, Bvevards, Springs, Myers and Bleeckers of North Carolina. On the paternal side to the Hendersons, Craigs, Spotswoods ("Cousin Sally Dillard"), Jones, Kendricks, Greers and Blockwoods. His great great-grandfather commanded a regiment in the Revolution, which assisted in driving the British from Mecklenburg City. Since the war has been connected with railroad interests.

DASHIELL, GEORGE, enlisted as a private in Company B, One Hundred and Fifty-fourth Tennessee, April 28, 1861; became paymaster of Cheatham's Division, and served as such until the spring of 1863; was then ordered by the war department to report to General N. B. Forrest, and served with him

as chief paymaster of his corps until the surrender at Gainesville, Ala. Was paroled May 9, 1865, and was one of the
early members of this Association.

DAVIS, ISAAC N., Major on General Forrest's staff;
entered the service February 28, 1861; paroled May, 1865.
Proposed for membership by W. A. Goodman, W. D. Stratton and J. H. Erskine, and elected April 28, 1870.

DeSAUSSURE, CHARLES A., born in Beaufort District,
S. C., September 21, 1846; of Franco-Swiss descent on paternal side and English stock on maternal side. Enlisted October, 1862, in Beaufort Volunteer Artillery (continuous organization since 1800) at Pocotaligo, S. C., Captain H. M. Stuart
commanding. This battery was then attached to Walker's
Brigade, in charge of the lower coast defenses of South Carolina, the special object being to defeat the determined efforts
of the Federal forces, under Admiral Farragut, to cut the
Charleston & Savannah Railroad, the base line between those
two cities. The battery participated in the battles of Pocotaligo, Honey Hill, Tullifinny, Averysboro, Smithfield and
Bentonville, besides numerous minor engagements. It also
took part in the coast defenses at Adams Run and on John
and James Islands before Charleston. After leaving the coast
before Sherman, the battery was incorporated into Burnet
Rhett's Battalion of Artillery, Hardee's Corps, A. P. Hill's
Divison, Johnston's army, and was finally paroled at Greensboro, N. C., in May, 1865.

Mr. DeSaussure has been engaged in the railroad passenger
service since the war, and at this writing (1896) is General Passenger Agent of the Memphis & Charleston Railroad and located at Memphis, Tenn.; joined this Association several years
ago and became a member of Company A, Confederate Veterans, and has since been an active and most valued member:
was with the company at Chattanooga in 1895 and at Richmond
in June-July, 1896, on which occasion he not only slept in
the barracks on the straw with "the boys" and marched
with them in the grand procession, but looked after their
interests in various ways, and secured for them and the ladies

in attendance from Memphis through transit each way without change in the quickest possible time—thus showing that he is thoroughly practical as well as in sympathy with comrades and friends.

DICKINSON, J. R., First Lieutenant Company K, Forty-seventh Virginia Regiment, Army of North Virginia; enlisted July, 1861; was wounded three times at Seven Pines, lost his right arm at Fredericksburg, Va., December 13, 1862, and was offered a discharge, but preferred to remain and perform light duty in the enrolling service at Richmond; was First Lieutenant of President Jefferson Davis' Guards when he left Richmond and went with him as far as Abbeville, S. C. Paroled May, 1865. Admitted to Confederate Historical Association March 15, 1895.

DICKSON, BARTON, Captain Company A, Sixteenth Alabama Regiment; enlisted May, 1861; was under Zollicoffer in the early part of the war. Paroled May, 1865.

DONELSON, R. S., private Company II, Thirteenth Tennessee; enlisted April, 1862; was wounded at Chickamauga and permanently disabled; was furloughed to the hospital, where he remained unable to do active duty until the close of the war; paroled May, 1865, in Memphis. Admitted to the Confederate Historical Association April 14, 1896.

DOUGLASS, C. A., private Company E, North Mississippi Regiment; enlisted March 27, 1861; was wounded the 23d day of August, 1864, at Abbeville, Miss., and paroled the 11th day of May, 1865. Joined this Association some years ago.

DOUGLASS, I. E., was at first a private in Company I, First Tennessee Cavalry, but does not remember exact date of enlistment. Went out with Captain M. J. Wicks; later was under Captain Jackson; still later under Captain A. C. Bettis; was elected or promoted to third lieutenant April, 1862. Later was promoted to captain and assistant quartermaster and assigned to duty with Wharton's Regiment, afterward Harrison's. Then promoted to rank of major and assistant quartermaster Wharton's Division, Wheeler's Corps, but never received a commission as major. Paroled May 10, 1865. Became a member of this Association at an early day.

DROESCHER, A. R., entered the service as a private May 8, 1861, in Forrest's old regiment; paroled May 12, 1865, after fighting all through the war. Entered this Association upon his own motion July 15, 1870. Died some years ago in Memphis.

DuBOSE, J. J., was born in Shelby county, Tenn., educated in the schools of this county and city, and at the Cumberland University at Lebanon, where he took a full course of law. Enlisted early in the war in the Ninth Arkansas Regiment; was in Bowen's Brigade, and was in active service at and around Columbus, Ky.; was at Feliciana, passed through Nashville and on down the line to the battle of Shiloh. After that was transferred to General Hindman in the Trans-Mississippi Department, with rank of first lieutenant; was promoted to captain and made chief inspector and ordnance officer for the Department of North Arkansas and the Indian Territory. He participated actively in the Banks campaign, and was in the last battle at Yellow Bayou. After that he was with General Magruder and rendered special service; was sent into the Federal lines several times to obtain information. The last time he came out to find that the surrender had taken place. Returning to what had been headquarters, he found all deserted and he the only soldier left. He was never captured, wounded or paroled. After the war he came to Memphis, practiced law, edited the *Public Ledger* for a year or two, resumed the law again, took an active part in local politics, and was elected to the State Senate and served one term. Married a Miss Polk of Columbia, Tenn. Served one term as Judge of the Criminal Court, and returned to the practice of law, in which he is now (1896) actively and successfully engaged. He became a member of the Confederate Historical Association July 1, 1869.

DUFF, WILLIAM L., entered the service in May, 1861, and remained four years; was successively Captain, Major and Lieutenant-Colonel of the Seventeenth Mississippi In-

fantry and afterward raised and was Colonel of the Eighth
Mississippi Cavalry in 1863, and was in Chalmers's brigade,
Forrest's command. Became a member of this Association
May 26, 1870.

DUNN, W. C., enlisted March 28, 1861, as a private in
Company C, Ninth Mississippi Regiment, for twelve months;
mustered out of service at Grand Junction in April, 1862;
joined Company G, Fourth Mississippi Cavalry in July, 1862.
Surrendered and paroled at Gainesville, Ala., May 12, 1865.

DUPUY, JOHN J., enlisted as a private in the Shelby
Grays of Memphis, from which, it is said, there were more
officers commissioned than there were names on the original
roll. This became Company A, Fourth Tennessee Infantry,
whose first battle was Belmont. J. J. Dupuy was in that and
in most of the battles of the Army of Tennessee, and received
wounds enough to have killed half a dozen men ordinarily.
At Shiloh he received a minnie ball in the right arm while
on the skirmish line after his regiment had captured a seven-
gun battery. He was in the battle of Perryville, and at
Camp Dick Robinson was detailed as aide-de-camp on the
staff of Colonel Strahl, commanding brigade, and served in
that capacity until after the battle of Murfreesboro. At Shelbyville he was commissioned Adjutant of Rapley's Battalion
of Sharp Shooters from Arkansas, composed of 400 men.
He reached the command at Bayou Pere on the retreat in
front of Grant, and was in the battle of Baker's Creek and
Big Black Bridge, and then was locked up in the siege of
Vicksburg, during which he received a flesh wound from a
shell one night during a sortie. At the surrender of Vicksburg he was the senior lieutenant of the only two officers of
the battalion left and turned over a roll of forty men. When
Lieutenant Dupuy's parole expired he returned to his old
command, became aide-de-camp to General Strahl, and was
with him in close touch to the end of his military life. At
the battle of Atlanta, July 22, 1864, Lieutenant Dupuy was
wounded three times by a volley from sharp-shooters, and
lingered between life and death for months. Went to Vir-

ginia on crutches; heard the last guns fired by Lee's army, and was paroled at Lynchburg.

Afterward lived in Bolivar, Tenn., and served two terms (sixteen years) as attorney-general of his district; came to Memphis in 1886, and has since practiced law here. He comes of illustrious Hugenot ancestry; was a typical, high-toned soldier and is yet a sentimental Confederate, and has expressed a desire to be buried as his two soldier brothers were, in a plain, simple, unostentatious style. He was admitted to this Association May 4, 1895.

DWYER, JOHN, born June 21, 1840, in Limerick, Ireland. Enlisted in Company L, Fifteenth Tennessee, Colonel Chas. Carrolls' Regiment, April 10, 1861, and was elected first lieutenant; served in Bushrod Johnston's Brigade; was wounded in battles of Shiloh and Kenesaw Mountain ; captured at Kenesaw June 21, 1864, and released 16th of February, 1865 ; paroled April, 1865; has since lived in Shelby county, Tenn. Is a member of this Association.

EDMONDSON, E. A., enlisted in April, 1861, in the Bluff City Grays, Forrest's Regiment; served through the war and was paroled at Gainesville, Ala., May, 1865. Admitted to this Association December 9, 1890.

ELAM, F. E., private Company A, Eleventh Texas; enlisted April or May, 1861; was crippled by a fall of his horse at Chickamauga; furloughed January 15, 1865, in South Carolina to come home and recruit; returned on horseback to South Carolina and met his company, which had been surrendered and was coming home; paroled at Grenada, Miss., May, 1865. Admitted to C. H. A. March 10, 1896.

ELAM, W. S., enlisted November 18, 1861, in Jones' Battery; after the twelve months' service expired became a member of Company I, Second Kentucky Cavalry, Morgan's command; was wounded at Green River Bridge; captured at Mill Creek, Ohio, and released from prison after the surrender. Admitted to C. H. A. July 17, 1895.

ELCAN, ARCHIBALD LIEBIG, born near Belmont, Fayette county, Tenn., October 29, 1844. George Hooper Elcan, his father, was born in Buckingham county, Va., in 1800, and removed to West Tennessee in 1819, locating in Fayette county, where he died in 1855. A. L. Elcan received his early education in the neighborhood schools and at the Tipton Male High School at Covington, Tenn.; was mustered into the Confederate service in Captain Sam. T. Taylor's Company of Cavalry in March, 1862, before he was 18 years old, and served as private secretary for Captain Taylor until transferred to Company B, Seventh Regiment Tennessee Cavalry; was with this regiment in all the campaigns under Colonel W. H. Jackson (afterward general) and Generals Armstrong and Van Dorn in West Tennessee and North Mississippi until the early part of 1863, when, together with Company B, he was detached for special service at Major-General Loring's headquarters, and took part in all the operations under General Loring looking to the relief of Vicksburg, and in the siege of Jackson, Miss., and the retreat of the army from Jackson to Meridian; rejoined the Seventh Tennessee Regiment in February, 1864, and followed General N. B. Forrest in his campaigns to the close of the war; was wounded by the side of General Forrest at Prairie Mound, Miss., February 22, 1864, in a charge on the enemy, led in person by General Forrest on foot, his horse having been shot a few minutes before; was appointed First Sergeant Company B on night of June 9, 1864, in place of Sergeant W. N. Mason, who was killed, leaving the company without a muster roll, which necessitated a hard night's work for him to make a roster of the company and get everything ready by daybreak, when they were ordered forward to Brices Cross Roads; was with the company in Middle Tennessee under Generals Forrest and Hood in the advance to and retreat from Nashville; made a midnight search alone and rescued a detachment of Company B from a perilous position right under the enemy's line around Nashville. There was great rejoicing in the company when they were brought in. Continued with the company on the retreat from Nashville until his horse was shot in an engage-

Major Genl. B. J. Cheatham.

ment with the enemy at Richland creek; then made his way
to the rear, crossed Tennessee river and rejoined the company
in time to go with the command to Selma, Ala. He and
Lieutenant H. T. Sale of Company B were ordered to close
up the rear by General Wirt Adams, which they did, and
surrendered with the company at Gainesville, Ala., in 1865.

After the war he read medicine, took a full college course,
and practiced in Tipton county; served as a member of the
Legislature, was also a justice of the peace, and belonged to
several medical societies. Removed to Memphis in 1888 and
has since practiced here successfully, and joined the C. H. A.
several years ago. Has written much for the medical papers
and the daily and weekly press. He was married November
4, 1869, to Miss Bettie Taylor, daughter of Dr. Joshua Swayne
of Carroll county, Tenn. Their children are Joshua Swayne,
Lucy Elizabeth. Nathaniel Henry, Rosalie Eva and Pauline
Thompson Elean.

ELDRIDGE, J. W., entered the army as private in the
"Beauregards," Captain W. Y. C. Humes, April 12, 1861,
and continued in the service until the surrender in 1865.
Governor Harris soon after his enlistment as private appointed
him one of the three General Assistant Quartermasters of
the State, and ordered him to report for duty to General B. F.
Cheatham in May, 1861, at Union City, Tenn. He assumed
the duties assigned, but soon resigned the place and sought
more congenial service in the field. Was commissioned captain of artillery by the Secretary of War, and ordered to raise
a battery and report to General Albert Sydney Johnston for
duty. This he did, and joined the Confederate forces at Bowling, Green, Ky. After the retreat from Kentucky, his command followed the Army of Tennessee and participated in
all of its campaigns. Resigned his captaincy in December,
· 1862, at Shelbyville, in favor of his nephew, Eldridge Wright,
who lost his life in the battle of Murfreesboro. Was then
appointed major of artillery and ordered to report for duty
to General A. P. Stewart at Shelbyville; was chief of the
artillery of his division and was acting with him in that
capacity until he was promoted to command of another corps

in 1864, after he had participated in the great conflict at Chickamauga, and the signal engagement and victory at New Hope Church, in the Georgia campaign. This last conflict was the most desperately contested one during the war. Stewart's Division of 2900 men repulsed and drove from the field Hooker's entire corps of 11,000 men, who vainly endeavored to penetrate Johnston's line of march and cut the Confederates in two. The artillery did the most effective work on that occasion. It remained right in the ranks with the infantry and did havoc at close fire for two hours, giving confidence and encouragement to the boys on all sides. General Sherman, in his "Memoirs of the War," says the Federal soldiers called the fight at New Hope Church by the euphonious name of "Hell's Hole." Verily, it was well named. Major Eldridge's loss there was sixty-five men and sixty-five horses killed and wounded, and not a charge of ammunition was left in the boxes. Major Eldridge distinguished himself on many occasions. After the war he practiced law in Memphis, and now makes his home in Mississippi. He became a member of the Confederate Historical Association October 14, 1890.

ELLIOTT, GEORGE B., private Company G, Twelfth Kentucky Infantry, entered service May 16, 1861, and retired May 16, 1865. Proposed by W. J. Pollard and elected a member of this Association March 20, 1870.

ELLIOTT, C. S., private Company A., Fourth Tennessee, enlisted April, 1861; was wounded at Shiloh and at New Hope Church and was discharged in June, 1862, for disability, caused by the wound; was reinstated in Ballentine's Regiment September, 1862; was totally disabled by the wound at New Hope Church for the rest of the war; reported daily at hospital; paroled June 6, 1865. Admitted to the Confederate Historical Association May 4, 1895.

ELLIS, W. W., Sergeant Company C, Thirteenth Tennessee Infantry; enlisted December, 1861; wounded at Murfreesboro and Atlanta; paroled April 13, 1865, at Augusta, Ga. Admitted to Confederate Historical Association March 10, 1896.

ENGLISH, RICHARD T., joined the Confederate Relief and Historical Association July 1, 1869, and died in this city October 13, 1871. He was a man of noble impulses and universally popular in all circles. He resided in this city for six years previous to his death, and it may be safely asserted that he had more genuine friends than most newspaper workers among all of the list, being liked not only by his personal intimates, but also by those who served opposition journals. Captain English was a native of Chester county, Pa.; born July 4, 1832: attended college in Wisconsin and removed to Natchez, Miss., with his father and family in 1852. He was there engaged in civil engineering until the war began. In April, 1861, he was third lieutenant of the Quitman Artillery, and three months later was unanimously chosen its captain. Served a year at Mobile and Pensacola under General Bragg, then raised a battery of light artillery at Natchez, Miss. At Port Hudson Captain English was appointed provost marshal, but he operated his battery in all of the engagements about that place until he was captured in 1863, when he was sent to Camp Chase, Ohio. Before his capture he had been promoted to a lieutenant-colonelcy of artillery and was on his way to serve under Kirby Smith when taken prisoner. One of his daring exploits was to place his battery on the bluffs at Ellis Cliffs, some twenty miles below Natchez, to fire on passing war ships compelled to move close along shore, owing to the nature of the river channel. On one occasion he used a Maynard rifle while in ambush half way down the side of the cliff to fire upon an officer occupying the quarter deck of a big ship, supposing it to be Commodore Farragut, as he wore a red sash of command at the time. The officer was hit and fell from the chair upon which he was seated. A broadside from the ship sent cannon shot and shell into the bluff at the feet of Captain English, which seemingly raised the side of the cliff as if a mine had been sprung. When Captain English died his funeral was attended by the Masonic brotherhood, of which he was a worthy member. Few can count upon as many and as lasting friendships as Captain English. His sense of honor was the highest. He was incapable of selfishness, and in his intercourse with all, his manners were most genial, prompted by a heart filled to overflowing with the milk of human kindness.

ERSKINE, Dr. JOHN H., was Chief Surgeon of the Army of Tennessee on the staff of General Joseph E. Johnston at the surrender in North Carolina and was one of the original charter members of this Association. In the great epidemic of 1878 he fell a martyr to a high sense of duty that others might live. A more extended sketch will be found in the second part of this book.

ERMAN, L. W., entered the Confederate service at New Orleans April 6, 1861, and was commissioned first lieutenant of First Louisiana Infantry and detailed on recruiting service. At the expiration of his commission he joined the Twenty-eighth Mississippi Regiment at Jackson, Miss.

ESTES. L. H., was a private in Company A, Sixth Battalion of Tennessee Cavalry, and served until the close of the war. He is now serving his second term as Judge of the First Circuit Court of Shelby County, having been re-elected at the last August election. Became a member of this Association in 1885.

FARABEE, BENJ. F., First Sergeant Company H, Thirteenth Tennessee Regiment; enlisted June 4, 1861; was in the battles of Shiloh, Richmond, Perryville, Murfreesboro, Missionary Ridge, Chickamauga, Marietta, Atlanta, and in all the Georgia campaign; also in the battles of Franklin and Nashville; was wounded at Nashville and also slightly at Franklin; captured December 16, 1864, and released June 22, 1865. Admitted to the Confederate Historical Association October 8, 1895.

FARRER. CHAS. SMITH, enlisted in 1861 as a private in the Ninth Tennessee Infantry; served under Generals Bragg, Hood, Johnston and Patton Anderson; was at Pensacola and Cumberland Gap: was wounded in battles of Cumberland Gap, Perryville and Chickamauga; was captured at Perryville and exchanged at Vicksburg.

FARRIS, O. B., was Captain of Company K, Second Tennessee Regiment. Bell's Brigade, Forrest's Cavalry, and served until the end of the war as such. Paroled in May, 1865.

FARROW, G. F., born in 1842, in Marshall county, Miss.; removed to Tennessee when 11 years old; enlisted at Germantown April 20, 1861, in Company C, Thirteenth Tennessee Regiment; was in the battle of Belmont, and soon after was transferred to McDonald's Battalion, Forrest's old regiment; was in all the important fights in which that regiment took part; was captured at Britton's Lane, Tenn., and exchanged ten days later; remained in the command to the end and was surrendered and paroled at Gainesville, Ala., in May, 1865. Has since lived near Memphis; joined the Confederate Historical Association June 13, 1894. His brother, John P. Farrow, in the same company, was killed at Belmont at the first volley, and is believed by General Vaughan and others to have been the first man killed in battle in the West. The death of this brave young soldier, belonging as he did to a prominent old family, created a great sensation at the time, and his remains were brought home and buried with all possible military and civic honors in an old church-yard a few miles south of the city.

FAZZI, J., private Company C, Forrest's old regiment, and served in all its changes; was wounded at Shiloh in the side and also at Holly Springs in the leg; was all through the war and paroled May 11, 1865.

FENTRESS, FRANCIS, Sergeant Company E, Seventh Tennessee Cavalry; enlisted in May, 1861; was first in Neely's Cavalry, afterward merged into W. H. Jackson's regiment, afterward commanded by Colonel W. F. Taylor as the Seventh Tennessee Cavalry; served until the close of the war in Company E; paroled May, 1865. Became a prominent member of the bar at Bolivar and removed to Memphis a few years ago and joined the Confederate Historical Association.

FINLAY, LUKE W., was born near Brandon, Rankin county, Miss., October 8, 1831. His father, Hon. Jas. Finlay, was of Scotch parentage and a native of Baden county, N. C.;

a citizen of Rankin from 1829 until his death in 1860; a
farmer by occupation; for six successive terms was Judge of
the Probate Court of that county. His mother, Cady Lewis,
was a native of South Carolina, whose ancestors served in the
Revolutionary war with General Francis Marion. Three sons
survive, all lawyers—Hon. Oscar E. Finlay, the county judge
of Young county, Texas; Hon. George P. Finlay, often of the
Legislature of Texas, city attorney of Galveston and now
surveyor of the port in that city, and Colonel Luke W. Finlay.
He was graduated at Yale in 1856; had charge of Academy
at Brandon a year; settled in Memphis August 1, 1857; January 1, 1860, he entered upon the practice of law; appeared
in Supreme Court, April term, 1861; April 19, 1861, he enlisted as First Lieutenant of Company A, Fourth Tennessee
Infantry; was wounded at Shiloh; on reorganization was
elected major; was in the battle of Perryville October 8, 1862,
where he was wounded the second time. He was engaged in
continuous service in the movement of the Army of Tennessee to Camp Dick Robinson; thence back into Tennessee by
way of Cumberland Gap, Knoxville, Chattanooga and Bridge-
port up to Tullahoma, and thence to Murfreesboro. At Murfreesboro he was the occasion of a singular and thrilling incident. In the furious onset of General Patton Anderson's
Brigade they for a moment faltered as they drove the Federal lines back, and upon being reformed Colonel Bright
Morgan asked him how he could get the Twenty-ninth Mississippi to the front. Major Finlay at once spoke to Colonel
Bratton, commanding the Twenty-fourth Tennessee Regiment, requesting him to let Colonel Morgan pass with his
regiment and cheer him as the colors touched each other.
Colonel Bratton immediately removed a file of men next to
his colors so the Twenty-ninth could pass. As the latter
advanced, so the two color bearers stood together, Colonel
Bratton, amidst the roar of battle, shouted, "Three cheers
for the Twenty-ninth Mississippi!" and amidst the storm of
cheers that regiment passed on to its place in front. He
rejoined his command, after a short absence on detached service, the second day of the battle of Chickamauga, and was

continuously with it and in charge of the Fourth Regiment at Missionary Ridge, where during the engagement he commanded the Fourth and Fifth Tennessee Regiments, who were stationed in rifle pits near the left of the line, and continued the engagement until he was ordered by his superior to move to the top of the ridge. This engagement was characterized by a withholding of fire until the Federal lines approached within easy range of the rifles. At this moment the command was given, "Ready, aim, fire!" After the advancing Federals, by the steady fire of the Fourth and Fifth, were driven back and the ensigns moved to their left in order to rally them, Major Finlay gave the command, "Right oblique, fire!" At the word the rifles were obedient to the command and the rallying ensigns again fell back. He was with his regiment on Chickamauga's banks, at Chickamauga station, as it passed the camp fires of the Federal bivouac at dusk; crossed the Chickamauga at Ringold Gap with Strahl's Brigade, supporting Cleburne there. His service continued at Dalton, Mill Creek Gap, Snake Gap, Resaca, Adairsville and New Hope Church in the successive engagements along the line of battle.

On May 27th, while holding an advanced position with the Fourth Tennessee, he was severly wounded in the head. This disabled him until the latter part of November, 1864, when he rejoined the Fourth on the night of the battle at Franklin. He had charge of his regiment at Nashville and on the retreat until it crossed the river. With the army he went to North Carolina and participated in the battle of Bentonville, where Joe Johnston held at bay the army of Sherman, and at Greensboro was paroled with his command.

For the past two decades he has been continuous in the practice of his profession, participating in politics only as a private citizen, never failing to exercise the right of the ballot and always striving for what he believed to be the best interests of the public. In 1894 his son Percy, whom he had given a complete education at Yale and a course in the Yale Law School, entered upon the practice with his father.

He has always been a Democrat in politics, a churchman

in religion, being a member of the Episcopal Church, and a practitioner at law in all the courts of his State. Became a member of this Association many years ago.

FISHER, J. B., private in Hickerson's Arkansas Regiment, Trans-Mississippi Department; enlisted July, 1863, and served until the close of the war; was wounded at Helena, Ark.; was on sick leave of absence at the time of the surrender and a few days before; therefore was never paroled. Admitted to Confederate Historical Association May 4, 1895.

FISHER, JOHN H., private in the Bluff City Grays, One Hundred and Fifty-fourth Tennessee; enlisted April 26, 1861.

· FLANNAGAN, P., was born in Strokestown, County Roscommon, Ireland, in 1828; came over to the States in 1850, reaching Memphis in 1852. He enlisted April 15, 1861, in Company E, Captain Casper W. Hunt's Company; went to Nashville and joined Bate's Regiment in May, 1861. This regiment went to Virginia and about the 12th of that month was mustered into the Confederate States service at Lynchburg. The regiment moved on to Richmond; thence to Fredericksburg and Brooks' Station and participated actively in the capture of Federal mail packets; was first under fire at Acquia Creek June 1, 1861. (See Lindsley's Annals, p. 132.) Was stationed at Evansport on the Potomac; ordered to the front, and although under fire and on a forced march was a day too late for the battle of Manassas. After that returned to Evansport and resumed the erection of defenses, and with other forces constituting a corps of observation facing the commands of Generals Sickles and Hooker; remained there until January, 1862. The regiment re-enlisted for the war and was furloughed for sixty days; met at Huntsville, Ala.; reformed there, went to Corinth, was assigned to Cleburne's Brigade and was in the battle of Shiloh, where the regiment lost in killed and wounded 225 men. Colonel Bate was severely wounded, and was promoted to brigadier-general before he was able to return to the field.

The regiment was in the Kentucky campaign under E. Kirby Smith, and in the bloody battle of Richmond private

Pat Flannagan lost his arm, and was taken prisoner. He was paroled and sent to Jackson, Miss., rejoined his command when able and was with the Second Tennessee Regiment at the battles of Chickamauga and Missionary Ridge, not carrying a gun, it is true, but rendering such service as he could, especially for the wounded. He was in winter quarters at Dalton, and with his regiment in the campaign at Atlanta. He never was in a hospital except when absolutely necessary, preferring to be with the boys at the front and in the ditches even after he lost his arm. His arm, however, whilst shattered at Richmond, Ky., was not amputated until January 4, 1863, at Mobile, Ala. He was paroled at Meridian, Miss., May 3, 1865; returned to Memphis and has been here ever since and has never married. He became a member of this Association in 1891. For some years he has been connected with a small business in one corner of the courthouse, and is a general favorite with all the officials and all who have business there. For a year he drew a pension from the State, but as it was discovered that he was not a pauper his name was stricken from the list of beneficiaries. He is a cheerful, jolly character and fine specimen of the surviving volunteer Confederates who fought for the love of the South.

FONTAINE, OGDEN, born and reared in Louisville, Ky. Being in New Orleans when the war broke out, joined Dreux New Orleans Cadets; went with that command to Pensacola, Fla.; with the command was ordered to the peninsula of Virginia; was in all the fighting along Warrick Run, when Magruder stood off McClellan's big army with a little thin line of 5000 men.

Dreux Battalion was then mustered out under the twelve months' enlistment law; then joined John H. Morgan's Kentucky Cavalry, then rendezvouing at Knoxville, Tenn.; was in all of Morgan's raids and marches, including the Ohio raid. Was captured in the Ohio raid at Buffington Island, Ohio, succeeding in escaping at Cincinnati. Rejoined what was left of Morgan's command and was with it under Forrest at the battle of Chickamauga; was severely wounded at the battle

7

of Cynthiana, Kentucky; again at Augusta, Ky., and again at Rhea Town, Tenn.

On Morgan's escape from Tennessee was ordered by General Morgan to report to him, to stay with him on his personal staff, to be commissioned as a captain and given a company on his prospective raid into Kentucky, he (General Morgan) expecting to recruit largely on that raid. General Morgan was killed a few weeks afterward. Was sent by Generals Breckinridge and Duke into Kentucky in the spring of 1863, aiding the straggling Confederates to rejoin their commands in Virginia. Surrendered to General John M. Palmer, with eight men, in Louisville, Ky., in April, 1865, after Lee's and Johnston's surrender of their armies. Joined this Association September 9, 1869.

FORREST, W. M., enlisted June, 1861, when quite a youth in White's Mounted Rifles; served on the staff of his illustrious father, General N. B. Forrest, as first lieutenant and aide-de-camp all through the war and was wounded in the battles at Fort Donelson, Harrisburg and Spring Hill, Tenn. Paroled May, 1865. After the war married and settled in Memphis and became a successful railroad contractor. Is a quiet business man and strongly resembles his father. Admitted to this Association October 9, 1894.

FRAYSER, ROBERT DUDLEY, was born in Memphis June 4, 1840, being the oldest child of Dr. John R. and Mrs. Pauline Frayser; attended city schools and in 1858 was sent to the Kentucky Military Institute, where he remained three years and was graduated as valedictorian of his class June 4, 1861. Meantime during vacations he had read law under Judge Thomas B. Monroe and received the degree of Bachelor of Laws. Although of slight physique, weighing only from 109 to 120 pounds at his best, and always apparently delicate, he had great powers of application, was very ambitious and resolute, and accomplished a great deal in his life.

As soon as out of college he cast his lot with the South. Went to Knoxville with Colonel (afterward General) Wm. H. Carroll, joined Company F, Thirty-seventh Tennessee, drilled the regiment, and in August, 1861, he was appointed adjutant by Colonel Carroll. He was with the regiment on duty when it came to Germantown, near Memphis; then went back to Chattanooga and Knoxville and marched across the mountains to Mill Springs, Ky., in time to cross the Cumberland river and participate in the closing scenes of the disaster to Confederate arms at Fishing Creek, made notable by the death of General Zollicoffer.

At the reorganization of the regiment, when it had become a part of Marmaduke's Brigade, at Corinth, Miss., after the battle of Shiloh, Adjutant Frayser was elected lieutenant-colonel and held this rank until the end of the war. He was sick and unable to go with Bragg's army into Kentucky, but was in the battle of Murfreesboro December 31, 1862, where he was shot from his horse early in the action. But he recovered in a few months.

At the consolidation of the Fifteenth and Thirty-seventh Tennessee Regiments, near Wartrace, Middle Tennessee, in the summer of 1863, he was retained as lieutenant-colonel and was with it with but few absences until the surrender at Greensboro, N. C. He was in the battles of Chickamauga and Missionary Ridge and in the campaign from Dalton to Atlanta, and particularly distinguished himself as officer of the day in command of a heavy picket line from Bate's Brigade; engaged all of one day in front of Kenesaw Mountain at a point known then as Bald Hill or Bald Knob. He was under fire almost every day, and in command of his regiment from there to Atlanta, where he was wounded on the 22d of July, 1864. He was rescued by the infirmary corps and sent to the hospital at Griffin, Ga. In a few weeks he resumed command of his regiment and was with it nearly all the time until the end in North Carolina. Toward the close he was in command of Bate's old brigade, known as Tyler's or Tom Benton Smith's, a mere skelton brigade. He endured intense hardships and sufferings with an inspired sort of faith and patience. Although a strict disciplinarian, he was just and considerate; was very grave and thoughtful, and enjoyed the respect and good will of his men. There were jealousies after the consolidation of those two regiments which gave him much trouble, but his conduct at Bald Knob, in the presence of both armies, closed the mouths of his enemies.

Colonel Frayser returned home and became a member of the law firm of Morgan, Jarnagin & Frayser. He married Miss Mary F. Lane, of an old and prominent family. He was a Mason and an Odd Fellow; was once Grand Master I. O. O. F. of the State, and joined this Association July 15, 1869; was a very active member. He became interested in the street railway business, made money very rapidly and branched out into various enterprises, and at one time was part owner of the *Public Ledger*, and was president of the Memphis City Bank. He was considered quite wealthy, but financial reverses overtook him about 1890–91, and he was a heavy loser. Overwork broke him down, and he died October 25, 1893, but left his wife and three children, a son and two daughters, in easy circumstances. His funeral was conducted by the Odd Fellows and attended by many of the best people of the city.

FRAZER, J. W., Brigadier-General, was in service in Washington Territory in the old army as captain; resigned, went to Montgomery, Ala., and offered his services to the young Confederacy in March, 1861; was put in recruiting service at once; that spring was appointed Lieutenant-Colonel of the Eighth Alabama Infantry and served in Virginia: raised the Twenty-eighth Alabama Regiment and elected its colonel; was appointed brigadier-general June, 1863, and sent to the command of Cumberland Gap with 1700 raw troops. In August the Gap was invested by General De-Courcey on the Kentucky side, which was followed by skirmishing until General Burnside, in September, with 23,000 veterans, crossed the Gap fifteen miles below, and having occupied Knoxville returned to the Gap. There were no troops or assistance in East Tennessee, and no adequate force short of Richmond, and these could not be spared. After two days, in which demands for surrender were made and shelling kept up, General Frazer called a council of his field officers, which decided that there was no other alternative, and the post was surrendered to General Burnside in person.

(See War Records and Jefferson Davis' "Rise and Fall of the Confederacy.") From that time to the close General Frazer was in prison, and was finally paroled from Fort Warren in July, 1865. He is now living at Clifton Springs, N. Y.

FRAZER, C. W., Major and Assistant Adjutant-General; was educated at the University of Mississippi; enlisted May, 1861, at Memphis; was Captain of Company I, Twenty-first Tennessee Regiment in 1861, Captain of Company B, Fifth Confederate Infantry, in 1862–63, and served on the staff of General J. W. Frazer as Acting Adjutant-General. The Twenty-first and Second Tennessee Regiments were consolidated after the battle of Shiloh, forming the famous fighting Fifth Confederate Regiment, for the war, in Cleburne's Division. Major Frazer was slightly wounded at the battles of Belmont and Murfreesboro; was captured, confined at Johnson's Island, and finally paroled there on the 11th day of June, 1865. He returned to Memphis, resumed the practice of law, attained the foremost rank at the bar, and is still in the practice. He became President of the Confederate Historical Association of Memphis in 1884, and has continuously served as such up to the present time, December, 1896, with great zeal and efficiency.

Major Frazer is the author of a strong war drama entitled "Johnson's Island." It is strictly historic, and realistic to a degree seldom produced on the stage, especially when the chief actors are ex-Confederate soldiers and their friends. It was played to crowded houses in Memphis last season and to appreciative audiences in Richmond last summer by and under the auspices of Company A, Confederate Veterans of Memphis. He was married to Miss Letitia Austin of Mississippi February 15, 1862, and they have three children—Mrs. Virginia Frazer Boyle, the well known Southern poetess, C. W. Frazer, Jr., and Miss Phœbe Frazer.

FREDERICK, E., private Company G, One Hundred and Fifty-fourth Tennessee; entered service April 23, 1861, and remained to the end. Admitted to the Confederate Historical Association July, 1869.

FRENCH, J. C., enlisted as a private May, 1861, in the Richmond Howitzers; was in the Army of North Virginia two years; was elected lieutenant, and served as aide-de-camp on the staff of General E. Kirby Smith; was in the Trans-Mississippi Department, and paroled in May or June, 1865. Joined this Association June, 1895.

FUCHS, VICTOR D., was born in Alsace (then France) in 1837, and came to Memphis, with other members of his family, in 1856. The next year he became a member of the old Washington Rifles, a local company composed entirely of foreign-born citizens. An incident in its history, remembered yet by a few, was the part it took in the reception tendered Governor Harris in Memphis soon after his election in 1857. Mr. Fuchs belonged to this company four years, and it was a part of the old One Hundred and Fifty-fourth Tennessee Regiment State troops or militia. The company did not go into the war with the One Hundred and Fifty-fourth Sr. Regiment, but did enlist in June, 1861, for twelve months in the Fifteenth Tennessee, Colonel Chas. Carroll's Regiment. Mr. Fuchs was elected Second Lieutenant of Company I, and Nick Frick was elected Captain. The regiment went to Columbus, Ky., where it afterward wintered; and Lieutenant Fuchs was with it in the battle of Belmont, Mo. In February, 1862, the regiment was ordered to march to the relief of Fort Donelson, but the order was countermanded, and in the spring proceeded to Corinth and thence to the front, and was hotly engaged in the battle of Shiloh, having nearly 200 men killed and wounded. Lieutenant Fuchs participated in this engagement, but was suffering from a chronic ailment which had troubled him for several years. He was shortly afterward permanently discharged and did not again enter the service. Had never really been fit for hard duty, and it is only within the last few years that he obtained entire relief. Is married, has children, and is a prosperous business man. He joined the Confederate Historical Association October, 1894, and has since been a useful and enthusiastic member of Company A, Confederate Veterans; attended the reunion at Richmond in June–July, '96; and has been on other trips with the company.

JUDGE J. S. GALLOWAY.

GALLOWAY, J. S., was born at the then home of his father, the Rev. Samuel Galloway, Mendham, N. J., on February 14, 1836; spent his early life at the home of his grandfather, Dr. Jacob Scudder, at Princeton, N. J.; was graduated from Princeton University in June, 1858, taking the highest honors in metaphysics and philosophy; removed to Georgia the same year, taught school until 1860, when he removed to Memphis, Tenn., where he continued teaching until April, 1861, when he enlisted in the Shelby Grays, Company A, Fourth Tennessee Regiment; was severely wounded at the battle of Shiloh, April 6, 1862; was afterward assigned to light service in the enrolling department, with the rank of first lieutenant, and served as such till the end of the war, having surrendered at Macon, Ga., in May, 1865. Like most of the young men of that day, he returned to his home impoverished in everything save youth and ambition. Two generous uncles — Mr. Benjamin R. Scudder of New Jersey and Mr. Alex. M. Scudder of Georgia — had advanced him considerable money with which to pay his way through school and the university, a large part of which he still owed. To liquidate this obligation, and to obtain the means to acquire a legal education, he again taught school. By means of the generous patronage afforded him by the good people of Memphis, he was soon enabled to pay off this debt of honor and prepare himself for the practice of law. Was admitted to the bar in 1866, and, after the "*lucubrationes viginti armorum*," was elected probate judge in 1886, having previously served ten years as justice of the peace and one term in the State Senate. The magnificent system of Shelby county turnpikes exemplifies his usefulness as a lawmaker; looking to that work alone, he can safely say "*exegi monumentum.*" In 1894 he was re-elected Judge of the Probate and Second Circuit Courts of Shelby county to serve another term of eight years. While leading a busy life, he has found ample time to indulge his natural fondness for politics, and has figured prominently in most of the political struggles that have occurred in county and State for the past twenty years, having been twice nominated by his party for justice of the peace, twice for State Senator, and twice for Judge of the Probate and Second Circuit Courts, practically without opposition. His greatest political battle, on his own account, occurred in 1890, when he offered for Congress in the Tenth Congressional District. His opponent was the Hon. T. K. Riddick of Fayette county. The contest, under the two-thirds rule, lasted for thirty days; upon the five thousand and fiftieth ballot Judge Galloway, lacking thirteen and one-third votes of being nominated, withdrew from the contest; whereupon Colonel Josiah Patterson was selected as a compromise candidate: this was a memorable contest—a record breaker. Judge Galloway is proud of the Democracy that has so often honored him, loyal to the State of his adoption, attached to the friends who have so often served him, and only hopes that his efforts to forward the interests of Democracy, State and friends will repay their partiality and devotion. He became a member of the Confederate Historical Association many years ago.

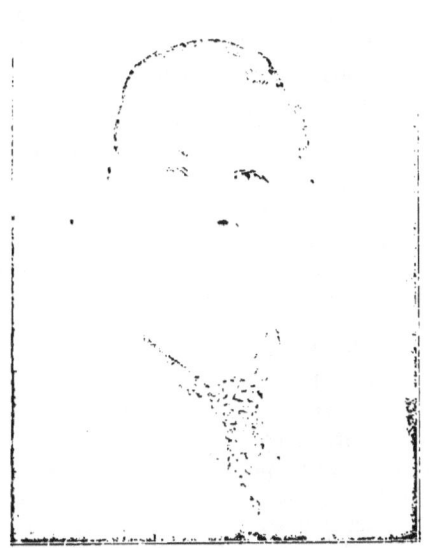

MICHAEL T. GARVIN.

GARVIN, MICHAEL T.. born September 16, 1840, in Cumberland, Md., of Irish parents, whose genial temperaments and sturdy traits of character have been inherited by the son. With his parents he moved to Memphis in 1845, then a town of about 3000 inhabitants, grew up here, and is now one of the best posted men in the city as to its growth and the biography of old-time citizens. When the war broke out he joined the Tennessee Guards as a private April 22, 1861, which organized as Company H, Fourth Tennessee Infantry, at Germantown, Tenn., on May 15, 1861; was made lieutenant of Griswold's Battery in January, 1863, and consolidated with Harris' Battery, Marmaduke's Brigade, in September, 1863. Resigned in December, 1864, and joined Stewart's Scouts; was captured May 2, 1865, at Dickson, Ala., and paroled at Iuka, Miss., on May 15, 1865, arriving in Memphis June 3, 1865. Was wounded October 8, 1862, at

Perryville, Ky.; also at Village Creek July, 1863, and in a
skirmish near Memphis in December, 1864. He was at Bel-
mont and the bombardment of Island No. 10, at Shiloh,
Mumfordsville, Perryville and the battle of Little Rock. Pine
Bluff, Poison Springs, Saline River and Ditch Bayou, in the
Trans-Mississippi Department, and in various smaller engage-
ments. Is now an active member of Company A, United
Confederate Veterans; was a member of the drill team when
Company A won the $1000 prize in the national military
contest at Memphis, Tenn., in May. 1895, and has been with
Company A on several trips, including the greatest of all to
Richmond last June–July, 1896.

For quite a time he was Deputy County Court Clerk; was
Constable of the Fifth Civil District and Deputy Sheriff, and
was in 1888 elected Magistrate, and is a leading member of
the County Court, which position he has held ever since. In
1890 was made City Recorder and still holds that position.
Being a man of sterling qualities and a strong judicial cast
of mind, as well as being a quick, intuitive judge of human
nature, he dispatches business with rapidity and fairness.

He was married on the 11th of January, 1872, to Miss
Maggie Moloney, and this union has been blessed with ten
fine children, six of whom are sons, constituting altogether
as happy a family as ever gathered around hearthstone or
center table. Esquire Garvin is yet a young-looking man,
and to his friends seems still younger at heart.

GARRETT, J. H., Sergeant Company A, Seventh Tennessee; enlisted May 6, 1862, and paroled at Marion, Ala.,
May 13, 1865. Admitted to C. H. A. February 11, 1896.

GIBSON, F. L., Lieutenant Company C, Second Kentucky
Cavalry, Morgan's command; served throughout the entire
war; was captured at Lebanon, Tenn., in the fall of 1861, but
escaped. Paroled May 13, 1865.

GILLOOLEY, FRANK, Captain Company F, G. B. Pickett's Engineer Corps; enlisted in 1861; was wounded at
Vicksburg. Shiloh and Tishomingo Creek; captured at Vicksburg July 4, 1863. Paroled at Gainesville, Ala., May, 1865.
Admitted to C. H. A. February 12, 1895.

GEN. GEORGE W. GORDON.

GORDON, GEORGE W., was born in Giles county, Tenn., and reared in Mississippi and Texas. Received a collegiate education and was graduated at the Western Military Institute, Nashville, Tenn., in the class of 1859; also receiving there about the same military education and training as were given at West Point. Practiced civil engineering, for which he had made special preparation at college, until the outbreak of the war. Entered the military service of the State of Tennessee, from the county of Humphreys, in June, 1861, in the capacity of drill-master for the Eleventh Tennessee Infantry Regiment; soon after transferred to the service of the Confederate States. Was successively a captain, lieutenant-colonel and colonel of this regiment, and in the summer of 1864 was made a brigadier-general and served with that rank till the close of the war. Though captured three times — once at Tazewell, East Tennessee, and again at the battles of

Murfreesboro and Franklin, Tenn., he was in every battle
fought by his commands except that at Bentonville, N. C., at
which time he was a prisoner at Fort Warren, Mass., where
he was retained till August, 1865, several months after the
close of the war. Upon his release from prison he studied
law and practiced that profession until 1883, when he was
appointed one of the railroad commissioners of the State.
In 1885 he received an appointment in the Interior Department of the Government and served four years in the Indian
country. Then resumed the practice of law until 1892, when
he was elected Superintendent of the Memphis City Schools,
which position he still occupies.

GORDON, C. M., enlisted August 29, 1863; was a private
in the Eighteenth Mississippi Regiment, and belonged to
Chalmers' escort; was wounded at Johnsonville, Tenn., in
November, 1864. Paroled at Gainesville, Ala., May 12, 1865,
and joined this Association February 17, 1895.

GOLDBAUM, MORRIS, private Company A, Fourteenth
Mississippi Regiment; enlisted April, 1861; was captured at
Fort Donelson and at Franklin; was wounded at the battle
of Franklin and the bullet was cut out May 10, 1893; was
released from prison April, 1865. Admitted to this Association November 13, 1894.

GOODBAR, JAMES M., was born in Overton county,
Tenn., and reared principally in White county. In the early
part of 1862 he assisted in raising a company of cavalry in
the counties of White and Van Buren. This company was
commanded by Captain George W. Carter, of Sparta, Tenn.
Mr. Goodbar was elected second lieutenant of said company.
At a later period this company was assigned to duty in the
Fourth Tennessee Cavalry, commanded by Colonel John P.
Murray, of Gainesboro, Tenn. Colonel Murray selected Lieutenant Goodbar for quartermaster of said regiment, with the
rank of captain. He was in the battle of Perryville, Ky.,
and many smaller engagements. This and other regiments
were reorganized at Shelbyville, Tenn., about January, 1863,
when Captain Goodbar was assigned to duty as purchasing

agent in the commissary department, and served in this capacity the remainder of the war. Upon one occasion he was captured by the Yankee cavalry, but being mounted on a good horse he made a sudden dash and a race of two miles, interspersed with many shots, and made his escape. After the war was over he returned to Memphis and engaged in the wholesale shoe business, in which line he had been before the war. He is now at the head of the wholesale shoe firm of Goodbar & Co., perhaps the largest establishment in that line south of the Ohio river, and is largely engaged in manufacturing; is a very active man and in the full prime of life.

GOODMAN, WALTER A., Major in the Seventeenth Mississippi; served in the army of Northern Virginia, and was engaged in the first battle of Manassas. His commission was dated July 31, 1862. He served as Assistant Adjutant General of Chalmers' Brigade of Infantry until transferred to Chalmers' Division of Cavalry, and then served with the same rank until the end of the war. He was one of the early presidents of the old Confederate Relief and Historical Association; succeeded General Jno. C. Fizer in 1872, and served for more than one term.

GOTTEN, NICHOLAS, private Company C, Forrest's old regiment; enlisted March 10, 1862; was wounded twice—at Bolivar, Tenn., and near Lafayette, Tenn.; was captured and left for dead by the Federals in May, 1864; captured second time at Greenbottom, Tenn, and exchanged at Vicksburg, Miss.; served under General Forrest until the surrender in May, 1865. Admitted to this Association October 9, 1894.

GRAY, J. E., private in Company D, Third Battalion, Lee's Brigade, Army North Virginia; entered service April 20, 1861, and retired April 3, 1865. Recommended for membership by Isaac Rosser and elected in this Association January 20, 1870.

GRAY, W. P., steward in General Dick Taylor's Department; entered service August, 1861; paroled May 5, 1865. Elected a member of this Association, upon his own application, September 9, 1869.

GREENWALD, LEE, private Company B; enlisted April 1, 1861; wounded at Franklin, Tenn.; was sent home sick from Chattanooga, as the army went east to North Carolina, and did not recover until after the close of the war; was not paroled. Recommended for membership by Ed. Whitmore and J. P. Young; admitted to C. H. A. February 11, 1896.

GREER, JAMES M., was born in Holly Springs, Miss., and comes of Revolutionary stock. His great-great-grandfather of Bedford county, Va., was a lieutenant in the struggle for American independence, and others could be mentioned in connection with the same cause. When the war broke out J. M. Greer was a cadet at the Virginia Military Institute and belonged to Company A in his battalion of cadets. This small but spirited corps was regularly enlisted in the Confederate service in 1864 and was called out just as the emergency dictated, and after a few weeks service returned to the barracks. The cadets were at the battle of New Market; assisted in repelling Hunter at Lynchburg; fought also in some skirmishes around Lexington, and assisted in defending Richmond against Sheridan's attack early in 1865. They had the spirit and fire of tried soldiers and fought with the coolness of veterans as often as permitted to take part in the war. After the surrender J. M. Greer returned home, read law, was admitted to the bar, came to Memphis, and has since been prominent in his profession, and is also quite well known for his literary acquirements outside of the law and for his oratorical abilities. He succeeded Judge Horrigan as Judge of the Criminal Court and served in 1883–84, and is now attorney for Shelby county. He was married to Miss Bettie Allen, daughter of Dr. Allen, in 1877, and they have three sons at the University of Tennessee.

GROVES, ROBERT DOUGLASS, was Orderly Sergeant of Company L, Seventh Tennessee Cavalry, Rucker's Brigade; enlisted April 4, 1862; was wounded at Harrisburg, July 14, 1864; was at home on wounded furlough when the surrender took place. His colonel obtained a parole for him May 11, 1865, but never delivered it. He was reputed to be one of the most dashing soldiers in Forrest's command.

COL. HUGH D. GREER.

GREER, HUGH DUNLAP, was born at Paris, Tennessee, February 4, 1836. Son of David Searcy Greer and Martha Jane Dunlap, representatives of two of the pioneer families of the State. His mother's father and mother, Hugh Dunlap and Susanna Gilliam, were married near Knoxville in 1794. His grandfather Greer settled in the State about 1811.

He graduated at the Mississippi University in 1856, and at the Lebanon Law School in 1858. He was married June 1, 1865, to Mary Ida Christian, daughter of Dr. James R. Christian, at Holly Springs, Miss. She died, without issue, June, 1867. He was married again in March, 1870, to Susan I. McLean, daughter of Colonel Charles D. McLean, of Memphis, Tennessee, and editor of the first newspaper published west of the Tennessee river; and has by this marriage four living children—Charles D. M. Greer, a lawyer in Memphis; David Searcy Greer, a farmer in Shelby county, and a pair

of twin daughters, Susie and Ida, now at school. He enlisted
in an infantry company organized by Robert F. Looney, at
Memphis, about the middle of April, 1861, and was elected
second lieutenant. Soon after, at the organization of the
Thirty-eighth Regiment, R. F. Looney was elected colonel;
First Lieutenant John C. Carter was elected captain, and he
first lieutenant, and served with that rank until April, 1862,
when he was elected Lieutenant-Colonel of the Thirty-eighth
Tennessee. He was shot down near the old church on the
evening of the second day of the battle of Shiloh in what is
known as the "Last charge at Shiloh," and was carried off the
field. When the army reached the old church that evening
on retreat, General Cheatham discovered that a large number
of caissons, ammunition wagons and ambulances containing
many of the wounded, had halted at a deep ravine, a hundred
yards south of the church, that was spanned by a little rail
or pole bridge that was difficult to cross. He ordered the
Thirty-eighth Regiment to move back to the crest of the hill
and hold the old church until the ambulances and wagons were
safely over. The regiment was formed across a little grave
yard about twenty or thirty steps north of the church and
ordered to sit down, as the men only had one round of ammunition left, and it was determined to hold that charge for the
supreme moment. The enemy, flushed with success, was
moving down in magnificent style and his skirmishers were
delivering a murderous fire. Generals Beauregard, Breckinridge, Cheatham and other prominent officers dismounted
under the hill and walked up to the church and remained for
a few minutes to encourage the men. All felt that the position was desperate, but not one man of those three or four
hundred Tennesseeans faltered. They had been in the bloody
fight for nearly thirty-six hours, without rest, without sleep,
but when the order came for that last sacrifice each soldier sat
quietly in line and looked at that magnificent Federal army—
first the skirmishers, then the infantry, and in the rear of each
brigade a battery of field pieces. The line extended to the
right and to the left as far as the eye could reach through the
open timber. General Cheatham, with his great big generous

heart, could not leave without a parting word. He walked
out to the front of the regiment and stepping up on a little
new-made grave, said, " My brave boys, I've ordered you to
halt here and hold this church until your wounded comrades
and the wagons are safely over the ravine. All that I have
to say to you is, when the shock comes remember that you are
Tennesseeans." When the enemy had come to within about
two hundred yards, Governor Isham G. Harris, acting aid-
de-camp to General Beauregard, rose up and said: "Colonel
Looney, the time has come; order your men to charge." The
regiment rose up, fired its last round of ammunition and
raised a yell, and with fixed bayonets drove back that part of
the line in front for nearly a quarter of a mile, and then
turned and marched back in good order under a fire from the
rear and both flanks, and halted at the old position at the
church long enough to see the last wagon cross the ravine.
During the whole of that trying ordeal and desperate charge
Colonel Robert F. Looney sat astride his old sorrel charger
and encouraged the boys by his superb courage and gallantry.
Soon afterward, when Colonel Greer was prisoner at General
Sherman's headquarters, he was asked by the General why
that regiment did not fire oftener than one round, and was
told the regiment had no more ammunition. General Sherman, in the presence of his adjutant, Major Hammond, grasped
Colonel Greer's hand warmly and congratulated him upon
being a member of so gallant a command. In the absence
of Colonel John C. Carter, Colonel Greer commanded the
regiment through the heavy skirmishing in front of Corinth
and through the battle of Farmington, but was taken sick
and asked for a furlough, but the surgeons of the brigade
had taken umbrage at some order of General Bragg's, and
all tendered their resignations. Bragg refused to accept, and
they refused to perform any duties except waiting on the sick.
No furloughs were granted except on surgeons' certificates,
and surgeons refused to comply with any such order. General Hindman suggested that if he would tender his resignation he would hold it for thirty days and give him a pass to
the rear, and before the time expired he could return and

8

withdraw the paper and resume his position in the regiment;
but before the thirty days had expired he was captured in
DeSoto county, Miss., by the Sixth Illinois Cavalry, carried to
Memphis and sent to Alton, Ill., and exchanged late in the fall
at Vicksburg He reported to General Pemberton, headquarters at Jackson, Miss., and upon a full statement of the facts,
General Pemberton gave him a commission to go into West
Tennessee behind the enemy's lines and organize a cavalry
command, and he organized a magnificent company at Denmark in Madison county, and joined the Fourteenth Tennessee Cavalry regiment commanded by Colonel J. C. Neely,
as Company C. That regiment became a part of the famous
Forrest Cavalry of the latter part of the war. He took part
in much of the hard riding and harder fighting through Mississippi, Tennessee, Alabama and Georgia, and was wounded
again at Lafayette, Ga., in the summer of 1864.

Colonel Greer is one of the few officers now alive who were
on the famous raid into the city of Memphis. The command
moved in on the Hernando road, the Fourteenth Regiment in
front, Company C in front of the regiment, and Captain Bill
Forrest about fifty yards in front as advance guard. They
broke into a gallop when they crossed Nonconnah creek, six
miles out from the city; not a word was spoken above a whis-
per. The signal to swing into line of battle was the firing of
the enemy's pickets on the advance guard; the city and suburbs were enveloped in a dense fog; it was impossible to dis-
cern objects beyond a few feet away. The pickets were not
far from the Female College. Company C went into Hernando
street at the intersection of College avenue, turned up Hernando, and charged a battery about where Looney's switch is
now located; moved down to Beale and up Beale to Main,
crossed into McCall street, and halted in the alley in the rear
of the Gayoso Hotel, Captain Bill Forrest going to the front.
It was hoped to capture General Washburn, supposed to be
stopping at that hotel, but it was soon learned that his headquarters were on Union street, at General Williams' house,
A great number of subordinate officers were at the Gayoso,
and they came down and chatted very pleasantly, and ac-

knowledged that they were not expecting such a call. Two videttes, who were stationed at McCall and Main and Gayoso and Main streets, galloped in and reported an infantry command closing in from each end of Main street. Colonel Logwood, with a part of his regiment, had moved up and halted on McCall street, and Captain Greer, with part of the Twelfth, had halted on Gayoso street. Colonel Logwood, the ranking officer, commanded Captain Greer to take the advance and pilot the command out of the city. When Company C moved into Main street, the enemy opened fire from both ends of the street; Company C wheeled to the right and charged the column at the intersection of Beale street, driving them into a church that formerly stood on the northeast corner of Beale and Main; moved down Beale to Hernando and out Hernando to near the old Poston residence, and found General Forrest with a part of his command fighting six or seven thousand of the enemy; then turned to the right, rode through the camp of the Fourth Illinois Cavalry, halted, swapped a few horses, then passed out between the enemy's right flank and the river, moved up to the front, formed on the left of the command, skirmished for an hour or two, and moved back toward Hernando in a walk; the Federals followed as far as Nonconnah, but did not cross the creek. General Washburn came over under a flag of truce, receipted for and carried back with him six or seven hundred prisoners that had been captured.

Owing to a disagreement with a superior officer, Captain Greer requested General Forrest to detach him from the regiment, which he did late in the fall of 1864, and ordered him into West Tennessee on recruiting service. During the winter and early spring he gathered up some men and skirmished against Hawkins' and Hurst's regiments, who were raiding and depredating upon the citizens in West Tennessee. Upon learning of the surrender of the Southern army, he rode into Memphis and was paroled on the 17th of May, 1865. Was elected to the Legislature of Tennessee in the fall of 1874, and served one term; since, has remained quietly on his farm in Shelby county. He became a member of the Confederate Historical Association over twenty years ago.

GRIFFIN, JOHN C., enlisted as private in Company A. Twenty-ninth Georgia, in October, 1862; again enlisted September, 1863, in Company I, Sixty-sixth Georgia, and afterward served in the Thirteenth Mississippi in 1864. He was wounded in the battles of the Wilderness and of Cedar Creek; paroled May, 1865.

GWYNNE, A. D., was born January 18, 1839, County Londonderry, Ireland. Came to Memphis, Tenn., with his parents December, 1849; advantages of schooling limited. At the age of fourteen was put to work in the hardware house of Holyoke, Lowndes & Co., now Orgill Bros. & Co. Married September, 1859, to Eliza A. Henderson, daughter of the late Andrew and Susan Henderson. When the South seceded he was clerking for the hardware firm of McCombs & Co.

Enlisted for the war in the Sumpter Grays early in the summer of 1861. This company was enrolled in the Thirty-eighth Tennessee Infantry, commanded by Colonel R. F. Looney, and formed part of Wright's Brigade, Cheatham's Division. He was elected second lieutenant and soon thereafter was appointed adjutant of a Tennessee battalion. April 3, 1862, was promoted to major and assigned to duty with the Twenty-sixth Alabama Infantry; served with that command in the battle of Shiloh and was wounded by a fragment of shell fired from one of the gunboats. The shell exploded overhead; one piece cut away the point of his cap, striking the button on his breast, glanced and shattered the bone of his right arm, and another piece struck his horse just back of the saddle. After the battle, and at the age of 23, he was promoted to lieutenant-colonel, and on June 28, 1862, was assigned to duty with the Thirty-eighth Tennessee Infantry.

The magnificent record this regiment made under the gallant Looney at Shiloh was repeated at Perryville, Murfreesboro, Chickamauga, Mill Creek Gap, Resaca, New Hope Church, Kennesaw Mountain, Peach Tree Creek, Atlanta, Jonesboro and Franklin, as well as in the daily skirmishes in which it took part, and in all of which it contributed its full share in making the imperishable war record of Cheatham's

COL. A. D. GWYNNE.

Division; in all save Jonesboro and Franklin he participated. On May 7, 1864, his regiment was ordered to hold Mill Creek Gap against a strong attack of the enemy; obeyed orders and Colonel Gwynne came out of the fight with a severe scalp wound.

February, 1864, Jno. C. Carter, Colonel of the Thirty-eighth Tennessee, was promoted on the field at Resaca to brigadier-general. He had been in command of the brigade for a long period prior to his promotion, and Colonel Gwynne was, therefore, at the time in command of the regiment and continued with it until wounded on the breastworks of the enemy at the battle of Atlanta, July 22, 1864, a minie ball striking his left arm, shattering the wrist joint and fracturing eight inches of the bone. He was taken prisoner and remained on the field ten days, and was afterward sent to the Federal hospital at Marietta, Ga. In speaking of this episode to the writer, he said : " I have no words at my command to give expression of my admiration of the ability and skill of the Federal surgeons who attended me when taken from the field. I was placed side by side with their own wounded, and when my turn came I was placed on the table and received the same care and successful attention as those who wore the blue."

When wounded he weighed 165 pounds; three months after, when again able to stand on his feet, he weighed 90 pounds. He was a prisoner on Johnson's Island for nearly three months. February, 1865, was exchanged and sent to Richmond, Va., arriving in that city late in the afternoon, and engaged supper, lodging and breakfast, for which he paid fifty dollars. Next morning started on foot to join the army in North Carolina.

When the war ended Colonel Gwynne had one Mexican quarter, given him by a brother Confederate, and it was every cent of value he possessed on earth. He borrowed money to bring his wife and child from Jackson, Miss., to Memphis. Landing in Memphis with his left arm totally disabled and bandaged to his side, he felt in poor plight to start afresh the battle of life. His first employment was on a Yazoo steamboat as second clerk. Early in 1866 returned to Memphis and found a situation with Galbreath, Stewart & Co. August, 1866, he moved to DesArc, Ark., and was admitted into a firm which opened business in Memphis in 1871 and had a New Orleans branch, as originally organized in 1866. He is connected with many Memphis enterprises. Has been with the State National Bank since 1873, as director, vice-president, and for the past five years president. Is a director in the State Savings Bank, Factors Fire Insurance Company and the Memphis Cotton Compress and Storage Company, etc.

As relics of army life he has the Mexican quarter already mentioned, the button he wore at the battle of Shiloh, the bullet that struck him at Atlanta, and a furlough (the only one) he received during the war; it is of date June 2, 1863, and for eight days leave of absence. He values it very highly for the indorsement it carries from Brigadier-General Marcus

J. Wright, who commanded the brigade at the time the furlough was granted. It reads as follows:

HEADQUARTERS THIRTY-EIGHTH REGIMENT TENN. VOLS.
In Camp near Shelbyville, June 2, 1863.

COLONEL—I have the honor to ask for a leave of absence for eight (8) days. In making this application I beg leave to state that I am desirous of visiting LaGrange, Ga., for the purpose of procuring a place for my family, who have been compelled to leave their home in West Tennessee, and more recently in North Mississippi, on account of the advance of the enemy. Hoping that compliance with the above request will not be detrimental to the good of the service,

I am, very respectfully, your obedient servant,

A. D. GWYNNE,
Lieutenant-Colonel Thirty-Eighth Regiment Tenn. Vols.

To Colonel Kinloch Falconer, A. A. G.

INDORSEMENTS.

In forwarding the application I desire to say that Colonel Gwynne is one of the best qualified, most attentive and industrious officers I have ever met in the army. He has done more important special duty in my brigade than any officer in it; is never absent from his post of duty, and makes this application only under the circumstances mentioned, which I regard as an extreme case.

Approved and respectfully forwarded: MARCUS J. WRIGHT,
Brigadier-General.

Approved: Approved:
  B. F. CHEATHAM,   LEONIDAS POLK,
  Major-General Commanding.   Lieutenant-General.

Approved, by command of General Bragg :   H. J. THORNTON,
Adjutant.

To commence from June 9.
  B. F. CHEATHAM,
  Major-General Commanding.

Colonel Gwynne bears the marks of wounds received in battle, and will as long as he lives. He is a busy, quiet man, and notwithstanding his record, as briefly outlined above, he seldom talks of his war experiences unless some old soldier introduces the subject. He has but recently applied for membership in the C. H. A.

HANCOCK, J. B., First Lieutenant and Adjutant Fortieth North Carolina Infantry, enlisted in Company C March 29, 1861; left for the coast May 20, 1861; company captured at Hatteras August, 1861; after that he was detailed as drill-master for recruits at Washington, N. C.; was wounded at Newbern, N. C., March 16, 1862; at Henderson February 17, 18 and 19, 1865; Neal Fork, near Kingston, N. C., March 7, 1865, and at Bentonville March 16, 1865; paroled May 1, 1865, at Bush Mill, near Greensboro, N. C.

HARRINGTON, JNO. N., private Company H, Crockett Guards, First Arkansas, enlisted June 2, 1861; was wounded three times—at Corinth, Chickamauga and Franklin. He captured the flag of the Sixteenth Iowa Regiment on the right of Atlanta in the battle of July 22, 1864; paroled June 4, 1865. Admitted to the C. H. A. February 12, 1895.

HARRIS, J. S., private Company F, Seventeenth Mississippi, enlisted April 19, 1861; was discharged from service July, 1863, on account of physical disability. Admitted to C. H. A. February 12, 1895.

HARTMUS, T. H., enlisted early in 1861; served on General W. B. Bate's staff with the rank of Major; was paroled at Augusta, Ga., August, 1865. Became a member of this Association at an early day.

HART, B. NEWTON, Captain Company B, Eighth Missouri Infantry, entered service May 6, 1861; was paroled at Meridian, Miss., May 10, 1865. Practiced law in Memphis with his father for a few years and returned to Missouri. Elected a member of this Association July, 1869.

HAYS, JOHN B., private in Company E, Ninth Tennessee Infantry, Maney's Brigade, enlisted May 26, 1861; wounded and captured at Shiloh; released December 6, 1862; discharged April 12, 1863. Admitted to C. H. A. March 13, 1894.

HERBERT, B. F., private in Anderson's Scouts and served throughout the war. Proposed for membership in this Association by Major W. A. Goodman and elected April 28, 1870.

HON. ISHAM G. HARRIS,
OF TENNESSEE.

sufficient to run the Government econom-
ically administered, and am thoroughly
opposed to the fallacious idea of protection
which never did, and never will, protect.
I am glad to know the majority of the people of my State hold the same opinions,
for they recognize the value of commercial
freedom towards opening up the vast natural resources the State possesses. The only
fault with many of our people is that after
the evil experience of high protection, they
are running in the opposite direction and
expressing themselves in favor of free trade.

This is the result of extremes in any system, for the reaction generally carries them
as far in the other direction. It is gratifying
to know, however, that the Democratic
majority recognizes the benefits to be derived
from the middle course, and only raise the
revenue for the carrying on of the Government from a tariff, the difference in the
cost of labor forming the basis of its com-
putation. We have had considerable trouble with the convict-lease system, and it has
agitated our people so much that their
minds have been distracted from many of
the economic questions of the day,
but we have changed all that, for
at the session of our Legislature which has
just adjourned, we provided for the erection
of prisons and stockades, and the convicts
will be put to work to mine the coal for
the institutions of the State—for which
$100,000 a year for coal is used—and when
the present leases with the corporations
expire on January 1, 1896, they will not
be renewed, and the State will attend to
its own convicts. Now, this vexed question
is settled to the satisfaction of all, our people will turn their attention to the develop-
ment of the State, and they look forward
to the assistance tariff reform will give
them."

"The platform of the Democratic party on
tariff reform," said Representative Fitzger-
ald, "was indorsed by the people of our State
last November, for they believe that is the
only policy for the salvation of the South.
The principles of President Cleveland are
our principles, and if there should be any
disagreement it will be that he does
. . . for enough for us. We have

judging of the evil effects of a restri ted
commerce, it is the farmers, for they are
among the first sufferers, and to a ....
they denounce it. As far as they are concerned, the revision cannot come any too
soon, nor be too far reaching, for at pres ent
it stands as a barrier to their prosperity, A
consequently reacts on the whole country."

SHODDY WOLF IN SHEEP'S CLOTH-ING.

It is quite certain that free wool and low
duties on woolens would seriously injure
if it would not be the death of the shoddy
industry in this country. This fact is being
made clearer every day.

Mr. F. Muhlhauser, of Cleveland, O..
the proprietor of the largest shoddy mill in
the world, replies in the *Wool Reporter* of
April 6, to a letter in a previous number
from a "certain Mr. Osborne, of Wyoming,"
who claims that "protection made wool
cheaper."

Mr. Muhlhauser not only gives the "certain Mr. Osborne" a fearful drubbing, but
laughs at the Reform Club and the members of Congress who are attempting to
revise the tariff downwards.

He says, "this whole question will turn
out the greatest farce of the nineteenth
century."

Now it so happens that the "certain Mr.
Osborne" is not only the Governor of
Wyoming, but is a large wool grower who
favors free wool, to provide better markets
for American wools. It is presumed that
Mr. Osborne understands his business
Mr. Muhlhauser understands the shod
business. There is a conflict of interest
Mr. Muhlhauser wants the importation of
foreign wools prevented so that our m
facturers will be compelled, in order to g
their cloths a soft finish, to mix shoddy
instead of foreign wools, with our ow
wools. Mr. Muhlhauser does not dare to
give his exact reasons for favoring high
duties on wools; he knows it would injure
his cause, just as the circular letter of the
shoddy and rag men in 1888, declaring for
high duties and for Harrison and Morton

U. S. SENATOR ISHAM G. HARRIS.

HARRIS, ISHAM G., Governor, and as such commander of all State troops until transferred to the Confederate service, entered the service April 1, 1861. After the transfer he continued with the Army of Tennessee to the end of the war, as a civil officer and without command. Was with General Albert Sidney Johnston at the battle of Shiloh and held the general in his arms when he bled to death from a wound. After the surrender he went to Mexico on horseback, accompanied by a faithful colored servant. Governor Brownlo had offered a reward of $5000 for his head, and this stood until after Governor Harris went to England and returned to this country.

Governor Harris and General Pillow entered upon the practice of law in Memphis about the year 1868. He is now serving his fourth term in the United States Senate, and seems endowed with all the energies and powers of endurance of a man of half his age, and is recognized all the country over as a leader in the Democratic party. He is the last of the war governors living, North or South. He became a member of this Association July 1, 1869; was elected President and served as such for two years, attending meetings regularly and presiding with as much formality and decision of manner and regard for parliamentary propriety as if he had been in the United States Senate.

HENDERSON, BENJ. R., enlisted as a private in Company H, Fourth Tennessee Regiment, on May 16, 1861, and served in Strahl's Brigade, Cheatham's Division, until he was discharged in 1863 for ill health and disability. Became a member of this Association at an early day.

HENKEL, CHRISTOPHER, Corporal Company A, Tenth Mississippi, enlisted March 26, 1861. The regiment left Jackson, Miss., for Pensacola, Fla., and after reorganization Company A became Company D, same regiment. Served in the army of Tennessee until the surrender; paroled April 26, 1865, at Greensboro, N. C. Admitted to the Confederate Historical Association January 14, 1896.

HENNING, S. L., enlisted January 4, 1861, in Company H, Thirteenth Tennessee, Vaughan's Brigade; was commissioned lieutenant November, 1863, and paroled at Greensboro, N. C., May, 1865.

HILL, J. L., private Company D, Fifteenth Arkansas Infantry; entered the service May, 1861; paroled May, 1865. Proposed by T. P. Adams, and elected to membership in this Association April 28, 1870.

COL. C. W. HEISKELL.

HEISKELL, CARRICK W., was born at Fruit Hill, Knox county, Tenn., July 25, 1836, of an old and prominent family; his grandfather on his mother's side, Joseph Brown, was a soldier in the Revolutionary war; a brother of his father's mother was a colonel in the Continental line; his father, Frederick S. Heiskell, was for many years before and up to the year 1836, with Hugh Brown, his brother-in-law, editor and owner of the *Knoxville Register*, a newspaper of great influence in its day, published at Knoxville, Tenn. C. W. Heiskell was educated at the University of East Tennessee and Maryville College; read law while teaching school at Rogersville, Hawkins county, Tenn.; obtained his license to practice law from Judges Lucky and Patterson in 1857, and was engaged in practice when the war broke out. He was the first man in Hawkins county to enlist in the Confederate service, and aided in raising the first company raised in that county; this was Company K, Nineteenth Tennessee Infantry. He was elected first lieutenant of this company, and on the election of its captain, A. Fulkerson, to the majority of the regiment, was elected captain of the company. This position he held until after the battle of Murfreesboro, where the major of the regiment, the gallant R. A. Jarnagin, was killed, when Captain Heiskell was promoted to the majority of the regiment over the senior captain. He was major of the regiment until after the battle of Missionary Ridge, where the lieutenant-colonel, Beriah F. Moore, the bravest of the brave, was killed, and Major Heiskell was made lieutenant-colonel. At the battle of Chickamauga he received a very troublesome wound in the foot, which disabled him for twelve months. No memorial of that conflict is he prouder of than this : "Most of the field officers on my right were dismounted by having their horses shot under them, and Major Heiskell of the Nineteenth Tennessee Regiment, a gallant officer, was severely wounded in the foot" (extract from General Strahl's report, U. S. War Records, series 1, volume 30, page 131). When he rejoined the army, after twelve months on crutches, Hood was retreating from Nashville. He witnessed what came very near being a bloody conflict between Forrest and Cheatham, when they quarreled over which of them should cross the river at Columbia first, each contending that he had precedence : guns were cocked all along the line of infantry, but Forrest at length gave Cheatham the right of way, and the incident closed. While Major Heiskell was wounded, both the lieutenant-colonel (Moore) and the colonel of the regiment (F. M. Walker, afterward promoted to brigadier-general, and than whom no truer man or better soldier ever drew a sword) were killed, and Major Heiskell received his commission as colonel of the regiment. He commanded Strahl's Brigade, and was with Forrest, covering the retreat of Hood's battered and tattered legions from the fatal Tennessee campaign. In the fight at Anthony Hill, near Pulaski, and at Sugar Creek, were witnessed the most gallant feats of the war, at least, the most striking evidences of the matchless courage and endurance of Confederate soldiers : hatless, barefooted and hungry, through sleet and snow, they marched, and when a fight came they fought with matchless pluck; even those too feeble to carry a gun stayed in the fighting contingent, as one of them expressed it to Colonel Heiskell, " to see what was going on." He, with his regiment, followed the fortunes of the Confederacy through all its dark vicissitudes from Nashville to High Point, N. C., where they surrendered with that great captain, Joseph E. Johnston. In the battle of Bentonville, when the Federals attempted to cut off the only avenue of retreat from "Old Joe," Colonel Heiskell's (Strahl's) Brigade followed General Hardee, who with a Texas brigade of cavalry charged the foe; the infantry captured a whole line of picks and spades, and at once went to fortifying; at 11 o'clock that night they were ordered to cease work, and in a few days the surrender came. The writer must pause to say that no man in the Confederate army was more beloved, no commander of greater capacity on the field, and of more modest and deserving worth, than Lieutenant-General William J. Hardee. His memory is sacred to every Confederate soldier of Johnston's army.

After the surrender in 1865, Colonel Heiskell settled in Memphis, Tenn., where he has resided ever since. He was elected Circuit Judge in May, 1870; this position he held until 1878, when he was appointed city attorney, which position he held until 1882; since then he has been engaged in the practice of law. He was married about the beginning of the war to a daughter of Hon. John Netherland of Rogersville, an eminent lawyer and old-line Whig leader, and they have a family of grown children.

HILL, A. B., was born December 12, 1837, in Tipton county, Tenn.; enlisted as a musician in Company C, Ninth Tennessee Regiment, on the 6th of May, 1861; afterward served in the Fifty-first Tennessee Regiment, and was discharged in May, 1862; re-enlisted in the Twelfth Tennessee Cavalry and transferred back to the Fifty-first Tennessee, and at the close of the war was Captain of Company G of that regiment; never was captured or wounded; was paroled May, 1865. Afterward came from Tipton county to Memphis, and has been for many years Secretary of the Memphis City School Board.

HOLLOWAY, J. L., Sergeant-Major Twentieth Mississippi Regiment and belonged to Company B; afterward he served in Tighlman's Brigade, Adams' and Loring's Divisions, Army of Tennessee. General Tighlman was killed at Baker's Creek and General Adams at Franklin, Tenn. The regiment was in Loring's Division during the war.

HOLT, G. A. C., the subject of this paragraph, recently located here, is from Kentucky. The health of his wife, Mrs. Ina L. Holt (nee Berry), a relative of the late Dr. F. L. Sim, caused him to select Memphis as a residence. He was born in Salem, Livingston county, March 2, 1840; graduated from the Louisville Law School in 1859; entered the Confederate army in April or May, 1861; was elected Captain of Company H, Third Kentucky Regiment of Infantry, under the then Colonel Lloyd Tighlman, afterward Brigadier-General. Colonel Holt was in the battle of Shiloh, and was brevetted by General Beauregard for courage and gallantry. A paragraph from a prominent Kentucky newspaper gives a synopsis of his public life. The *Danville Advocate* of 1886 says:

" When the tocsin of the late civil war was sounded in 1861, young Holt was among the first of the young men of Kentucky to volunteer in defense of the Southern Confederacy; was soon elected captain of his company, and before he was 22 years old was promoted to the coloneley of the Third Kentucky Volunteer Infantry. C. S. A. He served with conspicuous gallantry on many bloody fields of battle, and returned to his home in 1865 with a parole in his pocket, resuming the study and practice of law. He served his State as Senator two terms, was elected Speaker of the Senate, and became Lieutenant-Governor, succeeding Governor Leslie."

His regiment became very much depleted, and in the last year or two of the war was assigned with the Seventh and Eighth Kentucky Infantry to General N. B. Forrest to enable them to recruit. He was wounded at Jackson, Miss., from which his right hand and arm are yet paralyzed. He was paroled at Gainesville, Ala., in 1865, with Forrest's command. Colonel Holt and his son are practicing attorneys in this city. He has but three children—Hon. J. Pat. Holt, Misses Mamie and Marguerite Holt. He joined the Confederate Historical Association several years ago.

JOHN M. HUBBARD.

HUBBARD, JOHN MILTON, private in Company E, Seventh Tennessee Cavalry, is a native of Anson county, N. C. He was educated at Centenary College of Louisiana and Florence Wesleyan University. In 1858, the year of his graduation, he married Miss Lucy Hawkins of Florence, Ala., who in 1859 became the mother of Ernest M. Hubbard, for several years an officer of the Boatmen's Bank, St. Louis, Mo. Mr. Hubbard enlisted at Bolivar, Tenn., and was mustered into the service at Jackson on the 24th of May, 1861. He served under Chalmers, Armstrong, Van Dorn, Jackson and Forrest, and was paroled below Gainesville, Ala., on the 13th of May, 1865. Having prepared himself for the profession of teaching, he was already the successful principal of a good male school at Bolivar when he enlisted. He was opposed to secession and voted for Stephen A. Douglas in 1860, but like thousands of others in the South when war was flagrant, he went with his own people in their movement for separate independence. Though having little confidence in the success of the Confederacy after the disasters of 1863, every instinct of honor prompted him to stand by the cause to the sorrowful end.

Returning to Bolivar in 1865, he took up the work of teaching boys in the old academy. He has had a varied experience in his profession, but has spent the last eight years as President of Stanford Female College, Ky., and of Howard Female College, Gallatin, Tenn., which latter position he has recently resigned.

In 1868 Mr. Hubbard married Miss Sallie Pybass of Bolivar, who became the mother of Eugene P. Hubbard and Arthur P. Hubbard, now residing in St. Louis in responsible positions. Having become a widower for the second time in 1887, Mr. Hubbard, in 1889, married Miss Mary MacAnally, a well-known teacher of Memphis, but at that time the presiding teacher of Marion Female Seminary in Alabama.

The subject of this sketch believes that duty faithfully performed is a quality of bravery, and as soldier and citizen has tried to live up to a fair standard, but he never did enjoy the presence of flying bullets or the proximity of the enemy, except when they were "running." Of the many exciting incidents in battle which he witnessed, and fiery charges of the Seventh Regiment in which he participated, there is not space here to speak, but he would be willing, if it were possible, to have the very small number of the original Company E, who stood by the cause and lived to see the surrender, to bear witness to his record as a soldier.

HUHN, JOHN D., private Company C, Seventh Tennessee Cavalry; enlisted June 6, 1861; was promoted to adjutant; served through the war with splendid courage and patience, and was paroled May 11, 1865.

HUMES, W. Y. C., was born at Abingdon, Va., and was a leading young lawyer in Memphis before the war. In April, 1861, was chosen as First Lieutenant of Bankhead's Battery

Lt-Gen. Leonidas Polk,

of Light Artillery; participated in the campaigns around Columbus, Ky., under General Polk; was promoted to captain and placed in command of heavy artillery at Island No. 10; after a gallant defense he was captured there and confined many months in prison on Johnson's Island; was exchanged in the summer of 1862 and placed in command of a heavy battery at Mobile, Ala., but his superior abilities caused him soon to be called to the field, where he rose to the rank of major-general, and was distinguished as a cavalry leader with and under General Wheeler. After the surrender he returned to Memphis, and for a number of years had a very heavy and lucrative law practice; overwork may have shortened his days; he died, leaving a wife (nee Elder) and several children. He joined this Association July 15, 1869.

HUNT, W. R., was born in Washington, Ga.; came to Memphis in 1858, when quite a young man, and engaged largely in planting. At the outbreak of the war he was given charge of the arsenal in Memphis under the Provisional Government of Tennessee. After the State seceded, General Polk had him commissioned as lieutenant-colonel of artillery. After Fort Donelson fell the arsenal was located at Columbus, Miss., and after Corinth fell it was removed to Selma, Ala., Colonel Hunt still in charge. In 1863 he became chief of the mining and nitre bureau, and continued to the end to render invaluable services to the Confederacy in supplying the munitions of war. He was a firm, quiet man, of great earnestness and large executive ability; handled large bodies of men easily without harshness, and was intensely Southern in his views. After he was paroled he returned to Memphis, where he had a large estate. He became a member of this Association September 9, 1869, and died in 1872.

HUSKEY, W. H., private Company G, Second Virginia Infantry, Stonewall Jackson's Brigade; enlisted on March 1, 1861; was wounded at Gettysburg and Cedar Run; captured at Gettysburg July 4, 1863, and released February 21, 1864; paroled May 9, 1865. Admitted to C. H. A. June 11, 1895.

9

HARRISON. B. P., enlisted as a private in Company A, Twentieth Tennessee, in May, 1861, and was paroled after the surrender. (Record incomplete.)

HAMBLET, J. G., was a private in Company B, Forrest's old regiment; owing to his youth served twelve months before he enlisted, in August. 1864; paroled May 11, 1865, at Gainesville, Ala. Joined this Association November 14, 1898.

HILLS, J. B., was a private in Company A, Fourth Tennessee Infantry. Previous to his enlistment in May, 1862, he had served in the same command at Columbus, Ky., Island No. 10 and at Corinth without enrollment. He was never paroled, never discharged, and in his application for membership says: "I am still a Johnnie without an army to follow."

IVEY, A. J., Corporal Company A, Seventh Tennessee Cavalry; enlisted July 20, 1861, and served until the surrender at Gainesville, Ala., May 11, 1865.

JAMES, FRANK L., enlisted in service October 3, 1861; was Adjutant of the Twenty-second Louisiana Infantry; paroled May 10, 1865. After the war he was city editor of the *Appeal* under General Albert Pike; became a physician, as he had already studied abroad, and afterward removed to St. Louis. Elected a member of this Association July 1, 1869.

JANUARY, W. W., enlisted January 15, 1864, as a private in Harvey's Scouts and served in General W. H. Jackson's Division. These scouts were not attached to any regiment; paroled at Canton, Miss., April, 1865. Admitted to this Association January 14, 1896.

JARNAGIN, JOHN HAMPTON, was born at Cleveland, Tenn., September 18, 1843. At the beginning of the war was living at Austin, Tunica county, Miss.; joined Confederate States Army May 21, 1861, as a private in the Young Guards, Captain John Cameron, Ninth Tennessee, Colonel Carroll; June 20, 1861, was transferred to Hindman's Legion: June 10, 1861, made Second Corporal: September, 1861, promoted to Fourth Sergeant: was at the battle of Green River,

Ky.; at Bowling Green when the Confederates were shelled out; at Shiloh, Farmington, Perryville, Mumfordsville, Murfreesboro, Tenn., Missionary Ridge, and in the general fights from Dalton to Atlanta; after the retreat from Atlanta was stationed at Griffin, Ga.; ordered from there to Augusta and camp near Augusta to help Colonel Leroy O. Bridewell in organizing troops to be forwarded to General Jos. E. Johnston in South Carolina, where he was until the surrender of General Johnston's army; rode horseback to Meridian, Miss., and surrendered to Colonel Bertram, Twentieth Wisconsin, in May, 1865; thence on horseback home. He was commissioned captain and acting quartermaster February, 1863, and served on staff duty with General John S. Marmaduke and General Granberry. After the war engaged in cotton planting in Bolivar county, Miss., and moved to Memphis, 1889. Joined the C. H. A. February 12, 1895.

JETT, DUNCAN FRIERSON, enlisted as a private in Company B, Fourth Tennessee, April 26, 1861; three months later was promoted to captain and A. C. S., and served as same, and as assistant district commissary, with headquarters at Atlanta, Macon and Augusta, Ga.; was paroled May 3, 1865, at Augusta. Admitted to this Association June 13, '94.

JOHNSON, A. W., First Lieutenant A. P. Hill's Artillery; entered the service May, 1861; paroled May, 1865. Admitted to this Association, upon personal application, July 15, 1870.

JOHNSON, JOHN, enlisted as a private May, 1861, in the Sixth Tennessee Infantry; was discharged at Tupelo, Miss., in 1862; joined the Fourteenth Tennessee Cavalry in January, 1864, and surrendered at Gainesville, Ala., with Forrest's command, May, 1865.

JONES, D. C., Second Lieutenant of Artillery; enlisted in Company A, Thirty-eighth Tennessee Infantry, August 15, 1861, and remained in the same company throughout the war; served with it in heavy and light artillery. After the battle of Shiloh this company, Captain J. W. Rice, was transferred at Corinth to heavy artillery and remained in that branch of the service until the spring of 1864, when the command was supplied with light artillery and assigned to General Forrest's corps. In February, 1865, was transferred to heavy artillery again, sent to Mobile and remained there until the end of the war.

JONES, A. D., was a private in Logwood's Battalion; was captured near Gains Landing October 20, 1862; was seriously wounded at the battle of Belmont and afterward discharged on that account.

JONES, J. C., son of the late Governor James C. Jones; joined the Confederate service in 1862, when he was quite young and just from school; became first lieutenant of cavalry and was assigned to duty with General W. H. Jackson's escort, with which he served to the end of the war. Afterward returned to Memphis and engaged in mercantile pursuits for a time. He became partially paralyzed afterward and has since taught a select school for boys, for which work he has remarkable aptitude.

JONES, PHIL. B., was Adjutant of the Tenth Kentucky Cavalry, General John H. Morgan's Division; was captured at Buffington's Island, Ohio, May 26, 1862, and released from prison May 22, 1865. Admitted to this Association August 29, 1893.

JONES, R. L., Corporal Company C, Fifty-first Tennessee Regiment; enlisted May 5, 1862; was wounded severely at Chickamauga on September 19, 1863, and retired from the service by Dr. Frank Rice April 21, 1864, and did not recover from the wound until after the surrender.

JONES, RUSSELL, private Company I, Fifty-first Tennessee; enlisted February 5, 1862. After the Kentucky campaign his health failed and he was detailed to work in the government shoe shops at Atlanta, Ga., and afterward was removed to Augusta; was at the fall of Savannah. [The first captain of Company I was O. D. Weaver, who died at Knoxville and was succeeded by Captain Spivey. Colonel John Chester of Jackson commanding the regiment.] He was paroled May 5, 1865.

J. V. JOHNSTON.

JOHNSTON, J. V., was born in Adair county, Ky., and removed to North Mississippi at an early age; was engaged in mercantile business with R. H. Vance at Hernando when the war begun; enlisted in a company at that place known as the "Irrepressibles," under J. R. Chalmers as captain; went to Pensacola in March, 1861; the company became part of the Ninth Mississippi Regiment, with Chalmers as colonel; T. W. White was elected Captain of Company K, formerly the "Irrepressibles;" the regiment was composed of Mississippi companies mostly from the northern part of the State. Mr. Johnston's first real war experience was with this company and regiment in a night attack, October 9, 1861, on Fort Pickens, Santa Rosa Island, or rather on Billy Wilson's regiment of New York jail birds and other toughs in tents a few hundred yards from the fort. The leaders of the intended surprise were General Richard H. Anderson in command, J. R.

Chalmers in charge of the first regiment, J. Patton Anderson in charge of the second, and John K. Jackson in charge of the third; in all, about fifteen hundred men. The plan to capture the notorious Billy Wilson and his warriors of terrible repute, freshly recruited from Sing Sing and other prisons, was a failure, for the Zouaves fled to the fort, and Major Vogdas, with his regular troops, tried to intercept the Confederates and cut them off from their boats; a short and spirited engagement took place, with considerable loss on both sides; the Confederates got away with a loss of sixteen men, while the Federals were said to have lost more heavily. It was a foolhardy attack, but the experience gained was worth something. Major Vogdas, the gallant commander of the Federal regulars, was captured by Colonel Chalmers and taken over to Pensacola, where he was paroled the next day.

At the expiration of Mr. Johnston's term of enlistment, which was for twelve months, he returned to Hernando and joined a company under Captain J. B. Morgan, which became a part of the famous Twenty-ninth Mississippi Regiment; was appointed ordnance sergeant; was with the regiment, participating in every fight and never absent from duty a day, on down to Atlanta, where he was wounded and disabled on the 22d of July, 1864; was in the hospital at Griffin, Ga., and elsewhere for several months, and when able was assigned to duty under Captain W. P. Orne at Lauderdale Springs, Miss.; was paroled at Grenada, Miss., May 19, 1865.

After the surrender, Mr. Johnston came to Memphis and resumed a partnership with Mr. R. H. Vance, which has been continued for more than thirty years. He was married in Kentucky a few years after the war; has an interesting family; is a strict member of the Presbyterian Church, and has most strikingly illustrated the fact that a good Confederate soldier generally made a most exemplary and useful citizen. He became a member of the C. H. A. only recently.

JONES, JOE, private Company K, Second Alabama Cavalry; enlisted in 1862, served through the war, and was captured at Montgomery, Ala., April, 1865.

JORDAN, G. S., was Second Lieutenant in Company H, Thirteenth Tennessee Infantry; was discharged, but afterward served in the Twelfth Tennessee; paroled May, 1865, at Gainesville, Ala.

JORDAN, J. P., First Sergeant Company H, Seventeenth Virginia Regiment; enlisted April, 1861, and served throughout the war; was wounded twice at the battle of Frazier's Farm, Va.; captured there June 30, 1862, and released the following day; was mentioned in special orders by General Pickett as one of four scouts who performed specially valuable and heroic service; paroled April, 1865. Admitted to this Association October, 1894.

KEARNEY, J. R., private Company A, Pickett's Twenty-first Tennessee, enlisted May 16, 1861; paroled May, 1865. Recommended for membership in the Confederate Historical Association by A. R. Pope, B. F. Hawkins and M. T. Garvin. Admitted January 14, 1896.

KELLY, P. J., enlisted April, 1861, as a private in Company H, Fifteenth Mississippi Regiment; was wounded at Shiloh; paroled May 5, 1865.

KELLY, P. J., was born in County Clare, Ireland, June, 1842, and came to Memphis in 1858; enlisted May, 1861, in Company A, under Captain Shockey, Knox Walker's Second Tennessee Regiment; went to Randolph, Fort Pillow and Columbus, and was in the battle of Belmont with the regiment; went to Purdy and on down to Shiloh, in which battle he was wounded in the hand, losing two fingers. The regiment was consolidated with the Twenty-first Tennessee, and that became the Fifth Confederate under Colonel J. A. Smith. Mr. Kelly was at the battles of Farmington, Miss., and Perryville, Ky., and at the latter place was wounded in the thigh, which lamed him for life. He was discharged in 1863. After the war he married in Memphis, became a steamboat pilot and followed that calling for several years. Has three sons and a daughter: one son is a lawyer and the others clerks—all well educated. He became a member of the Association many years ago; has belonged to Company A, Confederate Veterans, since its organization; went to Chattanooga, Richmond and elsewhere, and is an active, enthusiastic member.

KENDALL, W. R., Orderly Sergeant Fourteenth Mississippi Regiment, enlisted May 29, 1861; was wounded at Fort Donelson, and afterward served in the Ninth Mississippi Cavalry; paroled May 10, 1865.

KENNEDY, A. E., enlisted April 18, 1861; was Sergeant Company A, Third Arkansas Regiment, Colonel Harrison commanding; served in the Army of Tennessee, and was paroled May 6, 1865.

KING, S. A., private Company I, First Confederate; shortly after the company was organized, it was put in H. Clay King's battalion, but later on was consolidated with two other companies from Wayne and Perry counties, and called the First Confederate; paroled May 11, 1865. Admitted to the C. H. A. February 12, 1895.

KING, W. C., private Company D, Fourth Tennessee Regiment, enlisted May 15, 1861; was captured at Missionary Ridge in 1863; escaped October 30, 1864, but never succeeded in reaching his command or getting through the Federal lines, though making repeated efforts to do so.

KINGSBURY, WILLIAM L., First Sergeant Company G, Nineteenth Alabama Regiment, enlisted May, 1861; was wounded at Marietta, Ga., and captured by Wilson's raiders just before the surrender; paroled May, 1865. Admitted to C. H. A. May 4, 1895.

KIRBY, JOHN A., enlisted as a private in the Fourth Tennessee Infantry, May 15, 1861; paroled at the close of the war. Proposed by J. E. Beasley and T. P. Adams for membership in this Association and elected March 3, 1869. Since the war has been merchant and planter; married Miss Ann Eliza Brooks at Ridgeway, Shelby county, Tenn.; they have two children, Joseph and Agnes.

KNOX, R. L., born in Fayette county, Tenn.; was graduated in the medical department of the University at Nash-

ville, and had just entered upon the practice of medicine at
Early Grove, Marshall county, Miss., when the war began;
enlisted as a private in Company F, commanded by Captain
Wm. Ivey, Seventeenth Mississippi Regiment of McLaw's
Division; was in the first battle of Manassas and at Ball's
Bluff, and in other engagements, serving as a private; was
made assistant surgeon of the regiment in the latter part of
1862. After the battle of Gettysburg was left in charge of
a hospital; remained six weeks and then was sent as a prisoner to Fort McHenry, Baltimore. where he was detained for
five months. The ladies furnished him and other prisoners
of his class with money to buy better food than furnished
prisoners. The treatment was not harsh, aside from strict
confinement. When exchanged he returned to his command
and was with it until the surrender at Appomattox, where he
was paroled. He immediately returned to Early Grove, resumed the practice of his profession and was thus actively
engaged for fifteen years. He was married to Miss Fanny C.
Steger of Fayette county, Tenn., came to Memphis in 1883,
and has since practiced his profession in this city. Joined
the C. H. A. February 12, 1889.

LAKE, WALTER S., enlisted September 26, 1863, W. F.
Taylor's Company, General Jackson's escort; was with the
Seventh Tennessee; was ordnance sergeant at the close of
the war, and paroled at Gainesville, Ala., May 12, 1865.

LANDSTREET, EDWARD, was born in Baltimore, Md.,
August 26, 1844; enlisted in Company A, First Virginia Cavalry, then commanded by Lieutenant-Colonel J. E. B. Stuart,
September 15, 1861, when he was a mere boy. When Stuart
was promoted to brigadier-general he detailed Edward Landstreet as courier, and he served with him and afterward under
Fitzhugh Lee, Mosby and other noted leaders throughout the
war. He was captured once, but escaped the same day; was
with General Lee's army at Appomattox, but escaped with
the cavalry, and finally surrendered with Mosby's command
at Winchester, Va.. and was paroled by General Augur in
May, 1865. After his return from the war he located in Bal-

timore, became a member of the Historical Society of the
Army and Navy of Maryland, and soon after his arrival in
Memphis, in 1888, was elected a member of the Confederate
Historical Association of Memphis, and was one of the first
to join the organization known as Company A, Confederate
Veterans; was elected second lieutenant of said company in
September, 1895, and as such attended reunion of U. C. V.
at Richmond in June–July, 1896.

LAVENDER, G. W., enlisted as a private in Company H,
Forty-first Tennessee, October 25, 1861; was captured at Fort
Donelson and was exchanged; put in all possible time in the
service until the regiment disbanded, after the battle of Nashville, to go home. He could not get back, and was captured;
was wounded at Marietta, Ga., and at New Hope Church.

LAWHON, H. C., Lieutenant in Company D, Faulkner's
Twelfth Kentucky Cavalry; enlisted May 15, 1861, and was
elected Lieutenant at the reorganization at Tupelo, Miss.;
was never absent, never wounded and never captured; was
paroled May 16, 1865, at Columbus, Miss. Admitted to this
Association July 17, 1894.

LEVY, DANIEL SEESSEL, was born in Attweiler, Prussia, on the 22d of October, 1826, and is therefore the oldest
active member of this Association. He came to the United
States in 1850 and to Mississippi in 1853, and was a citizen of
that State for thirty years. He was a merchant many years,
and was postmaster at Skipwith in 1858–59. Enlisted April
1, 1862, as private in Cowan's Battery, First Regiment Mississippi Artillery; was in Featherstone's Brigade, Loring's
Division, Army of Tennessee; was captured at Fort Blakely,
Ala., April 14, 1865, and released from prison at Vicksburg,
Miss., on the 16th of May, 1865; came to Memphis in 1883.
He was recommended on his application by Captain T. T.
Cowan and Lieutenant G. F. Tompkins, and became a member of C. H. A. in 1884. Mr. Levy has been an enthusiastic
worker in the Association, and a very active and efficient
member of Company A, Confederate Veterans, although the
oldest man in the company.

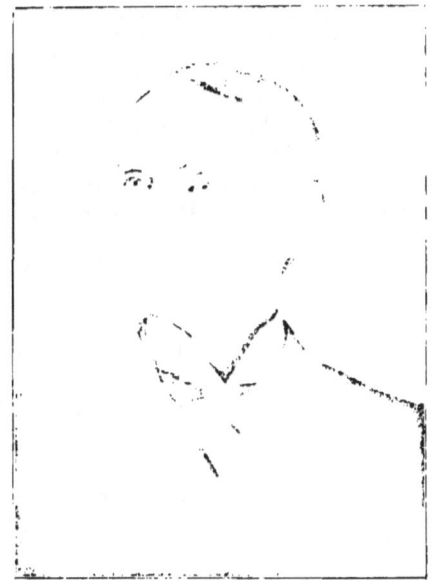

RICHARD P. LAKE.

LAKE, RICHARD P., born in Grenada, Miss., July 10, 1848; was the youngest of four brothers in the late war, and although only seventeen years old at the surrender he had been elected and served as second lieutenant of three different companies, and toward the last especially performed important service generally expected of much older men. He first enlisted in a boy's company at home, regularly drilled and disciplined by Captain, afterward Colonel W. S. Statham, of the Fifteenth Mississippi Regiment. He was elected second lieutenant of this company, and duty of some importance was performed without getting far from home. The older members one by one went off to the war. In 1864 the young man having reached the mature age of sixteen years enlisted in Captain R. E. Wynne's company, Colonel E. S. Fisher's regiment, State militia, and was again elected second lieutenant, and saw some active service. Early in 1865 acted as assistant in the Adjutant-General's office of Colonel Dennis' Brigade State troops, but was soon elected to the time-honored rank and position of second lieutenant in Captain G. P. Lake's company in Major H. C. Horton's battalion of cavalry. He was placed in charge of dismounted men, and went with them to Scooba, Miss., thence to Artesia, where he was in command of the dismounted men of his brigade and reported to Captain Virgil V. Moore of General Armstrong's command. The general lost his brigade after the battle of Selma and was reorganizing the remnants and some new material. It was this new brigade to which Lieutenant Lake was attached when he was surrendered in the field at Columbus, Miss., where he had been ordered to obtain paroles for his battalion. This was his last service. He has his parole yet, which he cherishes highly. Older men of his command desired him to lead them across the Mississippi river, to fight it out over there, but he reasoned that as the Confederates had failed on this side they would soon be exhausted on another field, so the project was abandoned. After the war Mr. Lake applied himself vigorously and successfully to business. He became a director and vice-president of the Mississippi & Tennessee Railroad Company, and continued as such until the road was bought by the Illinois Central a few years ago. He was a banker, merchant, planter, and general insurance agent. Was married in 1878 and has a grown son as large as himself. Removed to Memphis as a wider field for his energies and capital in 1894, where he and his wife soon became identified with the social life as well as business interests of the city. He soon became a member of this Association and of Company A, Confederate Veterans. He attended the Confederate reunion at Richmond with his company in June–July, 1896, and was appointed in Special Orders No. 5 as aid-de-camp with the rank of colonel on the staff of Gen. Stephen D. Lee, commanding the Army of Tennessee Department, U. C. V., and served in that capacity.

LEE. STACKER, private in Company A, Forrest's old regiment; entered the service February 18, 1863; paroled May, 1865. Proposed for membership by Colonel John W. Dawson of this Association and elected January 20, 1870.

JAS. A. LOUDON.

LOUDON, J. A., enlisted in Captain J. S. White's Cavalry Company in Memphis, May, 1861, when only 15 years old; was in an engagement with Federal cavalry at Charleston, Mo.; he wounded a soldier and released a number of citizen prisoners. N. B. Forrest (afterward general) was a private in this company. At Belmont young Loudon captured a Federal sergeant and a large gray mule; was tranferred to Captain Jack Stock's company; next fight was with infantry on the Big Sandy; there he captured another prisoner; next engaged the Federal infantry west of Paris; Confederates were outnumbered twenty to one; after sharp conflict fell back; Loudon lingered and had his hat shot off. Soon after the command under Colonel H. Clay King was surprised near Paris, but repulsed the enemy. The company reconnoitered Hickman, Ky., and had a return call next morning and a shower of bullets; a cannon ball killed a horse next to private

Loudon and scattered the blood all over him. The company became a part of the Seventh Tennessee Cavalry; made a dash on a Federal scouting party west of Paris and captured camp equipage. The next fight was at Diggs Mill, where Lieutenant Diggs was killed; then at Bolivar, Tenn., where the Federal Colonel Hogg in command was killed and a Dutch major was captured. Soon after had a fight at Britton's Lane; here private Loudon wounded a man and took him prisoner. He was in the attack on Corinth under Generals Price and Van Dorn; was under General Van Dorn on the raid to Holly Springs; the command afterward marched to Grenada with the prisoners taken and banners flying. During the next raid into Tennessee young Loudon was taken desperately ill and was sent by Surgeon Marable to a private house to take his chances of recovery. He finally met General Alcorn, who was under parole. The general advised him to reach his father's boat, the "Granite State," in the service of the Confederacy on the Arkansas river. Through the kindness of Colonel "Jim" Rogers he passed through the lines, reached his father and was nursed back to health. He was refused a pass to return to his command, and was assigned to duty as assistant pilot, with the rank of captain, on his father's boat. The army soon evacuated Little Rock and Pine Bluff, and he received orders to burn his father's boat, which he and his brother did at Swan Lake, in the fall of 1864. Soon after that he was elected first lieutenant of Captain Bart. Gillespie's company of cavalry, Colonel Charles Carleton's regiment. The first raid this regiment made was on a negro regiment commanded by white officers, entrenched on the Heiskell plantation near Pine Bluff. The attacking force had special orders and carried them out successfully to the letter. The command moved with General Price into Missouri and fought the battle of Pilot Knob, a battle near St. Louis, and one near Jefferson City, captured Boonville and Independence, and fought the battles of Mine Creek, Kansas, and Newtonia, Mo. The army reached its old camp terribly shattered. Lieutenant Loudon had participated in all its battles and marches. While recruiting for his company

he was captured by Major Davis, in command of Federal
cavalry, and imprisoned at Pine Bluff; was then removed to
the military prison at Little Rock, where he endured untold
and indescribable hardships for five months, and was paroled
from prison May 6, 1865. It was said of him that he killed
and captured more than his five of the enemy, and yet it was
all for a lost cause. After the war he returned to Memphis,
engaged in business, and except a few years spent on his Arkansas plantation has been a citizen of this city since. Was
married here to Miss Virginia Shanks in 1870; his wife died
in 1873, leaving a son, now grown. He became a member of
this Association among the first and has continued ever since.
Is a member of Company A, Confederate Veterans; attended
the reunion of U. C. V. at Richmond, June–July, 1896, and
the State reunion of the same, October 14 and 15 following,
at Nashville, as a delegate from Camp No. 28, and was elected
second vice-president of the State organization by acclama-
tion.

LEWIS, GEORGE W., Sergeant Company D, Fourth Tennessee Infantry; enlisted May, 1861; wounded three times—
at Shiloh, Perryville and Franklin; paroled April 17, 1865,
at Greensboro, N. C. Admitted to this Association in October, 1894.

LINDSTEDT, W. H., enlisted as a private in Company G,
One Hundred and Fifty-fourth Tennessee; was wounded at
Shiloh, and when he recovered rejoined his command after
the battle of Murfreesboro; was discharged February 4, 1863.

LINKHAUER, JOHN A., born in Prussia, July 8, 1825;
came to New Orleans in 1840, and to Memphis, where he has
since lived, in 1845. He enlisted in the First Alabama Regiment at Meridian, Miss., served six months in the field, was
detailed by Major Tom Peters and placed in charge of a large
government shoe factory at Cahaba, Ala.; was afterward
transferred to Montgomery and thence to Macon, Ga., where
he was captured by Wilson's raiders; was paroled on April 24,
1865, came home in the following September, and has ever
since been engaged in business. He joined this Association
at an early day.

LOCKE, CHAS. G., born in Memphis; is a son of the late Gardner B. Locke, who was mayor of Memphis in 1848; his mother's family came from New England. The Lockes came from England and settled in Virginia in 1710. Two of C. G. Locke's great-grandfathers were in the Revolutionary war, and one of them served on General Washington's staff. In April, 1861, C. G. Locke was temporarily in Arkansas, and enlisted in the Rector Guards of DesArc, a company which became part of the Fifteenth Arkansas Regiment, with P. R. Cleburne as colonel. In July, 1863, he was transferred to the Sixth and Ninth consolidated Tennessee Regiment, and was on its rolls to the end of the war. He served as a private, and once declined to be elected captain. At Perryville the drum of his left ear was broken by the cannonading, and he is deaf yet in that ear. At the battle of Chickamauga he was wounded in the left leg immediately above the knee. Gangrene supervened and the flesh sloughed off, leaving several large, ugly scars. This wound never healed until a year and a half after the war was over. Although in the hospital at West Point, Ga., he volunteered, in company with a handful of wounded soldiers and recruits, to go into the fort to fight Wilson's forces. Here he lost his right arm at the shoulder joint only a few minutes before the enemy poured over the breastworks. It was probably the last bloody fight of the war, having taken place April 16, 1865, a week after Lee's surrender and ten days previous to Joe Johnston's surrender. It was here that the heroic General R. C. Tyler of Memphis was killed on his crutches.

Private Locke was also in the battles of Richmond, Ky., and Murfreesboro, Tenn., as well as several lesser engagements. He treasures with commendable pride a certificate from T. H. Osborne, captain of his company at the time of his transfer to the Tennessee regiment, who wrote the following on his descriptive list: "The said C. G. Locke was not only present at the above mentioned battles, but acted with marked bravery in each, and especially at the battle of Murfreesboro. I recommend him for promotion as having been a dutiful, patriotic and gallant soldier."

He is the last of his immediate family, his nearest relative being a young nephew in Florida. He became a member of this Association March 20, 1870. Has been connected with the business departments of daily papers in Memphis nearly ever since the war, and is a leading member of the Masonic fraternity. He is the survivor of four brothers, who were all in the Confederate army for four years. The oldest brother, James Bowdoin Locke, was Captain of Company C, Sixth and Ninth Tennessee Regiments, and was in every skirmish and battle in which that regiment was engaged from Belmont to Franklin. William Locke was absent through sickness for several months in 1862, but was present and on duty at all other times during the entire war. Joseph Locke served first in the Thirteenth Tennessee Infantry, and being discharged on account of his youth at Tupelo, Miss., joined the cavalry with Richardson and afterward with Forrest. These three brothers were all wounded slightly several times each, the only severe wound being received by Captain Locke through the right lung at Franklin.

LOGWOOD, THOS. H., entered the Confederate service in May, 1861, as Captain of Memphis Light Dragoons, Sixth Battalion of Tennessee Cavalry. On organization at Columbus, Ky., Captain Logwood was elected lieutenant-colonel; at the battle of Belmont he crossed the river with two companies of cavalry and took a decisive part in that engagement. He was commissioned to raise a regiment of mounted Lancers but the idea was abandoned. In 1863, by authority from the Secretary of War, he organized a fresh regiment in West Tennessee, and was commissioned as Colonel of the Sixteenth Tennessee Cavalry. This was inside the Federal lines, and when General Forrest ordered the regiment to report at Oxford, Miss., it was scattered, and only about three hundred men responded. It was consolidated with the Fifteenth Tennessee Cavalry and a battalion of Mississippi cavalry, with T. H. Logwood as lieutenant-colonel. The regiment made a fine record. Colonel Logwood was in command of the troops that entered Memphis August 21, 1864, and was promoted to the full colonelcy of his regiment for gallant services rendered

10

on that day. The Fifteenth was at Johnsonville, with Hood in Tennessee, and in numerous heavy fights, and was paroled at Gainesville, Ala. Col. Logwood practiced law in Memphis before and after the war, and died several years ago, leaving a wife and son. He became a member of this Association April 28, 1870.

LOWRY, WILL J., private Company C, Seventh Mississippi Cavalry, under Forrest; enlisted July, 1862; paroled May 11, 1865. Admitted to C. H. A. March 15, 1895.

MAHONEY, E., was born October 17, 1844, in the city of Cork, Ireland; enlisted as private in Company A, Forty-third Alabama, in February, 1862; was detailed for duty in the ordnance department under Major Wagner and so remained until the end of the war, the Forty-third Alabama having been ordered to Virginia. Joined the Confederate Historical Association April 11, 1893.

MALONE, G. B., private Company E, Ninth Tennessee Infantry; enlisted June 7, 1861; discharged for being under age in 1862; served with the Twelfth Tennessee Cavalry, Reno's and Morton's batteries, and in Company H, Forrest's old regiment; rejoined the army; served in artillery as orderly sergeant for one year, then restored to cavalry as private; captured near Somerville, Tenn., March 9, 1863, and escaped April 27, 1863; paroled May 11, 1865. Joined this Association June 13, 1894.

MALONE, W. B., born 16th September, 1842; entered service as a private in Company A, Twelfth Kentucky, April, 1862; served through the war and was paroled May 16, 1865.

MANSON, J. A., Lieutenant Company A, Cobb's Georgia Legion; enlisted August, 1861; was wounded at Knoxville, Tenn., November 19, 1863, and at Sailor's Creek, Va., April 6, 1865; captured at the last place, and paroled June 19, 1865. He became a citizen of Hardeman county, Tenn., soon after the war; taught school and became a farmer, as he is yet; served several terms in the Legislature and was Speaker of the House of Representatives; was appointed United States

Marshal for the District of West Tennessee, by President Cleveland, in 1893, and still fills that position, with headquarters in Memphis. Joined the Confederate Historical Association August 13, 1895.

MARCUM, WM. J., Sergeant Company D, Ninth Mississippi Regiment; enlisted March, 1861; was wounded at Munfordville, Ky., September, 1862, and was discharged shortly after the battle of Missionary Ridge in 1863. Admitted to this Association March 15, 1895.

MARION, NATHAN, private in Company A, First Alabama Cavalry; enlisted April 19, 1861; was afterward transferred to Russell's Battalion, which was merged into the Fourth Alabama Cavalry, under Colonel A. A. Russell, serving under Forrest to the end of the war; was wounded at Shiloh and Shelbyville; paroled May 14, 1865. Admitted to this Association December 11, 1894.

MARTIN, J. H., was born in Winston county, Miss., October 28, 1840, and came to Memphis with his father's family in 1848, then moved to Arkansas in 1850; after completing his education he returned to Memphis in 1857 and remained until the beginning of the civil war; became a member of "Logwood's Light Dragoons" before hostilities began, and on May 16, 1861, almost the entire company was mustered into service of the Confederate States Army and left Memphis at once for active service around Randolph, Tenn., where General Gideon J. Pillow was in command. Their first actual engagement was at the battle of Belmont, and it is the testimony of survivors that not a man of the company, when drawn up in line on the bank of the Mississippi river, showed the least degree of fear, though they were within three hundred yards of General Grant's line of infantry, who were exchanging a heavy musketry fire with Colonel Charles Carroll's regiment, Fifteenth Tennessee Infantry. This entire absence of emotion was doubtless owing in part to a lack of appreciation of the danger, as some of them confessed to great trepidation in many much less dangerous positions in succeeding years of the war. At the reorganization of the army after the ninety-day enlistments expired, the company was reorganized as Company A, Seventh Tennessee Cavalry, under that brilliant commander Colonel W. H. Jackson, and when he became general the company was detached from the regiment to act as his escort. About February, 1863, Mr. Martin was promoted, upon the recommendation of General Jackson, for meritorious performance of duty, to the rank of first lieutenant, and assigned to duty on his staff. In December, 1863, Captain James Crump, aid-de-camp to General Jackson, was killed in battle near Sharon, Miss., and again, at the request of General Jackson, Lieutenant Martin was appointed to succeed him, and still holds his commission as such, and served in that capacity until the close of the war.

After the surrender Captain Martin came to Memphis, and has ever since been actively and successfully engaged in large business affairs; he married Miss Nina D. Wood, and they have reared an interesting family. He is a quiet, energetic man, and has built up large interests, without losing sight of old friends or forgetting the strong ties of comradeship existing between old soldiers. He was on the general's staff at the inter-State drill held in Memphis May, 1895, and contributed much to the success of that brilliant event. He joined the Confederate Historical Association in 1884.

MARTIN, JOHN C., was born in Shelby county, Tenn., December 2, 1843; enlisted December 1, 1862, in Company E, Twelfth Tennessee Regiment. At West Point, Miss., this regiment and Forrest's regiment, or McDonald's battalion, were consolidated, and then Colonel Kelly became the commander; fought through the war under Forrest, and was paroled May 6, 1865.

MASON, FRANK, private in Company D, Eleventh Tennessee, Preston Smith's Brigade; was born May 22, 1844, in Davidson county, Tenn.; enlisted May 1, 1861; was in the battle of Wild Cat, Ky., siege of Cumberland Gap and various other engagements; was in the Dalton, Ga., campaign, and was wounded on the 22d of July, 1864, in front of Atlanta; paroled May 3, 1865, at Augusta, Ga.

J. HARVEY MATHES.
Adjutant Thirty-Seventh Tennessee Regiment in 1863.

MATHES, JAMES HARVEY, was born near Dandridge, Jefferson county, East Tennessee, on the old place where his grandfather lived and where his father, Rev. William Alfred Mathes, still lives; he comes of revolutionary stock on all sides; received an academic education at Westminster English and Classical School and was prepared to pass through college in a year or two when the war began; was in Alabama when Fort Sumpter fell; returned home, raised a company for Confederate service, was elected captain and drilled the company for two months, but it was distributed in different commands and he enlisted as private in a company intended for service in Virginia; this became Company C, Thirty-seventh Tennessee Regiment, organized at Knoxville by Colonel W. H. Carroll of Memphis. Private Mathes was elected orderly sergeant, and was soon after appointed sergeant-major by Colonel Carroll. The regiment was brought to Germantown, near Memphis, then ordered back to Chattanooga and Knoxville, and became inured to marching and about-facing before ever smelling a battle. While at Knoxville Sergeant-Major Mathes was detailed to serve in the Adjutant-General's department on the staff of Major-General Geo. B. Crittenden, and saw some very pleasant service in hotel headquarters. When the midwinter march to Mill Springs, Ky., began he shouldered a gun, joined his regiment and shared the fatigues and dangers of that ill-starred campaign. Crossed the river at Mill Springs on January 19, 1862, and was under fire at the end of the battle of Fishing Creek and aided in bringing up the rear of the retreat. After the battle of Shiloh he was elected first lieutenant of his company and commanded it for a time, being then in Marmaduke's Brigade, and participated in the minor engagements about Farmington. Accepted a commission direct from the War Department, and was assigned to duty as adjutant of the regiment, with which he served in B. R. Johnson's Brigade, Buckner's Division, in the Kentucky campaign, and was in the battle of Perryville (see Lindsley's Annals, page —), and on the return to Knoxville served temporarily as adjutant of brigade; was in the battle of Murfreesboro, December 31, 1862, all day long, under Cleburne; the field officers of the regiment were all three shot down, and he was left practically in command of the regiment, though outranked by a captain of the line. In the spring of 1863 was stationed at Chattanooga; was adjutant of camp direction and inspector of posts on the line to Dalton; was sent to Vicksburg on a special mission, remained a few days and came out on the last train before the surrender of the place; after that was ordered to report to General Bragg at Shelbyville, and received special orders to look after posts and recruiting stations, which took him to various parts of the Confederacy, and involved some arduous and perilous work. Tiring of this he asked to be reassigned to his old regiment, where he was offered command of a company; was returned, but at Dalton was assigned to duty as inspector of Tyler's Brigade; served actively at Dalton and on the campaign to Atlanta; was almost constantly at the front, and was under fire seventy days out of seventy-five, and was act-

J. HARVEY MATHES,
Honorary Member Company A, Confederate Veterans of
Memphis, December, 1896.

ing adjutant-general on the staff of General Tom Benton
Smith when desperately wounded on July 22, 1864, in front
of Atlanta. The shell that wounded him killed his horse.
That night the leg of the young staff officer was amputated
by Surgeon J. C. Hall, now of Anguilla, Miss., in the presence
of several surgeons and friends. Colonel L. J. Dupre, who
was present as a war correspondent, wrote a very pathetic
account of the event. He saw no more active service: was
in the hospital at Columbus, Ga., several months, and had the
gangrene and another operation upon his leg. Came to Memphis after the surrender, and was paroled here May 13, 1865,
and has his parole as well as commission yet.

Captain Mathes became connected with the press, was on
the *Argus*, the *Avalanche* and the Louisville *Courier*, and for

many years was editor of the Memphis *Public Ledger*. Has been elected to public office several times : served two terms in the Legislature ; was a commissioner to the Paris Exposition from Tennessee in 1878 ; was for twelve years a member of the board of visitors to the University of Tennessee at Knoxville ; was elector on the National Democratic ticket in 1884, and has held other positions of honor and trust ; is a Mason ; belongs to the Knights of Honor, A. O. U. W., and other organizations. A few years after the war he was married to Miss Mildred Spotswood Cash of Forest Hill, Shelby county, Tenn. By this marriage were born five children— Mildred Overton, Lee Dandridge. Benjamin Cash. J. Harvey, Jr., and Talbot Spotswood, all living and at home except the oldest son recently married in Chicago and now living in Norfolk. Va. Captain Mathes was one of the early members of the C. H. A., and is an honorary member of Company A, Confederate Veterans.

MARTIN, E. J., served in the A. C. S. Department of Forrest's corps, and was captured at Durhamville, Tenn., March 1, 1865 ; released from prison and paroled following month.

MAULDIN, W. D., First Sergeant Company H, Twenty-second Tennessee Infantry, Gordon's Brigade ; enlisted July 18, 1861 ; wounded at Belmont, Mo.; captured at Nashville on Hood's raid December 18, 1864, and exchanged at Camp Chase, Ohio. February 28, 1865 : paroled on April 25, 1865. Admitted to C. H. A. August 13, 1895.

MAY, LAMBERT, entered service early in 1861 ; served on the staff of General Withers with the rank of major; paroled on the 26th of April. 1865. His name was proposed for membership in this Association by General Patton Anderson, and he was elected September 9, 1869.

MAYO, ALBERT. First Sergeant Company I. Fourth Tennessee ; enlisted May 15, 1861 : paroled May 26. 1865. Admitted to the C. H. A. May 4, 1895.

McCALLA, J. G., born June, 30, 1834, in Lincoln county, Tenn.; enlisted in the C. S. A. May, 1861 ; became Captain of Company D, Twelfth Tennessee Cavalry ; served through the war and discharged in March, 1865. Recommended for membership by General A. J. Vaughan and Dr. W. S. Rogers.

McCALLUM, JOHN F., was one of the boy soldiers of the war. He was born in Shelby county, Tenn., November 25, 1848. He became a private in Company A, Seventh Tennessee Cavalry, in 1863, having run away from home to join the army, which he found near Holly Springs. He weighed then less than 100 pounds, and owing to his extreme youth was hardly considered a soldier by his comrades and officers. Still he performed full duty and was with the command nearly a year. His company was detailed as escort for General W. H. Jackson, and he served as courier for a time. He was seriously wounded in the fight at Coffeeville, Miss., December 5, 1863, and was left on the field and narrowly escaped capture. His friends and his negro boy thought it impossible to remove him; gave him some money and other comforts and left him to his fate. But he slipped out that night and soon turned up at Grenada. After that he was unfit for service, and is to this day a sufferer from his wound. After the war he became a successful business man; was a charter member of this Association under the application made in 1884.

McCARVER, ARCH., enlisted October 1, 1861, in Company E, Twelfth Tennessee Cavalry; was a gallant soldier throughout the war, and was paroled April 25, 1865. He has since been in business in Memphis, and served one term as sheriff of Shelby county.

McCLURG, P. M., private Company K, Thirty-first Alabama Regiment; enlisted April 12, 1862, and served in the Army of Tennessee. (No other record appears.)

McCROSKEY, H. A., born on the 9th of July, 1842, in Shelby county, Tenn.; enlisted in Company B, Ninth Mississippi Regiment and afterward served in Company C, same regiment; was on the staff of General Marcus J. Wright, commanding post and department; was wounded three times in battles of Murfreesboro and Chickamauga and as General Bragg retreated out from Corinth, Miss.; paroled on the 17th of May, 1865. Joined the C. H. A. September 15, 1891.

McFARLAND, L. B., enlisted as private in Company A, Ninth Tennessee, May 24, 1861; became sergeant-major of the regiment; appointed second lieutenant in Ninth Tennessee in April, 1863; served as volunteer aid-de-camp to General George Maney; was wounded in the left arm at the battle of Shiloh; was in every battle of Cheatham's Division except Franklin; was captured at West Point, Ga., April 16, 1865, and finally released in the following month. He returned to Memphis, and has been for many years a leading member of the bar. Joined the C. H. A. August 13, 1869.

McGHEE, W. T., private in the "Como Avengers," of the Eighteenth Mississippi Cavalry. The company was organized in April or May, 1861, at Memphis; he was at Fort Pillow, Columbus, Ky., Bowling Green, at Shiloh, Vicksburg, and after that was in General Forrest's escort and with him in all his campaigns until the end of the war; was first in General J. S. Bowen's Brigade; paroled May 11, 1865.

McGOWAN, E. L., private in Company A, Seventh Tennessee Cavalry, Rucker's Brigade, Jackson's Division; enlisted August, 1862; served through the war, and paroled May 17, 1865; was afterward sheriff of Shelby county and a prominent Front Row merchant in Memphis. Admitted to the C. H. A. October, 1894.

McDAVITT, J. C., enlisted while practicing law with the late Chancellor Kortrecht, May 10, 1861, as a private in Bankhead's Battery. He was soon made second lieutenant, and in November, 1861, was promoted to senior first lieutenant of the battery, which he commanded at Shiloh, where he was wounded. In the fall of 1862 he was transferred to General Maury's command at Mobile, Ala., as instructor and inspector of artillery, and for several months in 1863 commanded the ironclad floating battery and Battery McIntosh (of eleven heavy guns) off Mobile. In June, 1864, he was transferred to the general staff of Lieutenant-General Polk, where he was inspector and adjutant of artillery of Polk's corps, participating in the battles of the Georgia campaign from Kennesaw Mountain to Atlanta, including those around

J. C. McDAVITT.

the latter place. Early in September, 1864, he was again transferred to Mobile as inspector of artillery under Colonel Burnett, and was stationed at the heavy batteries in the bay until the surrender of Mobile in April, 1865. He was paroled at Meridian, Miss., May 4, 1865, with the rank of first lieutenant of artillery. Joined the C. H. A. May 29, 1884.

After the war he was of the law firm of McDavitt & Bond, and of Estes, Jackson & McDavitt. For the last fifteen years he has confined himself to examinations of titles to real estate.

The only surviving officers of the battery engaged at the battle of Shiloh, as far as known, are J. C. McDavitt and Wm. Mecklenburg Polk, son of General Leonidas Polk, who was at that time junior lieutenant of the battery. The latter is now one of the noted physicians in New York city. Mr. McDavitt was born in Kentucky, and is descended on both sides of the house from Southern ante-Revolutionary ancestors. His grandfather, Jas. McDavitt, was born in Charleston, S. C., in 1767

McHENRY, E. B., born in Jefferson City, Mo., in 1840, and lived there until 1861; entered active service May 10, 1861; was with General Sterling Price in all his campaigns in Missouri and Arkansas in 1861–62; was under fire first at Carthage, Mo., in July, 1861, where Sigel was met and driven back to Springfield. Mo.; was in the battle of Wilson Creek August 10, 1861, and in siege of Lexington in September of same year; wintered at Springfield, which place was evacuated February 13, 1862: was in the battle at Elk Horn Tavern on Pea Ridge, Ark., March 6 and 7, 1862. He crossed to the east side of the Mississippi river with Price and remained there until December, 1862, when he returned to Arkansas and assisted in recruiting Wood's Battalion of Cavalry, of which he was made adjutant (afterward a full regiment). Served in the brigades of both Marmaduke and Shelby, and with the latter went to Missouri in 1863, leaving Arkadelphia, Ark., and striking the Missouri river at Boonville, and from there to Waverly, Mo., and thence south to Washington, Ark.

In 1864, unattached, the regiment went again to Missouri under General Sterling Price to make a diversion in favor of Hood's army; "diverted" enough of the Federal army to send the Confederates back in a hurry from Westport, Mo., after having traversed the State from Doniphan to that place, passing in the close vicinity of St. Louis and Jefferson City. The army camped one night in sight—in gunshot—of Adjutant McHenry's father's house, which he had left June 15, 1861. His regiment was active in the fights at Poison Spring, Jenkin's Ferry, Monticello, Mark's Mill and all the battles fought by General Price in his raid to Missouri in 1864. He surrendered at Shreveport, La., June 8, 1865, and returned to his old home in August of that year, where he was permitted to remain two days, being served at the end of that time with an elaborate paper setting forth that, "whereas certain traitors to the government of the United States by the name of George F. Rootes, Ashley W. Ewing and E. B. McHenry, have recently returned to this city fresh from the ranks of treason and rebellion," etc., etc., "therefore, we

MAJ. E. B. McHENRY.

pledge to each other our lives and sacred honor to remove
said parties from this community, peaceably if we can, forci-
bly if we must, and that within the next twenty-four hours.
Witness our hands, etc., Aug. 26, 1865." (Signed by twenty-
nine.) Accompanying these "whereases" was the following
notice: "To E. B. McHenry—You are hereby furnished with
a copy of an instrument we have signed by which you will
see that you are required to leave this community within the
next twenty-four hours or else take the consequences of remaining." This notice was signed by the same twenty-nine
who had promulgated the "whereases" and resolution. It
is needless to say he did not require twenty-four hours to
shake the dust of his native place from his feet and leave
them in peace and quiet.

Mr. McHenry came to Memphis in September, 1865, where
he has since resided. He married Miss Mary Taylor of Clin-

ton, La., in 1871. They have had born to them only one child, Edgar T. McHenry, now a grown man. He was Clerk and Master of the Chancery Court of Memphis under Chancellor Estes, and has been a member of the Memphis bar for many years; was one of the early members of the Confederate Relief and Historical Association, and after dropping out for a time rejoined the present organization January 8, 1895.

McKINNEY, JOHN FLETCHER, enlisted as a private in Company B, Forrest's old regiment, May, 1861; served through the war and paroled at Gainesville, Ala., May, 1865.

McKNIGHT, W. T., private in Company H, Armistead's Alabama Cavalry; enlisted in October, 1863; was paroled in May, 1865. Transferred to this Association from Camp Sumpter U. C. V, No. 332, Livingstone, Ala., November 24, 1894.

McLEAN, WM. L., left Memphis. Tenn., bound for Pensacola, Fla., to join the Fifteenth Mississippi Regiment, April 1, 1861; found that regiment full and returned. The Twelfth Arkansas Regiment was then camped near his father's house and hundreds were down with the measles. Ladies organized an aid society to nurse them. His mother was elected president. Colonel E. W. Gantt, through gratitude. offered to fill the first vacancy with young McLean if he would join, and he did so near New Madrid, Mo.; was assigned to duty as operator in the signal corps under Captain C. C. Cummings, General Beauregard's staff. In a few weeks he was made lance sergeant and ordered to Corinth, Miss. When the army fell back to Tupelo was recommended to General Maury and appointed First Lieutenant Twelfth Battalion Arkansas Sharpshooters. four companies of fifty picked men in each, W. L. Cabell's Brigade, Maury's Division, Price's Corps, Army Mississippi and East Louisiana. Soon after this Captain Cunningham was promoted to major, and McLean was by him recommended to General Earl Van Dorn and by him recommended to the Confederate War Department; was appointed captain of signal corps and assigned to General Maury's staff. The former captain of Company B, Twelfth Battalion, Jas. A. Ashford, was ordered to Arkansas to recruit. Captain McLean was again assigned to the company. After participating in all the battles from Corinth to Big Black, Miss., Company B was cut down to seven men and one officer, and surrendered May 17, 1863, to General Grant's army, that being the day he invested Vicksburg. Captain McLean was sent to Johnson's Island and arrived there June 5, 1863; occupied room No. 18, block 3, and with his bunk mate, John H. Morgan, slept on the same two-foot bunk, grinding their wallet of straw—filled once—into powder. On the 24th day of February, 1865, left the island on the ice over Sandusky Bay to Sandusky; thence to Pittsburg, Baltimore, down the Chesapeake Bay, Fortress Monroe, Hampton Roads, Norfolk and up the James river to Richmond; paroled there March 1, 1865. Went through Virginia, North and South Carolina, Georgia, to Opelika, Ala.; walked from there to Columbus, Miss., across the entire State of Alabama, and walked most of the way from there to Memphis, arriving May 15, 1865. Went to farming and gardening at once; followed it fourteen years. In 1879 became a commercial traveler, and is engaged in that pursuit now. Joined this Association January 12, 1888, and is an enthusiastic member of Company A, Confederate Veterans.

McNEAL, A. T., was a private in Company B, Fourth Tennessee; enlisted May 15, 1861, and paroled in April, 1865, with General Joe Johnston's army at Greensboro, N. C. He served first at Randolph and Fort Pillow, then at Columbus, Ky., under General Polk, and subsequently in the various campaigns of the Army of Tennessee. After the war he returned to his grand old home at Bolivar, Tennessee, and became one of the leading lawyers of the State, as he is yet. He has been a prominent and potential factor in State politics, and was often suggested and urged for Governor or other high office, but has always declined political preferment, and adhered to the pursuit of his profession and the serene enjoyment of a happy home life. Joined the Confederate Historical Association September 9, 1884.

MERRIN, T. C., born December 25, 1845; enlisted in the C. S. A. as a private in Company F, First Arkansas Cavalry, September 1, 1861; captured at Lexington, Mo., October 19, 1864, and released from prison June 19, 1865; was a second lieutenant at the close of the war.

MILLER, GEO. W., joined Captain Wm. Miller's Company of Light Artillery at Memphis April, 1861, as a private, and at the reorganization was placed in the First Tennessee Artillery, Colonel Andrew Jackson, Jr., commanding; after the fall of Vicksburg, served as ordnance officer for Batteries Hager, Tracey and Spanish Fort, in Mobile Bay, until the evacuation by troops; was elected first lieutenant at the reorganization; was wounded at Spanish Fort; was never sick so as to lose a day's duty; went to Meridian, and was there paroled May, 1865. Joined the Confederate Historical Association June 13, 1894.

MILLER, M. J., private, enlisted April, 1861; was wounded once in the battle of Redlick Church, Miss.; was in the commands of Pillow, Polk, McCown and others, and with I. N. Brown of the Confederate States Navy.

MILLER, MARSHALL JEFFRIE, who became a member of the Confederate Historical Association November 11, 1884, was born at Princeton, Ky., August 28, 1822. His father, Reuben B. Miller, of Fauquier county, Va., was next to the youngest of ten brothers who had only one sister. Eight of the brothers served in the Revolutionary war. Reuben B. Miller was in the battle of New Orleans and in the Creek war. His wife was a Bradburne; her brother John D. served in the army of Mexico from 1821 until the breaking out of the war with the United States, when he resigned. Meantime he had been military governor of the Mexican State of California. The Bradburne family was connected by marriage with the Blackburns, Shelbys, Johnsons, Flournoys, and other prominent families of Kentucky. In early life M. J. Miller became a pilot and settled in Memphis in 1850. At the beginning of the war he was ordered to command a small steamer called the Grampus. The vessel was 132 feet long.

24 feet beam, and 4 feet hold, with 3 boilers and 5 foot stroke of engines. Captain Miller armed his men with muskets and mounted three pieces of artillery—one twenty-pounder amidships, and two six-pounders placed fore and aft. A larger wheel was constructed, and the vessel could then make the trip from Columbus to Memphis in nine hours. The Grampus was used as a scout, performed some marvellous exploits, and was finally sunk at the bombardment of Island 10. Captain Miller afterward reported to Secretary of War Mallory at Richmond, came back to the West, and was in active service in various capacities on both sides of the Mississippi until the end of the war; he was near Selma when that place fell. After the surrender he came to Memphis, and on June 5, 1865, procured license as master and pilot and continued in active service as such until 1895. He still has his license, but has been disabled temporarily by the grip. He has a wife and one son.

MITCHELL, JNO. R., was born in Carroll county, Tenn., where his parents had just removed from South Carolina; lived there temporarily, and was taken to Mississippi when a child. His father, Jno. C. Mitchell, became a wealthy planter of DeSoto county, Miss., and gave three sons to the Confederacy. John R. enlisted, when a mere youth, in State service August 22, 1862; after serving twelve months under General J. Z. George, was discharged; re-enlisted for three years or the war with General Frank Armstrong's escort; was in numerous cavalry engagements, in one of which, near Holly Springs, his horse was beheaded by a cannon ball, and he himself was wounded and left for dead on the field. He was in many fights in Georgia; was cut off from his command while on a visit to his father, who had refugeed to South Carolina. When Hood's army left Atlanta he remained with Wheeler's Cavalry, and was in numerous skirmishes on down toward the sea, seeing much hard service. After the battle of Franklin he rejoined his command at West Point, Miss.; was wounded at Wall Hill and captured at the battle of Selma, Ala., about April 2, 1865, and received a parole about three weeks later with the forces of General Wilson, near the

11

State line in Georgia, with whose cavalry he had marched on foot two hundred miles; after that he and six other members of his company walked all the way to DeSoto county, Miss., in sixteen days; coming on to Memphis, he was sent back to Senatobia and paroled there. His home was one of desolation and mourning, as so often found by returning Southern soldiers; the family was only half the size as when he left; his mother and youngest brother had died in 1862, and soon after two brothers were killed in battle in Virginia.

Mr. Mitchell married Miss Adelia Robertson, a niece of two company comrades, in 1867, and lived on his father's old homestead until 1873, and has since been engaged as clerk, a large part of the time, in the county trustee's office. He is now a member of Company A, Confederate Veterans, and has done much to keep up the organization to a high standard of zeal and efficiency, and was with it at the sixth annual reunion of U. C. V. in Richmond in June and July, 1896.

MITCHELL, ROBERT WOOD, son of General Guilford Dudley Mitchell, was born in Madison county, Tenn., and removed to Mississippi when very young; was educated at Centenary College, Jackson; read medicine in Vicksburg, graduated at the University of Louisiana, returned to Vicksburg, and was elected physician of the hospital there in 1857. He removed to Memphis in 1858; was elected secretary of the board of health; organized the Memphis City Hospital, and was made physician in charge. In 1861 he became Assistant Surgeon in the Fifteenth Tennessee Regiment, Infantry, and in the autumn of the same year was made Surgeon of the Thirteenth Tennessee Regiment; afterward became brigade, and then division, surgeon, and served continuously with the Army of Tennessee until the end of the war. He returned to Memphis, and married Miss Rebecca Park in 1872; was very prominent in the epidemics that visited Memphis years ago, and is still an active practicing physician. He was one of the original incorporators of this Association, and his membership dates from July 15, 1869.

MOCKBEE, R. T., was born August 17, 1841, in Stewart county, Tenn.; enlisted in April, 1861, in Company B, Fourteenth Tennessee Regiment; served in General Lee's campaign in Northwest Virginia in 1861; then with Stonewall Jackson in his Romney campaign of June, 1862; then with the Army of Northern Virginia, and was surrendered and paroled at Appomattox April 10, 1865; was wounded three times in battle—at Sharpsburg, Spottsylvania Court House, and the second battle of Cold Harbor. He was captured once in March, 1863, near Clarksville, Tenn., but escaped during the same month. He had been sent inside the Federal lines on recruiting service by order of the War Department; was captured by a Federal scout and sent to Nashville, where he made his escape from prison with Major J. H. Johnson and others, and at the end of the war was a sergeant. Became a member of Forbes Bivouac at Clarksville, Tenn., and upon removal to Memphis was transferred upon proper certificate to this bivouac March 15, 1895. Mr. Mockbee has interesting old papers showing that his ancestors came from Wales to Loudon county, Virginia, and took part in the Revolutionary war on the patriot side.

MONROE. D. W., enlisted July 8, 1862, as a private in Company C, Davis' Regiment, Trans-Mississippi Department; entered the army as commissary clerk; was with Turnbull's Twenty-fifth Arkansas Regiment after the retreat from Corinth, Miss., until the command reached Lexington, Ky., at which place he became connected with Major J. W. Calloway, division commissary, and went to the Trans-Mississippi Department, where he served as commissary clerk until the close of the war; paroled July 1865. Admitted to this Association October 9, 1894.

MOORE, M. J. M., private in Company F, Twenty-sixth Mississippi, enlisted September 1, 1861; this regiment was formed at Iuka, Miss., went from there to Union City, thence to Bowling Green, and back to Russellville and Fort Donelson; served around Jackson, Miss., and went to Virginia in April, 1864; paroled May, 1865.

MORGAN. ROBERT JARRELL, was born in Putnam county, Ga., and came of Revolutionary ancestry in Virginia;

graduated from University of Georgia at Athens and admitted to the bar in 1850; practiced law successfully; married, and removed to Memphis in 1859. He was a Whig and opposed secession, but when the war broke out he raised and organized at Chattanooga the Thirty-sixth Tennessee Regiment, and was colonel of it two years, when he was assigned to duty as adjutant-general on the staff of Lieutenant-General Leonidas Polk; had special charge of court-martial proceedings in the corps, and afterward commanded a department. Early in the war he was stationed at Cumberland Gap, and saw service in Tennessee, Kentucky and Georgia, participating in the battles of Murfreesboro and Chickamauga; was with General Polk when he was killed on the Georgia campaign, and after that was assigned by the War Department at Richmond to the duty of adjusting claims against the State of Georgia, and continued in that service until the surrender, when he was paroled at Atlanta. Returning to Memphis with his family, he resumed the practice of law, and in 1867 was elected city attorney and served three years. Governor Senter, without solicitation, appointed him chancellor, and he was afterward twice elected by the people, serving in all about ten years, to the great satisfaction of the bar and people. In 1878 he voluntarily retired and resumed a very lucrative practice. In 1880 he was elector on the Hancock ticket, and at different times took some part in politics; was regarded as an available man for Governor, and once received a very complimentary vote for nomination. Strong intellectually and physically and a fine speaker, he has always wielded a large influence in public and private. He was made a Mason at LaGrange, Ga., and also took the Chapter degrees. He became a member of this Association September 9, 1869.

MORRISON, GEORGE E., private Company B, One Hundred and Fifty-fourth Tennessee; enlisted April, 1861; was in McDonald's Battalion of Forrest's old regiment; paroled May 11, 1865.

MOSBY, C. W., enlisted in Company I, First Confederate Regiment of Cavalry, Captain M. J. Wicks, who was promoted; the next captain, Sheppard Jackson, was killed in covering General Beauregard's retreat from Corinth. Was with General Joseph Wheeler in advance of General Bragg into Kentucky; was at the battle of Munfordville and Perryville; was with General Wheeler, who covered General Bragg's retreat from Kentucky; was at the battles of Murfreesboro, Chickamauga, and the various battles from Dalton to Atlanta; went with General Hood into Middle Tennessee; was at Franklin and Nashville; surrendered with General Forrest at Gainesville, Ala., to General Canby, who proved himself to be a generous foe, a thorough soldier and gentleman, by his magnanimous treatment of the worn-out troops of the command. He did not require the Confederates to lay down their arms in the presence of his troops, but allowed them to go to a designated place under command of their own officers, where they dismounted, grounded arms, laid their accoutrements by them, mounted and went back to camp. General Canby sent his wagon train and gathered up the arms afterward. He allowed the men to keep their horses, the officers their side arms and horses. Mr. Mosby relates these facts with great pleasure. He joined this Association in 1884.

MULLINS, THOS. B., private Company H, Thirteenth Tennessee Regiment, Vaughan's Brigade, enlisted June 4, 1861; "was in the fracas from beginning to end;" was in the battles of Belmont, Shiloh, Richmond, Ky , Perryville, Murfreesboro, Chickamauga, Missionary Ridge, New Hope, Peach Tree Creek, Atlanta, Jonesboro, Ga., and Franklin, Tenn.; was paroled May 23, 1865. Joined the Confederate Historical Association October 9, 1894.

MUNCH, GEORGE P., First Lieutenant Company D, One Hundred and Fifty-fourth Tennessee; enlisted April 26, 1861; served through the war; was wounded in front of Atlanta; paroled April 26, 1865. Admitted to the Confederate Historical Association January 8, 1895.

MUNSON, S. A., Captain Company H, Thirteenth Tennessee; enlisted June 4, 1861; served until the consolidation with the One Hundred and Fifty-fourth Tennessee, and was a prisoner from the battle of Missionary Ridge until the close of the war at Johnson's Island; released June 13, 1865. Admitted to this Association October 9, 1894.

MURPHY, J. J.   Early in 1861 General Leonidas Polk invited his old friend J. J. Murphy to accept a position as chief commissary upon his staff, and the position was accepted in the fall of 1861 at Columbus, Ky.   Major Murphy's large experience as a merchant, his suavity of manner and great executive ability peculiarly fitted him for this important trust. He was ever a great favorite with General Polk, who only complained of him on account of his propensity to rush into every fight, when it was not required or even allowed.   Major Murphy served with great efficiency and credit throughout the war.   He was present when General Polk was killed and helped to remove his body from the range of the enemy's artillery.   One of his cherished treasures was a lock of the general's hair cut off just before he was laid away forever from human sight.   The Major served to the end and was among the last to lay down arms with General Joseph E. Johnston at Greensboro, N. C.   After the war he resumed business and was successful in large affairs.   He was a man of wide reading and knowledge of men, was pre-eminently charitable and benevolent, kind-hearted, and a most lovable man.   He died February 11, 1891, in the 75th year of his age, respected and regretted by the entire city.   The immediate cause of his death was a long ride on horseback to the Confederate reunion at Montgomery Park the previous fall, an occasion upon which he was cheered by the entire audience when he appeared in front of the grand stand.   This was a happy day for him, but his last appearance in public.   The exposure was too much for him, and hastened the end of a long, honorable and useful life.   Major Murphy became a member of the C. H. A. July 15, 1889.

MURRELL, D. A., private Company G, Fifty-first Tennessee; enlisted December, 1861; was wounded twice in the battle of Atlanta, July 22, 1864, and paroled, with the rank of orderly sergeant, May, 1865.   Joined the Confederate Historical Association June 30, 1892.

COL. HENRY C. MYERS.

MYERS, HENRY C., is the youngest of six brothers and two half-brothers (his father having been married twice), all of whom were in the Confederate army. 1. George B. Myers was Lieutenant-Colonel of the Tenth Mississippi Infantry; was shot through the right lung and captured at the battle of Munfordville, Ky., and afterward paroled; he lost his left arm in the battle of Jonesboro near Atlanta in July, 1864, and was captured and held as a prisoner of war on Johnson's Island until June, 1865; he died at Holly Springs in the fall of 1879. 2. Calvin R. Myers resides at Byhalia, Miss.; was a member of Company A, Eleventh Mississippi Infantry, Army of Northern Virginia; he was wounded five times and wounded and captured at Gettysburg and paroled just about the close of the war. 3. Absalom G. Myers resides at Dallas, Texas; was a member of Company B, Thirtieth Mississippi Infantry, Walthall's Brigade. 4. Albert Myers resides near Byhalia, Miss.;

was a member of Company A, Eleventh Mississippi Infantry.
Army of Northern Virginia; was twice severely wounded.
5. Patrick S. Myers was a lieutenant in Company B, Thirtieth
Mississippi Infantry; was captured at battle of Missionary
Ridge and was held a prisoner of war on Johnson's Island
until the close of hostilities; he died at Byhalia in 1880. His
two half-brothers (6) Martin P. and (7) William R. Myers,
were both in the Confederate army; the former died at his
home in Texas a few years after the war; the latter is still
living and resides at Charlotte. N. C.

Henry C. Myers was born in Marshall county, Miss., and
was the baby boy of the family. After some desultory service
around home, which led to the conclusion that the front might
be the safer place, he joined Company H, Second Missouri
Cavalry, McCulloch's Brigade, in June, 1863, before he was
fifteen years old, and served under Forrest and with the Army
of Tennessee until the end of the war, participating in various engagements and hard campaigns. He was paroled with
his command by General E. R. S. Canby at Gainesville, Ala.,
in May, 1865. He afterward edited and published *The South*,
a paper at Holly Springs, Miss.; married a daughter of Colonel H. W. Walter, the eminent lawyer who served as adjutant-general on General Bragg's staff; took an active part in
local and State politics, and held different positions, the most
notable being that of Secretary of State for seven years. He
removed to Memphis with his wife and young daughter, their
only child, a few years ago, and has since been successfully
engaged in business. He has attended different general reunions of United Confederate Veterans, and is quartermaster-
general, with the rank of colonel, on the staff of General
Stephen D. Lee, commanding Confederate Veterans, Department of Tennessee, and served as such at the Richmond reunion in June and July, 1896. He became a member of this
Association in September, 1891.

MYERS, J., was surgeon-steward in the navy; served on
the receiving ship St. Philip and gunboat Gaines, and was
wounded at Battery Gaines, Mobile Point; paroled at Demopolis, Ala., May 18, 1865. Joined C. H. A. June 30, 1894.

CAPT. H. M. NEELY.

NEELY, H. M., is the son of Moses Neely, who married Jane P. McDowell, both parents being born and reared in Mecklenburg county, N. C.; was born in Madison county, Tenn., but since his childhood has lived in Shelby county, Tenn., and grew to manhood on a typical *ante bellum* Southern plantation, about fifteen miles east of Memphis. Judging from his appearance, he must have been well taken care of in his young days; he is of splendid physique, florid both in style and manner, is six feet two inches tall, and weighs about two hundred pounds. When the war broke out he enlisted as a private in Company I, officered by Captain Wright, First Lieutenant Ad. Coulter and Second Lieutenant W. D. Ridout; the company joined the Thirty-eighth Tennessee Regiment, and had its first experience in the stern realities of war at Shiloh. On the reorganization of the army, Colonel Looney resigned as colonel and received a commission to raise a brigade, and Captain John C. Carter was elected colonel and later promoted to the rank of brigadier-general; First Sergeant O. M. Alsup was elected captain of the company, and H. M. Neely was elected first lieutenant. Captain Alsup a few months later resigned on account of ill health, and Lieutenant Neely was promoted to the rank of captain and took command of the company.

Captain Neely followed the fortunes of the Army of Tennessee under Generals Albert Sydney Johnston, Beauregard, Bragg, Joseph E. Johnston and Hood, and was present and fought in all of the important engagements except the battle of Stone River, being absent at the time on account of a severe wound received while storming a battery at the battle of Perryville, Ky.; in that engagement his position in the Confederate lines brought him directly in front of the battery, but just before the enemy's position was taken he was shot down by a minie ball, and still carries the lead comfortably in his shoulder; he was often hit with bullets, but never severely hurt except in this instance. In 1864 he was appointed acting adjutant-general on the staff of Brigadier-General Jno. C. Carter, and served the last year in that capacity conspicuously in Northern Georgia and during Hood's raid into Tennessee. He was at the battle of Franklin, and was by the side of Carter in his reckless ride in front of his brigade in the assault upon the enemy's breastworks, but when within about one hundred and fifty yards of them he received a mortal wound, from which he died a few days after. Noticing General Carter reeling in his saddle, Captain Neely leaped from his horse and amid a perfect shower of shot lifted him to the ground and turned him over to a couple of soldiers, with orders to take him to the field hospital; by that time the brigade had passed on and reached the breastworks, but in such shattered condition that it was unable to go over or dislodge the enemy. Impressed with the necessity and duty of notifying the next ranking officer of General Carter's condition, Captain Neely remounted his horse, intending to ride on, but was scarcely in his saddle before he was slightly wounded and his horse severely shot four times; he then abandoned his horse and, amid the dead and dying strewn thickly upon the ground, footed it to the breastworks, but speaks of it as the lonesomest and most uncomfortable walk of his life. He was in the fighting around Nashville, and with the Tennessee troops under the command of Major-General E. C. Walthall, selected by General Hood as a breakwater against the pursuing columns of General Thomas and to protect the main army in its retreat. Everyone with that rear guard has a vivid recollection of the privations and trials to which they were subjected, but all were cheerful, brave to a fault, and able to appropriate to themselves a strange and reckless pleasure wrung from the hard and desperate conditions by which they were surrounded.

Throughout the war Captain Neely was known as an energetic and conscientious officer, who would dodge no duty nor responsibility; a good disciplinarian, who at all times won the respect and confidence of the men and his superior officers. In September, 1865, he settled in Memphis, and the next year, having gathered together the remnants left him out of the wreck wrought by war, was admitted as a partner in the then established mercantile house of Brooks, Neely & Co., which firm is still in existence, and has done a large and successful business. Some years ago he married a charming lady, Mrs. Mary B. McCown, daughter of William Morgan Sneed of Vance county, N. C. Since his residence in Memphis he has held positions in the highest business and social circles, and it can be truthfully said of him that he has made as good a citizen in time of peace as he did a soldier in time of war. He became a member of the old Confederate Association September 9, 1869.

NABORS, T. P., private Company I, Seventeenth Mississippi, Barksdale's Brigade, A. N. V.; enlisted March, 1862; was wounded twice — at Gettysburg and Corryville; served throughout the war in the same command, and was in every battle in which it was engaged, except two; paroled April 7, 1865. Admitted to the C. H. A. February 12, 1895.

NEALE, THOMAS R., enlisted in Captain McNeal's company, and to enable him to get through the Federal lines was transferred to Company D, Bell's Virginia Cavalry, with which he served till the close of the war; was wounded three times, and paroled at Clarksburg, W. Va., about May 1, 1865.

NELSON, F. M., enlisted as a private in Company A, Seventh Tennessee Cavalry, April, 1862; re-enlisted in Alabama Infantry, and was paroled at Gainesville, Ala., in May, 1865. Joined the C. H. A. at an early day.

NETHERLANDS, J. J., private Company E, Fourth Virginia Regiment; enlisted in spring of 1861 and was always in the same regiment. On the day before the surrender of General Lee he was sent by his captain with several others to Lynchburg, where they heard of the surrender; they started west, but could not get through the Federal lines on railroad; went home and afterward to Richmond, and was paroled in June, 1865.

NEWBORN, JOSEPH L., Second Lieutenant Company B, Thirteenth Tennessee; enlisted May 28, 1861; served first as a private in the State service, and when mustered into the C. S. A. was elected lieutenant; was in the battles of Belmont, Shiloh, Richmond, Perryville, Murfreesboro and Chickamauga, besides numerous smaller engagements and skirmishes. Admitted to this Association August 14, 1894.

NORFLEET, F. M., private Company C, Eighteenth Mississippi, Wirt Adams' Brigade; enlisted in 1863; served for a short time in Berton's Regiment of Infantry and in Fourth Mississippi; was wounded at Plantersville, Ga., in an engagement with the Seventeenth Indiana; paroled May 13, 1865. Joined the Confederate Historical Association June 13, 1894.

NORRIS, J. W., private Company F, Third Mississippi Cavalry, Adams' Brigade; enlisted February 1, 1864; served with same command to the end, and was with it in every engagement after he enlisted; paroled at Gainesville, Ala., April, 1865. Admitted to C. H. A. February 12, 1895.

NUTZEL, CONRAD, born in Kretz, kingdom of Bavaria, Germany, in 1838, and came to Memphis in 1853; enlisted June 5, 1861, in the old Washington Rifles, Fifteenth Tennessee Regiment. When the army was reorganized at Corinth comrade Nutzel was elected second lieutenant of his company. The regiment went into Kentucky with Bragg, and suffered very heavily in the battle of Perryville, losing nearly half its men, also sustained severe losses in the battle of Murfreesboro. After the battle of Murfreesboro Lieutenant Nutzel was assigned to the staff of Colonel Ben. Hill, Provost Marshal, and when the army was at Dalton he commanded the guards as military conductor on the Western & Atlantic Railroad. After the fall of Atlanta Lieutenant Nutzel and two other officers from his regiment, Captain Harry Rice and Lieutenant John Dwyer, were ordered to Augusta, Ga., and around there they recruited a good-sized regiment of 600 men, half of it from the different Federal prisons. Lieutenant Nutzel made up a company 100 hundred strong, nearly all Germans, who could not speak a word of English. They had only been in this country three or four months, and were easily induced to take the oath of allegiance to the lost cause. The new regiment was known as the First Confederate Galvanized Yankee Regiment, and it was no doubt the last. It was commanded by Colonel Jno. G. O'Neal, with Lieut.-Colonel Burke second in command, and Lieutenant Seymour, an old soldier from the Crimean war, as adjutant. This grotesque command was sent to Mobile, and then ordered to follow Hood's army into Tennessee. About one-half the regiment moved off by rail, but was ordered to stop off at Egypt station. Captain Nutzel's company was thrown out on picket duty the same afternoon and remained in the woods over night. Early next morning Grierson's scouting force came in sight and they opened fire. Captain Nutzel and three or four men were wounded, but not very seriously. The galvanized rebels made a gallant fight behind a railroad embankment, without loss, for three or four hours, repelling several charges, but finally were forced into a small stockade, where their ammunition was exhausted in about one hour and they surrendered late in the afternoon. The prisoners were marched across to Vicksburg, and from there Captain Nutzel and a host of others were sent up the river by boat.

At Memphis he was permitted to see a brother, get a good outfit and some money. He was sent to prison at Johnson's Island, where he was released on the 18th of May, 1865. He joined the C. H. A. January 8, 1895, and became a member of Company A, Confederate Veterans, in which he takes great pride.

O'BERST, C., private Company A, First Tennessee Artillery; entered service early and remained to close of the war. Proposed for membership in this Association by T. N. Johnson and C. W. Frazer, and elected May 12, 1870.

PAPE, A. R., private Company A, Fourth Tennessee; enlisted in May, 1861; was in the signal corps, but returned to Company A and fought in the battle of Shiloh, then back to the signal corps, in which he served until the end of the war. He was captured at Perryville; was exchanged and rejoined the army at Shelbyville, Tenn.; paroled April, 1865.

PEARSON, R. V., private Company F, Fifteenth Mississippi, Adams' Brigade, Lowry's Division; enlisted May 27, 1861; was wounded twice, first at the battle of Fishing Creek, where the regiment was in command of Lieutenant-Colonel E. C. Walthall, and the second time in front of Atlanta July, 1864; paroled May, 1865. He was admitted to this Association September 14, 1864.

PERKINS, A. H. D., was a private in Company E, Seventh Tennessee Cavalry, Rucker's Brigade, Forrest's Cavalry; enlisted in November, 1862, and was paroled May 2, 1865.

PERSONS, C. P., private Company C, Fourth Tennessee Infantry; enlisted May 15, 1861; was wounded April 6, 1862, and discharged from the service; recovered and joined Porter's Company, Ballentine's Regiment, Forrest's Cavalry, in 1862; was captured at Water Valley, Miss., December 1, 1863; released in February, 1864, and joined Forrest's old regiment about three months before the close of the war; paroled May 11, 1865. Admitted to the C. H. A. December 11, 1894.

WM. GARNETT PARKER.

PARKER, W. G., son of Robert A. and Lamira Parker, born at Somerville, Tenn., May 1, 1841; enlisted in Company A, Shelby Grays, Fourth Tennessee Regiment, May 15, 1861, and served throughout the war, surrendering at Goldsboro, N. C., April 26, 1865; was wounded at the battles of Shiloh and Franklin. Returned to Memphis June 1, 1865, and engaged in the cotton warehouse business. Died at the home of his mother, No. 187 Vance street, March 8, 1878. He was a brave and loyal soldier; sincere, tender and true in all his friendships; a loving and devoted son and brother. Joined this Association December 16, 1869.

PERSONS, RICHARD J., was born February 5, 1843, and is descended from a prominent old Revolutionary family of his name in North Carolina. The Persons family came to Shelby county early in this century. He was graduated from the Kentucky Military Institute at Frankfort, after four years attendance, in 1861, with the rank of captain in the Kentucky State Guards. He left college for the camp, and soon became Captain of Company B, Twenty-first Tennessee Regiment, and was afterward major of the famous fighting Fifth Confederate Regiment of Cleburne's Division, composed almost entirely of Irishmen. Major Person was in the battles of Belmont, Shiloh, Perryville, Murfreesboro, Chickamauga, and nearly all the heavy fighting on down to the front of Atlanta, where he was captured July 22, 1864, and after that was confined at Johnson's Island until the end of the war. He had been in command of the regiment from December, 1863. He was a thoroughly trained soldier, and the writer, who fought almost by his side more than once, regards him as one of the most intrepid men in the army. He was married in 1863 to Miss Annie E. Finnell of Lexington, Ky.; she died in 1866. He was again married in 1868 to Miss Alice Winchester, daughter of Major George B. Winchester, a prominent lawyer of this city, since dead. They have four children, two of whom are sons. Major Persons joined the Confederate Relief and Historical Association in 1869.

PETTIGREW, JAMES L., private in Company C, Second Mississippi, Army of Northern Virginia; enlisted March 8, 1862; was wounded three times—at Antietam, September 17, 1862; Gettysburg, July 3, 1863, and at Petersburg, October 14, 1864. After the wound at Petersburg he was furloughed and went home to Mississippi, and was never able to return to Virginia; was paroled at Okolona, Miss., May 29, 1865. Admitted to the Confederate Historical Association January 8, 1895.

PEPPER, S. A., was born in Johnson county, Mo., October 27, 1842, and taken to Virginia when very young by his parents, who had gone west only a few years before; was reared near Big Spring (now Elliston station), Montgomery county; there had good social and educational advantages. When the war broke out he enlisted June 5, 1861, as a private in Company F, Eleventh Virginia Infantry, and afterward

S. A. PEPPER.

served in the Twenty-fourth and Twenty-ninth Mississippi Regiments, Army of Tennessee. He went all through the war and was in a number of great battles, including Lookout Mountain and Missionary Ridge, and smaller fights; was wounded at the battle of Williamsburg, Va., and at Jonesboro, Ga., but never lost much time from the service. He was paroled when Johnston's army capitulated at Greensboro, N. C., and has his parole yet carefully framed as a souvenir of the great war, of whose history it is a part. He came to Memphis in November, 1865; went to Huntsville in December same year; remained there four years and returned to Memphis in January, 1870. He was married to Miss Anna Lee Polk of Helena, Ark., February 17, 1887, and there are three children from this union — Misses Allan Polk, Zelda Fontaine and Anna Fitzhugh Pepper. Mr. Pepper was one of the early members of the Confederate Historical Associa-

12

tion, and for many years was an active member of the Chickasaw Guards; became Orderly Sergeant of Company A, Confederate Veterans, about a year ago, and attended the reunion U. C. V. at Richmond June–July, 1896.

PHELAN, JAMES, Colonel and Judge of Military Court in 1864–65. Proposed for membership in this Association by Jefferson Davis and Isham G. Harris, and elected May 26, 1870; has been dead eighteen or twenty years.

PITTS, J. M., born July 29, 1840, in Meriwether county, Ga.; lived with his parents in Alabama and Mississippi, and went with them to St. Francis county, Ark., in 1856; enlisted June 10, 1861, in Company B, Fifth Arkansas Regiment, and was elected first lieutenant; was at the battle of Belmont, crossing the river under fire, and there took a prisoner and sent him to the rear. He was in the fight at Tompkinsville and afterward at Bowling Green, Ky.; was sent to hospital at Nashville. After the fall of Fort Donelson was given charge of eighty convalescents and sent to Atlanta; returned to his command about the time of the battle of Shiloh; was in the battle of Farmington. At the reorganization at Corinth was elected first lieutenant; resigned and refused transfer, and served the rest of the war as a private in the same company; was ordered from Tupelo to report to Dr. Westmoreland at Atlanta; was refused permission to leave, but left anyhow to follow the army into Kentucky. His captain, L. R. Frick, asked for his papers, and as he had none told him he would be reported as a deserter from the hospital. He sent for Lieutenant-Colonel J. E. Murray and General Hardee, stated the case, and they said they wished they had 20,000 such men. He was at Munfordville, Perryville and Crab Orchard with his regiment and back to Knoxville; was sent to hospital again, but escaped in time to be at the battle of Murfreesboro, where he took two stands of colors. After the battle of Liberty Gap, in which Captain Frick was killed, Mr. Pitts was again sent to the hospital at Atlanta, but got out in time for the battle of Chickamauga, and was in the Georgia campaign; was taken prisoner near Atlanta and placed in an old church, but escaped the first night, leaving a guard *hors du combat;* was wounded in the right hand on July 22 in front of Atlanta; was in the battle of Jonesboro and captured, but escaped with his clothing and accoutrements full of bullet holes; was also in the battle of Franklin and the fight at Nashville, and was in the last fight of the war at Bentonville, N. C., and was on guard with his company at General Joseph E. Johnston's headquarters at Greensboro, and was surrendered there May 10, 1865. Since the war he has lived both in Arkansas and Memphis, having been here since 1880. He married after the war, but his wife died years ago, and a married daughter is their only surviving child. Mr. Pitts is an all-round mechanic, and has been quite prosperous at times, but of late years he has suffered much with rheumatism and not been able to work at all times. He lives with and supports his aged mother, now (1896) in the eighty-first year of her age. He is a member of Company A, Confederate Veterans, under Captain W. W. Carnes, by whom he is highly regarded, and in spite of his sickness and rheumatism he attended the great reunion of veterans at Richmond, Va., in June–July, 1896.

PODESTA, LOUIS E., born near Genoa, Italy, June 9, 1846; came to this country with his parents in 1847; grew up in Natchez, Miss., and enlisted there April 9, 1861, in the Natchez Fencibles, an old company that had served in the Mexican war, and became Company G, then under Captain Ed. Blackburn, of the Twelfth Mississippi Regiment; went with the company to Jackson, Corinth, Union City and Lynchburg, and reached the battlefield of Manassas at 4 P.M. on the 21st of July. He served in Ewell's Brigade and Van Dorn's Division; afterward in Rhodes' Brigade, Longstreet's Corps; was next in Roger A. Pryor's Brigade; then Featherstone's, Posey's, and last in Harris' Brigade in Anderson's and Mahone's Divisions; was wounded at New Turkey Ridge, sixteen miles below Richmond, June 6, 1864; at Boydton Plank Road, below Petersburg, October 27, 1864; at Hatcher Run, where Pegram was killed, February 6, 1865, and at Fort Gregg, near Petersburg, April 2, 1865; was on crutches for twelve months. The last ball was cut out long afterward. He was in all engagements of any consequence with his regiment from Williamsburg, Va., 1862, to the surrender at Petersburg April 2, 1865, and has his parole dated June 16, 1865. He was in both the campaigns across the Potomac, and was barefooted much of the time; still he survived to enjoy robust health in spite of lameness for life. He came to Memphis soon after the surrender and engaged in business on Front Row, and joined the old Confederate Relief and Historical Association July 15, 1869. In 1872 he was married to Miss Parmelia Perasi (Rocco), the latter being an adopted name. From this union were born four boys and four girls, all fine young people, one of whom is a teacher in the public schools.

POLLARD, W. J., rank Major in the ordnance department; entered the service February 1, 1861, and paroled 10th of May, 1865. Elected a member of this Association upon his own application July 1, 1869.

POSTON, D. H., enlisted early in the war as a private in Company A, Fourth Tennessee Infantry, and was in most of the battles in which that regiment took part; was severely wounded in the leg at the battle of Perryville by a wounded Federal soldier to whom he had just given a drink of water. It is charitable to suppose that the man was crazed by heat and thirst or fright, and was not responsible. After the war Mr. Poston, although quite young, soon became the law partner of General W. Y. C. Humes, and had a large practice as long as he lived. His death was caused by a shot fired on the street by a brother lawyer and ex-Confederate. The tragedy greatly shocked the public mind and will be remembered for a generation. Mr. Poston was twice married. His last wife and children by the first survive him. Joined this Association August 12, 1869.

POSTON, JAMES, entered the service as a private in the Bluff City Grays, McDonald's Battalion, May, 1861; served throughout the war and paroled May, 1865. Proposed for membership by W. D. Stratton and elected January 20, 1870.

POSTON, WM. K., private in Company A, Fourth Tennessee; was born in Shelby county, Tenn., October 2, 1844; enlisted May 15, 1861; served through the entire war in the same command; was wounded twice—once at the battle of Shiloh once at Missionary Ridge; paroled May 23, 1865.

POWEL, JOHN A., born in Winchester, Tenn., March 81, 1844, and was reared in Memphis; enlisted in the Bluff City Grays, One Hundred and Fifty-fourth Tennessee, under Captain J. H. Edmondson, about May 1, 1861; was in the battles of Belmont and Shiloh. His brother Benjamin was wounded at Shiloh, and he dragged him off the field under heavy fire; on the retreat he found a four-mule team without a driver, mounted himself, drove to a field hospital and loaded up with wounded men, including his brother, Louis Vaccaro, Fred Wœller, Wm. Linsted and Billie Fleshart, and hauled them thirty miles to Corinth over terrible roads. This took two days and nights, without food or attention given to the wounded. Linsted only lives out of the five. John and Ben Powel fought side by side both days at Shiloh; assisted in capturing a battery; got into the "hornets' nest" and carried Ollie Patterson out of it mortally wounded; Patterson died the same evening. John Powel was in the battle of Richmond, which he describes yet as the fairest and squarest fight he ever saw. There he saw General Pat Cleburne shot through the jaws as he gave the command "Forward!" It was there Preston Smith, Colonel of the One Hundred and Fifty-fourth Tennessee, made a flank movement which, John says, whipped the fight and made him a brigadier-general. Mr. Powel's next battle was at Murfreesboro, where his company again had a hand in capturing a battery; they had seven men killed, including Lieutenants Creighton and Burch, and six men badly wounded. After that the company was mounted, and he took part in the battles of Chickamauga and Missionary Ridge. There he was rejoined by his brother Ben, who had been absent on account of his wound received at Shiloh. They were both with General Forrest on his memorable raid when he captured Colonel Streight and 1800 men near Rome, Ga. He was with General Forrest on his raid into West Tennessee in 1863, and was severely wounded by a shot through his right lung at Jack's Creek, and was confined to his bed for two years. He has since been a great sufferer, but hopes to live to a green old age. He was a lieutenant in McDonald's Battalion, and his name appears conspicuously in Lindsley's Military Annals. His brother Ben, who died only a year or two ago, followed Forrest to the end of the war. John A. Powel became a member of the C. H. A. September 9, 1884; his brother Benjamin was also a member.

PRESCOTT, J. A., private in Company F, Second Regiment; enlisted in October, 1861; was in the Army of Northern Virginia; was captured at Bolivar, Tenn., and discharged in 1863; released from prison in 1865. Recommended in application to this Association by J. J. Brown and J. P. Young.

PULLEN, BENJ. K., enlisted in 1861; was a member of Captain J. T. Begbie's Confederate Guards Home Regiment; afterward served with Colonel J. G. Ballentine's Cavalry Regiment, with the rank of captain, up to January, 1864; transferred to post duty at Grenada, Miss., under Major J. S. Mellon, Chief of Subsistence, until the surrender in 1865. Admitted to C. H. A. October 8, 1895.

QUINTARD, CHAS. TODD, is of Huguenot descent and came of a noted family. He was born December 22, 1824, at Stamford, Conn., in the room in which his father first saw the light, and the father lived to be 90 years old. He became a physician in early life, but took a course of theological studies under Bishop Hervey Otey, D. D.; was ordained deacon in Calvary Church, Memphis, in 1854, and in 1865 succeeded Bishop Otey. During the war he was chaplain of the First Tennessee Regiment and served at Valley Mountain, Cheat Mountain and Big Sewell in Virginia, holding daily services as often as practicable. He was at the battles of Perryville, Murfreesboro and Chickamauga; was in the Georgia campaign from Dalton to Atlanta, and was at the battle of Franklin, as well as other engagements. He was a practical, working chaplain, and it was through his zeal and labors that several generals and other soldiers became devout christians at

Dalton while the army was in winter quarters there. He became a member of this Association May 12, 1870.

RADCLIFF, T. D., private Company A, Seventh Tennessee Cavalry; enlisted May, 1861, and served through the war. Recommended for membership in this Association by T. P. Adams and Henry Moode, and elected March 8, 1869.

RAINEY, I. N., born April 6, 1845; enlisted in Company A, Seventh Tennessee Cavalry, at Columbia, Tenn., March 20, 1863; the company was known as " Memphis Light Dragoons " and was on special service as escort for General W. H. Jackson; went from Columbia to Spring Hill and continually raided and were raided by the Federals who held Franklin until about June 1, 1863; then with General Jackson's Division, joined J. E. Johnston's army in rear of Vicksburg; after the fall of Vicksburg, was at the siege of Jackson by Sherman, and in all the maneuvers in Mississippi at that time and until the command went to take part in the Georgia campaign; joined Johnston's army at Dalton; was on retreat to Atlanta, and at fall of that place; was with Hood on his advance to Nashville and during the campaign in Tennessee; retreated with army into Mississippi; at Corinth, in January, 1865, got a thirty days furlough, which was spent with friends in Kemper county, Miss.; followed Wilson in his raid through Alabama to Selma; was near Selma at its capture by Wilson; shortly after, surrendered at Gainesville, Ala., May 11, 1865; the number of his parole is 52. Was never wounded, but had three horses killed under him. Joined the Confederate Historical Association June 13, 1894.

RAMBAUT, G. V., entered the Confederate States Army as a private in Company H, McDonald's Battalion, Forrest's old regiment; was promoted from private to major July 20, 1862, and served on the staff of General Forrest through all his different promotions; was wounded twice—once at Shiloh and again on the march from Pontotoc, Miss., to Harrisburg and Tupelo. He enjoyed the full confidence of General Forrest and was with him " from start to finish." Major Rambaut was a very busy, active man, and only began to write his recollections of Forrest's campaigns in the spring of 1896, and soon after was taken suddenly ill and died in a few days, an irreparable loss to his family, and to his old comrades and many friends. He was peculiarly fitted for the work he had begun, and no one else can finish it for him as he would have done. He was one of the early members of this Association.

RAWLINGS, R. J., private Company B, Forrest's old regiment; enlisted May, 1861, in Welby Armstrong's Company, Second Tennessee Regiment Infantry, and was afterward transferred to Forrest's Regiment Cavalry; meantime had served in the One Hundred and Fifty-fourth Tennessee; was captured sick just before the battle of Perryville, paroled and came home, but subsequently escaped and rejoined his command at Como, Miss., and served from that date, December, 1863, to the end of the war; paroled May 11, 1865. Admitted to this Association October, 1895.

REAVES, BEN. T., enlisted as a private May 15, 1861; served in Cheatham's Division to the end of the war; paroled April 26, 1865. Entered this Association upon the recommendation of C. W. Frazer July 1, 1869; lived at Bartlett; taught school and practiced law. Died some years ago.

RENIG, CHAS., private in Company I, Fifteenth Tennessee; served through the war. Recommended for membership by Captain F. Wolf and elected in this Association January 20, 1870. Died several years ago.

RHEA, W. H., entered the service in April, 1861; was a Captain in the Second Tennessee Regiment; paroled May, 1865. After the war became one of the editors of the *Avalanche*, and afterward was connected with the Board of Underwriters of Memphis. Became a member of this Association April 28, 1870; name proposed by Dr. John H. Erskine. Died several years ago.

RITTENHOUSE, DAN. G., private in the West Rangers, McCulloch's Regiment; enlisted January 1, 1862. Filed a certificate of discharge from the army on account of chronic illness with application for membership in this Association.

RICHARDSON, W. G., Second Sergeant in Company A, Seventh Tennessee Cavalry; enlisted May 16, 1861, and went all through the war; was paroled at Gainesville, Ala., May 11, 1865. Became a member of this Association May 12, 1870, upon the recommendation of Colonel T. H. Logwood and Dr. R. W. Mitchell. Died several years ago.

ROBERTSON, W. M., enlisted May 1, 1861, as a private in Company A, First Mississippi Regiment, Pillow's Brigade; was wounded at Fort Donelson and captured; released July, 1862; also captured at Nashville under General Hood; was in all the battles of the Army of Tennessee from Fort Donelson to Nashville; paroled June 12, 1865. Admitted to this Association October 9, 1894.

ROBSON, B. P., enlisted as a member of Company B, Logwood's Battalion, May 15, 1861, and was detached as Quartermaster's Sergeant in Jackson's Division of Cavalry, and was with the command during the entire four years of the war; paroled in May, 1865. Admitted to the C. H. A. October 8, 1895.

RODEN, GEORGE, born in County Cavin, Ireland, in 1842; grew up in the city of Toronto, Canada; came south in 1859; enlisted June 13, 1861, in Company A, Captain F. A. Montgomery, First Mississippi Cavalry, commanded by Colonel Dick Pinson, and served with that command three years; was in Forrest's command nearly all of the war; was in the battles of Belmont, Shiloh, Franklin and many battles and innumerable skirmishes. In the winter of '63 the company was furloughed to go home and re-equip. Private Roden was cut off by Sherman's raid up the Yazoo, reported to General Wirt Adams and assigned to headquarters of scouts under Captain W. A. Montgomery; served with him to the end of the war and was surrendered at Gainesville, Ala.; paroled May 12, 1865. Lived in Washington county, Miss., until four years ago, when he came to Memphis. Joined the C. H. A. in 1893 and became a member of Company A, Confederate Veterans. When he applied for membership in this Association he presented very flattering testimonials from his former captain, W. A. Montgomery, R. N. Miller, prosecuting attorney of Hinds county, Miss., and other comrades. He is an active member of Company A, and was on its visits to Chattanooga, Richmond, Little Rock and elsewhere.

RODGERS, W. S., enlisted May 1, 1861, as a private in Company K, First Tennessee Cavalry, Humes' Brigade; paroled May 3, 1865. Joined this Association May 14, 1889.

ROGAN, H. A., Major in the Ninth Tennessee Infantry; entered the service in May, 1861; paroled May, 1865; occupation, lawyer. Proposed for membership by L. B. McFarland, and elected January 20, 1870. Died many years ago.

ROSSER, ISAAC, entered the service April 21, 1861, and was Second Lieutenant in Tobin's Battery, and paroled May 10, 1865. Proposed for membership by Colonel Jno. W. Dawson, and elected July 1, 1869. Died several years ago.

RUCKER, Colonel commanding brigade in Forrest's Cavalry corps; lost one arm in the war. Proposed for membership in this Association by W. S. Pickett, and elected January 20, 1870. Now lives in Alabama; occupation, civil engineer; was a conspicuous figure in nearly all of Forrest's campaigns.

RUST, J. W., private Company K, First Kentucky; enlisted May 18, 1861; released from service May 18, 1863, on account of ill health; served in the Army of Virginia. His discharge was regularly signed by General Joseph E. Johnston.

RYAN, CHARLES ROSCOE, born in Monticello, Jasper county, Ga., January 31, 1845; in 1859 the family removed to Des Arc, Ark., and in 1861 he joined the Twenty-fifth Arkansas Infantry at Corinth, Miss.; participated in the battles of Corinth and Iuka; his regiment was sent to Port Hudson; he was there during the whole siege, and was under fire for forty days continuously when the place fell. After he was exchanged he went to Georgia and became connected with the medical department, his chief being Dr. Bateman, formerly of Memphis; he continued until May, 1865, when he volunteered, against the expostulations of his chief, to go into the fort at West Point, Ga., to try and repel the invasion of the Federal cavalry under General Wilson. They were forced to surrender, but were not long detained. After the war he came to Memphis and engaged in the grocery business successfully. In 1884 he contracted a severe attack of pneumonia; after lingering for one year he died in Manitou, Col , November 24, 1885. His remains were brought back to Memphis, and now lie in Elmwood Cemetery. He was one of the early members of the old Confederate Historical Association.

SANFORD, G. W., private Company B, Seventh Mississippi Cavalry; enlisted in 1862; paroled May 16, 1865. Was recommended for membership in the C. H. A. by J. P. Young and C. W. Frazer, and admitted February 11, 1896.

SCALES, DABNEY M., Midshipman in the Confederate States Navy; enlisted May, 1861; was a midshipman in the United States Navy, but resigned when his native State Mississippi seceded; reported for duty at Savannah, Ga., under John N. Maffitt, on steamers Savannah and Charleston, and cruised along the coasts of Georgia and Florida; also served under J. N. Brown, commanding the steamer Arkansas, on Yazoo and Mississippi rivers; was engaged at Port Royal, Old River, and on Mississippi river at Vicksburg, with fleets of Farragut and Davis, and with Envoy and consorts under Commodore Porter; was sent by C. S. Government to Europe to join the cruiser Shenandoah, which played havoc with the United States merchant marine on the Pacific coast, and was never captured, but returned to Liverpool in 1866. Midshipman Scales was not paroled. He returned to this country long after the war, and married a daughter of the late Major Geo. W. Winchester; has practiced law successfully, and was a member of the last State Senate. He became a member of this Association August 12, 1884.

SCOTT, WM. L., came from Knoxville, Tenn., and practiced law and married in Memphis before the war; was chosen Second Lieutenant of Bankhead's Battery of Light Artillery; his brother-in-law, W. Y. C. Humes, was first lieutenant, and Smith P. Bankhead captain; the other second lieutenants were James Clare McDavitt and W. B. Greenlaw, Jr.; the battery spent the winter of 1861-2 at Columbus, Ky. Lieutenant Humes was promoted to captain and assigned to command a heavy battery, and Lieutenants Scott and McDavitt were promoted to the rank of first lieutenant. At Shiloh, Lieut. Scott had a horse killed under him, and was severely wounded in the neck by a musket ball. When the battery was reorganized, May 14, 1862, he became junior first lieutenant; Captain Bankhead was promoted to the rank of major and was made chief of artillery, and was afterward advanced to the rank of brigadier-general; Lieutenant Scott became captain of the battery, known afterward as "Scott's Battery;" it engaged in the battles of Perryville, Murfreesboro and Chickamauga where a number of the men were killed and wounded; at the battle of Missionary Ridge most of the men were killed, wounded, or taken prisoners; those who escaped were assigned to other commands. Captain Scott returned to Memphis after the war and resumed the practice of law; became chancellor of the Second Chancery Court of Shelby county, at Memphis; at the end of his term he resumed practice, and in 1875 removed to St. Louis and followed his profession there. Joined this Association September 9, 1869. Died several years ago.

SEARCY, MARK W., enlisted early in the war in Company A, Fifth Arkansas Regiment, Hardee's First Brigade, and served until May 1, 1862. His health was failing from hard service, and he was discharged at the suggestion of General Hardee, and then joined what was known as Saunders' Confederate Scouts. This company was organized for the purpose of acting as headquarters scouts for General Albert Sidney Johnston, and was merged with Saunders' Battalion. After General Van Dorn's death the command reported to General Joseph E. Johnston, and was attached to his army until the end of the war. Joined the Confederate Historical Association November 4, 1869.

SELDEN, M. L, enlisted February, 1862, as a private in Company A, Seventh Tennessee Cavalry, and remained with this company, known as the "Memphis Light Dragoons," until the close of the war, and was paroled in May, 1865. Joined this Association May 29, 1884.

SEMMES, B. J., was born June 15, 1823, in County Charles, Maryland, and was a member of the Maynard Rifles, an independent company organized in Memphis before the war. This (Company F) became a part of the One Hundred and Fifty-fourth Senior Tennessee Regiment, and served in the Army of Tennessee under Generals Bragg, Johnston and Hood. B. J. Semmes was for a time sergeant of his company, but was soon promoted to the rank of major in the commissary department, and served with marked fidelity and credit until paroled May 16, 1865. He has since been a highly successful merchant in Memphis, and reared a family occupying the highest social position. From a reference to the books of this Association it appears that he became a member in 1866.

SEMMES, P. W., was born in Washington, D. C., March 12, 1841; enlisted May 28, 1861, in Company C, Louisiana Guards, First Louisiana Regiment; became lieutenant and adjutant, and served in the Army of Northern Virginia; was transferred to the Army of Tennessee in 1862, and served under Bragg, Johnston and Hood with the engineer corps, and remained until the close of the war; was wounded in a skirmish at Warfield, Ky.; paroled May, 25, 1865.

SEMMES, RAPHAEL, Jr., Second Lieutenant in Semmes' Brigade, Johnston's army; entered the service November 8, 1863; paroled April, 1865; son of Admiral Raphael Semmes. Proposed for membership in this Association by Colonel Jno. W. Dawson, and elected September, 1869, and was for several years an active member. Lives now in Mobile.

SEMMES, S. S., eldest son of Admiral Semmes; was Second Lieutenant Company E, First Louisiana Infantry. This regiment went to Pensacola, thence to Corinth, Miss., where it formed the nucleus of the Army of Tennessee; remained in that regiment until the close of the war; paroled May 20, 1865. Joined the Confederate Historical Association September 13, 1894.

SHAW, THOS. J. W., private in Company D, Sixth Tennessee Infantry; entered early and remained to the end. Proposed for membership in this Association by J. E. Beasley and elected February 8, 1870.

SHELBY, J. M., private Company D, Fourth Tennessee; enlisted May 1, 1861; was captured at Shiloh April 7, 1862, and released the 11th of that month; was wounded at Perryville and Franklin; paroled May 1, 1865. Admitted to this Association January 8, 1895.

SHICK, JOHN, private in Company I, Fifteenth Tennessee, Tyler's Brigade, Bate's Division; entered the service May, 1861, and remained four years. Proposed for membership by F. May and R. Semmes, Jr., and elected May 12, 1870. Has been dead several years.

SHIPPEY, W. F., enlisted April, 1861, and was First Sergeant of Company A, First Virginia Cavalry, Stuart's Regiment, during the first year of the war; was transferred to Company D, Eighth Virginia Infantry, Hilton's Brigade, Pickett's Division, Army Northern Virginia, in June, 1863; commissioned in Confederate States Navy in the autumn of same year and served in James River Squadron until evacuation of Richmond; fell back with naval brigade and surrendered with it at Greensboro, N. C., April 26, 1865; was wounded nine times.

SHOUP, FRANCIS A., was a graduate of West Point; entered the service in May, 1861, and served four years; served as chief of artillery under Generals Hardee and Joseph E. Johnston and was promoted to rank of Brigadier General and commanded department of Alabama and Florida. After the war he lived in Memphis; was professor of mathematics in the University of Mississippi for several years and was the author of several books; he became an Episcopal minister and for many years filled a chair in the University at Sewanee; died at Columbia, Tenn., September 4, 1896, aged 63 years. His military career was brilliant and his subsequent life full of good works. He was proposed for membership in this Association by Hon. Jefferson Davis and General Gideon J. Pillow and was elected April 28, 1870.

SHOUSE, W. W., born in Woodford county, Ky., came to Memphis and engaged in business when quite young, just before the war; enlisted in the Memphis Light Dragoons, with W. F. Taylor as Captain, afterward under Captain J. Wes. Sneed; was in the Seventh Tennessee Cavalry; was in the battle at Holly Springs, under General Van Dorn, and in the battle of Corinth; again was under Van Dorn at the first battle of Franklin, and at Thompson's station. After General Van Dorn's death was transferred with his regiment to General Joseph E. Johnston's army in the rear of Vicksburg, when the relief of that place was contemplated; was in the fight at Jackson, and assisted in covering the retreat to Meridian; then ordered to join the army of Tennessee, and served throughout the Georgia campaign; was at the battles of Franklin and Nashville, and was in winter quarters at Tupelo; had a furlough from there, and was captured near Memphis, March, 1865, and started to Camp Chase; jumped from a train above Cairo; escaped to Union City, Tenn.; was recaptured there, carried to Hickman, Ky., and placed in a stockade for ten days, when news of the surrender came and he was released. Returning to Memphis in the fall he resumed business, and has been almost continuously since then connected with a large establishment, being for many years past a partner and the general manager; was married in 1884, and has five children. Joined this Association at an early day in its history.

SIMS, W. R., enlisted as a private in Company F, Eighteenth Mississippi Cavalry, Starke's Brigade, Chalmer's Division, in August, 1864, and was paroled in May, 1865. Joined Confederate Historical Association June 30, 1891.

SIMMONS, J. F., Major, and acting quartermaster; served on the staff of General Robert Ransom, Army of Northern Virginia; had typhoid fever in the summer of 1862; went back to the field too soon and relapsed; ordered from field for duty in Mississippi; served there until he applied for field service and was ordered to report to General W. H. Jackson as chief paymaster of cavalry; never captured, never wounded. Has since edited the Sardis, Miss., *Southern Reporter*. Joined this Association March 13, 1894.

SMITH, J. N., enlisted as private in Harris' Zouave Cadets, One Hundred and Fifty-fourth Tennessee, April, 1861, and was afterward transferred to Carnes' Battery; was captured at Saulsbury, N. C., April 12, 1865; paroled in June, 1865. Joined C. H. A. June 13, 1894.

SNOWDEN, ROBERT BOGARDUS, born in New York and came of Revolutionary stock; was brought to Nashville when three years old, his father being a leading merchant there; was educated in Nashville and at the Western Military Institute, Kentucky. He entered the war early, and became First Lieutenant and Adjutant of Maney's First Tennessee Regiment, and served the first year in the Army of West Virginia, the next two years in the Army of Tennessee, and the last year in the Army of Virginia. As Adjutant of the First Tennessee he served in the campaign of West Virginia under Generals Lee, Stonewall Jackson and Loring at Cheat mountain, Sewell mountain, Bath and Hancock.

After the battle of Fort Donelson his command was ordered back to Tennessee, to the army of Albert Sidney Johnston, and took part in the battle of Shiloh. After this he was made adjutant-general and assigned to the staff of General Bushrod Johnson, in whose command he served until the close of the war. His next battle was at Perryville, then at the battle of Murfreesboro, December 31, 1862, where he distinguished himself by leading a faltering regiment into action, and was promoted to the lieutenant-colonelcy of the Twenty-fifth Tennessee, the only instance of the kind in the West. He was wounded three times, once at Perryville, once at Murfreesboro, where he had a horse killed and two wounded, and once at Fort Harrison in front of Richmond. After the battle of Chickamauga the Twenty-fifth and Forty-fourth Tennessee Regiments were consolidated just before the battle of Missionary Ridge, when Johnson's Brigade, of which it was a part, was ordered with Gracy's Brigade to reinforce General Longstreet at Knoxville. The command was at the storming of Fort Saunders, and fought at Bean's station. From there they were ordered to Petersburg, Va., where Johnson's Division, composed of Gracy's and his old brigade, arrived in time,

COL. R. B. SNOWDEN.

as General Grant said, to effectually bottle up General Butler, who was trying to take Petersburg with 30,000 men. The command remained in the Virginia army, and took part in the fights around Petersburg and Richmond until Richmond fell, and it finally surrendered at Appomattox, along with the remnant of Archer's old brigade, with which it had been consolidated. Colonel Snowden commanded the Twenty-fifth and Forty-fourth Tennessee in numerous engagements, including the battle of Fort Harrison.

He was at Appomattox when General Lee surrendered, and made his escape with Captain W. T. Blakemore; went to Danville, Va., thence in the car with President Davis to Greensboro, N. C., where Johnston's army surrendered; then to Augusta, Ga.. where he surrendered to and was paroled by General Wilson, who gave him transportation to Nashville; then he went to New York and engaged in mercantile life

13

for a time.   In 1868 he married Miss Anna Brinkley, a young lady of wealth, and of an old and noted pioneer family of Tennessee; they have reared a lovely family, and entered largely into the social and business life of Memphis. Colonel Snowden is in the prime of life and looks after large affairs, but his cheery nature is unchanged by prosperity, and he loves to relate in his easy, charming manner, many stirring reminiscences of the war, especially when in a group of the old boys who wore the gray.   He became a member of this Association May 12, 1870, and was commander-in-chief at the inter-State drill held in Memphis in 1895, with the rank of major-general.

SPICER, JNO. E., private in Forrest's old regiment; entered the service May 4, 1861; retired at the surrender in May, 1865. Proposed for membership in this Association by J. A. Loudon, and elected January 20, 1870.

SPILLMAN, R. B., a native of Virginia, but lived in Memphis at the breaking out of the war; enlisted in the One Hundred and Fifty-fourth Tennessee Regiment; was in the battle of Shiloh; made the Kentucky campaign with General Kirby Smith, and was in the battle of Murfreesboro; was terribly wounded in the head by a shell when supporting a battery, and was taken prisoner and placed in a small room in the Female College in Murfreesboro with eleven other prisoners badly wounded, all of whom died in his presence, he being the only one in the room that survived; when well enough to move was taken to Camp Morton, Indianapolis, Ind., where he remained until exchanged at City Point, Va.   He returned to his regiment, then at Shelbyville, Tenn., but being unfit for active service reported to General Joseph E. Johnston, who assigned him to post duty at Marietta, Ga., and afterward at Thomaston, and then at Americus, Ga., where he was when the war closed.   He returned to Memphis and was paroled by Captain Kyle of the Federal army, who was on duty here at the time.   He was one of the early members of this Association, and at all times has been active and useful, and has been especially efficient upon annual memorial occasions when the graves of Confederates were strewn with flowers at Elmwood.   Has been vice-president since 1885.

SPOTSWOOD, EDWIN A., was born September 12, 1836, in Orange Grove, Orange county, Va.; came to Memphis in August, 1860, and engaged in business. In the spring of 1861 he was elected major of a regiment of State troops and commissioned. In January, 1862, became a member of McDonald's Battalion, and joined Forrest at Hopkinsville, Ky.; went with the command to Fort Donelson, and was one of the few who swam the back water and escaped; was furloughed with the regiment at Huntsville, Ala., and came home; was detained by sickness, and upon recovery was married May 22, 1862, to Miss Jeannette Armour. June 1st reported to General Forrest at Tupelo, Miss.; detailed to act as sergeant-major, and was soon promoted to the position of adjutant, with the rank of first lieutenant; was with General Forrest in covering the retreat of Bragg's army to Chattanooga; came with Forrest's command to Department of Mississippi and West Tennessee. In January, 1864, was promoted by General Forrest from adjutant to major of the regiment for gallantry on the field; was detailed with others to enter the lines, look up recruits and obtain information. Returned with General Forrest to North Mississippi after the battle of Fort Pillow, in which he participated; was in the battle of Harrisburg and various other engagements; was wounded in the thigh at Athens, Ala., September 22, 1864; joined his wife at Macon, Ga., and remained until January, 1865; rejoined Forrest at Tupelo, and was in the various moves and engagements on down to Selma. After that fell back to Gainesville, where the surrender took place, and he was paroled on the 11th of May, 1865. Except when sick or disabled by his wound, he took part in every fight in which his regiment was engaged from Fort Donelson to Selma. He was one of the early members of the old Relief and Historical Association, and has lived in Memphis ever since the war.

STARKE, E. T., Captain Company B, Sixth Missouri Infantry; enlisted in August, 1861; went to Pensacola in July, 1861, with Colonel Lomax, Alabama Volunteers; remained there until March, when relieved. The regiment enlisted for the war as the Third Alabama; went to Missouri and joined

General Price; served with him until the fall of Vicksburg, and then went with General Pillow until the surrender, May 29, 1865, date of parole. Joined the C. H. A. August 14, 1894. Dead.

STEINKUHL, CHRIS. D., became a member of the old Confederate Relief and Historical Association August 13, 1869; enlisted in Company B, commanded by Captain James G. Barbour, Forrest's old regiment, and at the reorganization of the regiment Mr. Steinkuhl was elected first lieutenant. He served throughout the war; was often in command of his company, and he was noted for his daring, his ever-present good humor and self-control. He was in some hand to hand sabre conflicts, had horses shot under him and was wounded more than once. He was surrendered and paroled at the end of the war. His wife is the daughter of W. C. and Rose P. Thompson, so long identified with the New Memphis Theater. After Mr. Thompson's death Captain Steinkuhl was for a time manager of the theater. He died of yellow fever in 1878, after many refugees had returned, and is yet remembered with affection by his old comrades and all who knew him.

STEWART, C. M., Captain Company E, Twelfth Tennessee; enlisted May 1, 1862; paroled May 11, 1865.

STILES, M., enlisted as a private in Company A, One Hundred and Fifty-fourth Senior Tennessee Regiment, April 26, 1861, and served throughout the war. Joined the C. H. A. February 9, 1886. Dead.

STRANGE, J. P., was Assistant Adjutant General on General Forrest's staff, with rank of Major; appointed July 21, 1862, and remained as such through all of the General's promotions; he was wounded at Fort Donelson in February, 1862; near Nashville December 2, 1862, and at Bolivar, Tenn., May 2, 1864; was with General Forrest at the surrender at Gainesville, Ala.; resumed business in Memphis after the war. Joined the C. H. A. March 3, 1870, and died a year or two later sincerely respected and mourned by all who knew him.

STRATTON, W. D., was born in Smith county, Tenn., on January 12, 1836; his parents were Virginians, and in 1852 moved to Shelby county and settled near the Mississippi State line. He entered the service as Lieutenant of the Memphis Rangers, Ninth Tennessee Regiment, Hal Rogers captain, and commanded the first detail to work on the fortifications of Columbus, Ky.; was promoted to the rank of captain on the battlefield of Shiloh, and at his request commissioned in the cavalry, which he received at Tupelo, Miss.; with his brother, T. T. Stratton, crossed the Mississippi river with a train of ordnance for General Hindman at Little Rock, which consisted of one hundred and six wagonloads, and was the first and only successful expedition that ever reached that department; returning he joined General R. V. Richardson in organizing a brigade of cavalry inside the enemy's lines, and served on his staff until General Forrest took charge in Mississippi and West Tennessee, when he was put in command of the provost guard in January, 1864, and served in this capacity until a few weeks before the battle of Harrisburg, Miss., when he was transferred to the Nineteenth Tennessee, Colonel Newsom commanding, and was acting major of this regiment when he lost his leg, leading it in a charge on a battery at the battle of Harrisburg. After the war he returned to Memphis, his old home, and was one of the active members of the C. R. and H. Association; was a member of the first committee on entertainment, together with Dr. Robert Mitchell, Captain Tom Johnson, Captain Steinkuhl and Colonel Dawson. He had six brothers in the service — one was killed at the battle of Atlanta, two were maimed for life, and three came out unscathed. He now lives in Atlanta, Ga.

SYKES, JOSEPH P., born September 2, 1844, in Maury county, Tenn.; entered the Confederate States Army as a cadet and served at Nashville; transferred to Pensacola and assigned to the Tenth Mississippi Regiment, then to Lumsden's Alabama Light Artillery; was in the battles of Perryville, Murfreesboro and Chickamauga, and in all the battles from Dalton to Atlanta; was transferred to L. S. Ross' Brigade of Texas Cavalry, and became inspector of same; was

with Hood's army in Tennessee, and in the engagement on
the retreat at Anthony's Hill, near Pulaski; paroled at Jackson, Miss., May 13, 1865. Joined the C. H. A. August 8,
1898; married a daughter of General Preston Smith, and has
practiced law in Memphis for many years.

TALLEY, RICHARD H., at the age of 16 years left his
widowed mother and enlisted in the Thirty-eighth Tennessee; served throughout the war, and was paroled May 1,
1865, at Macon, Ga. He then took service with the M. & C.
R. R. at Collierville, having his office and station in a box-
car. A few years after he was transferred to Memphis, where
he was employed in the treasurer's office. After fourteen
years' service he became ticket agent of the C. O. & S. W.
R. R. Co., and afterward represented other railroads. He was
secretary of the Memphis Passenger Association when he
died in 1895. Joined the C. H. A. March 10, 1885. He was
the youngest of four sons of Mrs. Emily B. Talley, all of
whom went into the Confederate army, as well as two sons-
in-law of this noble Southern mother. The other brothers
were Foster D., Fletcher H. and Wm. F. Talley.

TATUM, HENRY A., private in Company I, First Confederate Regiment; was born on the 8th of September, 1837,
in Guilford county, N. C.; enlisted early in the war, but does
not remember the day: he left Memphis with Captain M. J.
Wicks' Mounted Rifles; was captured at Murfreesboro, but
held only twenty minutes; was paroled at Gainesville, Ala.,
May 14, 1865.

TAYLOR, THOS. J., private in Company F, Twelfth Tennessee Cavalry; enlisted January 16, 1863; born 20th of May,
1847, in Haywood county, Tenn.; was wounded slightly at
the battle of Pulaski; captured at Athens, Ala., and paroled
May 14, 1865, at Gainesville, Ala.

TAYLOR, W. F., enlisted early, and the services of his
company were tendered to the Secretary of War before the
firing on Fort Sumpter. He became lieutenant-colonel and
colonel of the famous Seventh Tennessee Cavalry and served

with distinction throughout the war; was twice wounded, though not seriously; was in many engagements, and was a dashing, fearless leader, enjoying the full confidence of his men; was paroled in May, 1865, and has since been and is now (1896) a leading merchant of Memphis. Elected a member of this Association in 1869 or '70.

TAYLOR, THOS. C., was born in Clinton, East Feliciana parish, La., October 10, 1845; enlisted April, 1861, in Company B, Hunter Rifles, which went to New Orleans and was made a part of the Fourth Louisiana; the regiment was sent to Vicksburg, Miss., and built the first fortifications of that stronghold. The Fourth Louisiana, under that gallant colonel, H. W. Allen, went to Jackson, Tenn., and thence to Shiloh; it was in all the campaigns in the West and at Baton Rouge under Breckinridge, and at the first siege of Port Hudson, La.; on leaving Port Hudson the regiment rejoined the Western army at Dalton, Ga., and was in the battles of Atlanta, Peachtree creek and Jonesboro, Ga.; at the latter place Comrade Taylor was wounded, and has carried the bullet from August 31, 1864, to this day; rejoined his company and regiment in time for the battle of Franklin, and was captured on General Hood's retreat from Nashville on December 19, 1864, and sent to Camp Douglas at Chicago, Ill., where he remained until June 20, 1864, having belonged through the entire war to the same company and regiment. He returned to his home in Louisiana after being discharged from prison, and in October, 1865, went to Texas, where he was married in October, 1866, to Miss Fannie Vickers of Waco. He has been a resident of Memphis since 1871, and is a member of the Confederate Historical Association.

TAYLOR. J. R. ("Tobe"), went out early in 1861 as captain of a company in Miller's Battalion, afterward Pinson's First Mississippi Cavalry; was slightly wounded at Shiloh, and was with Armstrong and Jackson on the raid into Tennessee; was wounded at Denmark and left in the hands of the enemy, but nursed by Memphis ladies, and escaped; was with Van Dorn on his Tennessee campaign, and with Gen-

eral Joseph E. Johnston at Jackson, Miss., and in numerous
fights; was with Forrest, and wounded on the bridge at Moscow; served with Armstrong's Brigade, Jackson's Division.
through the Georgia campaign; was under Hood in Tennessee, and in the battles of Franklin, Nashville, Murfreesboro
and Anthony's Hill; was wounded and had a horse killed
under him while on outpost duty, and was one of the last to
get over the river; was in other engagements, and last of all
at Selma, where he was captured; was taken to Macon and
paroled. He was never sick and never missed a fight except
on account of wounds. He says now that he fared just as his
men did; is proud of his record, and hands it down to his
children and grandchildren as that of a plain soldier fighting
for what he knew to be right. He was married to Miss Eu-
genia Morgan in 1857, both of them being of fine Revolutionary stock; they have four sons and two daughters. Captain Taylor joined the C. H. A. on May 12, 1885.

THOMPSON, J. H., Corporal Company E, Twenty-ninth
Mississippi Regiment; enlisted in March, 1862; was captured
at Lookout mountain November 24, 1863; released from
Rock Island prison by parole for thirty days March 29, 1865,
and the war closed before the parole expired. Admitted to
the C. H. A. December 10, 1895, and became a member of
Company A, Confederate Veterans.

THOMPSON, JACOB, was born in Caswell county, N. C.,
in 1810, and died in Memphis, March 24, 1885. His life is
thus epitomized on a tablet dedicated to him in Memorial
Hall, Chapel Hill University of North Carolina: "Class of
1831; Member of Faculty, 1831; Representative in Congress,
1839–1853; Secretary of the Interior, 1857–1861; Lieutenant-
Colonel and Inspector-General C. S. A., 1862–1863; Confidential Agent of Confederate States to the Dominion of Canada,
1864–1865." Mr. Thompson became a lawyer, and located at
Pontotoc, Miss.; went to Congress, and was a distinguished
figure there for many years; after that was Secretary of the
Interior under James Buchanan, and served with marked efficiency and distinction; when Mississippi seceded he resigned

HON. JACOB THOMPSON.

and returned to his home. He was at the battle of Shiloh; became Lieutenant-Colonel of Ballentine's Regiment of Cavalry, and later on had a horse shot under him; subsequently he was sent on a mission to Canada, with a view of aiding in the escape of Confederate prisoners. After the war closed, a reward being offered for his head, he sailed for Europe with his family, and remained away for some years. He returned to Oxford, Miss., came to Memphis, built an elegant home, and passed the rest of his life in a manner becoming a retired statesman, soldier and true christian gentleman. Colonel Thompson was loved and respected by all who knew him, and especially by the members of the Confederate Historical Association, of which he was an honored member. His name was proposed for membership by Jefferson Davis, late President of the Confederacy, and by Rev. J. Carmichael, and he was elected April 28, 1870.

THOMPSON, J. N., born September 22, 1841, in Yalla-
busha county, Miss.; enlisted April 27, 1861, as a private in
Company E, Blythe's Forty-fourth Mississippi Regiment: was
wounded twice in the battle of New Hope Church, Ga., on
the 27th of May, 1864; served to the end of the war. Joined
the C. H. A. September 13, 1892, and is a member of Company A, Confederate Veterans.

THORNTON, GUSTAVUS BROWN, born February 22,
1835, at Bowling Green, Caroline county, Va., and came to
Memphis with his father's family in 1847. His collegiate
course was taken in Richmond, Va.; graduated at the Memphis Medical College in 1858, and at the University of New
York Medical Department in 1860; practiced medicine in
Memphis one year; spring of 1861 joined the Southern Guards
under Captain James Hamilton, One Hundred and Fifty-
fourth Tennessee Regiment, and served as a private three or
four months; was then commissioned as Assistant Surgeon
of State troops; when transferred to the Confederate States
Army retained the same rank. While assistant surgeon he
served at Belmont, New Madrid, Island No. 10 and at other
points, and acted as brigade surgeon with Brigadier-General
John P. McCown. After the battle of Shiloh was appointed
surgeon by the Richmond authorities and became chief surgeon of McCown's Division when McCown was made Major-
General, and was at the battles of Richmond and Perryville,
though not immediately present at the former. He was with
the same division at Murfreesboro. General McCown in his
official report said: "Division Surgeon G. B. Thornton was
untiring in his labors with the wounded. He is entitled to
the thanks of the command." See Series 1, vol. xxi, page
915, Official Records Union and Confederate Armies.

In the summer of 1863 he became chief surgeon of General A. P. Stewart's Division, and was with this division at
the battles of Chickamauga and Missionary Ridge; was in
winter quarters at Dalton, and on the Georgia campaign.
After the death of General Polk, General Stewart was promoted to command his corps, and Surgeon Thornton remained
with the old division, placed in command of General H. D.

DR. G. B. THORNTON.

Clayton of Alabama. He was at the battle of Franklin, but his division did not participate; was in service around Nashville. At the reorganization of the army in North Carolina in the spring of 1865, Dr. Thornton was assigned to Walthall's Division, with which he remained until the capitulation, which soon followed.

Returning to Memphis in the summer of 1865, Dr. Thornton resumed the practice of medicine. In 1866, when cholera prevailed, he was appointed assistant physician at the Memphis Hospital with Dr. J. M. Keller, and saw much service. In 1868 he became hospital physician, and held the position for eleven years. In the yellow fever epidemic of 1867 Dr. Thornton again saw hard service, and in '73 he was entrusted with great responsibilities and inaugurated some important reforms, one of which resulted in the separation of the smallpox hospital from the city hospital. The Doctor was also mainly instrumental in securing, through Hon. Casey Young and Senator Harris, the passage of the bill under which the Marine Hospital was located in Memphis. In the great yellow fever epidemic of 1878, while yet in charge of the City Hospital, Dr. Thornton was prostrated with the disease and narrowly escaped with his life. In 1879 he voluntarily resigned, and was appointed by Dr. D. T. Porter, President of the Taxing District (city of Memphis), President of the Memphis Board of Health; served ten years and then resigned. His services, papers and arduous labors were recognized by sanitarians and the profession at large throughout the country, as well as by the public and local government. Realizing the necessity of a new hospital for Memphis as no other man perhaps did, he was largely instrumental in securing the levy of a special tax of 9 cents on the $100 for three years ($80,000) for a new hospital, which is now assured.

After the installation of Mayor Clapp, Dr. Thornton was again called into service as President of the Board of Health, and at this writing (December, 1896) holds the position. He was a member of the State Board of Health several years, and belongs to several medical societies. He was ever a strong advocate of national, maritime and inter-State quarantine as a protection against yellow fever, and used his influence to secure the passage of the existing national, maritime and inter-State quarantine law, passed by the Fifty-second Congress January 13, 1863. It is no flattery to say that he is universally esteemed as a leader in his profession and as a most courteous and genial christian gentleman.

Dr. Thornton has been twice married—first to Miss Martha Louisa Hullum, December 1, 1869, who died June 27, 1875, leaving two children. Anna Mary and G. B. Thornton, Jr.; second, to Mrs. Ella Walker (Winston), widow of the late Colonel Gustavus A. Henry of Alabama. He became a member of the C. H. A. September 9, 1869.

TUCKER, W. W., captain of a company in the Fifth Mississippi Cavalry; entered the service March, 1861; paroled in May, 1865. Proposed for membership in the C. H. A. by General Patton Anderson and elected May 12, 1870.

THOS. F. TOBIN,
January, 1861.

TOBIN, THOMAS FRANCIS, born in County Tipperary, Ireland, January 1, 1840; came to this country with his family when 11 years old; was educated at St. Joseph's College, Perry county, Ohio; came to Memphis in 1859, and was given a position in the postoffice under General Wm. H. Carroll. At the outbreak of the war was elected captain of a company of infantry in June, 1861, and transferred to artillery, with the understanding that a West Pointer was to be captain. Captain W. Orton Williams, inspector on General Polk's staff, was given this place, and T. F. Tobin became first lieutenant. The seventy-six men were mustered into Confederate service for three years or the war July 4, 1861. The company went into camp four miles north of Memphis; ordered to Columbus, Ky., about the last of July, and placed under command of General Cheatham; took small part at Belmont; fired across the river in support of Tappan's regiment; wintered at Feliciana, Ky., and was in numerous artillery duels near Paducah; ordered to Corinth, and held as reserve at Shiloh; was in the battle of Farmington, and after that had a series of artillery duels on General Van Dorn's line with one of General Pope's batteries. In one of these Lieutenant Tobin was wounded, and had a horse shot under him. General Van Dorn was ever after his warm friend. In June of that year Lieutenant Tobin was promoted to captain, and he was slightly wounded at the battle of Iuka. He was in the thick of the attack on Corinth, and on the second day's fight, while trying to save a disabled gun, he was wounded and captured, but exchanged through the courtesy of General Rosecrans. In December, 1862, he was transferred with his battery to Vicksburg, and was actively engaged in and about this place until its fall, participating in fourteen engagements before the siege began. During the siege proper, which began early in May, 1863, Captain Tobin was chief of artillery of Gen. Forney's division on the Baldwin Ferry road, which was the center of the Confederate lines. He commanded nine redoubts and seven batteries with twenty-eight guns, and was wounded May 28, but returned to duty in two weeks. He went there with one hundred and five men, and at the end of the siege had only thirty-one fit for duty. On July 10 they were paroled and went to Selma, Ala. There Captain Tobin was prostrated with typhoid fever. He reorganized his battery at Enterprise. Miss., late in October. While at Vicksburg he had been commissioned as full colonel, with orders to report to General Van Dorn as chief of his artillery, and at the same time had been commissioned as captain of the Fifth Regular Artillery, but General Van Dorn had in the meantime been killed, and the captain preferred to remain with his old company. He reported to Major-General Maury at Mobile, and recruited his battery up to 200 men. Sections of his battery were sent to Florida and various points between Mobile and New Orleans, on detached service, and were in nine skirmishes with the Federals—at Pascagoula, Pensacola and other points. When the Confederates left Mobile Captain Tobin was ordered to report to Colonel Phil Spence, to assist in covering the retreat to Meridian, and his battery was placed at Cuba station on April 26. On May 11, after four years of arduous service, in which many lives were lost, Tobin's battery was paroled at Cuba station. A touching address of sympathy, respect and affection, signed by the officers and one hundred and seventy-six men, was delivered to Captain Tobin upon the eve of their final separation. He returned to Memphis and soon engaged actively in business. He was ticket agent for the Mississippi & Tennessee Railroad for one year, then engaged in cotton buying and storage, and is still in the cotton business. In August, 1886, he was appointed collector of the port of Memphis and served about five years; since that time has served a term in the State Senate in 1892–93, and has in the meantime managed large affairs entrusted to him for settlement. He has always been a popular man in social life, and has been a prominent member of all the clubs and commercial organizations. Joined the Confederate Historical Association when first organized, and was a member of the general staff at the inter-State drill held in Memphis in May, 1895. He was married in October, 1877, to Miss Julia Semmes, daughter of Major B. J. Semmes. She died two years later, leaving an infant son, who is living.

TUCKER, JOHN O., enlisted at Columbus, Miss., near where he was born, in October, 1863, in Company K, Sixth Mississippi Cavalry, before he was 15 years old. This was a regiment of young men, very few of them being 21 years old. He served actively until the end of the war; was in the battle of Harrisburg, where Captain Fields of his company was killed, also the colonel of the regiment, Isham Harris; he was in other engagements; was paroled at Gainesville, Ala., May, 1865. He married in Columbus, came to Memphis six years ago, and joined the C. H. A. December 11, 1894; holds a position in the postoffice.

TUCKER, W. D., was Assistant Surgeon of the One Hundred and Fifty-fourth Tennessee Regiment and promoted to rank of full surgeon at Shelbyville, Tenn., in 1863; was with General Polk at the battle of Chickamauga when he was relieved of his command, which was assumed by Lieutenant-

General W. J. Hardee; remained on General Hardee's staff as inspector until relieved by the Secretary of War through Surgeon-General Moore; then ordered to the Department of Alabama, Mississippi and Louisiana as inspector of department. Joined the C. H. A. June 30, 1892. Dead.

TUCKER, WM. W., was a private in Company K, Ninth Mississippi Regiment; after being wounded at the battle of Missionary Ridge, he reported back to his command at New Hope Church, Ga., but being still disabled was granted further time, and returned to his home in North Mississippi; there he secured a horse, reported to General Chalmers for duty and was with him at the end of the war; was paroled in June, 1865.

TUCKER, A. F., enlisted as a private in Company I, First Mississippi Battalion, May 1, 1861. After the battle of Shiloh was discharged on account of sickness; upon recovering he joined Forrest's command and remained until the end of the war; paroled in May, 1865. Joined the C. H. A. September 15, 1891.

TURLEY, THOS. B., born in Memphis, Tenn., April 5, 1845, in the house in which he now lives. His father was the late Thos. J. Turley, who died in Memphis August 1, 1854. His mother was Mrs. Flora C. Turley, a daughter of William Battle, Esq., one of the earliest settlers in this county. She died a few years ago. His father's family were Virginians, his mother's North Carolinians. He attended various schools in Memphis up to the breaking out of the late civil war. He enlisted the first year of the war in the Maynard Rifles, Company L, One Hundred and Fifty-fourth Tennessee Regiment. The first Captain of Company L was E. A. Cole. Its second captain was the late Walter R. Lucas of this city. He was wounded twice—once at Shiloh and again at Peachtree creek in front of Atlanta; was captured in the battle of Nashville and carried to Camp Chase, Ohio, where he was held until March, 1865, when he was exchanged and returned South. After the war he passed two years at the University of Virginia, where he studied law. Since about 1869 or '70 he has

been practicing law in this city. He is at present a member
of the firm of Turley & Wright; has never held office of any
kind; was married about 1870 to Miss Irene Rayner, daughter of the late Eli Rayner of this county; five children have
been born to himself and wife, all of whom are living. He
joined the C. H. A. October 9, 1894.

TYLER, F. A., enlisted April, 1862, as a private in Company G, Third Mississippi Cavalry, Adams' Brigade; paroled
May, 1865. Proposed for membership in this Association
by W. P. Gray and elected January 20, 1870; was editor of
the *Ledger* after the war, and also of the *Appeal* for a time;
afterward published a paper in Holly Springs and lives there
yet well advanced in years.

VACCARO, A. B., born near Genoa, Italy, in 1837, and
came to Memphis in 1852 and went into business with his
brothers; enlisted in McDonald's Battalion in the spring of
1861, going out at first in a sixty-days company; when that
disbanded he re-enlisted in Forrest's old regiment, and was
in the battle of Shiloh; after that he was detailed in the quartermaster's department and served in that capacity to the end
of the war, being with the army of Tennessee in all its campaigns in Kentucky, Louisiana, Alabama and Mississippi.
After the war resumed business successfully in Memphis. In
1867 married Miss Ida Bradford, daughter of Simon Bradford.

VACCARO, B., born near Genoa, Italy, in 1835; came to
Memphis in 1850 and engaged in business; enlisted in Company L, Captain E. A. Cole, One Hundred and Fifty-fourth
Tennessee, March, 1862; was in the battles of Shiloh, Perryville and Murfreesboro; wounded in the last named and disabled for ninety days; was in winter quarters at Shelbyville;
was in the battles of Chickamauga and Missionary Ridge; in
winter quarters at Dalton and on the Georgia campaign to
Atlanta, and in nearly all the principal fights under General
Johnston; was under Hood in the battles on Peachtree creek
July 20 and in the battle of July 22, and wounded severely
there the last day. Rejoined his regiment in time to be in
the battle of Franklin, and was in the fight and captured in

14

front of Nashville, along with the most of his command. After that was carried to Camp Chase, Ohio, and remained several months, when the war ended and he was released and sent home. After the battle of Shiloh he became a sergeant and served as such as long as in the army. Resumed business on Front Row, and has been actively and successfully engaged ever since. Was married in 1868 to Miss Celestina Sturla, and they have reared a family of five interesting children. Joined the Confederate Historical Association November 11, 1884.

VENN, FRANK H., enlisted at Holly Springs, Miss., May 25, 1861, as private in Company I, Nineteenth Mississippi Regiment; served in the Army of Virginia; took part in the battles of Williamsburg, Seven Pines and second Manassas; was in the campaign of General Lee in Maryland and Pennsylvania; was at the capture of Harper's Ferry and other engagements, and was wounded in one of the battles around Richmond, and paroled June, 1865. Joined the Confederate Historical Association September 9, 1869.

VANCE, R. H., son of the late Judge John W. Vance of Hernando, Miss., was born at Bowling Green, Ky., and with his parents removed to Hernando at an early age; went into mercantile life with his present partner, J. V. Johnston; enlisted in Company I, Captain J. B. Morgan, Twenty-ninth Mississippi Regiment, Walthall's, and was elected fifth sergeant, and in 1864 was made first lieutenant; was in the battles of Chickamauga, New Hope Church, Resaca, Peachtree creek, Atlanta and Franklin, and in numerous smaller engagements, particularly in the Georgia campaign, and was wounded July 9, 1864, at Chattahoochie river in front of Atlanta, and wounded the second time, under General Hood, in front of Nashville; was surrendered at Greensboro, N. C., on May 1, 1865, and paroled there. He was rarely ever absent from his command, except for short periods when wounded; saw much hard service, but came out cheerful, hopeful and ready for the other battles of life.

Returning home and to Memphis, Mr. Vance resumed bus-

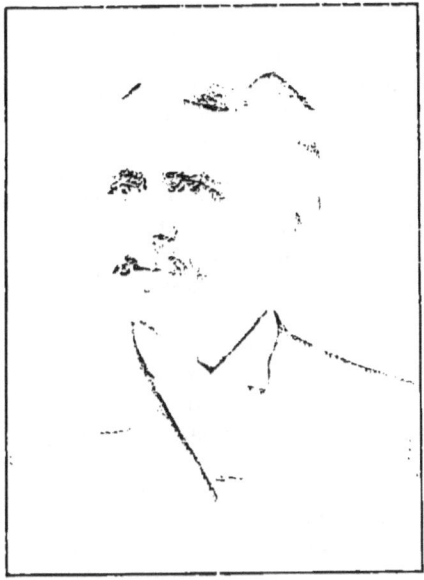

R. H. VANCE.

iness with his comrade and former partner, and they have been associated together most pleasantly and successfully ever since. He joined the C. H. A. July 15, 1869. He was married to Miss Mary Carroll, daughter of General William H. Carroll, February 5, 1877, and by this union they have two children—a son, Carroll, and daughter, Elise Vance. He became a member of the C. H. A. when it was first organized, and has taken an active part in the social and business affairs of the city, and has been exceedingly liberal in matters of charity and the general welfare. His success in life and high social position and natural geniality of character have enabled him to enjoy life and at the same time find greatest pleasure in doing good to others in a quiet, unostentatious manner, and the same can be said with equal truth of his life-long business partner.

VAUGHAN, A. J., born in Dinwiddie county, Va., May 10, 1830, and graduated at the Virginia Military Institute in 1851; went west and adopted civil engineering as a profession. While engaged in making a survey of the Hannibal & St. Joseph R. R. received the appointment of Deputy U. S. Surveyor of California, headquarters at Los Angeles, under Colonel Jack Hays, operated on the Kern river. In 1855 was appointed private secretary to Colonel Alfred Cummings of Georgia, then superintendent of Indian Affairs, who had been appointed on a commission to make a treaty with the Blackfeet and other tribes for the right of way for the Northern Pacific Railroad.

In 1856 he was married in Mississippi to Miss Martha Jane Hardaway of Virginia, his present wife, and was engaged in planting when the war broke out. Though a Union man, as soon as his native State, Virginia, and his adopted State, Mississippi, passed the ordinance of secession, he at once raised a company and tendered it to the Governor of Mississippi; but his company could not be received and was disbanded, many joining companies that had already been mustered into service.

About this time Governor Isham G. Harris of Tennessee called for 75,000 volunteers. He then united in forming a company at Moscow, Tenn., and was elected captain, and at the formation of the Thirteenth Tennessee, shortly thereafter at Jackson, he was elected lieutenant-colonel; served until after the battle of Belmont, when he was unanimously elected colonel of the regiment. At the reorganization of the army at Corinth he was re-elected colonel. As colonel of the regiment he fought at the battle of Shiloh; made the campaign into Kentucky under Kirby Smith; was engaged in the battle of Richmond, Ky., and was at the battle of Perryville, and fought in the battle of Murfreesboro.

In January, 1863, shortly after the battle of Murfreesboro, or Stone river, while the army was at Shelbyville, Tenn., the Thirteenth and One Hundred and Fifty-fourth Senior Tennessee Regiments were so reduced in numbers that they were consolidated. Colonel A. J. Vaughan of the Thirteenth was

GEN. A. J. VAUGHAN.

retained as colonel. Captain R. W. Pittman of the Thirteenth, who had been promoted already, was retained as lieutenant-colonel and Major John W. Dawson of the One Hundred and Fifty-fourth Senior Regiment was retained as major. Though these two regiments were consolidated, neither one ever lost its identity, and each was known to the close of the war as the One Hundred and Fifty-fourth Senior and Thirteenth Tennessee Regiments. From Belmont to Murfreesboro they had fought side by side on every battlefield. In daylight and in darkness, in victory or defeat, they had stood shoulder to shoulder. Each knew the worth and value of the other and both had a purpose in view, and that purpose, even to the extent of their lives, was to maintain the honor of Tennessee and to uphold the Confederacy. From this time forward to the close of the war the history of these two regiments was a common history; the glory of the one was the pride of the other, and neither ever lost hope until the Confederate banner went down forever.

In command of these regiments, Colonel Vaughan marched to Chattanooga, and fought in the battles of Lookout Mountain and Chickamauga, where the gallant Preston Smith was killed. He was then promoted on the field by President Davis in person, and assigned to Preston Smith's Brigade, which was composed of the following Tennessee regiments: Eleventh, Twelfth, Forty-seventh, Thirteenth, One Hundred and Fifty-fourth, and Twenty-ninth. They were the first troops to drive the enemy off the Missionary Ridge. He with the brigade was then ordered to reinforce Longstreet, who was at Knoxville, but before reaching there Longstreet was repulsed, and the brigade was ordered back to Missionary Ridge. He fought in the battle of Missionary Ridge, and the army was repulsed and driven back, but his brigade retired in perfect order. His next operations were in the memorable campaign from Dalton to Atlanta, where his brigade was engaged in every skirmish and engagement until it reached Vining station, just below Marietta, where on July 4, 1864, he lost a leg, which unfitted him for further service.

From first to last General Vaughan had eight horses shot under him in battle, and nearly all were killed. The wound which permanently disabled him was one of the freaks of war, and was received, as stated, on July 4, when by common consent hostilities were suspended, except some artillery practice, which was not seriously regarded. He was back on the third line in the rear, resting against a tree and chatting with some friends, when a shell fell and exploded immediately under his foot, tearing it off and making a hole in the ground big enough to have contained his whole body.

The devotion of General Vaughan to his men, and their love for him, as well as their heroism, patriotism and fidelity to the Southern cause, was illustrated by an incident which occurred while the army was in winter quarters at Dalton, Ga. While this formed perhaps a small part of the history of the Thirteenth Tennessee Regiment, it left a memory which will remain until the "shadows gather for the eternal night." The regiment was reduced to less than 200 men, and in generosity and love these few men determined to make their colonel (now promoted to brigadier-general) a present of a horse. It was a difficult matter to find such a horse as they wanted, but Dr. Yandell of Louisville, who belonged to the medical staff, had a magnificent Grey Eagle horse for which he asked $4000, but said that if the regiment wanted him for their commander, he would take $3000 for him. These few men, drawing $11 per month, with their ragged uniforms and living on half rations, agreed to buy the horse, and obstinately refused to allow any one outside of the regiment to give one cent. The money was scraped up among themselves and the present made. Captain Jerry Crook, Company I, Thirteenth Regiment, made the presentation speech, and Captain R. F. Lanier, Company G, on behalf of their commander, the reception speech. General Vaughan has lived to forget many things, but never will pass from his memory the gratitude he felt on that day when his war-worn soldiers in their ragged grey gathered around him to show their love and confidence. If nothing else, that act alone has made dear to his heart every soldier of the Thirteenth Tennessee Regiment.

General Vaughan removed to Memphis from Mississippi in 1873, and was elected Clerk of the Criminal Court in 1878, in which capacity he served two terms, this being the only civil office of importance he ever held. He joined this Association August 12, 1884, and is an enthusiastic ex-Confederate, and has attended national reunions of veterans at New Orleans, Birmingham, Houston and Richmond, and is now brigadier-general, commanding Second Brigade, Tennessee Division, U. C. V.; was one of the grand marshals at Richmond in June–July, 1896, and is chairman of the Battle Abbey committee for Tennessee, and in peace as in war is still a leader in the hearts of all his comrades and old friends.

WAGNER, A. E., private Company D, Sixteenth Mississippi Regiment, Harris' Brigade; entered the service early in 1861, and paroled in May, 1865. Proposed for membership by Henry Moode and J. C. Bennett and elected May 26, 1870.

WARD, B. F., enlisted March 27, 1861, in Company I, Ninth Mississippi; afterward was First Lieutenant in Company B, Forty-second Mississippi; attached to Joe A. Davis' Brigade, A. N. V., and was with Henderson's Scouts, Forrest's Cavalry, from March 20 to May 10, 1865; wounded three times—in the battle of Cold Harbor, Va., June 2, 1861, and twice in the entrenchments at Petersburg near the "crater" in 1864. He resigned as first lieutenant to accept the position as adjutant tendered him by Colonel W. G. Henderson of the Fifth Mississippi Regiment, General Chalmers' Brigade. Before he could reach that regiment his brother, Captain Albert G. Ward, was missing or killed at Franklin, and he chose to join Henderson's Scouts, and served in that company until the end of the war. His parole was dated Gainesville, Ala., May 10, 1865. He now (1896) lives at Marion, Ark. Joined the Confederate Historical Association several years ago.

WATSON, J. H., private in Company A, Corps of Cadets Virginia Military Institute; enlisted in May, 1864. The V. M. I. was adopted by the Confederate States as the national military academy, and sustained the same relation to the Confederacy that West Point does to the United States. The Corps of Cadets was in the service of the Confederacy as part of the regular army, but owing to the youthfulness of the cadets they were only called into active service in cases of emergency; paroled May, 1865. He became a member of this Association July 15, 1869; has practiced law with eminent success in Memphis for a number of years.

WALT, MARTIN, was born in Ohio and came to Memphis when a mere youth, and was captain of a steamboat at the age of 19 years. When the war broke out he was about of age, and went into the Confederate service with Captain Frank Gailor, of the old *Avalanche* staff, who was first on the staff of General Wm. H. Carroll and afterward transferred to the staff of General S. A. M. Wood of North Alabama. Major Gailor was killed at the battle of Perryville, October 8, 1862, and was succeeded by his assistant, Martin Walt, who was given the same rank. Major Walt served as quarter-

MAJ. MARTIN WALT.

master of division in the Army of Tennessee, and was for
two years on the staff of Major-General Pat Cleburne, and
was noted as a most business-like and efficient officer. He
had numerous stirring and trying experiences; among others
was that of his capture with his entire train in the rear of
General J. E. Johnston's army by Kilpatrick's raiding expedition in the summer of 1864. He was in the hands of the
Twenty-third Indiana Cavalry, held for twenty-four hours,
and then suddenly released by the approach of Confederate
cavalry. He was with the decimated army down to the end:
was captured at Lincolnton, N. C., and with fourteen hundred
others taken to Nashville and paroled there. After the surrender he returned to Memphis, where he has ever since been
in business, and is now (1896) a merchant on Front Row.
He married Miss Mary Trask in 1867. and has grown children. He joined this Association many years ago.

WATKINS, T. R., private in Company D, Sixth Tennessee Infantry; enlisted May 18, 1861; was wounded at the battle of Perryville and at Franklin; was captured at Franklin on Hood's retreat from Tennessee; was in prison at Columbus, Ohio, and at Point Lookout, Md., until June 4, 1865, when he was paroled. Joined the C. II. A. June 30, 1892.

WAYNESBURG, JOHN W., Company D, Harris' Zouave Cadets, One Hundred and Fifty-fourth Tennessee Regiment; entered service with the company at Memphis guarding the magazine the latter part of March, 1861; mustered into service April 26, 1861, at Randolph, Tenn., as orderly sergeant; was wounded first at the battle of Murfreesboro December 31, 1862, at Missionary Ridge September 20, 1863, and at Resaca, Ga., in May, 1864; participated in every battle of the Army of Tennessee, beginning with Belmont, Mo.; he was paroled at Greensboro, N. C., April 26, 1865, being one of only two of the company of ninety-two mustered in that was present at the surrender. He assisted in forming the Confederate Relief and Historical Association in Memphis in 1866 and was a member of Company A, Confederate Veterans. Died suddenly January 3, 1897, esteemed and respected in life and regretted in his passing away by his comrades and a large circle of friends.

WEAR, B. II., enlisted July 12, 1861, as a private in Company C, Twentieth Mississippi, and was afterward transferred to Company G, Grenada Rifles, Fifteenth Mississippi Regiment; was captured at Fort Donelson February 14, 1862, and wounded at Peachtree creek July 20, 1864; paroled at Greensboro, N. C., May 5, 1865. Has since been connected with the printing business and press of Memphis, and for the past few years has been successfully running a newspaper in Virginia. Joined the Confederate Historical Association May 8, 1894.

WEBBER, ALBERT, was drum-major of the Fifteenth Tennessee Regiment; consolidated with the Thirty-seventh Tennessee near Wartrace, Tenn., in 1863; enlisted April 23, 1861; was in the battles of Belmont, Shiloh, Perryville, Murfreesboro, Hoover's Gap, Chickamauga, Missionary Ridge,

Buzzard's Roost, and all the engagements from Dalton to Atlanta, and also at Jonesboro, where he was injured by the explosion of a shell; was with Hood in his campaign into Tennessee, and at the battles of Franklin, and in front of Nashville; was never sick, or absent from his command except on furlough, when he became separated from the army in the last few months of the war; was paroled in April, 1865; settled and married in Fayette county, where he has been and is yet a successful merchant and farmer, and has reared a large family. Admitted to the Confederate Historical Association February 18, 1896.

WEBB, JNO. L. ("Cap"), private in Hickory Rifles. One Hundred and Fifty-fourth Tennessee; enlisted April 28, 1861; paroled May, 1865. Admitted to the Confederate Historical Association February 12, 1895.

WHEAT, REV. J. T., Chaplain at Forrest Hill, N. C., 1864; retired only at the end of the war; he was rector of a church in Memphis after the war. Proposed for membership in this Association by W. A. Goodman and General Patton Anderson, and elected May 12, 1870. Died many years ago.

WHITE, MOSES, was born in Knoxville and educated at the East Tennessee University: came to Memphis and practiced law a few years; returned to Knoxville and joined Carroll's Regiment as a private; was elected lieutenant-colonel, and when Colonel Carroll was appointed brigadier-general he was promoted to full Colonel of the Thirty-seventh Tennessee, and at Corinth was elected colonel without opposition. Colonel White reached Mill Springs, Ky., January 18, 1862, in time to share a part of the disaster of the battle of Fishing creek the next day. He was with his regiment in the battle of Perryville, and was several times in Kentucky and Tennessee, in command of the brigade when Brigadier-General Johnston was in command of the division; was severely wounded in the battle of Murfreesboro, and in the summer of 1863 the Fifteenth and Thirty-seventh Tennessee were consolidated and Col. R. C. Tyler of the former was assigned command of both regiments. Colonel White was sent off on detached service at various points, and was in command at Eatonton, Ga.; was captured by Sherman's army and sent North in the hold of a ship with many others, all badly fed, treated and crowded together. While being transferred from one prison to another, to be held as a hostage, he jumped from a train at night in Delaware, reached Baltimore after great hardships, worked his way through the lines, and reported to General Marcus J. Wright at Grenada, Miss., just before the surrender. After that he practiced law in Memphis. He joined the C. H. A. July 15, 1869, and made one of the orations at an annual reunion of ex-Confederates at Elmwood Cemetery. He returned to Knoxville, and has lived there many years.

WHITE, R. T., private in Company E, Seventh Tennessee; enlisted in May, 1861; after consolidation was known as the Fifth Confederate Regiment; was in the battles of Belmont, Shiloh, Perryville, Murfreesboro and the various battles to Kennesaw mountain; paroled in May, 1865. Admitted to C. H. A. November 4, 1895.

WHITE, J. H., enlisted in Company A, Thirty-second Mississippi, in March, 1862; served in Lowry's Brigade, and was paroled at Corinth, Miss., at the end of the war.

WHITMORE, E., was born September 25, 1833, in Fayette county, Tenn., and was in railroad service before the war as conductor; enlisted in Company A, Foute's Battalion of Infantry, early in 1861, and served about one year; was sworn into Company L, Seventh Tennessee Cavalry, in August, '62; served in the brigades of Generals Villepigue, W. H. Jackson, Chalmers, Rucker and Alexander Campbell, and was in raids under Van Dorn and Armstrong; was slightly wounded in the fight at Medon, and the next day his horse was shot three times under him, but was not killed; was with his regiment directly under Forrest from November, 1863, until the end of the war, and was in all of its campaigns, except two months early in 1864, when he had pneumonia. The Seventh Tennessee was a great favorite with General Forrest, and therefore saw a great deal of hard and perilous service. Comrade

Whitmore was paroled at Gainesville, Ala.; from there he rode to Brownsville, where he had married early in the war. Afterward he founded the Memphis *Public Ledger*, and was its proprietor for many years. He joined this Association in 1895; became a member of Company A, and attended the late reunion at Richmond.

WIGGS, W. B.. Captain and Chief of Artillery on General M. J. Wright's staff; entered service May 15, 1861; captured at Jackson. Miss.; paroled May 12, 1865. Elected a member of this Association upon his own statement and application July 1, 1869.

WILLIAMS, L. G., was born September 1, 1844, in Desoto county, near Hernando, Miss.; was mustered into the Confederate service at Jackson, Miss. (his home then), November 4, 1861, as Second Sergeant Company A, Third Mississippi Battalion, and surrendered at Greensboro, N. C., May 1, 1865, as Captain of Company F, Eighth Battalion, Mississippi Infantry. After the battle of Shiloh the battalion became the Thirty-third Mississippi, then called Hardcastle's Mississippi Regiment for a short time, then properly numbered the Forty-fifth, and was so known until the War Department ordered it to resume its old and first name, the Third Mississippi Battalion Infantry. Captain Williams was in the battles of Shiloh. Perryville, Chickamauga, Missionary Ridge, and Ringgold Gap; also Atlanta, Franklin and Nashville, besides a number of skirmishes almost equivalent to battles. He was wounded at Ringgold Gap in the head, at Golgotha and elsewhere. At the surrender the regiment was known as the Eighth Mississippi, having reorganized at Smithfield, N. C., where all that was left of the Third Battalion, the Thirty-second Mississippi, Fifth Mississippi and the Eighth Mississippi, were consolidated into one battalion and named, in honor of the Eighth Mississippi Regiment, the Eighth Mississippi Battalion. Captain Williams had the skeletons of the Third Battalion and Thirty-second Mississippi in his company (F), about 34 men, hardly a modern drill team. He joined the C. H. A. June 13, 1894, and became a member of Company A, Confederate Veterans.

WILLIAMS, CLAUDE, private Company E, First Tennessee Infantry; enlisted April, 1861; was captured five times and escaped the last time from Camp Morton, Ind.; was transferred to Henley's Alabama Legion in January, 1864; when he escaped the last time he got as far south as Kentucky. In Louisville heard of Sam Quantrell near Crab Orchard Springs; joined his command and was with it until the end of the war; could never get out of Kentucky after the escape from Camp Morton.

WILLIAMSON, R. C., born November 4, 1836, at Covington, Tenn., and grew up in Tipton county; received a liberal education, and lived at Somerville; enlisted in Company D, Sixth Tennessee Regiment, and was elected second lieutenant, with W. M. R. Johns as captain; mustered into the service of Tennessee at Jackson, May 15, 1861. The regiment was mustered into Confederate service at Union City and placed under General Cheatham, in his first brigade. The command moved into Missouri; thence to Columbus, Ky., and spent the winter of 1862 there. The company went into the battle of Shiloh eighty men strong; lost eight killed and eighteen wounded. Among the wounded was Captain Johns. Lieutenant Williamson took command of the company. May 15 the company was reorganized and mustered into the service for the war. R. C. Williamson was elected captain, and his company and regiment participated in all or nearly all the great battles and skirmishing under Generals Bragg, Johnston and Hood, and finally surrendered with General Johnston at Bentonville, N. C. Dr. Watkins mentions in his unpublished diary that one day shortly before the battle of Missionary Ridge, when the regiment was on Lookout Mountain, Captain Williamson, seeing some foragers down in the valley, took five men off duty, made a sudden attack upon a heavy detachment of infantry, drove them off and captured their wagons. The command spent the winter of 1863–64 at Dalton, and was in all the fighting from there to Atlanta and Jonesboro and lost many men. Captain Williamson was wounded at the latter place and was detailed to go into West Tennessee. He rejoined the command after Hood came out

MAJ. R. C. WILLIAMSON.

of Tennessee and in the last days of the Confederacy was promoted (see Lindsley's Annals) to the rank of major and was in command of a consolidated regiment, a mere skeleton of less than one hundred men, at the surrender at Greensboro, N. C. After incredible hardships he and seven other men of the old company reached Memphis via East Tennessee, Nashville and the river. They rented one big room in the old Worsham House and remained until they could see friends, secure a little money and change their old gray suits for citizens' clothes. Then they returned to Somerville—8 men— all that was left of the original 104 of Company D. Major Williamson engaged in the practice of law, removed to Memphis, married Miss Delia Talbot, of a prominent old family, soon after the war, and was prominent in Masonry and many affairs. He was a chivalric, high-toned man, devoted to family, friends and duty. He died January 23, 1886, leaving a wife, two sons and two daughters. Became a member of this Association July 15, 1869.

WILLINS, JOHN T., born in Brooklyn, New York, July 5, 1841; came to Memphis in February, 1858, and entered the house of Orgill Bros. & Co.; enlisted in the One Hundred and Fifty-fourth Tennessee Regiment April, 1861; served with the Army of Tennessee about two years, then transferred to the Trans-Mississippi Department and served as chief clerk with Major John N. Norris, chief quartermaster under Major General S. B. Maxey, commanding the district of the Indian Territory, with headquarters at Fort Towson, Cherokee Nation. Under an order issued by General E. Kirby Smith at Shreveport, La., August 9, 1864, "Captain John T. Willins, A. Q. M. agent," was subsequently assigned to duty with Major Norris at Doaksville, Cherokee Nation, where he served until after the surrender; was paroled at Shreveport August 1, 1865, by Brigadier General George L. Andrews, U. S. A.; returned to Memphis and resumed business the same month, and for more than twenty years was a managing partner. In 1868 he married Miss Lizzie O. Nelson, daughter of Colonel Thomas A. Nelson. They had seven children, two of them daughters, and all survived him. He was one of the early members of the Confederate R. and H. A., a member and officer of Calvary Episcopal Church, a devoted husband and father, a good neighbor and citizen, and in every sense a true man. He died on January 28, 1892, aged fifty years and six months.

WILSON, T. E., born at Fort Smith, Ark., January 1, 1850; was a private in McCulloch's Brigade, Trans-Mississippi Department; went in the service at the age of 11 years and was with Ben McCulloch when he was killed at Pea Ridge; afterward went to General Henry E. McCulloch and remained with him as a courier until the end of the war; was never regularly enlisted on account of extreme youth, but served throughout the war. Admitted to this Association August 14, 1894. The following is a copy of an original letter he has in his possession:

CORPUS CHRISTI, TEXAS, Jan. 14, 1891.

Mr. Thos. E. Wilson, ex-Confederate Courier:

DEAR SIR—After your reference to your father's services with my chief quartermaster, Major W. G. King, I readily

T. E. WILSON.

call you to mind as the active courier and messenger boy soldier who served at my headquarters as such while I was in
command at Bonham, Texas, during the latter portion of the
Confederate war, and that although only a boy, I could and
did always rely implicitly upon you in carrying out written
orders promptly or delivering verbal messages intelligently
and faithfully; and thus remembering, I congratulate you on
living to become a man of family, and ask God's blessings
upon you and every member thereof.

Your friend,   HENRY E. McCULLOCH,
Ex-Brigadier-General C. S. A.

Mr. Wilson came to Memphis in 1873 and has been in business here since; he was married to Miss Mollie Murray in
Memphis in 1879, and they have a son and daughter.

WILROY, C. W., enlisted June, 1861, as a private in Com-
pany D, Blythe's Mississippi Battalion; was transferred to the
Forty-fourth Mississippi and to Henderson's Scouts; paroled
May 10, 1865. Joined C. H. A. June 13, 1894.

15

WILKERSON, W. D., enlisted May 28, 1861, as a private in Company A, Thirteenth Tennessee Infantry, and transferred to Company D, Sixth Tennessee, that summer; fought through the war and was paroled at Greensboro, N. C., April 28, 1865. Joined the C. H. A. June 13, 1894.

WINCHESTER, GEO. W., son of Major-General James Winchester of the old regular army, and prominently identified with the early history of Memphis; served on the staff of General W. B. Bate during the war; practiced law afterward here, and died several years ago. He became a member of this Association July 15, 1869.

WINFREE, SAMUEL, enlisted April 4, 1861, as a private in the Fourth Tennessee Infantry; served in Cheatham's Division; when the war ended was sergeant of engineers; surrendered with the army of General Jos. E. Johnston at Charlotte, N. C., in April, 1865. Joined this Association June 13, 1894.

WINSTON, W. B., First Lieutenant Company C, Seventh Tennessee Cavalry; enlisted August 9, 1861, in Logwood's Battalion. In 1863 and part of '64 commanded General Chalmers' escort, for which purpose Company C was detached; was wounded twice—at Harrisburg, Miss., July 14, 1864, and in front of Columbia, Tenn., November 25, 1864; was captured at Lamar, Miss., in November, 1862, and released the following month. After the wound at Columbia, was disabled completely, the shot being through the head, and was not recovered from until six months after the war; paroled in May, 1865; has been for many years a leading physician of the city. Admitted to the C. H. A. April 9, 1895.

WITHERS, R. Q., born in Marshall county, Miss., November 7, 1845; enlisted for twelve months in the Seventeenth Regiment, Mississippi Volunteers, in May, 1861, and in the Army of Northern Virginia until September, 1862; was discharged as under age; enlisted again in the Third Mississippi Cavalry in February, 1863; promoted to second lieutenant in October or November, same year. This command was with Chalmers' Division of Cavalry much of the time; was

on detached service at the end; paroled at Grenada, Miss., in April or May, 1865. Joined the C. H. A. June 13, 1894.

WOLF, FRED., born in Dieburg, Hesse Darmstadt, Germany, in 1835; came to New York city in 1851, and to Memphis in 1859; joined the Washington Rifles and was made second sergeant of the company, which became a part of the Fifteenth Tennessee; participated in the battle of Shiloh; after that was made quartermaster-sergeant; went through the campaign into Kentucky and back to Middle Tennessee. In the summer of 1863 the Fifteenth and Thirty-seventh Tennessee Regiments were consolidated near Hoover's Gap, and he went back to his company. Colonel R. C. Tyler had him appointed by the Secretary of War as A. Q. M., with the rank of captain, and he still has that commission (1896). He was at the battles of Chickamauga and Missionary Ridge; was in winter quarters at Dalton, and on the campaign from Dalton to Atlanta, having charge of all the ambulances of Bate's Division, acquitting himself with the highest credit under perilous and trying circumstances. At Tuscumbia, Ala., he was ordered to report to General Lawton in Richmond, who assigned him to General McCausland's Brigade, with which he served until the end. Captain Wolf was surrendered and paroled at Lynchburg, Va., one day after General Lee's surrender at Appomattox. He rode to Bristol, East Tennessee, sold his horse and fine saddle for $50, and worked his way slowly through to Memphis. He became an active member of the old Confederate Relief and Historical Association at an early day, and has been a member of Company A, Confederate Veterans, from its organization, and was with the company on its trips to Chattanooga, Richmond and elsewhere.

WOOD, JOHN W., enlisted March 1, 1861, in Company F, Twelfth Mississippi Regiment, Harris' Brigade; was commissioned as captain March 4, 1861, and served in the Army of Northern Virginia until the close of the war.

WOODSON, H. M., enlisted March 10, 1862, at the age of 17 years, while attending school in Mississippi, and was transferred to Company H, Thirteenth Tennessee Regiment,

Vaughan's Brigade, about February or March, 1864; was in about twenty-seven battles, not to speak of the almost daily fighting from Dalton to Atlanta; after that was assigned to lighter duty on account of his health. The only furlough he ever had was issued for sixty days by a surgeon at Columbus, Ga., on the 13th of April, 1865, four days after Lee's surrender; was paroled at Montgomery, Ala., May 10, 1865, and still has his parole. some railroad transportation and other cherished relics of that period. Returned to Germantown, married there, but has lived in Memphis many years. Became a member of this Association about the year 1891.

WOOLDRIDGE, OSCAR, enlisted in the Memphis Light Dragoons, Company A, Seventh Tennessee, September 25, 1862, just in time to take part in the furious attack at Davis' Bridge, Miss. He was in the battles of Corinth, October 4 and 5, 1862, Ripley, Old Lamar, Oxford and Coffeeville, and took part in the capture of Holly Springs, December 20, 1862, and was in the engagements at Davis' Mills and Bolivar December 21 and 24, 1862. In the spring of 1863 the company was engaged in the Vicksburg campaign; from thence it went to Georgia and was actively engaged in front of Sherman in the Atlanta campaign; from Georgia it went to Middle Tennessee with Hood, and the young soldier saw further severe fighting at Lawrenceburg, Campbellville, Rally Hill, Hurt's X Roads, Mount Carmel, Spring Hill, Franklin, Murfreesboro, Lynnville, Richland Creek, Anthony's Hill and Sugar creek, and in the engagements during the Wilson raid : he surrendered with his company at Gainesville, Ala., May 11, 1865. In all these trying days the young trooper bore himself as a hero. Cool, brave and determined, he was a very type of the Confederate veteran of that day; clean of life, proud, generous to a fault, he was an ideal messmate, and as a soldier worthy the race from which he sprang. He quitted the camp without an enemy, and though long since gone to a better home, his memory lingers green in the hearts of those who knew and loved him best in time of war. He joined the Confederate R. and H. A. September 1, 1870, and died several years afterward.

WOOLDRIDGE, EGBERT, enlisted March, 1862, in Company L, Maynard Rifles, One Hundred and Fifty-fourth Tennessee Regiment, for twelve months; was very young, a mere lad, and was under conscriptive age at the expiration of the time for which he was mustered into the service; he was then entitled to and received an honorable discharge and enlisted in the cavalry, joining the Bluff City Grays, Captain James Edmondson. His first captain, E. A. Cole, says of him: "If such a thing be possible, he was brave to a fault, always ready to meet the enemy and went into battle cheerfully and with alacrity; in other words, he was a good soldier and never shirked his duty; he was very companionable, with unexceptionable habits and noted for his extreme modesty. With credit and honor to himself he participated while in my command in the battles of Shiloh, Richmond, Ky., Perryville and Murfreesboro." After the surrender returned to Memphis, engaged in business and joined the C. R. and H. A. September 1, 1870: died several years ago.

In this connection it may be added that Oscar and Egbert Wooldridge had a brother, Charles A. Wooldridge, who belonged to the Hickory Rifles, One Hundred and Fifty-fourth Tennessee, a gallant soldier, who was killed, and fell into the arms of Captain Wynne Cannon at Peachtree creek, in front of Atlanta, July 20, 1864.

Another brother, W. H. Wooldridge, still living and an active business man, was too young to go into the army, but not too young to render valuable services in supplying his brothers with horses and clothing for several years, and in supplying other soldiers with medicines, clothing, etc. Being a mere boy he could run through the picket lines successfully and was really more useful than many who were at the front. C. P. Wooldridge, a cousin, belonged to the Hickory Rifles, and Alex. Wooldridge, another cousin, was a member of the Maynard Rifles, One Hundred and Fifty-fourth Tennessee, making in all six young Wooldridges in the Confederate service.

WRIGHT, JESSE C., Captain Company H, Seventeenth Mississippi Regiment, Army of North Virginia, enlisted May

27, 1861; started out as corporal of Company H; was captured at Farmville, Va., April 6, 1865; released at the end of the war. Joined the C. H. A. October, 1894.

WRIGHT, J. R., born in Norfolk, Va., December 25, 1841; enlisted April 18, 1861, in Grandy's Battery, Norfolk Blues, as a private; was made a sergeant soon after (his only promotion); was stationed at Sewell's Point, Va., and took part in the famous fight in Hampton Roads between the Merrimac and Monitor; at the evacuation of Norfolk joined the Army of North Virginia and followed Lee in all his campaigns; was at Fredericksburg, Chancellorsville, Spottsville, Gettysburg, and from the Wilderness to Petersburg, where he was captured April 2, 1865; sent to Point Lookout, Md.; released June 23, 1865, and returned to Norfolk; came to Memphis in 1868, where he still resides; joined the C. H. A. June 13, 1894, and became a member of Company A, Confederate Veterans; attended with it the reunion at Richmond, Va., where he met many old comrades and friends after long years of separation.

WRIGHT, LUKE E., enlisted June 4, 1861, in Company G, One Hundred and Fifty-fourth Tennessee Senior Regiment; became second lieutenant of artillery attached to the division commanded by Generals Breckinridge and Bate; was in the principal engagements of the West under Bragg, Johnston and Hood; was wounded at the battle of Jonesboro, Ga.; after the war was admitted to the bar; married a daughter of Admiral Semmes, who was an early president of the Ladies' Confederate Memorial Association; was elected Attorney-General of the Criminal Court of Shelby county and served eight years. Is recognized as one of the leading lawyers of Memphis and of the State.

WRIGHT, MARCUS J., born in McNairy county, Tenn.; practiced law in Memphis; was elected lieutenant-colonel of the One Hundred and Fifty-fourth Senior Tennessee Regiment April 4, 1861; commanded his regiment in the battles of Belmont and Shiloh, and served with the rank of lieutenant-colonel on the staff of Major-General B. F. Cheatham

the battle of Perryville; commissioned brigadier-general ;ember 13, 1862; assigned to the command of Hanson's .ntucky Brigade January 10, 1863, and relinquished this to take command of Donelson's splendid brigade, which he led in the battles of Chickamauga and Missionary Ridge; was twice wounded; afterward commanded the district and post t Atlanta and post at Macon, Ga. He was assigned to the command of the district of North Mississippi and West Tennessee, with headquarters at Grenada, Miss., February 3, 1865, and remained there until the surrender. After that he was connected with the press of Memphis and St. Louis. On the 1st of July, 1878, he was appointed by the Secretary of War to collect and prepare for publication by the government such records of the South relating to the war as might be available, and his services have been continued ever since. He has contributed much to secure a fair and impartial history of the civil war. General Wright comes of the best pioneer and Revolutionary ancestors and exhibits their sterling quali- *ies and brilliant gifts. He has been married twice and has a happy family and home in Washington, and still claims his citizenship in Memphis. Joined the C. R. & H. A. July 15, 1869.

WYNNE, J. W., enlisted in Company B, Third Texas ..valry, May, 1861; was commissioned as captain in May, 362; served in General Ross' command; discharged May, ^5. Joined the C. H. A. in March, 1891.

YOUNG, A. A., born January 5, 1847, in Shell county, ..nn.; enlisted October 1, 1863, in Company G, Third M s- .issippi Cavalry; served in Forrest's command and was paroled May 18, 1865, at Gainesville, Ala. Admitted to the C. H. A. December 11, 1894.

YOUNG, J. P., enlisted in Company A, Seventh Tennessee Cavalry, November 10, 1864, at Florence, Ala.; served in Rucker's and Chalmers' Brigades; was first for several months at Hardee's and Cheatham's headquarters and then with Com- ny A, Fourth Tennessee Infantry, Strahl's Brigade, but ng under age was never sworn into the infantry and was ...st regularly enlisted with the Seventh Tennessee Cavalry, and was with Forrest's command during the march into and in covering the retreat of Hood's army out of Tennessee, and surrendered with it at Gainesville, Ala., May 11, 1865 ; at the beginning of the war was an invalid ; as soon as able was engaged for a year or more in supplying the boys in camp with horses, equipments, clothing, etc., cutting telegraph wires, and such general Confederate deviltry as a boy could do. After the war he read law and was admitted to the bar; was connected with the Memphis *Avalanche* as city editor at one time ; wrote and published a valuable book, " The History of the Seventh Tennessee Cavalry"; admitted to this Association in 1884 and elected secretary in 1894, and has since served as such; was elected a justice of the peace in 1888 and has since been a prominent member of the County Court of Shelby.

NAMES WITHOUT SKETCHES.

The following are names of members appearing upon the books of the Association, mostly in early times, without record as to services. Some of them have died, others moved away, and still others are here yet, but were not reached by the writer and compiler of this book. Being on the rolls at all, is *prima-facie* evidence that they were all good soldiers and regularly admitted :

Adams, T. P.	Callahan, Daniel	Dickenson, B. F.
Auman, W. C.	Charles, Jas. L.	Duncan, R. P.
Baker, P. J.	Chisman, John R.	Edmondson, J. H.
Barth, Wm. G.	Collier, R. A.	Estes, Thos. H.
Bateman, Dr. R. P.	Collier, W. A.	Ewell, Gen. R. T.
Bate, James H.	Cook, John C.	Farris, James B.
Bell, D.	Colby, E. E.	Farrow, Chas. S.
Beatty, H. K.	Conner, James	Gammon, S. R.
Belcher, E. L. dead	Cox, James O.	Garvey, Thos.
Bridges, J. C.	Cressman, W.	Galloway, T. S.
Brown, Gen. W. M.	Curtis, H. R.	Gibson, John R.
Brown, E. H.	Darden, Thos.	Greene, Gen. Colton
Bulkley, Maj. dead	Davidson, Thos.	Hamblett, J. G.
Burnell, H. D.	Davis, Com. I. N.	Hampton, S. W.
Cannon, W. G.	Dailey, E. H.	Harper, W. F.

Hatcher, John S.
Heath, J. W.
Hill, J. L.
Holender, Ben.
Hoy, K. E.
Humes, A. R.
Hutchinson, R. B.
Hyman, Jas. H.
Johnston, A. H.
Johnson, T. N.
Jones, W. E.
Jordan, R. D.
Kealhofer, C. W.
Kean, Robert P.
Keefe, J. M.
Lawrence, J. B.
Lawler, John T.
Lamb, Lawrence
Lake, L. S.
Lewis, Jere
Logan, Marcellus
Lockey, W. B.
Matthews, S. W.
Martin, W. P.
Mason, R. M.
Maury, A. J.
Marye, Lawrence S.
Malone, P. C.
McClung, W. P.

McCulloch, Alex.
McGhee, J. P.
McHugh, J. A.
McKinney, W. B.
Miller, J. H.
Mingea, O. T.
Moode, Henry
Moores, J. W.
Murtaugh, Jno. D.
Nuttall, Dr. J. H.
Pain, G. N.
Parker, S. B.
Randle, J. D.
Pettigrew, J. M.
Pickett, W. D.
Pointer, Wm. B.
Poindexter, W. B.
Powell, J. R.
Powers, P. S.
Rand, E. G.
Rhett, T. M. S.
Richmond, B.
Rives, L. O.
Robins, Thos. D.
Robertson, F. W.
Rogers, W. S.
Safford, W. B.
Severson, Maj. C. S.
Sengstack, C. P.

Sherman, Victor
Sheeler, David
Simmons, W. F.
Smith, C. F.
Smith, W. E.
Smith, W. Spot.
Smith, Gen. J. A.
Stanley, T. L.
Styles, M.
Somerville, John
Tharpe, Capt. P. H.
Thomas, C. M. B.
Titus, John F.
Turnbull, Frank
Vance, John
Vance, T. W.
Ward, S. L.
Wenn, W. H.
Wheaton, Wm. H.
Wheeler, W.
White, B. F.
Wicks, Col. M. J.
Wilton, H. C.
Winchester, B.
Wilson, T. T.
Williamson, W. B.
Wright, W. H.

NOTE.—The foregoing lists and sketches embrace nearly all the names of those who have at any time belonged to the Confederate Historical Association from 1869 down to the end of 1896. A few, overlooked or prepared too late for classification, appear in the following pages, together with names and sketches of some well-known Confederates who never joined the Association. It is proper to say here, that while the conditions of membership were not laid down rigidly under the first charter, very strict regulations were prescribed under the new charter of 1884, which have been enforced ever since. All application papers have to be made out in regular form and referred to a committee for investigation and report a month later. Hence the present membership easily comes within the requirements of the United Confederate Veterans, with which this Association became identified several years ago. In going over records covering a period of nearly thirty years, and adding facts derived from other sources, it is to be expected that some omissions and minor errors would appear. These, if found, it is hoped will not mar the harmony or detract from the value of a book intended as a compilation of personal and historic data, to be preserved by ex-Confederates and their descendants and friends.

BALCH, ROBERT LANGDON, born in Virginia; he was a son of Rev. Thomas Bloomer Balch, who married a first cousin of General Robert E. Lee, and was a grandson of Rev. Stephen Bloomer Balch of Georgetown, D. C., who was a captain in the Revolutionary war in Georgia, though a native of Maryland. R. L. Balch lived in Memphis before the war, and was a man of means; enlisted as a private in Forrest's old regiment; was elected major just before the battle of Shiloh, and served until September, 1862, when Lieutenant-Colonel D. C. Kelley resigned and was succeeded by Major Balch. Major Rambaut, of General Forrest's staff, just before he died, spoke of Colonel Balch in the highest terms as a soldier and gentleman. In 1863 he was wounded in Middle Tennessee, lost health and spirits, was granted a leave of absence indefinitely, and dropped out of the service, as far as activity was concerned. After the war he was assassinated on his plantation, a few miles west of Memphis, in Critten-den county, Ark., when he was perhaps little over 40 years old. He never married.

BARNES, ROBERT WEAKLEY, oldest son of Bartley Marshall Barnes (major State militia); was born near Nash-ville, Tenn., August 4, 1832; enlisted with his father and two brothers in Munroe's Arkansas Cavalry in June, 1861. In July, 1863, was made captain of Company A, Munroe's Regi-ment; was in all the battles in which his regiment engaged—Helena, Poison Springs, Saline, through Price's last raid in Missouri, and was captured before Kansas City. He walked, with other prisoners, to St. Louis; was confined in Gratiot street prison; then sent to Johnson's Island; was released on June 16, 1865. On September 3, 1865, he was married to Miss Mary Jane Brownfield, at Van Buren, Ark.; removed to Memphis, Tenn., and engaged in the cotton business. He was the father of ten children, two of whom were twins. In the epidemic of 1878 he lost one son, Frank Bartley Barnes. He died January 20, 1885, leaving a wife and nine children.

BEARD, Hon. W. D., born in Wilson county, Tenn.; in May, 1862, he joined the Confederate army and was assigned to duty on the staff of General A. P. Stewart as brigade quartermaster; was in the Kentucky campaign under Bragg. At the battle of Murfreesboro, although not required to be with the troops, he performed field duty for General Stewart during the entire day. Colonel W. B. Ross of General Stewart's staff received his death wound at Major Beard's side, and was assisted to the ambulance by him. In the latter part of the summer of 1863 he was transferred to the Trans-Mississippi Department and reported to General Joe Shelby, who directed him to report to Colonel S. B. Jackman, then organizing a brigade. He was assigned to duty as assistant adjutant-general to Colonel Jackman, and did active work in this capacity both in Arkansas and Missouri. He was with the command of General Price in his move into Missouri in 1864. In the battle of Westport he was severely wounded in his thigh, and carries with him to this day the ball. He was brought out of Missouri in a wagon on the retreat of the army. In the spring of 1865, being still unfit for service, he was assigned to duty by General Kirby Smith, first at Houston and then at Huntsville, Texas, in charge of clothing, camp and garrison equipments. In June, 1865, was paroled at Galveston, Texas; from there went to St. Louis, and then returned to Memphis, practiced his profession and attained high rank at the bar. Several years ago he was elected Chancellor of the Chancery Court of Shelby county, Tenn., and has been recently elected to the Supreme bench of Tennessee, and is now one of the Justices of that court. Judge Beard had several brothers in the Confederate army. One was Captain James H. Beard, mentioned on page 180, Serial 51, War Records, by Colonel J. A. Smith, Third and Fifth Confederate Regiments, as being " the best and bravest soldier I ever saw." Judge Beard married a few years after the war, and has two grown sons, one of whom is Clerk and Master of the First Chancery Court of Shelby county.

BETHEL, W. D., born in St. Mary's parish, La., February 2, 1840; in 1860 married a daughter of Jerome B. Pillow of Maury county, Tenn.: he joined the Confederate army and served on the staff of General Gideon J. Pillow: lived in Memphis several years and reared an interesting family; was elected and served as President of the Taxing District; now lives (1896) in Denver, Col.

BRENT, JAMES, a well-known newspaper worker and printer of Memphis for twenty years past; was born in Maryland, grew up in Mississippi, and entered the service in 1861 from Vicksburg in J. C. Kline's company of cavalry, which became General Hardee's escort. After Shiloh he was one of 100 men detailed from General Wirt Adams' command to make a raid into Middle Tennessee under Captain (afterward General) John H. Morgan. He was in continuous service through the war, except when disabled by wounds, and was in many engagements under Forrest and other cavalry leaders. One instance of his bravery will illustrate many others: At the crossing of Estanaula river, near Calhoun, Ga., in 1864, when McPherson's corps flanked southward on Sherman's right, Jos. E. Johnston resisted the movement to allow his forces to retreat, and the battle of Resaca resulted. A four-gun battery under Lieutenant Beauregard—a son of the renowned general of the same name—fought a heavy column of the attacking force at close quarters, until every horse of the battery, and nearly all of the men, had fallen. Lieutenant Beauregard undertook to save his guns by drawing them off by hand, but his surviving force was too small and volunteers were called for. Mr. Brent, with others of Hardee's escort, moved to the work, and after hard labor pulled three guns of the battery across the bridge spanning the Estanaula, the other cannon being lost. As the pieces rescued were dragged to the south side of the river cheers went up from those who witnessed the incident. General Beauregard, a looker-on, ran up and gathered his son in close embrace as the lad—barely 20 years of age—crossed over to the south side, tears dropping from his eyes at the loss of one of his guns. General Johnston was an eye-witness of this act of heroism, and in general orders complimented Hardee's men for the gallant deed.

BREWER, A. CLARKE, born in Henry county, Va., in 1843, and came with his father to Chattanooga in 1856; was at college on Lookout Mountain; enlisted in a company raised

by Frank W. Walker; the company went with the regiment
to Cumberland Gap and saw service around there; was in the
battle of Fishing creek January 19, 1862, and was in the
battle of Shiloh, where the Nineteenth Tennessee took part
in the capture of Prentiss' Division and pushed on toward the
river, and Mr. Brewer believes that but for the order to halt,
the Federal army would have been driven into the river or
captured; he was wounded in the second day's fight at Shiloh.
He was in the battle of Baton Rouge; fought under Van
Dorn at Corinth, under Loring at Baker's creek, and in the
various engagements around Jackson, Miss.; was captured
near Vicksburg while on a scout in the latter part of 1864,
and was a prisoner at the time of the surrender; came to
Memphis and engaged afterward in planting down the river,
but is again a citizen of Memphis.

CAPERS, R. S., was at college at Clinton, Miss., when the
war began; came to Memphis and at the age of 14 years
joined Forrest's old regiment under Captain Fred Rogers,
went all through the war, and was in nearly all of Forrest's
fights; was wounded seriously in the shoulder at Shiloh and
disabled for four months; was also wounded at West Point
and Tishomingo creek and at the battle of Franklin. He was
captured thirty miles east of Memphis by Steger's command
on a raid, but released on account of his youthful appearance.
Another time when he came into Memphis to get a horse he
was picked up on the streets and thrown into the Irving
Block prison, and was released at the end of twenty-four
hours through the influence of Mr. J. E. Merriman, a kind-
hearted and very influential Union man: at the close of the
war he was paroled at Gainesville, Ala. Returning to Memphis
May 27th he went to work the next day in the office of Mr.
Alston, chancery court clerk, and remained in public service
in the courthouse for thirty years. Eight years of that time
he was Clerk of the Criminal Court and at last declined to run
for re-election.

CARY, HUNSDON, born in Marshall county, Miss., in
1842; came to Memphis in infancy; reared here; was teller
in the Gayoso Savings Institution in May, 1861; enlisted in

Captain John F. Cameron's company, Young Guards: attached to Hindman's Legion, Hardee's Brigade: Cary was made orderly sergeant of the company in the fall of 1861. The Young Guards became part of the First Arkansas Battalion, commanded by Lieutenant-Colonel John S. Marmaduke; this was filled out and became a full regiment in October and November, 1861, and was called the Third Confederate Regiment. Early in December, 1861, Cary was promoted to be junior second lieutenant, and assigned to duty with Captain Thomas Newton's company; was engaged in the fight at Woodsonville, Ky., December 17, 1861, acting as adjutant of the regiment on that occasion. In this fight the noted Colonel Terry, of Terry's Texas Rangers, was killed. Cary was with the command on its retreat from Bowling Green to Nashville, thence to Corinth, Miss., and was in the battle of Shiloh; was badly wounded, and was in feeble health for several years after, from effects of wound and chronic rheumatism; was honorably discharged in fall of 1862, and saw no more active service. After the close of the war was for a good many years a notary public and United States commissioner; read law, and was admitted to the bar in 1885; was chosen cashier of the German Bank in 1895, and is still occupying that position.

CARROLL, W. H., the grandson of Governor Carroll and the son of General W. H. Carroll, was born in Panola county, Miss., in 1842; he went to school in Memphis to that celebrated educator, W. H. Whitehorne; he also attended the Western Military Institute at Nashville. In 1861 he enlisted with his father, went with him to Knoxville and drilled a regiment which his father raised there, the Thirty-seventh Tennessee: came with the regiment to Germantown; was in camp some time; then back to Chattanooga and Knoxville; crossed the mountains to Mill Springs, Ky., in midwinter and received his baptism of fire and blood at the battle of Fishing creek January 19, 1862, where the youth quite distinguished himself by riding up and down the lines and trying to encourage the men to rally on the field. When General Chalmers took command of North Mississippi, in 1863, W. H. Carroll reported to him and was assigned to duty as acting assistant adjutant-general, which position he held for some time and until the arrival of Captain W. A. Gardner, the assistant adjutant-general. After this W. H. Carroll was elected captain of Company C, Eighteenth Mississippi Battalion, under Colonel Alex. H. Cheatham, and his company was detailed for escort duty with General Chalmers, and he continued in this position until near the close of the war, when his health was so much impaired that his life was despaired of and he was discharged and went to Canada. After the war he became a lawyer in Memphis, Tenn., where he soon took a good position and now stands in the front rank of the distinguished men who compose the bar of Memphis. As a politician he is widely known throughout the State, although he has never held or sought any political office.

CASH, PATRICK BOGGAN, son of Colonel Benjamin and Mrs. Mildred Spottswood Cash; born in Hardeman and reared in Shelby county, Tenn.; named after his great-grandfather, Captain Patrick Boggan, of Revolutionary fame in North Carolina, and came of patriotic ancestors on all sides. Attended Ralter's military school near Germantown, and when about 18 years old enlisted as a private in Company C, the Secession Guards, Thirteenth Tennessee Regiment, organized at Jackson, Tenn., and mustered into State service June 3, 1861. The regiment joined the " river brigade," commanded by Brigadier-General John L. T. Sneed, at Randolph, Tenn., July 25; went to New Madrid, Mo., and was mustered into the Confederate service; John V. Wright was colonel and A. J. Vaughan lieutenant-colonel. The regiment took a conspicuous part in the battle of Belmont and lost in killed and wounded 149 men out of 400. During the thick of the fight Boggan Cash, when at close quarters, wounded a Federal officer who refused to surrender to such a stripling and made the mistake of tantalizing his would-be captor on his boyish appearance. Appalled at what he had done the boy tried to stanch the blood of his expiring foeman and wept as he failed. The officer's sword was sent back to young Cash's mother and with it a note from Colonel Wright, saying: " You are the mother of a hero." The incident illustrates the horrors of war that come so often unexpectedly and in quick succession. Patrick Boggan Cash was only at home once after that, when he returned for a day to be at the funeral of his younger brother, Benjamin. He was at the battle of Shiloh ; went with his regiment into Kentucky ; was in the battle of Richmond and at the battle of Perryville, though the regiment was not engaged, and was seen last late in the afternoon of December 31, 1862, at the battle of Murfreesboro. His fate was not known for many years. He was reported as missing and it was supposed that he might have been taken prisoner. Inquiries were made and a man was sent by the family all over the North to points where Confederates had been imprisoned, but in vain. Only a few years ago General Vaughan learned from one of his old soldiers in Texas that Boggan Cash was killed in the advance of his regiment near dark on December 31, 1862, and thus was solved a long pending and sad mystery. The youth sleeps among the unknown dead on the field or in the Confederate cemetery at Murfreesboro.

COCHRAN, J. W., was born in Abingdon, Va.; came to Memphis before the war; left Memphis in 1861 in Captain McDonald's sixty-day company ; served out his time with said company ; returned to Memphis ; joined Captain Cole's company, which afterward was attached to the One Hundred and Fifty-fourth Senior Tennessee Regiment, just before the battle of Shiloh ; remained with it for some three years ; was in all the engagements that it was in during that time ; was detailed on General Preston Smith's staff at Shelbyville, Tenn., and was with him when he and two of his staff were killed at Chickamauga ; afterward was ordered to report to General Joseph Wheeler at Dalton, Ga., for staff duty, with rank of captain, and remained with him to the close of the war ; served four years and three months ; never had a furlough ; never was sick, badly wounded or in a hospital. Paroled at Gainesville, Ala., May, 1865.

COLEMAN, ROBERT H., was elected corporal in the organization of the Cuba Guards, and made a brave soldier throughout the entire war ; was twice wounded at the battle of Chickamauga in a charge on a battery ; he was knocked down by a piece of shell striking him on the left shoulder, but soon rising, continued in the charge, when he was again stricken down by a ball piercing his right shoulder and lodging in his lung. After recovering partly from his wounds he continued with his command until captured at Atlanta in 1864. Just before the regiment was captured Captain Beard, Ashner Stoval and R. H. Coleman, being separated from the regiment by the dense undergrowth through which they were passing, came suddenly into the road where General McPherson and his staff were making a reconnoissance. Captain Beard called on Corporal Coleman to fire on General McPherson, as he was the only one that had a loaded gun. At the report of the gun the distinguished officer fell from his horse a corpse. He was dead by the time he reached the ground. Coleman and a number of others were shortly afterward taken prisoners, and on his way to a Northern prison he arrived at Utica, N. Y., on the same day that the remains of General McPherson reached there. Mr. Coleman was not known then and there as the man who fired the fatal shot. He remained in prison several months. He has told the writer that he always regretted this shot, fired on the impulse of the moment. He was as modest and unassuming as he was true and brave. He finally died near Los Angeles, Cal., from the effects of the wound received at Chickamauga, the ball remaining in his right lung until the end.

COLEMAN, W. M., enlisted in the Cuba Guards of Cuba, Shelby county, Tenn. The company was organized, seventy-eight strong, March 1, 1861, by the election of the following officers: Dr. Ed. Irby, Captain; W. M. Coleman, First Lieutenant; Dr. W. D. Lewis, Second Lieutenant; E. H. Fite, Third Lieutenant; mustered into State service, ordered to Union City May 15, 1861, and organized with the Twenty-first Tennessee Regiment, with Ed. Pickett as Colonel, Hiram Tillman as Lieutenant-Colonel and J. C. Cole as Major. September 15th the regiment was ordered to Columbus, Ky., and on November 7th went into the fight at Belmont, Mo., 800 strong and came out with a loss of 128 killed, wounded and missing. It was ever afterward called " the bloody Twenty-

16

first." Company A, Cuba Guards, had its captain, first lieutenant (W. M. Coleman) and three privates badly wounded. After the evacuation of Corinth, Miss., the Twenty-first became a part of the famous Fifth Confederate, which was nearly all captured at Atlanta, Ga., in 1864. Lieutenant Coleman bears the scars of war, but is still an active and successful farmer in his old neighborhood.

COLLIER, CHARLES II., born and reared near Fortress Monroe, on the Chesapeake Bay, and educated at a military school in Virginia. At sixteen he commenced his preparation for the engineer corps, U. S. Navy. Before this was completed the war broke out and he was appointed to the Confederate Navy; reported to Commodore M. F. Maury, under whom he served. He was promoted to second assistant engineer and assigned to the Stono, Lieutenant Commander Rochele. The Stono was wrecked off Charleston breakwater, attempting to run the blockade. Mr. Collier was assigned to the flagship Charleston under Flag Officer John R. Tucker; he saw much service; had orders to join the Florida; went to Bermuda and had the yellow fever; was afterward ordered to report to the Stonewall, then recently completed in France, but too late; after the surrender he began teaching; came to Memphis; was principal of high schools, and for twelve years was superintendent of city public schools, and is now principal of a high school at Whitehaven, eight miles south of Memphis.

COOPER, LUNSFORD PITTS, born in Rutherford county, Tenn., January 8, 1830; his father, Micajah Thomas Cooper, was born in Salisbury, N. C., December 31, 1806, and his grandfather, a native of Maryland, served in the Revolutionary war and afterward removed to Rowan county, N. C., where he married the daughter of Captain William Hollis, of the Revolutionary war; his mother was a Vincent. This indicates the strain of blood from which L. P. Cooper came. He was reared in Bedford county; graduated in 1852; became principal of an academy first in Williamson and then in Bedford county; attended Lebanon law school one term; was mar-

JUDGE L. P. COOPER.

ried to Pauline Henderson Scales in Davidson county January 24, 1854; removed to Panola county, Miss., 1856; engaged in planting there on a large scale, and when the war began was rapidly becoming rich; he had more than one hundred bales of cotton burned, his stock was destroyed, his fifty negroes set free, and at the close of the war he had to start life over. He enlisted as a private in Captain Meek's company, Forty-second Mississippi Regiment; went to Virginia and after arriving at Richmond was made quartermaster with the rank of captain; served with this regiment until late in the war, when he became brigade quartermaster; he was in the field with his command all the time, except about sixty days, in 1863, when he returned home to attend his wife's funeral; when the end came he was soon after admitted to the bar, and was elected a delegate to the State Constitutional Convention, composed of the ablest men of the State, and the

Constitution was so amended as to recognize the new order of things. After this Captain Cooper entered upon a large and lucrative law practice. In 1875 he removed from Panola to Memphis and formed a partnership with the late Hon. Henry Craft; in 1894 he was appointed Criminal Judge of Shelby county, and in the August following was elected for the full term of eight years, from September, 1894; and thus a prominent lawyer, good and popular judge, was developed from an old-time Southern gentleman and planter. He was married to his second wife. Miss Cornelia Battle, at the residence of her sister, Mrs. Turley, in Memphis. December 10, 1868.

COUSINS, PETER R., born in Nottoway county, Va.; went in the army from Memphis, in the Southern Guards; at Columbus, Ky., the company was detached from the One Hundred and Fifty-fourth Regiment and assigned to the heavy artillery; took part in most of the engagements on the Mississippi river from the battle of Belmont to the siege and fall of Vicksburg; was made first lieutenant of artillery, and after the fall of Vicksburg (the army being paroled) was in parole camp at Marietta, Ga.; was sent to Richmond, Va., to have the command exchanged, and then ordered to Mobile, Ala., and assigned to duty at Fort Morgan, in Mobile Bay, which, after a long siege by navy and land forces. surrendered; was prisoner at Fort Lafayette and Fort Warren until General Lee surrendered; has since lived in Memphis and been in business here.

CRAWFORD, WEST J.. born in Mississippi; reared in Vicksburg; attended Madison College in Mississippi, and the Western Military Institute at Nashville, Tenn.; enlisted at Memphis in Company A, Shelby Grays, Fourth Tennessee. and was in the principal battles in which the Army of Tennessee participated; was in Kentucky on the Georgia campaign, and under General Hood back into Tennessee. and was paroled by General E. R. S. Canby at Meridian, Miss.. May 22, 1865; never was wounded seriously or captured, and rarely missed a battle or skirmish in which his regiment took part: after the surrender returned to Memphis, engaged in business and became a member of a leading firm, as he is yet; has been president of the Memphis Cotton Exchange; held various important positions in the business community, and has been for some years past president of the *Commercial* Publishing Company, and is a director in several financial institutions. He was married in November, 1874, to Miss Anna L. Thompson, a niece of the Hon. Jacob Thompson, and they have three children, Erasmus, Kate and Marianne.

CROFFORD, JOHN ALEXANDER, enlisted at the age of 16 in Company D, McDonald's Battalion, or Forrest's old regiment; was in the battle of Chickamauga; with General James Wheeler in East Tennessee, and around Grant's army, immediately after Chickamauga; transferred with General Forrest to the Department of Mississippi; was with General Forrest in all his campaigns and battles till close of the war, except time absent from wound and sickness; wounded at Columbia in October, 1864; captured a Federal flag in a charge near Okolona, Miss., on February 22, 1864. In the battle in which Colonel Jeff. Forrest was killed, Company D acted as escort for Colonel Forrest, he at the time commanding brigade; surrendered and paroled with the regiment at Gainesville, Ala., May 11, 1865. He is a member of the C. H. A. and of Company A, Confederate Veterans. (See p. 72).

DAVIS, W. C., born at Covington, Tenn., March 25, 1845; enlisted for Confederate service in the Tipton Rifles, Fourth Tennessee; served one year; discharged on account of being under age; became a substitute for his father, Lewis W. Davis, First Tennessee Heavy Artillery Regiment; went to Vicksburg, Miss., and remained until the surrender. During this time his father was taken prisoner by Colonel Hatch's cavalry command and sent to Alton, Ill., prison and there died August 12, 1863; afterward joined Captain Elliott's company, Fourteenth Tennessee Cavalry; at the battle of Franklin was by order of General N. B. Forrest promoted from private to lieutenant for gallantry; in the retreat from the front of Nashville was wounded in the right hip; his parole is No. 21, dated Gainesville, Ala.; he lacked only four days of serving four years; came to Memphis in January, 1870; was appointed a patrolman; in 1875 was promoted to the position of captain; in 1880, when the then chief of police, P. R. Athy, was elected sheriff, Davis was made chief of police, which position he held until July 1, 1895, when he resigned to accept the office of wharfmaster, which position he still holds.

DRAKE, JOHN B., born in Shelby county, and was a descendant of General James Robertson, the " father of Tennessee "; enlisted April 16, 1861, in Company B, Bluff City Grays, One Hundred and Fifty-fourth Tennessee, and remained until the end of the war; saw much hard service; was captured and held in prison at Alton, Ill., sixteen months; married Miss Frances Cash April 24, 1867; was proposed for membership in the C. H. A. by James E. Beasley and elected February 3, 1870; was cashier of a bank; died August 20, 1875; was buried in the Confederate lot in Elmwood Cemetery; left a wife, but no children.

ERSKINE, JOHN HENRY, born at Huntsville, Ala., December 23, 1834, and was one of three brothers, Drs. Albert and Alexander being the others, who went through the war as Confederate surgeons. He graduated in medicine at the University of New York in 1858, and at once began the practice of medicine in Memphis. Early in 1861 he was commissioned as assistant surgeon of Bate's Second Tennessee Regiment, served more than a year as such, was promoted to the rank of senior surgeon on the staff of General Cleburne, and was soon chief surgeon of Cleburne's Division; next was medical inspector of Hardee's Corps, became chief surgeon of the corps, and at the close he was acting as medical director of the Army of Tennessee on the staff of General Joseph E. Johnston. His promotions came rapidly, his services were continuous, and he filled every position with splendid efficiency and credit. He was a man of superb physique, great powers of endurance, intensely earnest and sympathetic, and drew about him hosts of loyal, loving friends. His was such a character as men love and women adore.

In all his army career, which was nearly all in the field, he

DR. JOHN H. ERSKINE.

never asked for or received a leave of absence or was disabled. His courage, zeal and skill, and unswerving kindness, endeared him to all. Returning to Memphis in August, 1865, he resumed practice, and was in the epidemics of 1867, '73 and '78, manifesting the same devotion and heroism that he had shown in the military service. He was three times chosen health officer of the city—in 1873, '76 and '78. In the last great epidemic he faced death for weeks to relieve stricken sufferers. But he overtasked himself, was prostrated with yellow fever, fell a martyr to duty and the cause of humanity and yielded up his life September 17, 1878. He died that others might live. It was not a time for much formality, but about fifty leading citizens united in a beautiful tribute to his memory. This was lithographed, surmounted by his picture and elegantly framed, and is yet cherished by surviving friends and relatives. Another tribute was in the form of a very heavy and beautiful golden medallion, prepared by army comrades and sent to his venerable mother at Huntsville, Ala. On one side was the inscription " Dr. John H. Erskine, Chief Surgeon Army of Tennessee, C. S. A., April 26, 1865, on General Joseph E. Johnston's Staff." On the reverse was a Confederate flag, surrounded with the stars representing the Confederate States, and inside a circular rim the words " Disbanded at Greensboro, N. C." This superb memento of loving regard was sent to the venerable lady at Huntsville and accompanied by the following letter :

RICHMOND, VA., AND MEMPHIS, TENN., Jan. 8, 1879. *Mrs. Susan C. Erskine, Huntsville, Ala.:*

DEAR MADAM—The medallion which accompanies this letter has been prepared by the friends and Confederate army comrades of your noble son, Dr. John H. Erskine, in testimony of his official rank and standing at the end of the South's struggle for independence. We do this because the Confederate government was able to give commissions to very few of the military officers who, like Dr. Erskine, were entitled to them. The medallion, with its inscriptions, will serve instead of a military commission as evidence of Dr. Erskine's well-earned military rank; and his relatives may hand it down as such to their descendants. We, who sign this letter, *know* that when the C. S. Army of Tennessee was disbanded by its commander at Greensboro, N. C., May 2, 1865, Dr. John H. Erskine was its Medical Director.

With assurances of very deep sympathy with you in your sad bereavement by the death of such a son, we are

Most respectfully yours,

J. E. JOHNSTON,	JAMES E. BEASLEY,
W. H. RHEA,	EDWARD L. BELCHER,
R. B. SNOWDEN,	G. B. THORNTON, M.D.,
W. A. GOODMAN,	A. J. VAUGHAN,
COLTON GREENE,	B. F. CHEATHAM.

The medallion and letter will doubtless be transmitted to posterity as a priceless family heirloom. Little more need or can be said of such a man. His memory is especially dear to many old Confederates who knew him. He became a member of the old Confederate Relief and Historical Association on the 15th of July, 1869.

ERSKINE. ALEXANDER, born in Huntsville, Ala., September 26, 1832, and came of old and notable families identified with the early history of Virginia and Pennsylvania. His mother was the daughter of Colonel Albert Russell, who was in the Revolutionary war and was with Washington in his marches. He took a thorough academic course at Huntsville, and studied four years at the University of Virginia, graduating in chemistry and German; read medicine in his father's office at Huntsville and then returned to the University, where he took a medical course; went to the University of New York and graduated there in 1858, and settled in Memphis the same year; practiced medicine, and was connected before and several years after the war with the Memphis Medical College. When the war broke out, Dr. Erskine entered the Confederate service, and was with Generals Cleburne, Cheatham, Bragg and Polk in Tennessee, Kentucky, Mississippi and Georgia. He was taken prisoner at the battle of Perryville and placed in charge of the sick and wounded at Harrodsburg; was afterward sent to Vicksburg and exchanged, and joined the army at College Grove, Tenn.; was at the battle of Murfreesboro; spent the winter at Tullahoma as a brigade surgeon in General Polk's command, and after that was in charge of the Law Hospital at LaGrange, Ga., until the surrender. After the war he resumed the practice of medicine in Memphis, and has ever since enjoyed the fullest confidence of a large clientele. He passed through all five of the epidemics in Memphis since the war and stood the severest tests at the post of duty and danger, and did his full part for the relief of suffering humanity. He is an elder in the Presbyterian Church, to which his ancestors belonged for several generations; belongs to medical societies and other organizations, and is otherwise identified with the best interests and moral influences of this city. Dr. Erskine has been twice married—first at Memphis, December 10, 1861, to Mrs. A. L. White (nee Law), to whom were born two sons. Mrs. Erskine died in 1868; second marriage to Miss Margaret L. Gordon, a cousin of General John B. Gordon, at Columbia, Tenn., December 19, 1872. She was a cousin of Dr. Erskine's first wife, and her father, Washington Gordon, a planter of Maury county, died in the Confederate service at Vicksburg. By this union there were seven children. He is now and has been since 1885 connected with the Memphis Hospital Medical College as professor of obstetrics and diseases of children.

FIZER, JOHN C., born in Dyer county, Tenn., in 1838; removed to Panola county, Miss., with his father's family when 10 years old; grew up in mercantile life; came to Memphis to live, but when the war broke out he went back to Mississippi, and was elected first lieutenant and became adjutant of the Seventeenth (Featherstone's) Mississippi Regiment; was in the first battle of Manassas and at Ball's Bluff. When the regiment was reorganized he was elected lieutenant-colonel; was soon after promoted, and was in the principal battles in Virginia and at Gettysburg. He came with Longstreet to Tennessee, and was in the battle of Chickamauga. It was at Knoxville that he lost his arm when in command of his brigade. He was afterward assigned command of a brigade in South and North Carolina, and was with General J. E. Johnston at the capitulation at Bentonville. This brief sketch gives only a faint idea of his brilliant career. After the war he engaged very successfully in business in Memphis and married here. He was proposed for membership in the C. H. A. by Major W. A. Goodman, Captain W. D. Stratton and Dr. J. H. Erskine, and elected April 28, 1870; succeeded ex-Governor Isham G. Harris as president of the Association in 1871, and died June 15, 1876, at the early age of about 38 years.

FLANNERY, DAVID, was born February 16, 1828, in Limerick, Ireland; he was superintendent of telegraph from Memphis to New Orleans for the Confederate government, and filled this, or a corresponding position, to the close of the war, as shown in a letter from General Stephen D. Lee; was paroled in May, 1865, and has since lived in Memphis, and is still connected with the telegraph service. His career throughout the war was one of great hazard, valuable service and thrilling interest, and would make a book of itself. He joined the C. H. A. several years ago.

FLIPPIN, J. R., born in Williamson county, Tenn., in 1834; removed to Fayette county, Tenn., and reared there on a farm; graduated at Old Jackson College, Columbia, Tenn., and at Lebanon Law School; removed to Memphis and located in fall of 1856; entered the One Hundred and Fifty-fourth Tennessee Regiment as a private in 1861; was in the battles of Belmont, Shiloh, Chickamauga and Missionary Ridge; detached from command and served as brigade quartermaster when not in active service, and was surrendered under General Joseph E. Johnston at Greensboro, N. C.; resumed practice of law in 1865 in Memphis; was elected and served with credit and distinction as Judge of the Criminal Court and as Mayor of Memphis; spent some years in Mexico in charge of large mining interests; married Miss Nelson of Brownsville, Tenn., in 1871; has three daughters and a son; is an elder in the Linden Street Christian Church, and is practicing law.

FORREST, NATHAN BEDFORD, Lieutenant-General of Cavalry, C. S. A. No attempt will be made in this limited space to give an adequate sketch of the life of this most remarkable man. His methods and achievements in war are well known, and have been fully described by the ablest critics and military men of this country and of Europe. He was a born leader of men, without any of the advantages of early education. In him strong common sense and quick perception dominated over a splendid physique. He had a big, sympathetic heart, as was often manifested in most trying situations, but he could restrain his emotions in the pursuit of any great purpose. Self-control and faith in himself inspired courage in others. He never ordered men to go where he would not dare to lead; if he was severe at times it was for a purpose; it was to enforce discipline and make the best out of trying circumstances. The testimony of all who were very near him in his great campaigns is that he was sympathetic, genial and companionable. He was a temperate man; had no small vices; was not given to levity or common-place small talk, but was frank, candid and sincere; positive and honest in all things. His men were ever ready to follow him into the jaws of death. In judgment and discretion he was a head and shoulders above most men. No general and concise history of the Civil War can ever be written without giving to him large space and the highest credit for military genius. His name will go down to future generations with a luster that the centuries will not dim or the admirers of real heroes permit to be forgotten. N. B. Forrest volunteered as private and surrendered as a lieutenant-general. He was a self-made, strong, broad-minded man ; was a leader in civil life as well as in war, and died universally regretted by his comrades and followers, and the Southern people, who knew him best.

GOODLOE, J. L., born in Madison county, Miss., September 3, 1840 ; enlisted in 1861 in Company E, Twenty-eighth Mississippi Cavalry ; detailed to Harvey's Scouts ; captured June, 1864, at Allatoona, Ga. ; imprisoned at Rock Island, Ill. ; wounded at Cassville, Ga., May, 1864 ; paroled February, 1865, and sent to Richmond, Va. ; practiced law at Memphis, Tenn., since 1867, joining this Association about 1886.

HAMILTON, HUGH A., born in Baltimore. Md., in 1834 ; was educated in that city ; became connected with an express company, and was in the Confederate army from 1861 to 1865 ; became a resident of Memphis in 1867 and died here in 1887 ; was married in 1882 to Mrs. Kate E. Dawson, daughter of Eugene Magevney, Esq.

HANAUER, LOUIS, born in Bavaria in 1820 ; came to America in 1838 ; lived at Pocahontas, Ark., and removed to Memphis in 1860 ; enlisted in the Confederate army and served for a time on the staff of General Hardee ; was a prominent merchant here for many years ; died in August, 1889.

HAYS, A. J., born in 1830, and graduated at the Lebanon Law School ; in 1861 became a member of the One Hundred and Fifty-fourth Tennessee Regiment and was appointed quartermaster of State troops with the rank of major by Governor Isham G. Harris. He served for a time, but had to retire on account of an acute case of chronic dysentery, which lasted him for seven years ; he remained the rest of the war at Hayswood plantation, near what is now Arlington, and rendered much valuable aid to the Confederates. After the war he engaged in planting and died of yellow fever in September, 1878, aged 48 years. He was a great nephew of General Andrew Jackson and was named for him; he was a man of a sunny nature, and is remembered by hosts of friends.

HIX, J. M., born in Albemarle, N. C.; came to Memphis in 1858; joined the Shelby Grays, Fourth Tennessee; participated in both days' fight at the battle of Shiloh, and was transferred on December 25, 1862, to Company B, of the Forty-eighth North Carolina Regiment, Cook's Brigade, Heath's Division; promoted to first lieutenant; was in the battle of Bristow station, and at both days' fight at the battle of the Wilderness and in nearly all the battles from the Wilderness in the campaign of 1864, including Spottsylvania Courthouse, Cold Harbor, Petersburg, to Richmond in March, 1865; at one time was in charge of a brigade train in Virginia; from Richmond he was sent to North Carolina on special duty, when deserters and bushwhackers abounded in the mountains; was paroled at Salisbury; returned to Memphis and has lived here almost ever since and connected mostly with one house, except about six years spent in New York and California.

HUGHES, BARNEY, a native of Louisville, Ky., and in boyhood a very bright lad, who could study his lesson by leaning his book against the fence while at a game of marbles. In 1861 he was connected with the railway and telegraph business, then in their incipiency; went out from New Orleans as lieutenant with a company of heavy artillery. One of the heavy batteries under the bluff at the chalk banks above Columbus, Ky., was manned by Hughes' company, and had a share in driving Grant's forces back from the field of Belmont, Grant leaving his mess chest, private papers, gold pen and a saddle horse on the field for the Southern troops to use at their convenience afterward. In the operations around Island 10 Lieutenant Hughes served on the staff of General Trudeau. When General Bragg moved into Kentucky Lieutenant Hughes was telegraph operator at Chattanooga, and he soon after became confidential operator for General Bragg. He served in this capacity at the battle of Chickamauga, and

also in the operations around Missionary Ridge.   At the latter place cannon balls went whizzing through his telegraphic
tent at so lively a rate that his quarters were quickly changed.
He continued in the service until peace was made; then went
West, and at Salt Lake City worked the first telegraphic
instrument ever operated there.   Later Lieutenant Hughes
returned to this city, taking position with the Memphis &
Charleston Railroad, with which he remained until his death
in September, 1892.   He married Miss Wittie Ellis of Kentucky, in 1872.   Lieutenant Hughes had a host of friends and
after his death a number caused a monument to be placed
over his remains in Elmwood, upon which is recorded his
virtues.

KELLAR, ANDREW J., was born in Kentucky, and his
ancestors were from Alsace and Lorraine, settling originally
in Virginia.   In politics he was a Douglas Union Democrat,
of Jacksonian ideas, and as a matter of fact was named Andrew Jackson, his ideal of statesmanship and heroism.   He
came to Memphis before the war, and engaged in the practice
of law when quite a young man.   When the trial came he
left some of his more ultra associates behind and went out as
captain of a company.   After the battle of Shiloh, in which
his sword belt was shot from him, he was elected colonel of
his regiment, the Fourth Tennessee.   Although in broken
health, he was a faithful, active soldier throughout the war.
He went into the battle of Murfreesboro so feeble that after
the battle his men lifted him from his horse; but he had
fought his fight.   After the death of General Strahl, Colonel
Kellar commanded the brigade, and he had received his commission as brigadier-general when the war closed.   He married Miss Margaret Chambers of Mississippi, a descendant of
Griffith Rutherford and of General Wm. Davidson of North
Carolina, both of Revolutionary fame.   Of this marriage was
born four sons and one daughter—Chambers, Andrew Conley,
William Henry, Philip Rutherford and Werdna, the latter
name being Andrew reversed, still in honor of Old Hickory.
After the war Colonel Kellar practiced law in Memphis;
became interested in and finally owned the old *Avalanche*, and

edited or controlled its policy for several years; sold out and engaged in other enterprises, and some years ago removed, with his family, to Hot Springs, South Dakota; entered upon the practice of law and is now a member of the State Senate.

KELLY, W. O., born in Franklin, Tenn., November 2, 1838; enlisted in Company H, Twelfth Tennessee, June, 1861; participated and was wounded in the battle of Belmont, Mo.; also took part at Shiloh; after that was detailed for duty in commissary department under Major Lee M. Gardner, Polk's Corps; later took part in resisting an advance of General Grierson in his famous raid through Mississippi, acting as aid-de-camp on the commanding officer's staff; paroled at Meridian, Miss., June, 1865; returned to Memphis and married the daughter of Mr. M. B. Elder, at Trenton, and has been for many years connected with a leading house in Memphis.

KINNEY, I. C., born near Covington, Tipton county; enlisted at the age of 16 years in Company I, Captain Alexander, Seventh Tennessee Cavalry; after the battle of Fort Pillow was on Colonel Rucker's staff as courier at the battle of Harrisburg; was in the raid under Forrest made into North Alabama and Middle Tennessee in September, 1864; was in various other engagements with his regiment in that campaign; came home at the end of the war; never was paroled or wounded, but saw much hard service; lived in Tipton county until last year, when he removed to Memphis and engaged in business.

LONG, Rev. NICHOLAS M., born in Somerville, Fayette county, Tenn., July 27, 1849; removed to Sullivan county when he was nine years old, with his mother, who had married the second time, and grew up on a farm. In 1864 enlisted in the Confederate service, in Witcher's company, Owen White's Battalion; after several months hard service for him, including picket duty in the mountains at perilous points, his command was ordered out of East Tennessee, and it was arranged that he should return home to care for his mother, as his stepfather was also in the army. Many of Mr. Long's near relatives

were in the Confederate army, and they all came of heroic
pioneer and Revolutionary stock. An excellent sketch of
him, with references to his family connections and ancestry,
appears in " Prominent Tennesseeans." (See page 172.)

LOONEY, ROBERT FAIN, a grandson of David Looney
and Richard Gammon; both resided in Sullivan county, East
Tennessee, and were members of the Convention that framed
the first Constitution of the State. His maternal grandfather,
Richard Gammon, was one of the commissioners appointed
to control the affairs of Tennessee while yet in a territorial
form. Colonel Looney is the youngest of a large family, of
which he and the Hon. A. M. Looney of Columbia, Tenn.,
alone survive. He was born in Maury county, Tenn., where
his father, Abraham Looney, moved at an early day; was
educated at Jackson College, Columbia, and studied law with
his brother-in-law, Judge Edmund Dillahunty; he moved to
Memphis when quite a young man. He married Miss Louisa
Crawford of Columbia, Tenn. Early in 1861 he raised a regiment, the Thirty-eighth Tennessee, which he commanded at
Shiloh and other battles. An old soldier of this regiment in
a recent letter says: " I have often thought that the history
of the Thirty-eighth Tennessee should be written; other commands and other commanders have become famous for doing
less." It won distinction at Shiloh, Perryville and Murfreesboro, and was conspicuous in most of the great battles of the
war. At Shiloh (on Sunday, the 6th) this regiment made a
charge across an open field that was matchless in execution
and results. Colonel Looney led the charge in person, riding
far in advance of his men. (Lindsley's Annals, pp. 505-6.)
Colonel Looney, in his official report at the time, said: " I
received an order to charge the battery and camp under cover
of the woods to the right, from Major-General Polk, through
his son, Captain Polk. I quickly examined the route and
saw that the order could be carried out in effect with but
little more risk by moving rapidly through the open field. I
ordered the charge, which was promptly and successfully
executed as to the camp and battery, and I suppose at least
one thousand prisoners were taken." Colonel Looney, in con-

.COL. ROBERT F. LOONEY
At Richmond in 1861.

cluding his report of the two days' engagement, says: "I
delivered the last volley to the enemy on Monday." Of the
distinguished gallantry of Colonel Looney in this battle the
captains of the companies composing the Thirty-eighth Tennessee Regiment, in a published account under date of April
8, 1862, say:

"Our regiment, the Thirty-eighth Tennessee, commanded
by Colonel Robert F. Looney, was engaged the 6th and 7th.
During the whole engagement our colonel was at his post,
riding up and down the line, encouraging and urging on his
men, and doing even more than might have been expected of
a veteran hero. On Monday, the 7th, it became necessary to
drive back the enemy and hold a position for a certain time.
Our regiment was ordered to the charge. It advanced under
a heavy and devouring cross-fire. Our colonel was every-

17

where, doing everything. His men were encouraged by his
bold and fearless conduct. The fire became terrific. Sometimes the line would stop and stagger back like a strong ship
when smitten by a wave. Then our leader, despising danger
and contemning death, with one hand pointing to the colors
still flying in the breeze, would shout, Forward! Still press
on!"

An old soldier, writing, recalls this charge when the gallant
colonel seized the colors in his hand and, riding to the front,
told the men to follow him and the flag. The brigade commander, Colonel Preston Pond, in his official report, compli-
ments Colonel Looney for his coolness and intrepidity. Col.
Looney's regiment was not in General Polk's Corps, and is,
therefore, not mentioned in his official report, but General
Polk complimented him and his men on the field for gallant
and valuable services.

General Marcus J. Wright, in his War Records, says:
"Among the many Tennessee commands which were conspicuous for gallantry at the battle of Shiloh, none won more
laurels than the Thirty-eighth Tennessee, commanded by Colonel R. F. Looney." Colonel Looney later in the war was
taken prisoner, and being exchanged he reported to General
Pemberton. When hostilities were over he returned to the
practice of his profession, the law, but after a few years he
became interested in various enterprises; he has always taken
an active interest in politics, exerting powerful influence and
laboring for party and friend; he is now one of the commissioners appointed by the government to make a great national
park of the Shiloh battlefield.

LOUDON, MILTON B., commander of the steamboats
Granite State, Q. L. Hyatt and Keokuk; was the second son
of John Loudon, and entered the Confederate service at the
age of 23 years, in Captain Wicks' cavalry company. His
first engagement was Perryville, Ky.; was in every important
battle afterward; attached to General Wheeler's command;
served throughout the war; died of yellow fever on board of
his boat Keokuk in 1873; buried at the Loudon vault, Elmwood Cemetery.

LOUDON, HOPKINS, third and youngest son of John Loudon and Minerva Trowbridge Loudon ; born in Cincinnati, O. ; graduated at Woodward High School, Cincinnati, O. ; in 1861 came to Memphis ; entered the Confederate service on his father's boat, Granite State ; was ordered with his boat to Little Rock, Ark., via Arkansas river, loaded with Confederate government stores ; boated in the government service until Little Rock and Pine Bluff fell. Knowing that the capture of the boat was only a question of time, he sunk her at Silver Lake and then set fire to her upper works ; he had removed her bell, which was a large and valuable one. At the close of the war his father, John Loudon, presented it to St. Patrick's Church, where its silvery tones are heard all over Memphis to this day. After the destruction of the boat he entered Company G, Captain Gillespie's cavalry ; was with General Price in his raid through Missouri and Kansas, and in all the battles of that arduous campaign ; at close of the war returned to his home at Memphis, and now resides in Kansas City, Mo.

MAURY, RICHARD B., born in Georgetown, D. C., February 5, 1834, but grew up at Fredericksburg, Va. ; graduated in several schools of the University of Virginia, and last of all in medicine ; afterward took the degree of M.D. in the University of New York. After a hospital career went to Natchez, Miss., and after recovering his impaired health engaged in the practice of medicine at Port Gibson, Miss. He entered the Confederate service as Surgeon of the Twenty-eighth Mississippi Cavalry. After one year of hard service was transferred to hospital duty, and remained in charge of hospitals until the close of the war. In 1867 Dr. Maury removed to Memphis, where he has since enjoyed a large practice. He is a member of various societies and has contributed largely to medical journals. His family history is exceedingly interesting. M. F. Maury of the United States Navy was his second cousin, and after his father's death became his guardian, as well as true friend and kind adviser. Dr. Maury was first married in Port Gibson, Miss., to Miss Jane T. Ellett, daughter of Hon. Henry T. Ellett. They had a family of six children; his wife died in Memphis in 1875. His second wife was Miss Jennie B. Poston of Memphis, and they have several children.

McGUIRE, WM. EUGENE, born of Virginia ancestry, November 17, 1839, in Christian county, Ky. He joined Company A, First Kentucky Cavalry, commanded by Colonel Ben. Hardin Helm, a brother-in-law of President Lincoln; was appointed chief of scouts at Florence, forty picked men, and watched the movements of Grant's and Buell's armies; was elected first lieutenant of his old company, but he was retained in the scouting service until the end of the war. He had many narrow escapes and thrilling experiences. He served with General Forrest in the Georgia campaign, and was with the last fragments of Johnston's army of grizzled and tattered veterans until it, with the executive department of the lost Confederacy, surrendered at Washington, Ga.

After the surrender Captain McGuire engaged in business in Christian county, Ky., and there met Miss Lula Lawrence of Memphis, and afterward married her and removed to this city. Her family came to Memphis from Virginia in 1818, and was of the same family as Commodore James Lawrence of "Don't give up the ship" fame.

MALLORY, W. B., was born in Hanover county, Va., and previous to the war was Captain of the Monticello Guards at Charlottesville, and by order of the governor took this company to Charleston as a guard to represent the State and preserve the peace, and was there in that capacity when John Brown was executed. When the war broke out Captain Mallory, in command of the same company, with the Albemarle Rifles of Charlottesville and about one hundred students of the University of Virginia, left Charlottesville the night of April 8; went to Harper's Ferry by order of Governor John Letcher, reaching that place on April 19, the State having passed the ordinance of secession on the 16th, which was to be promulgated the next day; remained two weeks; was then ordered back to equip his company; in ten days the Guards were ready and reported at Culpepper Courthouse, where the Nineteenth Virginia Regiment was organized, and of which

CAPT. W. B. MALLORY.

Captain Mallory's command was the senior company. He
served in the field for twelve months and then was ordered
to take command of the post at Charlottesville and be provost
marshal, upon the ground that he could be of more service
there than with the army. This was a strategic point of great
importance, and many efforts were made to take it. Captain
Mallory remained there in command until near the close of
the war. No Federal troops reached the place until March,
1865. Captain Mallory, with a small force partly recruited
from the hospitals, took a decisive part in averting the raid
made by General Custer. It was not until March, just before
the surrender, that General Sheridan passed through from the
valley to the rear of General Lee's army at Petersburg. Of
this movement Captain Mallory kept General Lee informed
daily until General Sheridan crossed to the south side of
James river. Captain Mallory had an opportunity to surren-

der at Appomattox, but started south; feeling further resistance or flight useless, he accepted the situation and surrendered a few days later. Soon after the war he came to Memphis, embarked in mercantile life and was pre-eminently successful. He has a palatial home, has a large family, and is fully identified with the business affairs and best social life of the city. Joined the C. H. A. June 18, 1894, and was a staff officer with the rank of colonel at the inter-State drill held in Memphis in 1895.

MARTIN, HUGH BRADSHAW, son of William Pitt Martin and Martha Harris Bradshaw: born in Columbia, Tenn., August 9, 1838: his father, W. P. Martin, was a brilliant lawyer, a jurist, a man of infinite wit and great personal magnetism; at the age of 21 Mr. Martin began the practice of law in Memphis, where two years later he was married to Miss Ruth Talbot, and two weeks after he joined Forrest's cavalry. He was soon promoted to the position of ordnance officer on the staff of General Forrest, where he served two years, 1862–63; in the latter part of 1863 he was transferred to the staff of General Starnes, who was soon after killed at Shelbyville. General Dibbrell succeeded to the command: with him Captain Martin remained till the close of the war. A machinist by the name of Casey, in the ordnance department, became very much attached to Captain Martin and made him at the ordinary forge a beautiful pair of spurs and a bridle bit with a star made of a silver dollar. These mementoes of affection in the times that tried men's souls are yet preserved in the family, and grow more valuable as the years go by. During the battles of Shiloh, Murfreesboro, Chickamauga, Franklin, and the later terrible struggles, Captain Martin was at his post. After the surrender, Dibbrell's Brigade, with others, was selected as an escort to President Davis and his Cabinet when seeking a place of safety; Dibbrell's men did not, however, remain in this service; the force was already so large that it rendered secrecy impossible. When leaving the President's escort General Dibbrell's command was paid in coin, the last disbursement by the Confederate States of America. Captain Martin kept this money

CAPT. HUGH B. MARTIN.

in his possession as an heirloom for his children. General
Dibbrell joined General Joe Johnston in North Carolina,
where he surrendered. Captain Martin returned to Memphis
and resumed the practice of law; he was a man of splendid
personal appearance, with a heart filled with gentleness and
kindness to the whole world; his nature was as genial as the
springtime that wakes in beauty all the flowers; and he died
a few years ago lamented by a devoted wife, loving sons and
daughters and hundreds of sincere friends.

MERIWETHER, MINOR, was born in Christian county,
Ky., January 15, 1827; his father was Garrett Minor Meriwether, of Louisa county, Va., and his mother was Ann Minor,
of Orange county, Va.: he is of Welsh and Dutch descent,
mixed with Scotch through the Douglas. A paternal Welsh
ancestor of the eighth generation back settled in Surrey coun-

ty, Va., in 1652; a maternal ancestor, Doodes Minor, of the seventh generation back, came from Holland in 1675 and settled in Urbana, Middlesex county, Va. If Minor Meriwether has any special ancestral pride it is on account of his Dutch ancestors, who for a century resisted the despotism of Spain and aided in establishing the Republic of the United Netherlands, as well as in other great improvements. He was educated at the Tennessee University, Nashville, for a civil engineer, and afterward had charge of important engineer work in construction of the Nashville & Chattanooga Railroad. In 1852 he married Miss Elizabeth Avery of Memphis; removed to this city, and as chief engineer mainly located and constructed the Memphis & Grenada Railroad; after that was Chief Engineer of the Mississippi River Levees from the Tennessee line to the mouth of the Yazoo. When the war began he closed up and dropped this work, and reporting to General Polk, assisted in constructing defensive works at Columbus, Island 10 and Fort Pillow, holding a quasi commission as Major of Engineers. He was afterward commissioned by President Davis as Major of Engineers, and later as Lieutenant-Colonel of Engineers. In April, 1861, the city of Memphis appropriated $25,000 for defense and appointed General Jos. R. Williams, W. A. Bickford and Minor Meriwether a committee to construct works on the river to prevent the descent of Federal gunboats and transports. The field work devolved upon Major Meriwether; he constructed Fort Harris above Memphis and was in the long and heavy bombardments of Fort Pillow, Island 10 and Columbus by gunboats and mortar fleets; he aided in the construction of works around Corinth; served on the staff of General Leonidas Polk in the battle of Shiloh; on the staff of General Price at Iuka, September, 1862, and Hatchie bridge in October, 1862; in the latter part of that year laid out and constructed fortifications at Grenada and at Abbeville, on the Tallahatchie river. Being familiar with the country he foresaw the attempt to send gunboats and transports through Moon lake and Yazoo Pass and on through a network of rivers to Haines' Bluff, where an army could attack Vicksburg from the rear, and he warned General

MAJ. MINOR MERIWETHER
At the Age of 38.

Pemberton of the danger. General Pemberton was advised otherwise. In January, 1863, when the floods came, the Federals cut the Pass levee and rode into Moon lake with their gunboats and transports and commenced the descent; too late Major Meriwether was ordered to Greenwood to sink steamboats and blockade the fleet; the water was too deep to render this effectual; the major erected defenses at Fort Pemberton, sank the Star of the West, an ocean steamer, and placed batteries in position: General Loring was in command of less than 1500 men; the Federals had over 15,000 and heavy batteries; General Grant cut the large levees on the Mississippi and the Confederates were well nigh drowned out; many were taken sick, and toward the end Major Meriwether was the only one of the engineer corps able for duty; yet the Confederates, weak, sick and worn out, held on, and the great movement to invest Vicksburg by that route was abandoned,

and General Grant ultimately made the attack from below.
After the fall of Vicksburg Major Meriwether was ordered to
Florida to assist in an important railroad connection and was
brought under the immediate command of General J. F. Gil-
mer, Chief Engineer of the Army; later he was under command of General Richard Taylor, and was surrendered under
him at Meridian in May, 1865.

Major Meriwether returned to Memphis and resumed the
labors of his profession successfully and eventually adopted
the profession of law, for which he had been prepared before
the war; he took an active part in public affairs and was
appointed receiver for the old municipality of Memphis, in-
volving great labor and heavy litigation. This being concluded
to the satisfaction of the taxpayers and people at large, he
resigned some years ago and removed with his family to St.
Louis, where he is now engaged in the practice of the law
and is as busy as ever. He was one of the early members of
the Confederate Relief and Historical Association, and was
for some years its secretary and treasurer.

MATHES, GEORGE ANDERSON. second son of Rev.
William Alfred Mathes, was born near Dandridge, Jefferson
county, East Tennessee, October 25, 1844; ran off from home
and enlisted in Company I, Thirty-seventh Tennessee Regiment. Carroll's Brigade. at Knoxville, in the latter part of
1861; was a delicate youth and had never known many hardships; marched to Mill Springs, Ky., and was in at the end
of the battle of Fishing creek January 19, 1862; after the
battle of Shiloh was in Marmaduke's Brigade; was in the
battle of Farmington and in minor engagements; fell back to
Tupelo and was sick there; was physically unable to go with
Bragg's army into Kentucky; was in the battle of Murfreesboro December 31, 1862; became a non-commissioned officer :
was in the battles of Chickamauga and Missionary Ridge;
was in winter quarters at Dalton, Ga.: in the campaign from
Dalton to Atlanta. On July 20, 1864, on the Peachtree creek
road, in a heavy engagement at close quarters, he was shot
through the right arm by a minie ball and would have bled
to death but for the prompt attention of his older brother, a

DR. GEO. A. MATHES.

staff officer, who happened to be on the line. The arm was tied up and the wounded youth sent to the rear. His arm was disabled for life and he performed no more active field service. After the surrender he attended college for a year or two, read medicine, took a course at a medical college and began practice, but turned his attention to newspaper life; became one of the editors of the Somerville *Falcon*; married Miss Mary English Dulin at Calvary Episcopal Church in Memphis in the fall of 1873; removed to Brownsville and successfully published and edited the *States* and *States and Bee*, but his health failed him, and after testing the climates of Texas and Florida he returned and died in Memphis at the home of his brother, July 31, 1881. His wife had died seven months before him. They left three little girls, Mary D., Viola Belle and Georgie Bolton, who have since grown up to womanhood. Dr. Mathes was a man of decided talent and popularity; he was cut off in the midst of success and usefulness.

MOYSTON, JOHN H., born in Wheeling, Va., in 1842; came of Revolutionary ancestry on both sides of the house, and has a most interesting family history, being on his mother's side a descendant of Oliver Cromwell, and running back several centuries; enlisted, at Harper's Ferry May 17, 1861, in the Shriver Grays. Twenty-seventh Virginia, which afterward composed a part of the Stonewall Brigade. His first engagement was at Falling Waters, six miles from Martinsburg; then went to Manassas and was in the first battle there; was in the campaign under Jackson, and was in all the principal battles under him, some thirty or forty in number; was in the battles of Seven Pines, at Fredericksburg, at Gettysburg, Sharpsburg, Cedar Mountain, and was wounded in the second battle of Manassas and in other battles, and served throughout the war without ever seeing his home; served as orderly with General Stonewall Jackson about two years and attended his funeral at Lexington; was captured near Knoxville, where his regiment was attempting to come to reinforce Longstreet; was sent to Rock Island prison; was exchanged in a few months and returned to Richmond at the time of the surrender; attempted to reach Johnston's army in North Carolina, and failing in this Mr. Moyston and eleven others, without being paroled, chartered a forty-ton lumber boat at New Orleans, hid in the hold and had the captain to clear for some distant port and made direct for Vera Cruz, and went to Cordova. Mr. Moyston remained in Mexico nearly four years and became a naturalized Mexican citizen and superintendent of a copper mine; then returned home and to Memphis about the year 1869 and has since lived here; married here Miss Anna Auer, a Baltimorean, and has three children, Blanche, Guy and Roy. Joined the C. H. A. at an early day and has always been an earnest, enthusiastic member. Mr. Moyston was conspicuous as a Knight of Pythias at the post of duty in the great epidemic of 1873 and rendered valuable services in other years, and has in every way proved himself as good a citizen as he was a daring, intrepid soldier. He is an enthusiastic admirer of the late President Davis, whom he knew personally, and whose portrait, splendidly painted in oil by

JOHN H. MOYSTON.

a New York artist, he not long since caused to be presented through his children to the Confederate Historical Association.

OMBERG, JAMES A., born at Lawrenceville, Ga., in 1839. His paternal ancestors came from Norway in the early part of the present century and settled in Georgia. His mother's ancestors came from the north of Ireland in the eighteenth century and became citizens of South Carolina. He prepared for a university course. Preferring a commercial life, however, he accepted at an early age a position as clerk in the Bank of Chattanooga with his uncle, William Fulton, the cashier, and soon succeeded to the position of teller of the Commercial Bank of Memphis. When the war broke out he promptly enlisted in Company A, Shelby Grays, Fourth Tennessee, from which he was soon transferred to the commissary headquarters of his brigade and division, remaining therein until the surrender with the army in North Carolina in April,

1865. In 1879 he became cashier of the Bank of Commerce, and has held the position ever since. Mr. Omberg was married in 1867 to Miss Eliza Graham, of an old and prominent family of Memphis. They have four children.

OUTTEN, WILLIAM T., was born September 26, 1840, in Baltimore, Md.; was present at the riot April 19, 1861; remained until Butler took possession of Annapolis, Md.; was mustered into Confederate service in May, 1861, in Captain J. Lyle Clark's company of Baltimore, Twenty-first Virginia Regiment, and went to West Virginia with Generals Lee and Loring; joined Jackson December, 1861; was under Jackson in the winter campaign to Bath, Hancock and Ramsey; saw much of General Loring and of Bishop Quintard, then with that command; was with Jackson at Kernstown, April, 1862; was a member of the Second Maryland Regiment; was organized in September, 1862, and operated independently until the Pennsylvania campaign; was with Stewart's Brigade, Johnston's Division, Ewell's Corps; was slightly wounded at Gettysburg; was at Cold Harbor June, 1864; in the several battles around Petersburg; was present at the breaking through of the Confederate lines; was wounded there and taken to a hospital at Manchester, opposite Richmond, and captured there; was paroled with thirteen others. Mr. Outten has been living in Memphis or vicinity since 1871, and is one of the very few Maryland ex-Confederates to be found in this part of the country.

OVERTON, JOHN, JR., born in Davidson county, Tenn., April 27, 1842; grew up on a farm, where his father, Colonel John Overton, still resides; attended the common schools until fifteen years of age; then went to school two years in Albemarle county, Va., in 1857–58; entered the University of Nashville in 1860 and remained until April, 1861, when he enlisted in Captain Reed's company, Forty-fourth Tennessee Regiment. In 1862 he was transferred to the staff of Brigadier-General Bushrod Johnston, with the rank of captain; served with him on the Kentucky campaign and at the battles of Perryville, Murfreesboro and Chickamauga, and minor engagements. When General Forrest was transferred to the

west, Captain Overton was transferred to his staff with the
same rank, and served in all of Forrest's campaigns, including the raid on Fort Pillow; was at Tupelo and Nashville,
and with Hood's army in Tennessee, and finally surrendered
with Forrest at Gainesville, Ala., May 13, 1865. He returned
to Memphis, where his father had large landed estates, and
went into the real estate business on a large scale. Although
a wealthy man, he is essentially a man of and for the people.
He has been elected to both houses of the Legislature and
served with distinction. He was a Commissioner of the Taxing District of Memphis. He takes an active interest in politics as a public-spirited citizen, but not for the sake of office,
as there is hardly a place within the gift of the people he
would accept, unless when special work was needed. He
enjoys the fullest confidence and good will of all classes.
Captain Overton was married October 23, 1866, to Miss Ma-
tilda Watkins of Davidson county, Tenn. They have three
children—two sons, who are married, and a young daughter
single and in society. The Overtons have been conspicuous
and highly connected since the days of the Revolution, and
have certainly held their own in public and private affairs,
in war and in peace.

PARKER, MINTER. born in Memphis October 24, 1842;
his father, Robert A. Parker, was one of the pioneer merchants of Memphis : was at college at LaGrange, Tenn., when
Fort Sumpter fell : joined the Shelby Grays, Fourth Tennessee
Regiment; after the battle of Murfreesboro was promoted to
a position in the corps of topographical engineers on the staff
of General Leonidas Polk, and after his death was with Generals Johnston and Hood, and was again on the staff of General
Johnston and surrendered with him at Salisbury, N. C., April
26, 1865; rode to Memphis on horseback and reached home
on the first day of June; was married November 20, 1867, to
Miss Fannie Pillow. daughter of Jerome B. Pillow, near
Columbia, Tenn.; wife died March 17, 1890, and he died October 7, 1894. They are survived by six children.

PATTERSON, Hon. JOSIAH, is the grandson of Alexander Patterson, who came from the north of Ireland before

the Revolutionary war, settling in Abbeville District, S. C.; became an officer in the patriot army; was severely wounded at the battle of Cowpens. Malcolm, the son of Alexander Patterson, born in North Carolina, removed to Morgan county, Ala., in 1817, where he married Mary De'Loache. Their son Josiah was born September 14, 1837; was admitted to the bar and began the practice in 1859. In 1861 he became first lieutenant in Clayton's First Alabama Cavalry, and was promoted to captain for gallantry in the battle of Shiloh; was on detached service in North Alabama; was highly complimented in a general order issued by General Bragg; became colonel of the Fifth Alabama Cavalry Regiment and was in command of it until the close of the war; he was in the battles of Corinth and Iuka and numerous other engagements; was in command of the District of North Alabama; resisted the advance of Wilson's raid; was captured in the battle of Selma, but escaped a few nights afterward and returned to North Alabama to reorganize his command; surrendered and was paroled May 19, 1865. Since the war he has been prominent at the Memphis bar and in politics, and is recognized as one of the ablest men in Tennessee. He has served two terms in Congress, making a national reputation, and will contest for the seat of E. W. Carmack in Congress, to whom the certificate of last election was given. Colonel Patterson was married to Josephine, the daughter of Judge Green P. Rice, of Alabama, December 22, 1859. They have three children, Malcolm R., Mary L. and Anna E. The son is Attorney-General for the Criminal Court of Shelby county.

PILLOW, GIDEON J., was born in Williamson county, Tenn., in 1806; was graduated at the Nashville University in 1827; was admitted to the bar and began the practice of law at Columbia, and was soon after appointed upon the staff of Governor Carroll, his relative, with the rank of general. His ancestors on all sides were in the Revolutionary war, and are mentioned in Ramsey's History of Tennessee. When the war broke out with Mexico he was commissioned brigadier-general by President Polk and led a brigade of Tennesseans. He was promoted to major-general, and commanded a divis-

MAJ.-GEN. G. J. PILLOW
During the Mexican War.

ion at Cherubusco, the storming of Chepultepec, and taking of the city of Mexico. He was wounded severely several times, and had some friction with General Scott, but came home crowned with honors and applauded by the people. He engaged in planting in Tennessee and Arkansas, and had acquired a large fortune when the late war began. Governor Harris appointed him to command State troops with the rank of major-general. He was a man of tireless energy and superb executive ability, and aided materially in the organization of some 25,000 men, advancing his own means to the State. When the State seceded he was commissioned as brigadier-general by Mr. Davis. This meager recognition of so illustrious a man was attributed, whether justly or unjustly, to personal prejudices engendered in the Mexican war. General Pillow took prominent part at the battle of Belmont, and made a splendid fight at Fort Donelson. Not believing the surrender necessary he left the place with his staff, and made his way

18

to Nashville. For this act of quasi insubordination he was suspended for some time, though General, then Colonel Forrest, was not. General Pillow was never again given a command in the field, though he was given charge of the recruiting service in several States with headquarters at Marietta, Ga., and rendered most efficient service which was highly complimented by General Bragg and others high in command. After the war he resumed planting, and in 1868 formed a law partnership with ex-Governor Isham G. Harris, which continued for several years. His first wife was Miss Mary Martin of Maury county, from which marriage the following children survive: Mrs. T. J. Brown, Nashville. Tenn.; Mrs. J. D. Mitchell, Helena, Ark; Mrs. W. F. Johnson, Atlanta, Ga.; Mrs. D. F. Wade, Mrs. Melville Williams, Mrs. L. C. Haynes, Nashville, Tenn.; Mrs. D. B. Fargason, Memphis, Tenn., and R. G. Pillow, Little Rock, Ark. General Pillow died October 8, 1878, near Helena, Ark., leaving a wife and three young children, one since dead, by his last marriage. He was a man of unquestioned courage, fine address and high culture, a charming conversationalist, and in all respects a typical chivalric Southern gentleman of the best school. His name deserves the respect and honor of all true Tennesseeans. He became a member of this Association July 15, 1869, and for some years attended the meetings regularly.

PICKETT, EDWARD. born at Huntsville, Ala., in 1828 and died in 1876. He was a graduate of the Kentucky Military Institute; studied law; was clerk of the House of Representatives at Jackson, Miss., in his youth; was afterward editor of the Natchez *Free Trader* and an editorial writer on the Memphis *Appeal*. When the war broke out he promptly espoused the Southern cause and became Colonel of the Twenty-first Tennessee Regiment, which was cut to pieces at Union City; was aid to General A. S. Johnston at the battle of Shiloh, and afterward commanded the post at Milledgeville until the close of the war; practiced law in Memphis until his death. His editorial talents and inclinations were transmitted to his son, Mr. A. B. Pickett, who for some years past has been editor and manager of the Memphis *Evening Scimitar*.

PIPER, O. H. P., enlisted April 12, 1861, in the Southern Guards, commanded by Captain James Hamilton, an experienced and accomplished officer from Columbus, Ga., who had been an officer before when quite young in the Mexican war. This was the first company to enter the service from Memphis and the first to go to Randolph, then considered the post of honor; became the nucleus of the One Hundred and Fifty-fourth Tennessee; was assigned to artillery service, detached and stationed on Hatchie Island under General John P. Mc-Cown; was sent to Columbus, Ky.; took part in the battle of Belmont; thence despatched to Island No. 10, and when that post was about to fall the men escaped to the woods and swamps, reformed and went to Corinth, and from there to Mobile and Fort Morgan, and was stationed at the last named place until it was captured. The first captain soon died; the second captain was Richard Hambleton of South Carolina, who died before the company reached Island No. 10; the third and last captain was Thomas N. Johnson, who returned to Memphis after the war and became a member of the Confederate Relief and Historical Association but died a few years afterward.

O. H. P. Piper was one of three brothers born in Somerset county, near Princess Anne, Md., who came from Ohio to Memphis when quite young and entered the Confederate service from here; he was only 21 years old; at Columbus, Ky., he was detached from his company to serve with Major Guy in the commissary department and was with him at various points, also later on with Majors J. J. Murphy and B. J. Semmes, thence reported for duty to General Bragg's chief commissary, John L. Walker of Mobile, and back to Major Guy; most of the time he was in the purchasing department. He was in the battles of Belmont and Perryville; at the latter place he and Maj. Frank Gailor, who were great friends, agreed the night before to go into the fight, though not required to do so; Gailor, a resolute, cool young man, gallant as ever lived, fully conscious of the situation, rode to his death in front of General Wood's Alabama Brigade, Hardee's Corps. Piper took a gun and went in front with his old friends the

Shelby Grays of Memphis in the Fourth Tennessee Regiment, Cheatham's Division, and escaped unhurt. After the battle he found his horse, which he had left tied in a deserted stable in Perryville, and soon after, on reporting at headquarters, learned the sad news of his friend Gailor's death. After that he saw much active service to the end of the war, when he returned to Memphis, and has since been engaged in various large business affairs.

His next brother, John George Piper, enlisted at the age of 19 in Captain M. J. Wicks' cavalry company early in the war, and shortly after serving in the battle of Murfreesboro was killed in a cavalry charge on a stockade on the pike near Nashville. His comrades who survived him praised in the highest terms his coolness and unwavering courage to the last moment of his life.

The third brother, William Augustus Piper, was in a different command, the Maynard Rifles, One Hundred and Fifty-fourth Tennessee, Captain Ed. Cole; he enlisted at the age of 18 years, took part in the battle of Shiloh for two days and was greatly exposed, bringing on a fatal illness; he died May 8, 1862, in Major Frank Gailor's tent, receiving every attention and being sustained by the sympathy of friends and the consolations of religion. Major Gailor wrote a beautiful and touching tribute to his memory which appeared in the old *Appeal* of May 11, 1862. His remains were buried in Elmwood.

These three brothers not reared upon our soil freely risked their lives and their all for the South, and only one came home alive. But they came of a fighting, liberty-loving stock. Their two grandfathers were in the Continental army, one from Philadelphia, the other from Bucks county, Pa. Both commanded companies in the war of American independence. Much is said of their patriotic ancestors in Davis' History of Bucks county, Pa.

PRICE, BERNARD FRANCIS, was born in Alexandria, Va., November 30, 1845; left there when small with his father, who went to Shreveport, La., to live, thence to Lyons, Ia., thence to Rock Island, Ill. Went to his trade of printer

BEN F. PRICE.

at the early age of 10 years at Lyons, Ia.; came to Memphis in 1857, and finished on the old *Bulletin* under J. M. Keating; went in the army at the first tap of the drum, as a drummer boy, with the Ringgold Guards, Captain G. W. S. Crook; disbanded at Lynchburg, Va., for want of quota to make the company. Young Price returned to Memphis and went out in the "Sumpter Grays," whose first captain was Jas. A. Lee, subsequently Captain T. W. Rice, and known as Company A, Thirty-eighth Tennessee Regiment, Colonel R. F. Looney, General G. M. Pond's Brigade, and General Ruggles' Division. After the battle of Shiloh the company was placed in heavy artillery service, in charge of a battery commanding the Farmington road. After the evacuation of Corinth it was placed in light artillery in Forrest's command. At this time private Price was detailed and sent to Selma, Ala., to assist in getting out the House and Senate journals of Mississippi; was subsequently moved to Montgomery for the same purpose, where he was when the war closed, and was paroled there. He never went to school except for three months, but has attained the highest position in the Masonic fraternity, Grand Master. He was married in 1867 to Miss Mary Virginia Price. From this union have been born eight children, six now living, two daughters and four sons, and there are two grandchildren. The children's names are Mrs. D. G. Dunlap, Velasco, Texas; Mrs. T. W. Avery, Memphis, Tenn.; Bun F., Jr., Robert N., Mack, and George C., are the boys. After the war Mr. Price was for some time in the printing business, but for some years past has been the secretary of a leading local insurance company. He has an elegant home in one of the fashionable suburbs of Memphis and a fine library, and finds time to make valuable contributions to Masonic literature through the daily press, as well as the magazines of the day.

PORTER, EDWARD E., born March 28, 1832, at Lincolnton, Lincoln county, N. C. His parents removed to Memphis in 1835. He graduated at Hanover College, Ind., and also at Princeton College, N. J., and was a graduate of the Union Theological Seminary, Hampton-Sydney, Va. He was married to Mattie C. Rice, daughter of Rev. Benjamin Rice, D. D., President of the Union Theological Seminary, of which he was a graduate. He was pastor of the Third Presbyterian Church of this city when the war commenced; went into the service from a sense of duty to country and from emotions of patriotism which could not be repressed, leaving his young wife and children at home. Early in the contest he received a commission from President Davis to raise an independent company, known as Porter's Partisans. With this command he repaired to Fort Pillow, continuing there and at Columbus until the evacuation of those places, when his company was regularly mustered into the Confederate service in the Department of Memphis; was connected with General Forrest's command at the time of the surrender. He lived to lay down his arms before the conqueror when success was no longer possible; but his health was broken in the contest, and on the 6th day of October, 1867, he entered "that low green tent whose curtain never outward swings." He had as noble a heart as ever beat in a man's bosom, and for gallant conduct and dauntless courage as an officer of the Confederate forces, he was not excelled by any other. He was finely educated, and a man of abilities equaled by very few of his age. He loved his country and his kind, and sought always to do good to both and wrong to none.

PORTER, Dr. JOSEPH T., born at Columbia, Tenn., in 1845; enlisted at Memphis, June 1, 1861, aged 15 years, under Captain John C. Carter, Thirty-eighth Tennessee (later brigadier-general) who was killed while commanding a division at the battle of Franklin; served until the evacuation of Corinth, and then was discharged as a non-conscript at Tupelo, Miss.; afterward joined Forrest; was captured near Fort Pillow in January, 1863, and remained in prison at Camp Douglas six months: exchanged at City Point, Va., joined his command, and surrendered at Gainesville, Ala., in 1865. Has practiced his profession and lived in Memphis since the war.

SEBRING, W. H., born near St. Louis; reared in Gibson county, Tenn.; came to Memphis just before the war broke out, when about 20 years old, and assisted in making up a company to go to Charleston, but the young men went to Nashville, joined Bate's Second Tennessee Regiment; served in the Virginia campaign from May, 1861, to February, 1862. The regiment came west and was in the battle of Shiloh. In 1863 young Sebring was promoted to lieutenant; sent west with dispatches to General Kirby Smith; captured, sent to Gratiot prison, St. Louis; tried and sentenced to be shot; was in prison eleven months and eighteen days, and was for five months in a condemned cell; on Christmas eve, 1863, tried with others to escape, and with comrade A. C. Grimes was chained to a post in the back yard of the prison five days and nights and nearly frozen to death. He was to have been shot June 25, 1864, but on the 18th he and eight others charged the sentries. Captain Douglas, Captain Jasper Hill and Lieutenant Sebring got through and back to the army; two were killed and two wounded; afterward he was detailed by President Davis and joined Captain T. H. Hines, John B. Castleman and George B. Eaton in an attempt to release the 10,000 prisoners at Camp Douglas; the movement was ultimately betrayed, but Lieutenant Sebring escaped back through the lines; reported back to Richmond, was promoted to lieutenant-colonel and sent down the James river on an expedition: later reported to General Giltner. of Duke's (Morgan's old) Division, and with it was surrendered at Mount Sterling. Ky., April 30, 1865. Colonel Sebring returned to Memphis and on June 30, 1866, was married to Miss Annie Perdue, one of Maryland's fair daughters who had been imprisoned in Memphis and subsequently banished South for her intense devotion to the cause of the stars and bars. They removed to Florida in 1873, where Colonel Sebring took a prominent part in reconstruction times and other affairs, and where he became Brigadier-General of State Militia in 1881. The general and his family removed to Memphis a few years ago.

SNEED, J. WES., enlisted as captain of Company A, Seventh Tennessee Cavalry, May 16, 1861, and fought throughout the war; was wounded and mentioned for gallantry at Corinth by Colonel W. H. Jackson, October 5, 1862. (See Lindsley's Annals.) He went through the war to the end: engaged in business here after the surrender; suffered much from old wounds and delicate health and died many years ago.

SNEED, JOHN L. T. The life of this eminent citizen, written out in full, would make many volumes of most entertaining and instructive matter relating to the military annals and jurisprudence of the State. He inherited the intellectual vigor, suavity of manner, high moral tone and magnificent physique of illustrious ancestors. After filling many positions of high trust and taking part in two wars, he is still in the prime of life, genial, industrious and cheerful, filling the position of Chancellor of the First Chancery Court of Shelby county, to which he was elected in August, 1894, by a vote that was practically unanimous, and as complimentary a popular tribute as could possibly be expressed. He was born

JNO. L. T. SNEED.

in Raleigh, N. C., in the home of his grandfather, Hon. John Louis Taylor, then Chief Justice, and for whom he was named. On the maternal side he is descended from Hon. Matthew Rowan, his great-grandfather, Judge Gaston, being a family connection. His father's ancestors, from England, settled in Virginia and soon after removed to Granville county, N. C. Major Junius Sneed, his father, was for many years cashier of the State Bank of Salisbury, N. C.

Receiving a liberal education, he came to West Tennessee when a young man, and soon became prominent at the bar and in politics, and was an officer in the Mexican war; after that was attorney-general for a number of years; was brigadier-general in the Provisional Army of Tennessee in the late war and was in the service of the Confederacy until the end; afterward was on the Supreme Bench for eight years; resumed the practice of law in Memphis and also established a law school, which he conducted successfully until elected chancellor. He has been elector for the State-at-large on the Democratic ticket and held various other positions of honor, and whilst of distinguished lineage and bearing, he has always been essentially a man of the people, affable with all, and a charming, easy talker in whatever circle he is found. He was married years ago in the prime of early manhood to his present wife, but never had any children; he is a good churchman, a generous giver to every worthy cause as far as his means will reach, and is loved alike by the rich and poor. An old-time Christian gentleman, he looks upon the sunny side of life, and by his example makes others happier and better, and with no class of people is he a greater favorite or more congenial than his comrades, the old Confederates. Upon one occasion, a dozen or more years ago, he delivered the annual address upon Confederate Memorial Day at Elmwood cemetery, a masterpiece of beautiful thought and pure English.

SOUTHERLAND, JAMES, was born on December 24, 1835, and came of distinguished Revolutionary ancestry, being descended from the old Virginia families of Pendleton, Claiborne, Rives and Clayton. While still quite young he engaged in the mercantile business in Memphis, being thus occupied at the breaking out of the civil war. At the first call to arms he volunteered his services in defense of his country and was shortly made first lieutenant of the Bluff City Grays under Captain Thomas F. Pattison. Captain Pattison's health failing, Lieutenant Southerland was placed in command of the company, which was engaged in many desperate conflicts, among them being the battles of Shiloh, Chickamauga, Missionary Ridge and Franklin. Lieutenant Southerland bore himself with conspicuous gallantry on the field, and was noted for his daring bravery and his remarkable coolness under fire. He followed the fitful fortunes of the Confederacy from the first outbreak of hostilities until the closing scenes at Appomattox. At the close of the war he resumed his commercial life and was several years later married to Miss Imogene Latham, a daughter of F. S. Latham, one of the pioneer editors of Tennessee. Lieutenant Southerland died on January 9, 1875, and is buried in Elmwood cemetery. One son, James, and three daughters, Imogene, Katherine and Mary, survived him.

STOVALL, GEORGE A., was born in Green county, Ky.; came to Memphis when quite young in 1848. After Memphis fell he joined Company A, Seventh Tennessee Cavalry; took part in the battle of Corinth and was in the raid to Holly Springs under Van Dorn; was in the fight at Thompson's station; took part in operations around Jackson, Miss., and was in the Georgia campaign: the company became the escort company of General W. H. Jackson after Captain Wm. F. Taylor became colonel of the regiment; after the surrender returned to Memphis and lives here yet. The company to which he belonged was made up mostly of Memphis boys, many of whom he still remembers and mentions in most complimentary terms: Captain (afterward Colonel) W. F. Taylor, Captain Henry Martin, John T. Hillsman, Mage Martin, Henry Bragg, Dick Ivey, Jo. and I. N. Rainey, Don. Dockery, of Hernando, Miss.: Clad. and Tell Selden, Foster Talley, Bruce Bow, W. W. Shouse, Bill Rollins, of DeSoto county, Miss.; George Holmes and many others.

STOVALL, W. H., brother of the above, now of Stovall, Coahoma county, Miss., went out as a lieutenant in the Beauregards, with the One Hundred and Fifty-fourth Tennessee Regiment, under General Preston Smith, and became adjutant. He came to Memphis from Kentucky in 1855 and was practicing law with J. R. Flippin when the war began; he married a daughter of Mr. J. W. Fowler: went to Mississippi, and is now (1896) a prominent planter near Coahoma; he became a member of the Confederate Relief and Historical Association of Memphis August 12, 1869.

STOVALL, JAMES R., a brother of the two named above, born in Greensburg, Green county, Ky.; came to Memphis in 1854 or '55, and removed to Mississippi: when the war broke out joined the Hickory Rifles, One Hundred and Fifty-fourth Tennessee Regiment: was wounded at Shiloh and again at the battle of Franklin, where he was taken prisoner; came here after the war and soon died in Mississippi.

TALLEY, WM. F., enlisted in Shelby county, Tenn., in
1861, in Captain Porter's independent company; was captured near Oxford, Miss., and sent North to prison; he then
returned to Vicksburg to be exchanged, but before reaching
Vicksburg all exchange of prisoners had stopped, and the
boat, loaded with prisoners, was sent back up the river. At
Memphis he made his escape and rejoined his command. But
his health and constitution had been destroyed by exposure
and want while a prisoner, and he died just at the close of
the war, aged 36 years. He was one of the four brothers
alluded to in other sketches.

TALLEY, FLETCHER H., was General Agent for the
Memphis & Charleston Railroad Company at Memphis at the
beginning of the war. Upon the capture of the city in 1862
he enlisted in Company A, Seventh Tennessee Cavalry, and
served continuously until detailed for railroad service at Meridian, Miss., as agent. Upon the capture of Meridian by
General Sherman he moved his office to Selma, Ala., where
he continued until the capture of that place by General Wilson. After the war he was re-employed by the M. & C. R. R.
Co. as General Freight and Ticket Agent until his death in
1871, being succeeded by the lamented Barney Hughes.

TALLEY FOSTER D., was one of four brothers who
entered the Confederate service from Memphis; saw much
active service and lived through the war, while two brothers-
in-law, who married their sisters, never returned. F. D. Talley
left the railroad service and enlisted in Company A, Seventh
Tennessee Cavalry; was in the movement against Corinth in
October, 1862; was with Van Dorn at Holly Springs, and
under him when he was killed; was under General Joseph E.
Johnston around Jackson, Miss., and afterward on the Georgia
campaign. After several days hard fighting on the New Hope
Church and Dallas line he was detailed for railroad duty and
stationed at Selma, Ala., until run out by Wilson's raid. His
parole, which he still keeps, is dated Memphis, May 11, 1865.
He has since been in business and has a home in Memphis.
Joined the C. H. A. in October, 1896.

TRASK, W. L.. born in Jefferson county, Ky.. in 1839, and identified with the western rivers and the sea in early life. He held a commission from Thomas Overton Moore, Governor of Louisiana, early in 1861, as Second Lieutenant of the Sumpter Grays, at New Orleans.   In the early autumn of that year he commanded the sidewheel steamer Charm, serving the Confederates at and about Columbus, Ky.   At the battle of Belmont, November 7, 1861, the Charm was busy conveying troops, stores and ammunition from the Kentucky side to the Confederates. who were driven back to the bank of the river. The Charm was exposed to the fire of the enemy and was considerably torn by cannon shot.   Several on board were wounded, but the vessel was kept to her work, carrying wounded soldiers to the east shore and reinforcements to the western side of the river, until General Grant and his little army were driven from the field, the General leaving his mess chest, saddle horse and gold pen and other camp equipage in the hands of the Southerners.   Captain Trask was permitted to write letters next day with the gold pen, and also to ride over the battlefield on the General's horse.   None of the steamers in the combat were disabled, though several were considerably cut up.   The masters of the vessels were complimented by General Polk in his report.   After that Captain Trask commanded the Charm and the Prince in the service until the fall of Island No. 10, and on one occasion a fragment of a thirteen-inch shell from a mortar fell through the hurricane deck of his boat, making a straight line of holes through the cabin or boiler deck, the lower deck and on to the bottom plank of the hull, upon which it lodged without going through. As the Union forces moved down the river, planting heavy guns along the Missouri shore at intervals, the passing of the batteries by transport steamers proved a serious business. Captain Trask's boat run the gauntlet whenever it was deemed necessary.   In May, 1862, the steamer Capitol, owned by the late Messrs. Bohlen, left this port with Captain Trask in charge, towing the unfinished gunboat Arkansas to a haven of safety in the Yazoo.   The feat of piloting so large a steamer as the Capitol, with a heavy and helpless gunboat in tow, up the narrow and tortuous Yazoo, as far as Greenwood, then down again to Yazoo City, where the war vessel was finished, was regarded by practical river men as one of more than ordinary hazard and daring. This work was done by Captain Trask and a skilled Mississippi river pilot named John Hodges at the wheel, and without injury to the war ship. Soon after the boats that had sought refuge in the Yazoo, to the number of fifty or more, were scuttled, burned or otherwise destroyed. Captain Trask went to Kentucky with General Bragg, serving as Adjutant of Austin's Battalion of Sharpshooters, a command of picked men from the Eleventh and Thirteenth Louisiana Regiments. This command, under General D. W. Adams, formed the extreme left of the Confederate line of attack at Perryville, Ky., and while in advance of the entire line of Confederates, as they fought with the Fifteenth Kentucky, the Tenth Ohio and Loomis Michigan Battery on their front, Wm. H. Lytle, a brigade commander of the Union forces, was taken by Adjutant Trask and one of his comrades. General Lytle was escorted to General S. B. Buckner, as a prisoner, by the adjutant, and General Buckner paroled him on the field. At Murfreesboro, and in the Atlanta campaign from Dalton to Lovejoy's station, Ga., including Resaca, New Hope, Kennesaw, Marietta, the Chattahoochee and the great combats in and around Atlanta the subject of this sketch bore a more or less conspicuous part, and made numerous escapes from very close calls. After the war he came to Memphis and engaged in business on Front Row, but soon became identified with the daily press, with which he has been connected almost ever since. He is a prominent Odd Fellow, and a solid, well-to-do citizen.

WALDRAN, C. M., one of the boy soldiers of the war, was born February 27, 1846, about six miles east of Memphis; he attended country schools until 14 years old; then was sent to the Iuka Military Institute. When Memphis fell, June 6, 1862, he came home and in July, 1862, went south and operated with independent scouts until January 1, 1863, when he was captured by a German company of Federals about eighteen miles from Memphis, on the Pigeon Roost road; he remained in the Irving Block but three days and nights, when he was released. On May 18, 1863, he left again for the army and joined Captain Flem. Sanders' company of scouts, with headquarters at that time at Panola, Miss.; served until November, 1864, when his company was ordered by General Forrest to report to him at once; joined General Chalmers and started on the Hood campaign; surrendered with his company (L of the Eighteenth Mississippi Regiment) at Grenada, Miss., and was paroled May 18, 1865; has since lived in Memphis; was married February 15, 1870, to Miss Estelle Golibart of Baltimore, and they have six children.

WHEATLEY, WILLIAM ARTHUR, was born in Memphis, Shelby county, Tenn., January 4, 1843, and educated at Randolph Macon College, Mecklenburg county, Va.; in May, 1861, he joined Captain Stockton Heth's infantry company, the Culpepper Riflemen, Thirteenth Virginia Regiment (A. P. Hill's), Elzer's Brigade, Joe Johnston's Division, at Winchester, Va., and after the battle of Romney, in Virginia, participated in the first battle of Manassas July 22, Sunday, 1861, serving two years in the Virginia campaign in the valley; he joined a wing of N. B. Forrest's cavalry under Captain Ned Sanders at Memphis, Tenn., in 1863, and fought at the battles of Corinth, Iuka, Courtland, Holly Springs and others, and on a thirty-day furlough went to his plantation in Carroll Parish, La., to refugee his slaves to Western Texas, having put a substitute in his place, and rejoined the Confederate army under his old commander, General E. Kirby Smith, of Shreveport, La., and surrendered, and was paroled by General E. O. C. Ord, U. S. A., at Shreveport, La., in April, 1865, at final end of the war. October 1, 1867, Mr. Wheatley married Miss Elizabeth Bowen near Front Royal in the valley of the Shenandoah, Va., and ever since has been in real estate business in Memphis, Tenn., and is also a United States commissioner.

WILKINS, W. G., enlisted May 5, 1861, in Company B, Bluff City Grays, One Hundred and Fifty-fourth Tennessee Regiment; took part in the battles of Belmont and Shiloh, and was wounded the second day at the latter place; he was engaged in the battle of Richmond, Ky., August 31, 1862; rejoined the main army in time to take part at Perryville; was in the battle of Murfreesboro December 31, 1862, and also in the engagements there from January 1 to 4, 1863. The company was mounted February 15, 1863, and placed in the Eleventh Tennessee Cavalry, commanded by Col. J. H. Edmondson, their former captain. This company was thrown in with a remnant of General Forrest's old regiment and organized as McDonald's Battalion, and as part of the Eleventh Tennessee Cavalry; took conspicuous part in the battle of Chickamauga September 18, 1863, (see Lindsley's Annals, p. 693), as well as in many other battles. At Tupelo this battalion was recruited to a regiment commanded by Colonel Kelley, and designated as Forrest's Old Regiment. In this the company remained until the surrender. Mr. Wilkins was paroled at Gainesville, Ala., May 11, 1865; returned to Memphis and engaged in business; married a daughter of the late Judge J. T. Swayne, and has lived here ever since.

WILKINS. CHAS. W., enlisted in the same company as his brother; served as corporal; was wounded at Murfreesboro, and wounded and captured at Athens, Ala., in September, 1864; was sent to Camp Chase, Ohio, and paroled just before the close of the war. Returned to Memphis, engaged in business, and died in 1870; never married.

WILLIAMS, JAS. M., born September 1, 1841, four miles east of Bartlett, Shelby county, Tenn. Later his father, Esq. Hal Williams, settled two miles south of Brunswick, on the L. & N. R. R., where he was brought up on the farm, receiving a country school education, with the addition of two years, 1859 and '60, at Shelby Military Institute, near Germantown, Tenn. He was the second child and only son of Henry and Mary A. Williams, his father being a native of Pitt county, N. C.; his mother, Mary A. Black, a native of Giles county, Tenn., near Pulaski.

He enlisted June 2, 1861, and was one of the organizers of the Yancey Rifles, Captain R. W. Pittman, and was elected orderly sergeant of that company, and attached to the Thir-

J. M. WILLIAMS.

teenth Tennessee. In June, 1862, at his own request, he was transferred by General Polk to cavalry service, and assisted in raising, mounting and equipping a company of cavalry in Shelby and Fayette counties, about 200 strong, commanded by Captain Ed. E. Porter of Memphis, which became a part of Ballentine's Seventh Mississippi Cavalry Regiment, Armstrong's Brigade. About six months before the close of the war this company, then only about thirty strong, was transferred to Forrest's famous old regiment, which surrendered May 11, 1865, near Gainesville, Ala.

He was, for the greater part of these three years of cavalry service, specially detailed with Captain Ad. Harvey's Scouts, which rendered valuable service to Generals Armstrong and W. H. Jackson. Being always well mounted, cool and deliberate, but determined and fearless, he was among the first to respond to a call for a volunteer to undertake a daring and

19

perilous scout within the enemy's lines, and oftentimes in the enemy's camp. Harvey's Scouts and Armstrong's Brigade made a record that will yet be vivified by the historian's pen and will thrill the hearts of future generations. He was in many battles and skirmishes, including Shiloh, Guntown, Holly Springs, Raymond, Big Black, Natchez, Brandon, Selma, Dalton, Ringgold, Big Shanty, New Hope, Atlanta, Jonesboro, etc. He was slightly wounded once, captured once and sent to Camp Chase, but escaped and rejoined his command.

He married Miss Sallie R. Wooten of Holly Springs, Miss., in 1872; has resided in Memphis since July, 1869; actively engaged in business since 1884, assisted by his son, Heber Williams, a promising young man of 20 years. He is prominently connected with several commercial, fraternal and benevolent organizations of the city of Memphis, and is well and favorably known; takes life philosophically, never sees the dark side, is genial, social, and of a happy disposition; is a member of the Confederate Historical Association, and an active member of Company A, Confederate Veterans of Memphis, being commissary of the company, and enjoys the honor and privilege of feeding the Veterans when in camp; is hale and hearty, and bids fair for many years to extend the warm hand of brotherly love to his old comrades.

WOOD, JACOB MABIE, born in New York City January 21, 1845; resided in Memphis since 1858; enlisted in the Maynard Rifles, One Hundred and Fifty-fourth Tennessee; the company joined the regiment March, 1862; was wounded late Sunday evening at the battle of Shiloh; received treatment in camp for two months; never entered a hospital; was in all the important battles of the Army of Tennessee: Murfreesboro, Chickamauga, Richmond, Ky., Perryville, Atlanta, Jonesboro, Franklin, Nashville, Missionary Ridge, Lookout Mountain, and was at the surrender at Greensboro, N. C., May 1, 1865; was senior officer in command of the One Hundred and Fifty-fourth Tennessee Regiment with twenty-three men at the surrender; arrived in Memphis May 26, 1865.

While in camp at Tullahoma, Tenn., took a furlough for sixty days, instead of discharge (being under age); entered

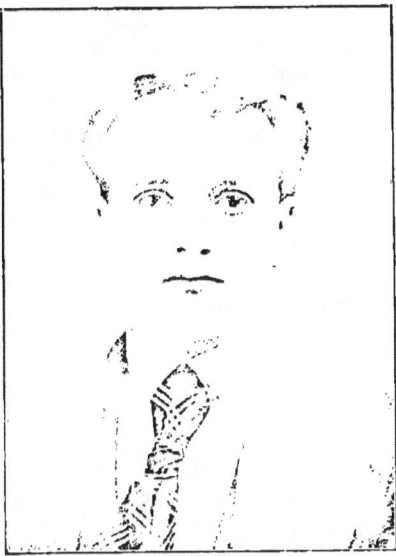

JACOB M. WOOD
In 1868.

the lines of Memphis disguised as a citizen and remained three weeks, long enough to write home to his mother in New York and get a reply to his letters. It had been reported that he was killed at Perryville; to correct this was his object in entering Memphis: he remained three weeks or until General Hurlbut issued orders to hang all Confederate soldiers found in the city: drove out of the lines on the passport of Misses Fannie Ballard and Mollie Noble as their boy driver; they lost their boy driver at Dr. Jos. Williams' residence, about three miles from the city, after loading him with smuggled clothing, etc., for the boys. He hid these in an old ox wagon and drove that night with these fast goers to Hernando, Miss., and thence to Grenada, and arrived at army headquarters, at Tullahoma, the day his furlough expired. After the war Mr. Wood entered the service of a large drug house on Main street, Memphis, and has since become a partner and general manager; he was married to Miss Blanche McConnell, daughter of George McConnell, a noted architect, who drew the plans of the old St. Charles Hotel of New Orleans. Mr. and Mrs. Wood have two sons. Percy and Eugene. He is a direct descendant of the Knickerbocker stock that first settled in New York. His mother, Elizabeth Mabie, was born on Pearl street, in 1813, the farm of her parents running back to where the city hall now stands. Her father, Jacob Mabie, was born in Holland and came to this country in his youth. On other sides of the house Mr. Wood is of English and Scotch stock. In the war he illustrated the sturdy, enduring, patient and good-natured qualities of his ancestry, and it is the testimony of his late captain, E. A. Cole, still living, that he was at one time awarded a medal by a vote of his comrades as the most gallant and popular soldier of his company. The late Mrs. Sallie Chapman Gordon-Law, the "Mother of the Confederacy," in her little book, written in 1892, pays him a beautiful compliment on pages 13 and 14, one of which he and his family may ever feel justly proud.

CARROLL, CHARLES MONTGOMERY, a native of Nashville, Tenn., born in 1821; chosen Colonel of Fifteenth Tennessee Regiment at Jackson, Tenn., in June, 1861. The soldiers of his command were mainly from Memphis and largely of Irish birth. The regiment moved to Union City, marched thence to New Madrid, thence into Missouri some distance from the river, afterward operated about Columbus, Ky., and also participated in the action at Belmont, being a part of Cheatham's Brigade. Evacuating Columbus in February, 1862, the regiment marched to Humboldt, then to Lexington, and later to Purdy, in time to take part in the two days' battle of Shiloh. Afterward, at Corinth, when the regiment was reorganized, at the expiration of its twelve-months service, Col. Carroll retired from the service. Col. Carroll, now in his seventy-sixth year, is a resident of Memphis. His father was the celebrated Carroll who led the Tennesseeans to victory on General Jackson's left on the plains of Chalmette. His grandfather emigrated to America from Ireland at the early age of 14 years. The mother of Colonel Carroll was a Montgomery, a niece of the Irish-American soldier who fell at the storming of Quebec in the winter of 1775.